THE HOME

An absolutely addictive psychological thriller

SALLY-ANNE MARTYN

Joffe Books, London
www.joffebooks.com

First published in Great Britain in 2023

Cover art by Sasha Alsberg

ISBN: 978-1-83526-216-0

For my son, Gabriel.

PROLOGUE

Hallow Croft

1972

His fingers crawled spider-like along her pale arm, mapping their way towards her neck. Tiny goosebumps appeared across her skin in the wake of his trailing touch. Emily shivered, eyes fixed on his fingernails. Neglectfully long, stained with oil paints and chemicals used to clean his overworked brushes. She snapped her eyes shut and tried to take herself away to another place. *Anywhere but here.*

'Like silk,' he purred, his admiring voice cracked and low.

She turned her head away as his fingers reached her ear, gently stroking the lobe, as if feeling the quality of her. A small cry left her lips. She opened her eyes and pulled away, stumbling to the side and falling into a small table of paints, multi-coloured tubes and hog-bristled brushes clattering to the wooden floor. The bark of a giant dog echoed from another part of the house.

'Don't be silly now,' he reached out a hand to her, his fingertips skimming her cheek, a nail catching her skin.

'No,' she slapped his hand away and raised her fingers to her face, soothing the skin where his had just been.

His brow furrowed and his eyes narrowed and darkened.

'Come on, Emily, you're my muse. Many an artist before has had a thing for his subject. It's tradition. Freud, Dalí, Picasso. It's an honour to be chosen.'

I'm fifteen,' she tried to say, but her throat had dried up, each word crackling like a broken radio.

'You're not a child anymore, look at you.' His eyes skimmed down her body, his breathing slow and deep.

Emily crossed her arms over her chest. 'I want to go home.'

He sneered, his lips curling at the edges. 'I thought you were more mature than this, Emily. You disappoint me.'

He stepped forward, grabbing her hair and pulling her back to him, a tube of paint exploding beneath his foot, cadmium red oozing across the walnut floor. She gagged as she inhaled his odour of sweat and whiskey. His grip loosened and he began stroking her hair as if trying to get a child to sleep, her face forced against his chest. She felt something hardening in his trousers, pushing against her hip.

'Like golden thread,' he purred.

Emily focused on the door, his words distorting in her head as if she were underwater, drowning. He pulled her back to the surface when she felt his hand clasp the strap of her pale blue summer dress and take it down over her shoulder. She jumped back, the strap tearing and the dress falling on one side. Emily held the material to her body and ran as fast as she could out of the room, kicking brushes across the floor, her bare feet skidding in the red paint.

She ran down the centre of the grand staircase, catching her toe in the worn Persian runner and stumbling forward, crying out, rolling down the stairs as the hallway span around her. A chandelier, carpet, oil paintings, carpet again.

She lay at the bottom of the staircase, her head spinning and intense pain radiating from her twisted ankle. She heard his footsteps padding down the landing after her and dragged herself up, crying out in pain as her right foot hit the ground. She ran to the grand entrance dragging her foot behind her, her hand shaking as she reached out for the brass handle.

'You'll catch your death out there,' he warned, clutching the ornate banister, taking the stairs one at a time. 'Come back, let's not be silly. I'll make us some supper.'

Emily limped barefoot across the gravel drive. She heard him following, then stop. She turned to see him stooped over with his hands on his knees, catching his breath, coughing and spitting dark phlegm to the ground. Tears burned her cheeks, her eyes wide with fear. She carried on running, past his old Jaguar and beyond the manicured lawns and topiary birds to the edge of the woods.

His footsteps picked up speed again, his heavy breath carrying through the cold air. Emily entered the woods, the trees enveloping her, drawing her further into the darkness. She darted between the ancient trunks, ducking beneath thorned branches, her feet numb to the sharp twigs and scattered debris that covered the ground.

She reached the clearing deep within the woods. The Nine Ladies ancient standing stones protruded from the ground like crooked teeth. In Hallow Croft's grounds, the ancient stones had public right of way. A place for the local teens to gather and smoke and drink cheap cider. She panted, the cold December air slicing her throat, each breath like a dragging blade. She heard twigs cracking and snapping in the woods as he followed. She ran behind one of the stones and crouched down, her back to the ice-cold rock, gripping both hands tightly to her mouth to keep the sobs in. Her heart jumped as an owl cried from above, flapping its wings as it swooped across the clearing.

The stalking footsteps halted somewhere nearby, and she froze, listening to his heavy breath.

Please God, she prayed, *keep me safe.*

As a dark shadow loomed across the ground beside her, she dared to look up. He gazed down at her, a triumphant smile on his ragged face.

'There you are, now let's get you back inside. You'll catch your death.'

He clasped his fingers around her thin arms and yanked her to her feet. Emily tore herself away and hit out, her hand slapping his cheek so hard that he froze for a moment, his pupils blackening.

'You silly little girl.'

Emily backed up to the standing stone, watching as he launched at her, his hands gripping her neck. She writhed and kicked out, catching his shin, but he didn't flinch. He just stared into her eyes, his face contorted with rage, fingers pushing against her windpipe until her cries and chokes silenced and she fell in a lifeless heap onto the wet grass.

CHAPTER 1

2023

Samantha reached over to the car radio, keeping one eye on the dark road as they sped along the M62. She switched stations, anything to get rid of the song that reminded her of *him* and a time when everything had been exciting and new. As she clicked the button, a chip of indigo polish fell from her nail.

'For f—'

Her daughter Lily held out her palm.

'Fifty pence for the swear jar if you continue.'

Samantha smiled at her daughter's frowning face.

'I need to get it removed before Monday anyway. Can you google nail salons in Nether Dale?'

Lily let the drawing pad and pencil fall into her lap and leaned forward to take her mobile phone from the glove compartment.

'Do we have to listen to this?' Lily said, as Noddy Holder cried out that it was time for Christmas.

Before Samantha could swipe her hand away, Lily had turned the music back to 90s indie and instantly Samantha was back in his office. Her flushed face in his hands, his groin pushing against hers. She reached down into the side pocket of the door and lifted the vape to her mouth, ignoring the burn of Lily's glare as the strawberry-mint scent filled the car.

Samantha tried to put the image of him out of her mind, concentrating on the road. The window wipers squeaked across the windscreen. Next to her, Lily scrolled through the search results on her phone. The bleak endless stretch across Saddleworth Moor felt like pathetic fallacy for the aftermath of the affair. What had begun with passion and excitement had ended in shame and dark regret. Samantha reached down and returned the music to the ChristmasMuzic station before her daughter could protest.

'Driver chooses music, sweet cheeks. It's an age-old law that if broken is punishable by removal of teenager's phone for the foreseeable.'

'The nearest one is ten miles away in Sheffield,' Lily said, holding onto her phone as her mum blindly swept her hand at it.

Samantha shook her head. 'Christ on a bike.'

'You said you wanted remote,' Lily said, taking 50p from the cup holder between them that held odd coins covered in unidentifiable sticky substances, various hairbands and a packet of chewing gum.

'Christ isn't a swear.'

Lily ignored her, put the 50p in her pocket and continued to scroll down her phone, listing the scant amenities that awaited them. 'A grocer's, some kind of café-post office thing that looks like somebody's back room, and a pub called the Skull and Feathers.'

'Ah, the delightful Skull and Feathers.' Samantha sighed, before mouthing curse words at a passing car that had driven right up behind her, flashing its lights.

'Didn't you know all this before you took the job?' Lily asked, watching the other car flash its hazards in retort, the shadow of a fist visible through the rear window.

'Not really, no. Our village was five miles away. Other than mixing at secondary school we rarely saw the other

6

villages. We all knew the Skull and Feathers though — they sold cheap booze to teens. So on the rare occasions I did venture there, I never saw past the pub and then it was very, *very* bleary.' Samantha winked at Lily, who gave her a disapproving look. Samantha looked back to the road, 'Anyway, never mind. Sheffield is just a car ride away, so it doesn't really matter.'

'I don't drive,' said Lily quietly, putting her phone back in the glove compartment and reopening her drawing pad, where a strip of passport photos of her and her best friend Sophie held the page. Lily's sketch was a stunning representation of the two friends. Her daughter's artistic ability was something Samantha was in awe of — her own time in art class was spent reading *Just 17* and gossiping about the sixth-form boys.

Samantha glanced down at the photos and felt a sharp pang of guilt. Lily and Sophie had been inseparable for the past two years, Lily's first best friend since junior school. Samantha had hoped that her job in A & E, her *dream* job, would have worked out for once and that they could have put down proper roots. Now here they were again, her entire life stuffed into the back of a Volvo estate and heading to yet another place to try and make a home.

'We could make plans for you to see Sophie soon? She could come here during the school holidays. It would be fun.'

Lily muttered noncommittally and Samantha felt another small chip of motherly success fall away like the damaged nail polish.

She turned her attention back to the road, which had transitioned from wide motorways and A roads to winding lanes. A wild grid of grey drystone walls criss-crossed the misty winter landscape, illuminated only by the car lights. Lost-looking sheep dotted the fields, a lamb cried for its mother from the wrong side of a hedge. A brightly coloured pheasant skittered out into the road and Samantha slammed on the brakes, causing a frying pan to slip out of a black bin bag and hit Lily's shoulder. 'Bloody hell!'

'Fifty pence.' Samantha held her hand out, smiling.

'Near-death experiences don't count,' said Lily, retrieving the pan and pushing it into a box of bottles and toilet paper by her feet.

Every inch of the backseat was taken up by their portable life. Clouds of duvets and pillows, bin bags of clothes and cardboard boxes filled with various plates and mugs clanking against each other.

'This is going to be a new start for us, Lily. The promotion means more money — we'll be able to travel and go to festivals together.'

Samantha caught the familiar look of horror on Lily's face at any mention of them socialising together. She had made the application for matron of the nursing home on a hope and a prayer. She had worked hard and had the experience but was aware well-paid nursing jobs were few and far between. Nobody had been more surprised than her to have been given the appointment. She had never intended to go back to the village, but the options had been limited.

'I need a wee,' Lily said.

'Can you hold it in?' Samantha looked out of the window. 'We're only about five miles of freezing cows, two thousand drystone walls and a haunted farmhouse away from our destination.'

Lily grimaced. 'This place really is in the middle of nowhere, isn't it? No wonder you wanted to get away.'

'The village at least has a chip shop.'

'Fancy,' said Lily, making light touches with her pencil, bringing a glint to Sophie's eyes.

'You'll soon make friends, and we'll settle.' Samantha put a reassuring hand on Lily's arm. 'This time for good, I promise.'

'You said that last time, Mum, and the time before.'

Samantha took her hand away, gently placing it on the steering wheel. The whisper of a tattooed *Lily* was just visible beyond her watch strap. Lily was fifteen going on fifty; it got harder by the day to get anything by her. She missed the days when her daughter believed every fairy tale and cobbled-to-gether explanation she had.

'If I remember rightly, there's somewhere along this road to stop,' said Samantha.

They both peered out into the dusk, purple heather now black shadows on a greying landscape. Samantha was about to lose faith in her memory, when she spotted the faint glow of flickering petrol station lights, and then a hand-painted sandwich board propped up on the narrow grey path.

Mo's Diner next left.

She could at least manage to find her daughter somewhere to pee if nothing else.

'Here we are,' said Samantha, with more enthusiasm than she felt. She looked down to the dashboard, the petrol-tank needle now in the red zone. 'I'll get petrol while we're here, God knows when I'll next find any.'

Samantha drove up to the rusty-looking petrol pump, relieved to see the LED numbers alight. Lily put her pad and pencil in the door pocket and peered out of the window as tiny specks of grey-white snow began to float past, illuminated by the dull yellow lights of the forecourt. She secured the beanie over her mousy blonde hair and got out of the car. Samantha was unscrewing the petrol cap.

'We'd better not be too long or we might get stuck here,' said Lily, holding her palm out flat and catching snowflakes, 'and you'll catch your death.'

'Yes, Mum,' said Samantha, smiling at her daughter and trying not to shiver as the tiny flakes melted on her bare arms.

She had been hot running around, packing the car, a ball of nervous energy. Now her skin was goose flesh in her retro Ramones T-shirt and skinny jeans that sat low on her hips, another inked line visible above the waistband, another fading memory.

'There'll be a loo in the diner. Grab us a tea and I'll join you.'

Lily nodded, burying her hands deep in the pockets of the mustard faux fur coat, her thin legs rooted in a pair of thick-soled Dr Martens. As Lily disappeared into the diner, Samantha looked around the deserted forecourt, her fingers red against the ice-cold pump handle. The reality of bringing her daughter to the place she had yearned to escape from all those years ago sent a shudder up her spine. Perhaps it would be better now.

She released the petrol pump handle, smug in managing to stop at a round twenty pounds. Samantha shook the nozzle and replaced it in the holder, before locking the car door and making her way over to the garage shop to pay. The windows were grimy and smeared. Outside, unsold newspapers fluttered on a metal rack. Samantha glanced at the *Nether Dale Chronicle* headline.

'Christmas cancelled for local youth centre.'

Christ, why had she brought them both here? The answer was simple: the chance of a job she was good at and which paid generously. She could only hope that, in time, her daughter would forgive her.

A bell rang above Samantha's head as she entered the seemingly deserted shack to pay for the petrol. A portable fire glowed orange in the corner, the smell of paraffin and damp heavy in the air. A single fluorescent strip light buzzed above, illuminating dusty chocolate bars and packets of ready salted crisps that lined a metal shelving unit, alongside baskets piled high with sponges and yellow chamois leathers. A radio crackled from somewhere in the back, playing plinky piano tunes that reminded her of stays at her nan's house. Those times when her parents needed more space to argue. Samantha took two Mars bars and wiped the dust away, taking them to the small, unmanned counter in the corner of the hut.

She looked through the grimy windows out to the diner, where she spotted Lily sitting down at a window table carrying a tray.

'Oh, hello, ducky!'

Startled, Samantha spun round to see the woman before her.

'Oh, aren't you a picture on this miserable cold night. What lovely red hair you've got, and those nails!'

The woman's own hands were encased in threadbare fingerless gloves, nails bitten down to nubs and blackened with oil and dust. She wore multiple jumpers and a thick woollen skirt with tights. Her ankle boots, though once sturdy, were now worn and scuffed. Her entire outfit was at odds with the tiny pompom snowman earrings that hung from stretched earlobes. The smell of cabbage stew wafted through to the counter from a back room and Samantha felt a swell of nausea. She opened her purse and took out a debit card. The woman dabbed a finger on a hand-written sign taped to the counter.

Cash Only.

Samantha gave a tight smile, opening up her purse, hoping she still had enough cash left over from her leaving do last week. Vodka shots and Asian fusion food, now a distant memory. She glanced around the shop and then out to the forecourt.

'Do you have a cash machine?'

The old woman giggled, revealing discoloured teeth.

'Nearest one to here is—'

'Sheffield?' Samantha didn't mean to sound exasperated, but her head was beginning to throb from the long day of packing and driving and the realisation she had willingly travelled one hundred miles east and fifty years back in time.

'No. Heather Brook — it's about five miles west of here.' The woman's smile faded, her lips now taut.

'OK, well, I only have a twenty, so I'll leave these.' She pushed the Mars bars away and handed over the money.

The woman took the note from Samantha but held onto her fingers. She turned her hand over, tracing the lines on Samantha's palm with a gnarled fingertip. Samantha tensed her hand; twenty years as a nurse meant her own hands were always immaculately clean.

'Life and soul of the party, I see,' the woman said, her eyes remaining fixed on Samantha's palm.

It didn't take a mystic to work that out. Samantha was aware she looked like she had just walked out of a gig, having forgotten to leave out suitable clothes when packing.

'A broken career line, lots of changes, a new challenge ahead. One child.'

Samantha looked over to the diner. The woman had seen them arrive — again, her insight was hardly outstanding.

'Now then, what's this?'

The woman held her fingers tightly. Samantha tried to pull away but the woman gripped onto her.

'I really have to go, my daughter's waiting. I'm not really into fortune telling—'

'Your *daughter*. Yes.'

Samantha looked down at her palm.

'What about my daughter?'

The woman's eyes met Samantha's, a flash of uncertainty in them. Then a glint of recognition. She dropped Samantha's hand and it hit the counter. Samantha withdrew her hand, cradling it in the other. The woman looked across the forecourt to the diner where Lily sat, her eyes glazed and dark. Samantha followed her gaze, then swiftly shook off the feeling of unease that the woman's change in mood had brought on.

'Here, have these on the house.' The woman pushed the chocolate bars back to Samantha.

'Right, erm, OK. Thank you, that's very kind.'

Samantha swiped them into her bag and hurried to leave, eager to get out of the place that served as a reminder of how crazy some of the villagers were. The bell above tinkled once more as she opened the door. Behind her, she heard the woman speak. Her voice was low, but she heard her perfectly well.

'She's here.'

CHAPTER 2

Lily took a bite out of her donut. It looked like it had been hit with a mallet. Flat, sweet bread with jam oozing onto the chipped white plate like a leaking wound. She glanced across to the petrol station, watching as her mum paid in the half-gloom of the garage. She narrowed her eyes. The cashier appeared to be holding her mum's hand.

On the café counter behind her, a mechanical toy Father Christmas wiggled his hips from side to side as 'Santa Claus is Coming to Town' played from a distorted speaker hidden under its faded Santa suit.

'Excuse me, is anyone sitting here?'

Lily looked up to see a boy slightly older than her pulling at the chair opposite. She pushed the second cup of tea across the table, feeling her cheeks burn.

'Yes, sorry, my mum, she—'

'Oh, er, no worries. I wasn't going to sit with you, just take it to sit with my mates.'

Lily looked across the diner to a group of builders clad in high-vis jackets. Hard hats were scattered across the table between mugs of tea and bread rolls stuffed with ham and cheese. They all watched with thick grins.

'Sorry.' Lily shrugged.

'You new round here?'

'Yes, we're moving to Nether Dale.'

'Where are you from?'

'Lots of places.'

The young man smiled. 'Mysterious.'

Lily smiled back. 'Not really.' She looked out of the window, watching as her mum exited the shop. 'Just life.'

Samantha was jogging across the forecourt, her arms tightly folded as the snow settled on her skin and hair.

'Riiight,' he said, following her gaze. 'Woah, is that your mum?' he asked, his eyes wide.

Lily looked at him, her irritation so clear he took a step back.

'I didn't mean . . . I—'

Lily tore a large chunk of donut away and stuffed it in her mouth, a forced hamster-cheek smile that didn't reach her eyes. Lily had had a lifetime of watching men do double takes when they saw her mum. As a child it had worried her, she felt these strange men would take her mum away, but now it just bored her, the predictability of it all.

A sharp waft of icy air blew into the diner as her mum flew in, rubbing her hands together and blowing on them. Lily looked over to the group of builders as the boy sat back down, a gnarled older man rough housing his hair like an amused parent.

'Who was that?' Samantha demanded.

'Nobody.'

Samantha raised her eyebrows and waited.

'He wanted to know if this chair was free, that's all.'

Samantha looked around. 'You mean rather than the one right behind him?' She winked.

Her mum had always been proudly open about boys and sex, though Lily would rather have read about it quietly in a book like other kids. Her mum took a sip of tea and let out a satisfied *ahh* as she sat back on the metal chair. The door blew open again, snow flurrying in, but no one entered. A tired-looking man, presumably the 'Mo' of Mo's

Diner, shuffled from behind the counter, drying his hands on a grubby apron and cursing his lot as he pushed the door closed. Outside the wind howled and dusk became more apparent as the petrol-station lights extinguished one by one, the pumps no longer in use.

'Finished?'

Lily nodded and Samantha reached out to Lily's plate and took the remains of the donut, sucking the sugar from her fingers.

'So this is Nether Dale,' Lily said flatly.

A ragged man at the next table slurped short, sharp sips of tea. Opposite him, a woman of the same age cradled a mug, her attention somewhere else, neither speaking.

'No, it's a mile or so further on. There'll be more to do there, and you can always get the bus into town. There used to be a bus stop somewhere in the village, I'm sure.'

Her voice was light and enthusiastic, but Lily sensed the uncertainty. She remembered her mum telling her that she had spent her entire childhood ready to move away, and now she was bringing her to live here. She was good at that, her mum, airbrushing history to suit the present narrative.

'Lots of beautiful scenery for you to draw.'

'Great, I'll look forward to it,' said Lily dryly.

'Speaking of which, shall we get going before we're snowed in here for the night?'

Lily looked over at the builders, one of whom eyed Samantha with cheeks full of sandwich and gave her a gurning smile.

'Don't fancy yours much,' said Lily, taking the 50p from her pocket and leaving it as a tip.

As they stood, the silent couple at the next table craned their necks and followed them with a stony gaze. Samantha threw Lily an amused grin, which Lily batted away, keen to get out of there and on their way.

Lily had only seen photographs of the nursing home, Hallow Croft, as it looked now. A technicolour advert for the final destination of the elderly. There had been a few black-and-white images of its heyday as a family estate too, manicured gardens and marble statues. It was certainly going to be one of the most impressive homes they had lived in.

A sound like chattering monkeys moved across the diner. Lily turned to see all the builders' eyes on her mum as she stretched her arms out, oblivious as always to the attention. Lily managed to catch the eyes of one and admonished him with a stare.

As they were leaving, Lily saw a noticeboard — a sofa for free, a basket of wide-eyed kittens needing homes, details of a local art group. She was about to take the contact information of the art group when she noticed something hanging from cotton and pinned to the cork.

Crafted from twigs and twine, with dried herbs and faded berries, hung a five-pointed star. Lily reached out to examine it and felt the scratch of a pin as her mum snatched it from her hand.

'Don't touch that.'

As her mum reached for the door, Lily held up her finger, squeezing a speck of blood into a minute bubble. The wind gusted in, causing Lily to gasp as the ice-cold air hit her cheeks. She glanced back to the star, before turning and following her mum out onto the snow-covered forecourt.

CHAPTER 3

The car revved past a greying metal sign welcoming them to Nether Dale, twinned with a town in Germany. Samantha looked out to the village pub, the Skull & Feathers, with its empty flower baskets and half-empty beers on damp pub benches. She couldn't help but think Bautzen had got the raw end of the twinning deal.

A phone box on the corner of the village square stood half lit, the receiver hanging from the base and swinging in the night breeze, hitting a graffiti-strewn Perspex panel. She glanced over to her daughter, who was fast asleep, her head resting on a bundled-up coat against the window. Perhaps all of this would look better in the daylight.

Samantha continued up the hill, the old Volvo spluttering like a twenty-a-dayer. It gave her some comfort to see the large houses dotted about on the hill, Christmas decorations sparkling against dark walls and the ghosts of images reflecting on the lounge windows. Beyond the houses a road wound further up the heathered moors, more drystone walls gridded out across the expansive land.

'*In three hundred yards take a right turn.*'

Lily muttered in her sleep and slowly lifted her head, wiping away a dot of drool from her chin. Samantha looked ahead, trying to locate the right turn in the gloom. It appeared suddenly, disguised by an unruly hedgerow. She indicated and took the turn, catching sight of a sign tilted into the hedge as if it had been knocked by a passing vehicle. The car headlights illuminated the sign:

Hallow Croft Nursing Home ahead.

'Nearly there, Lily,' she said, trying to rally herself as much as her sleepy daughter. Lily pulled her fluffy coat tight around her neck. Samantha reached out and touched her soft cheek. Lily pulled away.

'Don't be weird, Mum.'

Samantha felt the pang of grief that Lily was no longer a child and before she knew it would slip away to her own life. Lily stretched her arms and legs as far as the packed car would allow. Samantha looked back to the road, her headlights throwing orange beams onto the dark hedges that seemed to skitter with life from within.

'*In four hundred yards you will reach your destination.*'

The closer she travelled to their new life, the tighter the knot in her stomach pulled. Just as an urge to turn the car around came over Samantha, she spotted it. A behemoth in the distance, its presence looming as they approached the entrance at the front of the house. The sight of it made her heart race. Lily sat up straight, her eyes fixed on Hallow Croft.

'*You have reached your destination.*'

Samantha and Lily got out of the car and looked up to the grey stone walls that towered above them. The Victorian gritstone manor house loomed and the two women stood back to take more of it in, Samantha placing a reassuring arm around Lily's shoulder.

'It's amazing, Mum. Are we really going to live here?'

Samantha smiled, her body relaxing as relief washed over her.

'Yes, this is our new home; at least, part of it will be.'

Three shallow stone steps led up to a heavy wooden door with a small ramp curling up from the side. Warm lights glowed from tall windows and a Christmas tree glittered behind a leaded bay window. Samantha took a deep breath, the first day at a new job nerve-racking regardless of age.

She rang the doorbell and they waited, as heavy footsteps approached from inside, slowly making their way towards the thick oak door. Lily's eyes widened.

'If Norman Bates answers, I'm out of here.'

'Thanks for that, Lily.'

The door opened slowly, flakes of snow fluttering into the house. A face appeared round the door, skin powdered white, a thin line of red lipstick and eyebrows drawn in pencil.

'Can I help you?' the woman said, her forehead furrowed.

'Yes, I'm Samantha Rawley, the new matron.'

The woman looked her up and down. 'Are you sure?'

Samantha let out a splutter of a laugh, a puff of cold air rising like vapour. Lily elbowed her, the contact numbing her chilled skin.

'Yes, quite sure.'

The door opened and the woman ushered them through, her manner changing from suspicious to welcoming.

'Come on in then, you'll catch your death. I'm Valerie, the head care assistant.'

'Nice to meet you, Valerie, thank you,' Samantha said, as Valerie held the door for her.

She brought them into a spacious reception area, with peach walls and soft lighting. A giant rubber plant sat in a terracotta pot in the corner. A resident shuffled past, clutching a silver walking frame that scuffed across the wooden floor. There was another, less impressive Christmas tree in reception, silver branches with tiny coloured baubles hidden among the foil. On the wall next to a television room was a poster:

Hallow Croft welcomes
Merlin the Magician!
Saturday 16 December

'That's something to look forward to,' smiled Samantha, pointing at the poster.

Valerie grimaced and shrugged. 'If you ask me I think it's a bad idea. A lot of weak hearts around here.'

A chesty cough echoed from somewhere in the day room, as Samantha shot an amused look at Lily.

In the warm light of Hallow Croft reception, Valerie's face appeared softer. She was tall, with broad shoulders and thin, heavily veined legs poking out from beneath the candy-pink uniform. Samantha guessed she was in her late sixties, a hint of silver-grey visible at the roots of jet-black hair.

'Lovely to finally meet you, Samantha.' Valerie turned to Lily, whose wide eyes were scanning every inch of the space they stood in. She put a heavy hand on each of Lily's shoulders, bringing the teen's attention to her. 'And you must be Lily, lovely Lily.'

Samantha snapped to attention. 'How did you know her name?'

'I was privy to your application, Samantha. They value my opinion here, they do,' she beamed.

'Looks like I shouldn't get on the wrong side of you then,' Samantha joked.

Valerie said nothing, just smiled thinly.

The end credits to *Coronation Street* played out from the day room and a cacophony of buzzers began to ring. Samantha looked to Valerie, who rolled her eyes.

'Do you need to go to them?' Samantha asked. 'I can help, if you like.'

'No, no, Debby and Don, the other care assistants, will be along to answer those.'

Valerie marched over to a telephone, her black rubber-soled shoes squeaking with each step.

'Jonathan? It's Valerie. They've arrived. Shall I show them to their accommodation? Yes, thank you, Jonathan.' She returned the handset and smiled at the new arrivals. 'Now then, I'll show you to your room and the big boss will be along later.'

As Samantha swung her handbag over her shoulder, her car keys fell to the floor. Valerie snatched them up and held them in the light, reading the engraving on one of the key rings: *Sexy Samantha*

Valerie turned it over in her palm as Samantha flustered, 'Oh God, an ex bought it for me, I haven't got round to binning it.'

'A woman's got a right to express herself however she wants,' said Valerie. 'Personally I'd prefer something a little less obvious, but each to their own, eh?' she chirped, winking at Lily.

Samantha looked to her daughter, fully expecting the look of disdain her daughter returned.

* * *

Valerie led them up a grand staircase, Lily walking in front of Samantha, as Valerie pointed out some of the décor to her, talking in hushed tones. Samantha strained to hear, but only caught odd words: *Master Shuttleworth, cornicing, gallery*. When they reached the top, Samantha paused, looking around as Valerie and Lily continued on. The landing split in two directions, leading to the residents' bedrooms. Above each door was a dormant light, ready to flash at the touch of a buzzer. She peered round the corner of a corridor, following a glow of red light. It was coming from a door at the end; no sound, just the intermittent flash of light. Samantha watched as a young girl passed her, half running as she headed towards it. The door opened and the sound of groaning and crying drifted out, before it was closed again and silence.

Samantha looked back to where Valerie and Lily had disappeared and made her way towards them. She pushed through a heavy fire door and into a cold corridor, the walls shiny and grey like sealskin. She followed the voices up a spiral staircase, finding Valerie and Lily at the top, still deep in conversation. When Valerie saw Samantha she stopped and addressed her:

'I was going to send out a search party.'

'Just getting my bearings.'

Valerie nodded. 'Now then, we've come up through the nursing home, but at the bottom of the spiral staircase you can turn right and go down another set of stairs and there's a back door out of the building. It gives you more privacy. There's a key on here for it.'

Valerie held up a small bunch of keys before taking one and opening the flat door, a faint aroma of furniture polish and neglect wafting out on cold air.

'I did tell the cleaner to give it a good going over for you,' said Valerie, picking up a blown lightbulb from the brown carpet and shaking it to her ear, the tinkling of loose filament echoing in the empty hallway. She put the bulb into her pocket.

She led Samantha and Lily past two sparsely furnished bedrooms and into the living area. A small galley kitchen ran along the far wall. Two brown velour sofas faced a large bay window and a TV that looked like it had last been switched on to view the first moon landing. Samantha caught Lily's eye. Her daughter smiled weakly. Unlike the main part of Hallow Croft, there were no soft peach furnishings and lush foliage here, just a wash of magnolia paint and furniture that looked like it had been salvaged from next door's skip.

'There's a lovely view out to the quadrant from this window,' said Valerie from the kitchen, watching Lily rub at the glass with the side of her fist and peer out. 'You can't see much now, but come morning I'm sure you'll be very pleased.'

Valerie took the kettle from its stand and filled it with water.

'Tea?'

'Thank you for showing us the flat, Valerie, but I think we're going to get an early night, and tea will just keep me awake.'

Valerie's eye twitched, her smile fading. Then, as if realising, she lifted the corners of her mouth.

'Of course, I'll leave you to settle in.' She placed the kettle back on its base. 'I'm sure you'll make it your own little palace soon.' She took out the small bunch of keys from her pocket. 'Here are your keys, Matron.'

'Call me Samantha, at least when I'm off duty.'

Valerie smiled. 'No doubt Mr Shuttleworth will show you what's what tomorrow, Samantha.'

'And Mrs Shuttleworth?'

Valerie rolled her eyes, her fingers twisting a gold chain around her neck, a large locket glinting in the light.

'Between you and me, she's neither use nor ornament. Let's just say Mrs Shuttleworth was not created for the Yorkshire Moors. It's not everyone that can live somewhere like this.'

As if on cue, a gust of wind hit the window and rattled the glass. Samantha wished she hadn't asked; she could sense Lily shivering behind her.

'Well, I'm sure we'll be fine,' said Samantha, walking over to her daughter and reaching an arm around Lily's shoulder. 'Manchester wasn't exactly the Caribbean.'

Another gust hit, sending a window off its catch, the metal clanking onto the windowsill. Valerie looked at the window for a moment before returning her gaze to Samantha, then to Lily.

'I'm sure you will be quite fine. Now then, I must get on with things. Those residents won't get themselves to bed.'

CHAPTER 4

1975

Annie sat on her daughter's bed, a worn teddy bear clutched to her stomach.

'I'm off now, Emily.'

She stared ahead at the painting on the wall. Silence.

'I won't be too long, I promise.'

Emily's eyes stared back at her, a questioning look on her face. What had she been thinking as those delicate brush strokes were made? Did she know she was in danger? Her pale skin luminous in oils, it was a painting so out of place among posters of David Bowie and The Rolling Stones. So many times Annie had thought to get rid of it, hesitating by the front door, deciding whether to call back the bin men and give it to them. But the thought of her daughter's face alongside next door's potato peelings and old newspapers was too much to bear. She always retreated back into the house and hung it up on the bedroom wall once again.

It had arrived one morning, a week after Emily's murder. Annie had heard the latch on the gate clink, but by the time she reached the window whoever had been there had slunk away. The painting had been wrapped in a heavy blanket, leaning against the damp wood of the shed. She had looked out into the ginnel that ran the length of the terraced houses, a patchy ginger tom cat hissing at her, drawing her back into her yard. When she had uncovered the painting she had stumbled backwards, turning to throw up over the brittle remains of a hydrangea.

Her husband Kevin had urged her to destroy it: *'The work of a monster!'* he had shouted. But there was something about the painting, as if Emily was trying to tell her mum something from behind the protective glass: that she was OK now. In the painting she wore a pale blue silk slip, the same one she wore as her mother cradled her that night in the morgue.

My baby.

By keeping the painting with her, it meant that for the rest of her life she would feel Emily's gaze. It somehow felt that if she stared at her enough, Emily would know she was somewhere safe again.

Annie rose, putting the teddy bear back on the neatly made bed. She kissed the tips of her fingers and placed them on the glass.

'I'm going to make it all OK, I promise you, Emily.'

* * *

Annie turned off the television in the lounge, the winking presenter's coiffed hair disappearing into static blackness. Kevin was slouched over in his armchair, heavy snores and whinnies pushing from his nostrils.

'Kevin, Kevin!' Annie prodded him. 'Go to bed.' Annie tried to hook her elbow under his armpit to cajole him into moving, but he was a dead weight, and when she felt something strain in her lower back, she let him drop again like a sack of stones.

Annie stubbed out a cigarette in the metal ashtray on the arm of the chair, charcoal ash staining her pale fingers.

'Hey, I hadn't finished that!' he said, coming to life again.

Annie tidied up around her husband, squashing beer cans in her palm and holding the newspaper tightly under her arm. He eyed her tightly buttoned winter coat, her blonde hair falling to her shoulders.

'Where are you off to?'

'Out.'

He shrugged. She knew he wouldn't persist in asking. He had stopped caring about where she was or what she was doing from the moment the policewoman had delivered the devastating news of their daughter. He smacked his dry lips together, reaching for another can by the side of his chair and catching the ring pull beneath a tobacco-stained nail. It fizzed open and he lifted the drink to his mouth, catching the froth as it expanded from the confines of the metal tin. Annie shook her head.

'What?'

'Are you ever going to get up out of that chair and do something?'

'Like what?' He slurped at the can, the glug of liquid audible as it moved down his gullet in golf-ball-sized waves.

Annie dropped the empty cans in the bin and noticed a picture that had fallen. She lifted it up and cleaned the glass with the tip of her finger. She turned to Kevin, holding the photograph out to face him. He turned his head away.

'Look at her.'

He reached for a cigarette and lit it, his eyes focusing on the can in his hand. Annie marched over, pushing the photograph towards his face.

'I said, *look* at her.'

He tried to look elsewhere but couldn't avoid it. Annie watched as a pinprick of pain crossed his face.

'I don't need that to remember; this place is like a shrine.'

'It's like every other house that has a child — there are photographs.'

'Only this house doesn't have a bleeding child in it any-more, does it?' he growled, before glugging the rest of the beer.

26

Annie took a sharp intake of breath, the pain of his words stabbing her gut. Kevin crunched the empty can in his fist and launched it at the bin, missing by a foot. Annie let the photograph drop to her side.

'I'll be back in a couple of hours,' Annie said, walking towards the door, placing the photograph back on the mantlepiece as she passed.

As she left the room, she heard the familiar hiss of another can opening, and closed the door behind her.

* * *

The bottom of Annie's flared jeans dragged along the wet pavement, water seeping up the hem. She wore platform sandals, the only footwear she had that was anywhere near 'going out' shoes, her exposed toes turning red against the cold. A group of teens sat on the wall outside the Skull & Feathers, the Bay City Rollers booming out from the jukebox inside.

'Looking good, missus!' a teenager jeered, holding his crotch while the other boys cackled and screeched like hyenas out hunting.

Annie ignored their calls, pulling her coat around her shoulders, and kept walking up the hill. The voices of the young lads gradually faded beneath the sound of her heavy-soled shoes on the concrete path. Mrs Dukes from the post office caught her eye and then swiftly moved to the other side of the road, her head down.

When Annie reached the familiar wall, she noted the new graffiti that had appeared.

Beware of the Devil women.

The words didn't register in her head, just as the ones the month before hadn't, or the month before that. She turned into the drive of Sage End, her shoes tilting and sinking across the gravel. The house was a large Victorian villa with grey stone steps leading up to a violet-painted door. A wreath of dried flowers spun with holly and pinecones hung from a nail. Annie looked around her, before taking hold of the brass knocker.

Ginny looked out at the road as she opened the door, ushering Annie into the hallway.

'I saw the graffiti,' Annie said, taking her coat off and hanging it on a hook attached to the indigo wall.

'Just kids I expect, but you know how Sylvia gets with these things. If it were up to her, she'd string them all up.'

'That wouldn't look good in the papers,' said Annie, smiling.

Incense burning at a tall table filled the air with patchouli and jasmine. The effect was intoxicating, a welcome relief from the odour of stale beer and sadness at home.

'Exactly. The less attention we give them the better, I say.'

The hallway walls were covered in silver- and gold-framed photographs and artwork. A *This is Your Life* of Sylvia's existence. Smiling film stars and politicians stood next to Sylvia, who before moving to Nether Dale to form the coven had enjoyed a long career in film and television. She had appeared with the greats, the glamorous blonde ingenue to the dashing lead. She had lived a life that Annie could only dream of, and then she had met him, the man who had shown her a different path, one that she could control. Only it turned out she had not been in control at all, and when she had become strong enough, she had left.

Annie glanced at a photograph she saw each time she came. It was Sylvia wearing a long purple cape, edged with gold. On her head was a crown made of flowers and foliage, and in her arms a tiny baby with a shock of dark hair. It wasn't her clothes that intrigued Annie though, nor the open doorway behind Sylvia, where the glow of flames drew the eye. It was that the photograph had been cut in half, a piece of flowing black material just visible to her left-hand side and the existence of a man's long fingers touching the edge of her cape. The torn image of a man whose dark magic had caused her to leave the city of twinkling lights and star-laden pavements, and bring her mystical knowledge to the women of Nether Dale.

'Come on, we're ready to start,' Ginny urged.

Annie pulled herself away from the photograph and turned to her friend. She smiled, the warmth of Ginny's friendship guiding her as they made their way into the kitchen.

Smoke, chatter and hundreds of flickering candles filled the kitchen. In the centre was a large round table, sliced from an ancient oak, its veins and knots curling and extending through the varnished wood. A scattering of high-backed chairs were placed around it. Pots of tea and mugs of coffee sat on slate coasters, along with plates of biscuits and foil-covered chocolate bars.

On a sideboard beside a giant rubber plant, incense curled from joss sticks, shadows dancing on the walls of the candlelit room. A vase of exotic flowers spilled pollen onto a marble coffee table. Golden idols collected from around the world sat cross-legged on shelves, alongside crystal glasses and cascading pot plants. Under the magenta, gold and sapphire light filtering from the Moroccan lampshade above, the women turned as Ginny and Annie entered.

'Hi,' said Annie, taking her place between Donna and Corinne.

Donna had painted her hands with gold ink, delicate swirls and symbols that curled to her wrists.

'How are you doing, Annie?' Corinne asked.

Corinne had followed a long-haired hippy from her native France to Nether Dale in the late sixties, their dreams of setting up home in a yurt and living off the land coming to an abrupt end when the realities of Yorkshire winters hit home. Now they lived in a council house near Annie, Corinne taking a job in the village café and her hippy husband working as an office clerk in Sheffield.

'I'm doing OK,' said Annie.

'I had a hell of a night last night,' said Donna.

Annie smiled, thankful to have the attention off her.

'Another one-night wonder?' said Martha, an unmistakable barb in her voice.

29

'I wish,' Donna continued, ignoring her disdain. 'He wanted to talk.'

The women looked at her, waiting for the punchline. Donna shrugged her shoulders. 'Just talk,' she said with disgust. '*No* sex.'

'A gentleman, how awful,' said Martha.

Annie giggled, the openness of the women a light relief from the claustrophobic grief of everyday life. She had been part of this coven of women for a year now, ever since her cleaning job for Sylvia turned into something more. Here she felt protected and strong. When she was in the company of these women, she felt her life opening up.

'If I wanted a gentleman I wouldn't go to the Roxy, would I?' Donna ran her hands down her body. 'I just wanted a proper seeing to, is that too much to ask?'

Ginny stifled a laugh, holding her hand to her mouth to catch the crumbs of cascading chocolate biscuit. Martha gritted her teeth, furiously spinning a Parker pen around her fingers, a simple gold band on her wedding finger catching the light. Ginny's amusement faded as the candles on the table flickered, the table shaking slightly, causing ripples on the surface of the drinks. The women all looked up to the ceiling as the sound of thudding reverberated through the room.

'*Merde*,' said Corinne, shaking her head, 'she's bad tonight, no?'

Annie shuddered, still not used to the sudden changes in atmosphere that happened in the house. When they heard the sound of a key turning in a lock and footsteps crossing the landing, the women gathered themselves. Ginny relit the candles that had been extinguished and Donna dabbed at the spilled tea with a linen napkin. Martha scribbled on her notepad as if nothing had happened.

The kitchen door flew open and Sylvia entered, a pale pink satin kaftan flowing behind her. She smiled, but her eyes blazed, her cleavage heaving in and out as she tried to regain her composure. She took her seat at the table and placed her hands palms down on the velvet tablecloth, closing her eyes as the rhythmic tap of a tennis ball being thrown against a wall continued in the room above. Ginny poured whiskey from a crystal carafe into a heavy-bottomed glass and pushed it over to her, the glass touching the tip of her bejewelled hand. Sylvia opened her eyes and looked down at it, a smile appearing on her lips, her gaze softer.

'Thank you, Ginny, darling.' She patted Ginny's hand, put the glass to her frosted pink lips and drank it down in one.

'Is she OK? Do you want me to go and—' Annie ventured.

'She's fine,' snapped Sylvia.

Annie lowered her head, her cheeks reddening.

'Sorry, darling,' Sylvia added, reaching across and placing her hand on Annie's. 'She just seems to get more determined with age.'

Annie nodded. She knew Poppet was hard work. Sylvia had always shown great patience with her only child, but the sound of a calling child was like an alarm that blasted in Annie's insides. She looked up to the ceiling, urging the child to settle.

'Shall we start?' Martha said, pen poised.

The noise upstairs continued as Sylvia replied, 'Yes, let's.' She turned her attention to Annie. 'Annie, I understand you have something you want to talk to the coven about? I should say that Annie and I have already spoken, but as it's something that involves you all, I wanted you to hear together.'

All eyes turned to Annie and she shrunk back in her chair, her breath shallow as the moment arrived.

Donna held her hands up in an impatient gesture for her to say something, looking back to Sylvia, who remained focused on Annie.

'I wanted to ask you all something, if you'd . . . if—'

'Spit it out then,' said Donna.

'Donna!' Sylvia chided. 'Let her speak in her own time.'

Annie continued, 'I need your help, *all* of your help.'

'Of course, Annie, anything,' said Ginny, looking to Corinne, who nodded her head in agreement.

Annie took a deep breath and held her head up.

'I want you — us, the coven — to curse the Shuttleworth family.' She looked around at each of them, her fists clenched so hard the whites of her knuckles were visible. 'I've waited long enough for justice, and we all know it's not going to happen now. I must take it into my own hands, and that's why I'm asking for your help. It's time I had my revenge for Emily's murder.'

CHAPTER 5

2023

There was a knock at the door, short, sharp raps. Samantha made her way down the short hallway to the door, peeking into Lily's room as she passed, the teenager fast asleep, an open book by her hand.

Samantha put her mouth close to the door frame, her voice low. 'Hello?'

'Samantha? It's Jonathan, Mr Shuttleworth.'

She looked down at her hoodie and sweatpants, cursing herself. Too late now, she turned the Yale lever and opened the door.

On the other side stood a tall, bespectacled man with a tanned face and bushy moustache. He held out his hand to her.

'Samantha! Nice to meet you. Jonathan Shuttleworth.'

She took his hand and let him shake hers, his grip firm.

'I hope you're both settling in OK?'

'Yes, thank you, Lily's already gone to bed. Flat out.'

Jonathan grimaced. 'Sorry, I hope I haven't woken her?'

'No, you know teenagers, they can sleep on a washing line. Can I get you a cup of tea or—'

He whispered, 'Goodness, no, it's very late. My apologies for calling on you at this time, we've just got back from Majorca.'

'Lovely,' said Samantha, thankful that she wasn't going to have to entertain.

'I just wanted to introduce myself and welcome you.' He handed her a bunch of chrysanthemums wrapped in plastic, the tips of the petals already wilting.

'That's so kind, you didn't need to do that.'

'Nonsense, we're very glad you could start at such short notice.'

Samantha smiled. One of the benefits of having to leave her last job so swiftly.

'We, Diane and I, would like to invite you and your daughter over for drinks tomorrow evening. There will be a few of the staff there and we thought it would be a good chance for you to meet them before you officially start on Monday. She asked me to bring this over — it's your uniform. There's a spare in there too, of course. Anything more you need, just shout. Sorry again for disturbing you. See you tomorrow night?'

Samantha nodded. 'Yes, of course, thank you.'

Jonathan put his finger to his mouth in a *shhh* gesture and crept off down the corridor. Samantha looked down at the plastic-coated uniform. It was pale grey with maroon piping around the sleeves and pockets. Thankfully there was an elastic belt to give the starched dress some shape. She walked back towards her room to hang the uniform from the door frame, then placed the flowers in the sink, put the plug in and ran the tap.

She cast her mind to tomorrow, thinking about the tasks ahead. They would need to unpack and try to make the flat their own; she needed to help Lily feel at home. As she went to sit on the sofa, she noticed something outside and stopped. She switched the lounge light off and stood by the window.

An elderly woman ran across the quadrant, her long nightie billowing behind her in the icy wind and her thin white hair blowing across her face. The grounds were lit by street lamps, styled to match the history of the house. The woman's slippers left a trail of tiny footsteps in the light dusting of snow that had fallen. Samantha was about to grab her coat to go down to her when she saw Valerie scurry along the path, calling out and waving her arms. The old woman ignored her, running towards the woodland beyond the lawn.

Valerie grabbed for her arm, pulling the woman back. Samantha bridled at the way she handled her. But the woman now turned to Valerie. Her face was contorted, her mouth fixed in a tight grimace.

Samantha leaned forward, as if to be sure of what she was seeing, as the old woman grabbed onto Valerie's wrist and twisted it so far round that Valerie's whole body was bent over and down. Samantha couldn't hear Valerie cry out but she saw her mouth open and her eyes scrunch in pain as the old woman released her grip and let Valerie fall away.

For a moment Samantha thought Valerie would strike out in response. But she just drew her arm around the woman's bony frame and held her close, as she guided the reluctant resident back towards Hallow Croft.

CHAPTER 6

1975

They fell quiet, the rhythmic duff of the tennis ball above them punctuating the silence. Annie waited, daring to look at each of the women in turn. Ginny looked sympathetic, Corinne thoughtful. Martha wrote in the book.

'Isn't he on his last legs?' Donna said, leaning back in her chair.

'I heard he was really sick,' said Corinne, looking to Sylvia for confirmation.

Sylvia nodded. 'It's not him you want to curse though, is it, Annie?'

Martha looked up from her notebook, her forehead creased with confusion.

'No, it wouldn't be punishment enough,' said Annie. 'He's dying anyway. I want him to know that future generations of Shuttleworths will suffer because of him.'

'His son?' asked Ginny. 'I saw him once in the village shop, very handsome.'

'No. I want an eye for an eye. I want him to go to the grave knowing that his family will grieve like I have to. I want to put the curse on his first female heir, and I want him to know that it's going to happen.'

'It's never been proven though,' Martha said, pushing her glasses down her nose and looking at Annie. 'How do you know for sure it was him that killed your daughter?'

'Henry Shuttleworth was the last person with her, the only person with her. She had paint on her skin. He has a reputation, you all know that.'

'Creepy bastard,' said Donna. 'Makes my skin crawl. I had a friend sit for him once, he tried it on with her. Didn't reckon on her being a black belt, did he? He could barely walk for a month. The police did nothing. Zip.'

'It's been three years since she was murdered and the police have done nothing for Emily either. And why? Because the inspector drinks at the same men's club. Because Henry Shuttleworth has personally funded every single police initiative for the last few years. Emily was just a young girl from a council house; better to simply brush her death under the carpet and carry on taking the money.'

'Well, I for one vote yes,' said Donna, lighting a cigarette and blowing smoke into the air. 'These bastards shouldn't be able to get away with it. What with the Ripper at large as well, women aren't safe anywhere.'

'But the girl, his grandchild or great-grandchild?'

'I will never know what it is to have a grandchild,' Annie said, her head down.

'We *all* need to agree if we're going to put a curse on the family,' said Sylvia, looking to each of the women.

'I need to think about it,' said Martha. 'I know your pain—'

'You don't *know* my pain!' cried Annie, her head snapping up and hands in the air. 'How could you know what it is to lose your only child unless you've been there?'

Annie couldn't hold the tears back any longer; her grief began to flow.

'Ginny,' said Sylvia.

Ginny rose from her seat and walked over to Annie, urging her to take her hand and follow her. Exhausted and empty, Annie allowed Ginny to lead her from the kitchen and into the living room next door. Ginny offered her a glass of water, but her insides were too twisted to drink anything.

'Stay here awhile, rest for a moment.'

Ginny placed a jewel-coloured blanket over Annie's trembling body and left her. Annie could hear the low mumblings of chatter from the kitchen as she lay back into the velvet-covered sofa. As her sobs subsided, she became aware of the silence upstairs. Then her eyes darted to the door as footsteps padded along the wooden floor towards the room. Annie's heart raced as small fingers curled around the oak door, slowly pushing it open. Poppet appeared, speaking to Annie in a long whisper.

'Em-il-y.'

CHAPTER 7

2023

'Come in, come in.' Jonathan ushered Samantha and Lily into the hallway of Laburnum Cottage. 'Let me take your coats.'

The warmth hit Samantha as soon as she stepped into the narrow hall. She handed her coat to Jonathan. Lily just shook her head and pulled her faux fur jacket tightly around her. Jonathan smiled and hung Samantha's on a hat and coat stand by a painting of an ethereal-looking woman that gazed down at them.

'That's Mother,' Jonathan chirped.

'She's beautiful,' Samantha said.

'She was indeed.' He sounded wistful. 'Sadly a long time gone now.'

Jonathan met his mother's gaze, momentarily lost in thought until laughter from a room down the hall snapped him back.

'Now then, let me introduce you to the others.' He led them to a door at the end of the hall. The walls were lined with black-and-white school photographs, rows of glum-faced boys sitting behind and around glowering masters.

Samantha turned and gave Lily an encouraging smile, sensing her unease in the strange surroundings.

Jonathan turned a brass handle and opened the door to the lounge, slightly ducking as he walked beneath a low beam. 'Come in, everybody's here.'

The lounge was long and the beamed ceilings low. An open fire roared at the far end of the room, framed by two chintzy sofas and a scattering of antique chairs, inquisitive faces peering at them.

'What can I get you both to drink?' Jonathan offered, ushering them over to the seats.

Samantha wanted to say water, Diet Coke or tea, but the day had been long. She had unpacked as much as she possibly could and received several unsolicited texts from her ex, fruitlessly asking if they might continue the affair long distance. In the end she had blocked him, airbrushing him away, along with the rest of her past.

'Wine would be lovely, thanks.'

'Red? White?'

'Whatever's open, I'm not fussy.'

'What about you, Lily? Lemonade, perhaps a cider?' he winked.

'Lemonade please.'

Samantha spotted Valerie on the opposite sofa and smiled at her, waving a low hand in her direction. 'Hi, Valerie.'

Samantha scanned Valerie's arm for evidence of a bruise from the previous night, but there was nothing, just fleshy pale skin. Valerie caught her eye.

'How are you both? Settling in nicely?'

Samantha turned to Lily, a cue for her to answer. 'Good thanks.'

Samantha rolled her eyes. 'Do you want to expand on that?' Her voice was light but Lily's lack of response irritated her.

'Oh, never mind us, we don't bite. Come and sit here, Lily, it's good to have a young one around the place.' Valerie patted the seat next to her and Samantha watched Lily reluctantly walk across to it.

As soon as Lily sat down, Valerie poked her side, making the teen giggle, and for a fleeting moment Samantha resented the instant camaraderie between the older woman and her daughter.

Also in the room was a grey-haired man with glasses that sat halfway down his nose, icy blue eyes staring over the top, and a heavy-set girl wearing a Beyoncé T-shirt and leggings, her mousy blonde hair pulled tightly back into a ponytail.

A woman stood up from a worn velvet chair and held out her hand. 'I'm Diane. Nice to meet you, Samantha, and you, Lily.'

Diane's eyes seemed slightly unfocused and weary. She wore a bright flowery cocktail dress, her short hair styled and make-up fresh on skin as tanned as Jonathan's. Jonathan shot over to them. 'Of course, how rude of me. My wife Diane is an integral part of Hallow Croft.'

Diane huffed, causing Valerie and a girl sitting next to her to stifle sniggers. Samantha looked from them back to Diane. 'Lovely to meet you, Diane, thank you for inviting us tonight.'

Diane smiled and took a swig of her drink, leaving Samantha to find a seat on a slightly too high wooden chair opposite the sofa. Jonathan continued the introductions, pointing to the pony-tailed girl first. 'Now then, this is Debby, she's our wonderful junior care assistant, and this is Don,' Don smiled dryly over his glasses, 'another much-valued care assistant and member of the team.'

'It's so nice to meet you all, isn't it, Lily?'

Lily smiled politely at the staring faces.

'Yes, lovely.'

'Of course this isn't the whole team,' said Jonathan, 'but Valerie, Debby and Don are here most often. We didn't want to overwhelm you with faces.'

Showtunes from a stereo in the corner filled the silence. The lounge door flew open and a giant shaggy wolfhound bounded in, padding across the wooden floor towards them.

'Oh heck,' Valerie said, standing up and clutching her drink.

When Lily saw the dog she slid off the sofa onto her knees, arms outstretched.

The dog ran straight to her, its pink tongue lapping at her cheeks.

'Finn!' Jonathan bounded after the dog, reaching out for its collar and yanking it back.

'I love dogs,' Lily said, holding her hand towards it.

'Ah, good girl, not everyone's so understanding though.'

When Finn caught sight of the other guests he froze, his tail sliding beneath him, his ears back. A low growl issued from his throat, his wet nose pointing towards Valerie and Debby.

'It's Debby, he can sense her fear,' said Valerie, eyeing the dog with disdain. 'They smell it a mile off.'

Debby's feet were tucked up underneath her backside, her wide eyes fixed on the dog.

'I'll take him out,' Jonathan said.

Samantha hadn't seen her daughter so animated about anything in ages. She wished the others weren't so bothered so the dog could have stayed.

'Maybe you could offer to walk him sometime, Lily?' she said, watching as Jonathan yanked the growling beast out of the room.

Lily nodded, her enthusiasm simmering as the dog was taken away. Jonathan returned, picking wiry grey dog hairs from his trousers.

Diane held her glass in the air and Jonathan dutifully filled it. His wife was dressed immaculately and seemed out of place in this quaint old cottage, with her acrylic nails, thick gold jewellery and satin cocktail dress. Her age was difficult to guess; there were no grey roots to see on her brassy blonde coiffed hair, but Samantha thought late fifties — younger than Jonathan, who she knew from a previous Google search was sixty-seven.

'How have you been, Diane? Mr Shuttleworth says you've had a terrible flu,' Valerie said.

'It's the draughts in this old place. I'm prone to it. I wasn't made for the north of England, I haven't the skin for it.'

Don pursed his lips, as if holding sour words tightly in his mouth.

'We've spent two months in Majorca this year, Diane!' said Jonathan, bringing over a ramekin of olives and holding them under Debby's nose.

She screwed up her face but Valerie reached into the small bowl and scooped a few out, popping one in her mouth and manoeuvring it around her teeth as she navigated the stone.

'Have we not got cocktail sticks?' scorned Diane, rising from her chair, marching over to a cabinet and pulling down the front to reveal a small bar crammed with half-empty bottles of spirits. She took out a small plate laden with tiny plastic swords and placed it on the long wood and glass coffee table between the two sofas.

'Anybody else for sherry?' Jonathan asked, the bottle held aloft.

'Have you a house in Majorca?' Samantha asked, attempting to dissolve the fog-like tension that hung in the air.

'A villa, yes. I'd live there all year long if I had my way. Thirty-foot pool, balconies and just a mile or so from the beach.'

'Yorkshire in winter must be quite a shock to the system, then.'

'At least someone understands,' Diane said, waving her glass to get Jonathan's attention, 'See, Jonathan, it's not just me!'

A windowpane rattled and Diane shuddered theatrically.

'Valerie,' Samantha said, once again trying to navigate the obstacle course of conversation, 'I saw you had an escapee last night?'

Valerie's eye twitched, her mouth taut.

Don's head snapped to Valerie. 'Who was that?'

'One guess.'

'One of these days we won't notice, and Mrs Dawson will make it all the way to Sheffield,' he said.

'You should let her go,' Diane sniped.

'Diane!' Jonathan's jaw was tight, his teeth clenched. Valerie's eyebrows were as far up her forehead as they would go. 'We promised we'd take care of her, no matter what.'

'Well, it looks like you're doing a good job, if Valerie's actions last night are anything to go by,' said Samantha.

Valerie smiled and looked to Jonathan for recognition.

'Oh yes, I don't know where we'd be without our wonderful staff keeping everything going.'

'Majorca,' Diane sniffed.

Jonathan glared at his wife and Valerie failed to suppress a smug smile at the fractious interaction between husband and wife.

'Now then, let's have some more music,' Jonathan said, already swapping *Les Misérables* for Beethoven. 'So, you like dogs, Lily?'

Lily nodded enthusiastically. 'Yes, I'd love one, but . . .'

'Well, you are more than welcome to walk Finn whenever you like, isn't she, Diane?'

Diane nodded.

'Are you looking forward to getting stuck in?' Don asked Samantha.

'I think so, yes. There are twenty residents in total, aren't there? It's a nice number for a big home like Hallow Croft.'

'Exactly,' said Jonathan. 'We pride ourselves on giving the highest quality of care. We didn't want to pack them in like battery chickens.'

Samantha glanced around the room. 'I'm sure we'll all get along just . . .' she caught Valerie glaring at her with piercing eyes, 'just fine.'

'Cheers to that,' said Diane, slurring slightly and holding up her empty glass.

They all held their glasses aloft, Debby cracking hers against Valerie's, who playfully chastised the younger care assistant. Debby mouthed an apology. Samantha noted the power Valerie commanded over the others, even Diane.

Diane poured herself another glass of wine when Jonathan's back was turned to the window, as he looked into the darkness.

The music had now turned to disco at Diane's insistence. Baccara played as Samantha closed the downstairs toilet door. She could hear Lily's voice responding to a barrage of questions from Valerie, and felt a rush of maternal pride that her daughter was socialising so well. She pulled her trousers down and sat, thankful for a moment's peace. She looked to her left: yet more family photographs. Jonathan's mother on stage in a tutu, arms gracefully entwined in the air, ballet shoes en pointe. Next to it hung one of his father, she presumed, standing proud beside an unveiled painting in a gallery. Lives lived well, for all to see. She thought about the dreary flat; she would put some photographs up, make it look more homely.

One photograph in particular caught her eye. It was taken on the steps of Hallow Croft. His mother, now slightly older, but still beautiful, had a vacant, resigned look in her eyes. Next to her, Jonathan's father. The same rugged, handsome features, but his hair now flecked with grey, eyes dark. He looked to be in his late sixties and wore the clothes of a bohemian. On the step below them and separating them, a young Jonathan. Handsome, standing proud with chest out and chin high, the future lord of the manor.

Samantha flushed the chain and washed her hands at a small sink, rose and jasmine soap filling the air. The small window was open and she looked out to Hallow Croft, which was visible through a gap in the trees. She assumed that Diane and Jonathan didn't live there and were in this quaint but clearly cramped cottage for financial reasons, leaving more space for paying residents. It occurred to her that that might explain Diane's barbed comments. Who wouldn't want to be lady of the manor? Especially one as impressive as Hallow Croft. She unlocked the door, taking one last glance at his father's image, a faint recollection of stories whispered in her youth. She shuddered and closed the door behind her.

* * *

45

'Have you ever been married?'

All faces looked expectantly at Samantha, Valerie's eyes flickering to her ring finger. Samantha stifled a yawn, a new line of inquisition unwelcome at the late hour.

'No,' said Samantha, smiling tightly. 'I didn't have the best example growing up.'

'I don't blame you,' Don piped up. 'I managed six months before I left Stewart, but not before sewing frozen prawns into the hems of his curtains.'

'Ooh, a man scorned,' howled Valerie.

'Coffee anyone?' asked Jonathan, offering Samantha a mug and a sympathetic look.

'Not for me, thank you,' she said, putting down her glass. 'We must be getting back, lots to sort out tomorrow. We've barely unpacked.'

Samantha stood up and the others began to shuffle in their seats and follow suit. Jonathan disappeared and reappeared with an armful of coats.

'Now then, if there's anything you need, just shout,' he said.

'Thank you,' said Samantha, looking over to Diane, who had averted her gaze to the open fire, an orange glow intensifying her tanned skin. Her expression looked troubled, verging on fear.

'Right,' said Don, breaking the short silence, 'time I got my beauty sleep.'

Jonathan opened the front door and the guests piled through.

'Good night, Mrs Shuttleworth,' Valerie shouted through the doorway.

There was no reply.

'She's probably nodded off,' Jonathan said. 'We've had a tiring couple of months trying to run things ourselves, but all that should calm down now Samantha and Lily have arrived. Our knights in shining armour.'

'Well, a matron's uniform at least,' smiled Samantha.

'It's as good as, in my book,' Jonathan beamed.

Valerie and Debby linked arms and huddled together as they walked down the path and through the woodland. Lily followed, her coat buttoned up and arms crossed tightly against the wind. Valerie turned and called Lily to join them. Samantha watched as her daughter skipped forward and Valerie linked her arm through Lily's.

Samantha and Don walked behind. She was a good judge of character and felt of all of them Don was the one she would get on with best.

'Can I ask what happened to the last matron — I mean, why she left so suddenly without notice?'

His face blanked and he began to dig for his car keys in his pocket. Samantha waited.

'I'm not sure really, I'm not in the know with these things, you see,' he joked. 'Lowly care assistant and all that.'

'Right,' she paused, 'only it's very unusual for someone in the care sector to just leave before the backup arrives.'

'Nowt as queer as folk.'

'Right,' she said again, watching as Don opened his car door.

'See you Tomorrow, Matron!' he said, before disappearing into the driver's seat, the clatter of the closing door echoing in the cold night air.

Valerie unhooked her arm from Lily's and spoke to her, words imperceptible to Samantha. Lily laughed and waved as Valerie and Debby disappeared down the drive in a puff of engine fumes.

Samantha made her way to her flat, unable to shake thoughts of the previous matron from her mind. She heard Lily's footsteps approach and turned to her, offering her arm. Lily didn't appear to notice and carried on past her towards Hallow Croft.

CHAPTER 8

1975

Annie walked through Nether Dale holding her head up, for once. The wind snapped around her, her hair blowing over her face. Two teenage girls eyed her from the bus stop, whispering as she passed. When she turned to face them, they both giggled then looked away.

Each time she met with Sylvia and the women, something inside her grew in strength: a purpose, and a power. She entered the café in the village, the small bell above the door tinkling, the smell of toast and grainy coffee warming after the cold street.

'Good morning,' said Annie, chasing the woman's eyes with her own.

Mrs Harby, the café owner, tried to look away but forced herself to acknowledge Annie.

'Morning,' she replied, her voice clipped.

Annie heard the whispers from the two middle-aged women who stared at her without shame or fear of conse-quence. She smiled brightly at them.

'Hello,' she said.

The two women stopped whispering and looked down to their bone china teacups, neither replying to her greeting.

Even though it was *her* daughter who had died, it was Annie who had been rendered a ghost in Nether Dale. She had not been the centre of village life before Emily's murder, but somehow her loss had pushed her further beyond the boundaries of the people and places. Her passport to any kind of social life had been through Kevin: the Skull & Feathers darts team and his friends at the cement works. Now he had all but retreated within himself, she was left to fend for herself. Though it was not just loss that had rendered her a pariah, it was influence she was fighting against, and the suspicions around Sylvia and the other women. She glanced up at the notice board and read the poster.

The Shuttleworth prize for best-dressed shop window!
Winner announced at the Skull & Feathers Family
Christmas Party.
Kindly sponsored by the Shuttleworth family.

'What can I get you?' Mrs Harby asked, her face expressionless.

'Two teas, please.'

The waitress looked at the empty space opposite her, sighed and then scribbled into a small notepad.

When the door to the café opened again, Annie felt the pressure of aloneness dissolve instantly.

'Good morning!' Ginny beamed, plonking herself down. She freed herself from a large corduroy bag she carried over her shoulder and put it on the table, its contents clanking together. Then swept off her knitted bobble hat and heavy coat, dropping them on the back of the chair. Mrs Harby sneered at her soil-stained dungarees and departed.

'I come here for the warm welcome.' Ginny smiled. 'How are you, Annie?'

'Nervous.'

'We've another meeting tonight to discuss it.'

'Should I be there, to state my case ag—'

Ginny put her hands over Annie's, squeezing them gently. 'No, Annie. The rest of the coven has to decide now.

49

You've done all you can to put your case forward. Everyone else needs to be free to air their views and you may not like them. That's just how it works, you know that. It's the only way to make it fair.'

'I feel like I'm on trial, like I'm being judged.'

'You're asking us to do something that could have very serious consequences, not only for the Shuttleworths, but for us.'

Annie looked at her questioningly.

'You've heard about the three-fold rule?'

Annie shook her head.

'Well, when you . . .' Ginny glanced over to the women, making sure they weren't listening, 'when you cast a baneful curse like this, there's always the possibility it will pay you back three times as bad. That's a risk we take so it's only fair there's time given.'

'What could happen to the coven?'

Ginny shrugged. 'I don't know. Injury, loss of money . . . death.'

'Death?' Annie exclaimed, causing the two women to peer over.

Ginny waited for them to look away again and whispered, 'Well, maybe not that, but it's something we have to take seriously. We haven't cursed anyone for years, we say no to most requests, either it's not justified, or it's just not worth the risk.'

'And if one of the coven says no?' said Annie.

'Then the curse won't go ahead. It's how we've always worked, for hundreds of years. The coven is a democracy, it's the only way to make it fair.'

'I'll do it myself then,' Annie said, her bottom lip jutting out as she crossed her arms.

Ginny smiled. 'Now you sound like Poppet.'

Annie smiled. Sylvia's daughter had a temper like no other child, and when she decided to launch it on the world, everybody knew. Though Poppet was usually softer with Annie, because she was Emily's mum. When Emily had been murdered, Sylvia told Annie that Poppet had locked herself in her room for days, refusing all food and drink.

Mrs Harby returned, clanking the bone china teacups and saucers as she placed them down, along with a large pot of tea and a jug of milk.

'Sugar?' she asked.

'Sweet enough,' Ginny returned, a mischievous glint in her eye.

Mrs Harby grunted before retreating to her counter and wiping down the glass display cabinets that housed the pallid mince pies and currant-filled Christmas cakes. When a fly dared to land on the glass, she flicked the cloth and the insect fell to the floor in a beat, threadlike legs flickering as it squirmed in circles on its back.

'Are you quite sure you want to do this, Annie? You know it's almost impossible to reverse a curse, and by the time this one comes to pass there's a chance none of us will be here to stop it. You know what hell you've been through; do you really want to put another mother through that?'

Annie had thought about that. There was part of her that ached with the thought of inflicting that pain, but the Shuttleworth family had shown little care for her feelings, and any guilt for what happened in the future would lay squarely on their shoulders.

'I have to do it for Emily.'

Ginny nodded. 'I understand. I'm sure if I'd been through what you have, I'd do the same.'

'If the coven does agree, when do we tell Henry Shuttleworth?'

Ginny shook her head. 'We *don't*. People are suspicious enough of us here.' They both looked at the two old women who were engaged in chatter, occasionally peering over their cats'-eye spectacles to observe Ginny and Annie. 'If he got wind of anything like that it would put us all in danger. As it is, we're lucky they don't still burn witches at the stake.'

Annie slumped. The whole point of the curse was to punish Henry Shuttleworth. If he died not knowing, then why bother doing it at all?

'He will find out in time, Sylvia will see to that. You must be patient. That's if everybody agrees to go ahead,' she warned.

Annie looked beyond Ginny's shoulder and through the window. Poppet was crossing the village green that formed a triangle in the small village, her jet-black hair and coat stark against the snow-covered grass. She was thirteen years old, but her slight frame and hunched shoulders gave her the look of a much younger girl. The church bells rang out from beyond the heath as Annie ran out of the café door.

By the time Annie had reached Poppet, PC Pickford was already talking to her, leaning towards the girl, trying to make conversation with the sullen teen. Annie put her arm around Poppet's shoulder, the girl's coat damp from the mist.

'What are you doing out here, Poppet? You'll catch your death.'

'I wish Sylvia would keep a better eye on her,' said the constable. 'She shouldn't be out alone.' PC Pickford looked over to a group of much older-looking teens, who had gathered together. They were eyeing proceedings with menacing grins.

Poppet glared at the policewoman, who raised her eyebrows at Annie.

'She's thirteen — my Emily was playing out far younger than that.'

Neither said it, but both were aware that Poppet was not like other children. The coven was the focus of whispers and idle gossip, but Poppet was the source of fear and suspicion. A loner of a child sent home from school on more than one occasion for biting her tormentors or refusing to take part in lessons. It was noted that following several of these suspensions, her teachers would find themselves the victim of an accident or bad fortune and the finger of blame was always pointed firmly at Poppet.

'Well, maybe one of us should take her back home now.'

The teens restarted their games, throwing snowballs at each other, laughing and jeering. A stray snowball flew through the air and hit Poppet's coat, the icy ball causing her to step back. The teens fell quiet, perhaps because of the presence of the policewoman, but more likely because of the child that they feared and chastised in equal measures.

'Come on, love, let's get you home,' Annie said, brushing down her coat and turning her away from the kids.

'I saw you the other night,' PC Pickford said.

Annie's mind flashed back to the night of the coven meeting.

'Be careful what you get involved with, Annie — people talk.'

Annie's cheeks reddened. 'Talk is *all* people do around here.'

'I'm doing my best, Annie. I've tried to get answers for you.'

'It's not answers I need. It's justice, for Emily.'

'We all want that—'

'*All?* This village is practically on the payroll of the Shuttleworths, including your boss. You're as powerless as I am around here.'

PC Pickford was about to say something else, but Annie knew there was nothing more that could be said on the subject. As much as she despised the police of Nether Dale, she knew PC Pickford had done all she could, but to no avail.

'Just be careful, OK?' the PC warned. 'You know what the family is capable of.'

Annie smiled briefly, then took Poppet's hand and led her across the green.

Away from the stares of suspicious locals, Annie felt the child relax under the touch of her hand. Poppet pulled away slightly but Annie held tight, partly because she didn't want to risk her running away, but mainly because she missed the sensation of maternal touch. She felt the glare of the girl looking up at her.

'You shouldn't wander around the village alone; people can be mean. They don't understand us, Poppet.'

The child regarded her face, a look of defiance etched into her pinched features.

'Are you going to help Emily?' said Poppet.

Annie stopped walking. 'What do you mean?'

'You're going to hurt that man, curse him?'

Annie looked up and down the street: a man walking his dog, tennis ball in hand, heading towards the heath.

'No, Poppet, nobody is hurting anybody, OK?'

The child's eyes narrowed. She whispered in a low, growling voice, 'I heard you.'

'You really loved Emily, didn't you?'

The child's face softened for a moment. Emily had been Poppet's babysitter, friend and protector. The one she had called for when she didn't get her way, the one who had soothed her dark moods and irrational cries. Annie had barely given a thought to how her death might have affected this small child, who was only ten when it happened. The way adults went about their business and spoke in whispers, assuming the child's attention was elsewhere — but Poppet wasn't a normal child, and the death of her only ally had hit her hard.

Poppet leaned in closer to Annie, who crouched to hear her.

'I want him hurt too.'

CHAPTER 9

Samantha's first day at Hallow Croft began with a handover and introduction from the nurse coming off night duty: a list of the residents and their needs, those that had more serious health issues, and those with special dietary requirements. Samantha studied the paperwork, taking in all the information and asking the nurse to explain anything that was unclear.

'Oh, and one more thing,' the night nurse said, yawning and stretching her arms above her head. 'Mrs Dawson in room fifteen. She can be a little *tricky*, we just have a few named staff see to her. New faces worry her, according to Mr Shuttleworth. No serious medical issues, just apt to lash out.'

'Right,' said Samantha.

As soon as the night staff left, Samantha put the paperwork into the filing cabinet and made her way out to the residents. The kitchen at Hallow Croft was buzzing with the rattling of cups and saucers being loaded onto trolleys and the hiss of boiling water spluttering inside giant metal urns. Samantha watched from the doorway as the cook, Cathy, grabbed fistfuls of teabags with the delicacy of a prizefighter, dropping them into large white teapots before placing them under the urn taps and filling them with steaming water. She jiggled her hips as Christmas music played on a flour-covered radio in the corner.

Valerie brushed past Samantha, her face flushed.

'Morning, Matron.'

'Hi, Valerie, is everything OK?'

'Mrs Ollerton takes two of us. She's still not dressed, as Debby's been faffing around trying to find Mr Benton's favourite blue socks and—'

'Here, take a break for a minute.'

Samantha took a teapot from a tray and poured the dark liquid into a cup that sat on a white saucer.

Valerie looked aghast. 'The teas and biscuits won't hand themselves out.' She wiped the beads of sweat from her forehead.

'And you won't be able to hand them out if you collapse on the floor in exhausted stress. Trust me, I'm a matron.'

Cathy eyed Valerie suspiciously as she reluctantly took the cup and saucer. A mountain of custard creams bounced on a large white plate that Cathy dropped onto the serving trolley without a word to the two women. Valerie winced as she took a sip.

'This'll put hairs on my chest.'

'The old folk like it strong. That's proper tea, that,' Cathy said.

'I'll take the trolley this morning, it'll give me a chance to meet the residents,' said Samantha.

'You can't do that, you're the matron.'

'Which means I'm in charge, so I can do what I like. When you've finished your tea, go and help Debby find those socks and get Mrs Ollerton up. I'm sure I can handle this.'

Samantha began to push the trolley out of the kitchen, stopping as she reached the door and turning back to Valerie.

'The other night . . .'

'Yes?'

'Did Mrs Dawson hurt you?'

Valerie's face was blank as Samantha continued, beginning to doubt herself. 'I'm surprised you haven't got a bruise, that's all. It looked quite nasty.'

'You must have been mistaken. Mrs Dawson is tricky, but she didn't hurt me. Wisp of a thing like her?'

Samantha looked at Valerie's arm and then to her face, wondering if she'd been more tired than she'd realised.

'Right, OK. That's good then, no accident report to worry about.'

Valerie chuckled. 'No, Matron, all fine here.'

Samantha narrowed her eyes slightly, then shook the moment away, going back to her trolley and heading into the day room.

'Who are you?' a cross-looking woman with pinched features and paper-thin skin asked, her beady eyes fixed on Samantha.

'I'm your new matron.'

The old woman didn't look convinced. Samantha leaned forward, pointing to her badge:

Matron

Hallow Croft Nursing Home

The woman nodded. 'If you say so.'

'And what's your name?' asked Samantha.

'Mrs Potter to you.'

'Nice to meet you, Mrs Potter.'

'Huh,' the woman returned, snatching a biscuit from the tray.

Samantha smiled politely and wheeled the trolley to the next resident, a jolly man reading *The Times*.

'Tea or coffee?'

He dropped his paper down and smiled broadly.

'A new face, how lovely! Tea please, two sugars and a splash of milk.'

'My name is Samantha, I'm the new matron here.'

'Bert Lancaster, former member of Her Majesty's army.' He saluted her.

'Lovely to meet you, Bert.'

Samantha handed him his tea. His long fingers clutched the handle, trembling slightly, causing the china cup to rattle against the saucer.

'Biscuit?' Samantha held out the plate of custard creams.

'Terrible what happened, wasn't it?' Bert said, taking a bite of the biscuit, crumbs tumbling down his woollen cardigan.

Samantha had been watching two residents bickering over the remote control. 'Sorry?' She returned her focus to Bert. 'What was terrible?'

'Bert!' an elegant woman across the way scolded, raising an eyebrow, daring him to continue.

Bert looked puzzled, then something seemed to register and he turned back to Samantha.

'Are there any bourbons?' he asked, holding the remainder of the pale biscuit aloft.

'Pardon? Oh, I don't know, I'll check for you.'

An alarm rang out, not a light buzz, but a hard, constant ringing. The emergency alarm.

'Sorry, Bert, I have to go and see what that's about.'

Samantha ran out of the room and scanned a large board of numbers, each with a light next to it. A small red light flashed rapidly by room number 15.

She jogged up the stairs, taking two at a time, until she reached the first floor. Her eyes scanned the doors as she followed the numbers across the landing. Samantha turned the corner and looked ahead to the door she had been blocked from on her first night. The red light flashed rapidly, illuminating the surrounds.

Valerie ran past her, knocking her sideways, and rushed into the room. Samantha steadied herself and walked at a pace to the door. She pushed on the handle, but the door was locked. She could hear raised voices behind it and, she thought, light sobs. She rapped her knuckles on the door as the flashing light above turned off.

'Valerie, it's Matron, can you let me in?'

She put her ear to the door: muffled voices and a hissing of words. She knocked again and clutched the handle, rattling it up and down.

'Open the door this min—'

The lock turned and an eye peered at Samantha from the other side.

'All in hand, Matron,' said Valerie.

'I'd like to come in.'

Samantha went to reach for the handle again and Valerie slid through the door onto the landing, not letting it open an inch more than it needed to for her to exit. She closed the door and blocked it with her large frame.

'Whose room is this?'

'Nothing for you to worry about, Matron, it's only Mrs Dawson. Debby pulled the emergency cord by mistake.'

'Mrs Dawson?'

'It's best if we deal with this. Mrs Dawson doesn't like strange faces, it worries her. You'll only make it worse. Didn't they explain to you at your introduction, she's only to be looked after by limited staff?'

'Yes, but she might need medical help, Valerie. You're not qualified to judge that.'

'No, she's fine. Like I said, Debby just made a silly mistake.' Valerie tilted her head and put a cold hand on Samantha's forearm. 'Don't take it personally, she's a funny one. The last matron tried to care for her too and she had none of it from her either.'

The mention of the previous matron caused Samantha to pause, questions still unanswered about her swift departure. It occurred to her that part of the reason might be the woman whose glinting eyes were staring back at her now. But if Valerie thought Samantha could be intimidated out of a job, she had another think coming. The room had quietened and Samantha decided this was a battle she didn't need to fight right now.

'Well, if you're sure you have everything in hand, I'll leave you to it. Call me if you need anything.'

When she reached the end of the corridor, she heard the door open behind her. Debby exited Mrs Dawson's room clutching her scalp, her cheeks flushed and wet with tears. Samantha felt her heart stutter as Debby took her hand away from her head and revealed a small, bald, bloody patch of skin.

CHAPTER 10

Jonathan handed Finn's lead to Lily, along with a couple of small plastic bags, for picking up Finn's *business*, as he called it.

'Don't be afraid to be firm with him, Lily. Diane's spoiled him rotten so he can be a bit of a handful. Now, are you sure you're OK with him?'

Lily nodded. 'I used to walk my friend's German Shepherd.'

'Ah, very well then, you'll be fine with Finn. Now, keep him away from the residents as he can be a bit over-enthusiastic. We don't want to be sued!' He smiled and pointed towards a patch of open grass. 'Over there's a good spot, nice and open. Keep away from the woods, though: they're bigger than you think and once you're in there it's easy to get lost.'

Lily nodded, trying to take in all the instructions as Finn pulled eagerly on the other end of the lead. She held on tightly as Finn sniffed at the grass, the scent of a rabbit urging him forward. Up ahead the rabbit stood stock still, its nose twitching as it surveyed the danger no more than twenty metres away. Finn pulled Lily across the tufts of yellowing grasses poking through the wet snow. She tried to keep her balance in her Converse shoes, the canvas already sodden.

'Do gardens, Finn,' she commanded — the magic words her old friend Sophie had used for her dog Beau. Finn continued to sniff the ground. 'Wee wees?' Lily tried.

Finn cocked his leg against a fallen branch. His head froze, nose violently sniffing the air. Before Lily had chance to lead him away, Finn spotted the rabbit in the distance, and it seemed the rabbit knew, as it quickly turned and bolted towards the woods. Lily didn't have time to firm her footing as the dog lunged towards it, his long, muscular body flying through the air, grey fur tight to his frame. The lead that Lily had wrapped around her hand began to unravel and, before she could grasp the last few inches, the rope dragged across her skin, causing her to let go and cup her burning palm. She watched helplessly as Finn bounded after the animal and into the woods.

'Finn!'

When she reached the woods, Lily spun around, certain she would catch sight of the giant dog lolloping through the trees like a racehorse.

'Finn!' Lily called, her voice catching in the wind.

She imagined returning without the dog, the look on Diane and Jonathan's faces, and worse still, the look on her mum's. She'd lose her job and then they'd have to start all over again. The thought of her mum scouring yet more job adverts, leaving a life that had just started for the two of them, was unbearable.

Lily entered the woods, kicking the mulched leaves as ice-cold water squelched between her toes. She picked up a large knotty stick and pushed at the brambles around her, making her own pathway through the trees in the hope she could retrace it afterwards. Jonathan's warning about getting lost now rang in her head.

'Finn!'

She heard a distant bark and stopped in her tracks, hoping she would hear it again. She waited a moment and then it came, this time more manic, echoing around the endless trees that surrounded her. Lily ran as fast as she could, tiny thorns and daggerlike twigs catching on her striped woollen tights, as she leaped and raced through the trees, trying to follow the coarse barks of the dog.

Relief pulsed through her as she burst into a clearing and caught sight of him busily digging at the ground, unaware of the worry he had caused. He began to bark again, pawing at the snow-covered ground, sending dirt flying into the air. Lily called his name again, but he didn't turn to her; his snout had disappeared into the hole he had created. She reached his side and coiled the lead once again around her other hand, the red welt on her palm still burning from his escape.

'Finn, come on.' Lily tugged at the lead, anxious to get him back to the cottage. He didn't move. She pulled as hard as she could, but the stubborn dog held firm, sniffing frantically at the ground.

It was then she spotted it. The smooth white bone of a skull. Lily edged forward, pushing Finn away with her hip; he seemed to have calmed now, distracted by a pile of soggy brown leaves. She crouched down, lifted the skull up to eye level and peered into the hollow cavities where eyes once sat. The skull was long, two horns curled from the top. She ran her finger round the large orbital holes and down the narrow lines to where its nose had once been. She held it on her palm, lifting her hand to the light as skies darkened above her. A goat's skull maybe. Gently, she placed it back in the ground, noticing a burned-out tealight poking from the dirt beside it. She lifted it out and spun it on her palm, then clawed at the ground, revealing a further tealight. She shuddered, imagining the local goths carrying out some sort of occult ceremony here. She threw the candles back on the ground and hurriedly covered them over, along with the skull.

She gave a disapproving look to the unrepentant Finn, who was busy worrying a gnarled stick.

'Come on, let's get out of here before you desecrate another animal's grave.'

Lily hadn't noticed the standing stones when she had first approached Finn. Now she turned slowly: one, two . . . there were nine in all. No taller than gravestones, each a slightly different thickness and height, and all leaning at angles to the side or forward. She reached out and touched the cold surface of one. A crow above cawed loudly and she clamped her hand to her chest.

Jesus.

She laughed nervously, glancing through the trees, feeling suddenly alone and lost. Above, the clouds began to gather and the sky turned charcoal. Lily turned and ran. Finn galloped beside her, jumping in excitement at the new game.

She fled the small clearing chased by the screams of crows from above. Her fingers wound around Finn's lead as they ran, partly to make sure he didn't run off again, partly because she felt safer with him by her side. She stopped suddenly by an ancient-looking tree, noticing something hanging in the wind. Finn came to standstill, looking up at her as she peered through the branches, her eyes searching. Swaying above her head were small dolls tied to the tree by twine. Thin, hand-sewn cloth dolls, intricately made and weather-worn, each in a varying state of deterioration, each eye a stitched cross of black thread. The same thread crosshatched their stomachs, not neat like the seams of their bodies, but rather a crude, messy tangle made by an inexpert hand, as though attempting to fix a tear. The hair on the dolls looked human. They hung by their necks, swinging limply to the creak of the branches above.

Lily reached for one, but as she did Finn began pulling forward and she was forced to hold on and follow for fear of losing him again. She spun around, trying to remember this spot, but as the winter rain began to fall it all became a blur and before long she found herself back in the open air with Hallow Croft in sight.

Diane was waiting at the door to the cottage, a towel held out in front of her at arm's length. She was wearing a pale pink trouser suit and white gym shoes. Lily could smell her flowery perfume from the end of the path.

'Give him a rub down, would you, Lily? He'll ruin my new throws.'

Lily took the towel and crouched next to the giant dog, rubbing his body roughly with the towel. Every now and then she would catch that perfect spot and he would raise a leg and try to scratch himself.

'Good boy, Finn,' she said, her voice soothing and low.

'Did you have a nice walk?' asked Diane.

'Yes, he was really good.'

Diane tilted her head, arms crossed. 'How are you liking it here? Everything OK?'

Lily ruffled Finn's head with the towel, his jaws trying to catch it and pull it away.

'Yes, everyone's lovely.'

Diane took the towel from Lily, folding the wet material and holding it away from her clothes. 'That's good. I . . . I really hope everything goes well for you and your mum here.'

Lily waited, as if Diane might say more, the tone of her voice edged with something Lily couldn't put her finger on.

'In the woods,' Lily began, 'there was a tree with dolls hanging from it.'

Diane's face dropped. 'Dolls?'

'Funny little dolls with stitches for eyes.'

'I don't know about that,' said Diane. 'Probably children messing about, you know how it is. If I were you, I'd keep away from there. You never know who's about. There's some strange folk in this village.' Diane glanced towards the woods and then took Finn by his collar and scuttled into the cottage, closing the door, leaving Lily standing alone.

She heard Diane shoo Finn out of a room and a door slam, and felt sorry for him, wishing she could take him back to the flat for a bit. Jonathan wandered round from the garden.

'Good walk?'

'Yes, thanks for letting me take Finn.'

'Not at all, it's you doing us a favour. I'm afraid the poor boy is rather neglected during the day.' He bent towards her, his voice now a whisper. 'Diane was after a Pomeranian but I got my own way. Wolfhounds have been in our family for years.'

Lily smiled. They had a beautiful cottage and their own residential home, not to mention Finn. Lily had no sympathy for Diane if all that was making her angry was a big goofy hound. She was about to go back to their flat in Hallow Croft when she stopped.

'What are those stones?' Lily said.

Jonathan looked puzzled.

'The nine stones in the clearing. I tried to keep out of the woods, but Finn was determined to follow a rabbit.' She left out the part about him running free, for fear he may not let her walk him again.

She noticed Jonathan's eye flicker slightly. 'Oh, those? Nothing really, some historical significance, I suppose. Some myths about nine ladies who danced on the sabbath and got turned to stone — fairy tales, I'm afraid. Old villages like Nether Dale are full of them. Naughty Finn, doesn't listen to a word anyone says!'

When he had gone, Lily took her phone out of her pocket and googled *Nine Ladies, Derbyshire* and a raft of links appeared.

Jonathan was right. It was a story about the women who had dared to have fun on a Sunday and were frozen in stone for their punishment. She scrolled idly down until something else caught her eye and she felt a knot in her stomach.

The Strange Curse of Hallow Croft.

CHAPTER 11

'You OK, love?'

Samantha turned to the elderly woman behind her. A kind face and softly permed hair. She leaned on a walking frame, a small handbag swinging from her wrist.

'You look like you've seen a ghost,' the woman said.

Samantha caught herself and took a deep breath, the image of Debby's bleeding scalp still vivid in her mind.

'I'm absolutely fine, thank you for asking . . .'

'Renee,' she held out her hand, 'I'm in room four.'

Samantha took her hand and shook it. Renee's skin was soft and powdery.

'I'm Samantha, the new matron.'

'Well, Samantha, why don't you come to my room? I have just the thing.'

Before Samantha could answer, Renee was turning the frame and making her way to her room. Samantha followed, checking the board as she passed, the red light of number 15 now extinguished. Renee's room was filled with the fragrance of cinnamon and cloves. Samantha lifted a dried piece of orange from the bowl of potpourri and inhaled.

'Smells like Christmas.'

Renee handed her a small crystal glass containing a dark amber liquid.

'And this tastes like Christmas.'

'I shouldn't really,' Samantha said.

'Oh, go on, a little snifter won't do you any harm,' Renee urged, taking her own drink down in one gulp.

Samantha hesitated, then followed suit. As soon as the liquid hit the back of her throat, she gasped and held her hand to her neck. Renee quickly poured water from a glass jug into a tumbler and handed it to Samantha.

'Not used to the strong stuff?'

Samantha caught her breath. 'More of a wine person myself.'

'You young ones can't take the pace.'

Samantha looked around the room, instantly feeling at ease with the chintz armchair and crocheted throw over the bed. She was back in the safety of her nan's house, a place of solace and security, somewhere to escape the chaos of home. Renee sat on her bed and gestured for Samantha to sit in the floral armchair.

'How are you settling in?' Renee asked.

'Early days, but so far, so good.'

Renee regarded her for a moment, words seemingly on the tip of her tongue.

'How long have you lived here?' Samantha asked, breaking the silence.

'Just . . . don't let anyone put you off staying. Stand your ground, love.'

'Right,' she replied, not wanting to get into idle chatter about staff members with a resident. 'Plenty of experience of doing that after twenty years in the NHS.'

'I'm sure you have, but Hallow Croft has its own . . . peculiarities. Nether Dale has—'

The door opened and a face appeared, eyeing them both. Samantha stood and approached the small woman looking up at her. Her thick grey hair curled over her shoulder in a long plait that reached her stomach.

'That's our Aparna,' said Renee. 'I think she's forgotten where her room is.'

'Hi, Aparna, I'm the new matron, Samantha. I can help you get back to your room.'

Aparna looked up at Samantha. The woman's delicate hands reached out and gently touched Samantha's cheek. Aparna began to mumble under her breath, her brow furrowed. Samantha looked to Renee, who pushed herself up from the bed and took hold of her walker. She edged her way over to them and put her hand on Aparna's shoulder. At her touch, Aparna silenced, her agitation easing.

'Now then, Aparna, let me take you to your room. I could do with a little walk,' said Renee.

Renee winked at Samantha, who had to swallow down the second bitter pill of the day where her services weren't needed.

Samantha turned to Renee's dressing table and a faded colour photograph of two young women in flared jeans and platform sandals leaning against a car bonnet, their hair straight and long. Samantha loved seeing these snippets of the past. For most, the elderly were invisible. A dying strain on the system. The full, vibrant lives of beautiful women and handsome men forgotten with time and weakening bones.

A bell rang out in the corridor and Samantha gathered herself, peeking at the carriage clock on Renee's shelf. One o'clock. She sighed. Two hours until the end of her shift.

* * *

Samantha took a wire basket from a stack just inside the door of Nether Dale Stores & Post Office. Bright fluorescent lights illuminated two rows of metal shelving units that shook when the shop door closed. She took out a list from her pocket and scanned it, making her way down the first shelf. She put the list back in her pocket and picked up a packet of powdered mashed potato, eyes narrowing at the ingredients before putting it back on the shelf and opting for a tin instead. She would go into town as soon as she had a day off, but until then she would have to make do with random cans of food, a bag of pasta and a packet of frozen sweetcorn.

She placed the basket on the counter, waiting for the assistant to finish serving an elderly man at the post office counter. Samantha scanned the assortment of cheap toys that sat in a spinning rack: packs of Happy Families playing cards, cheap dolls and multi-coloured, glittery bouncy balls. God, she missed buying stuff like this for Lily. She looked back to the counter and across to a mobile that hung silently, small sparkly black pendants dangling under the harsh light.

'That's pretty,' she said to the assistant, who was now stood in front of her.

The woman glanced up and then back to Samantha. 'Did you find everything you needed?'

Samantha thought about her original list. Feta cheese, mixed salad leaves, balsamic vinegar and sourdough bread, accepting it was naïve of her to expect any small village shop to sell these things. She smiled, 'Yes, thank you.'

The woman jabbed at the till buttons, carefully placing the items in a plastic bag. The door opened again, causing the mobile to jangle. Samantha turned to see Valerie enter, an empty linen shopping bag hanging from her wrist.

'Hi, Valerie,' Samantha called.

'That's £5.65,' the shop assistant said, glancing nervously at Valerie.

'Do you take—'

The assistant held out a card terminal and Samantha found her debit card. Valerie's distinct herbal perfume wafted around, her presence ever closer.

'Cooking up a storm, are we?' Valerie beamed.

Samantha noticed the assistant take a step back.

'Sorry?' Samantha said, turning back to Valerie, who was opening her carrier bag and peering at the tinned vegetables.

'Of course, a young girl like Lily needs a healthy diet — not five a day, but ten a day, I say.'

Samantha clamped the carrier bag shut.

Valerie took a step back, a thin smile on her face. 'You're doing the best you can.' She looked to the assistant, her tone more demanding. 'I've come to collect my parcel. Can you hurry, only I've to be back at the home shortly.' She looked at Samantha. 'Hope you don't mind, Matron, Don is covering for me.'

Samantha shook her head, still annoyed at the not-so-thinly veiled barb about her shopping.

'Of course not, as long as the residents are in good hands.'

Samantha watched the assistant scuttle away from the counter and make her way back to the post office. The jangling mobile still tinkled as if the door were open and the winter air circulating. The assistant reached down behind the counter and handed a package to Valerie. Valerie held it protectively, gently running her fingers over the brown paper bundle, secured with string.

'Looks interesting,' called Samantha, 'I love the paper and string.'

Valerie turned to Samantha, her brow furrowed as if she wasn't sure where she was for a moment.

'Is it a gift?'

Samantha noticed the assistant staring at her. She was sure she was shaking her head.

Icy air curled between the three women.

'What?' Samantha said, nonplussed.

There was a beat of silence before Valerie answered her, 'Yes, Matron, a gift from an old acquaintance.'

Valerie put the package into her shopping bag and, without saying another word, left the shop and the black-jewelled mobile fell silent again.

* * *

Samantha attempted to open the tin of new potatoes with a tin opener she had found at the back of the cutlery drawer. The rusting kitchen utensil was one of many things that had been left by the previous matron, along with cupboards half filled with crockery. There were a couple of dresses hung beneath plastic on the back of her bedroom door, a gold necklace and ring, a medical journal and, most surprising, a pocket diary left in a bedside drawer. It was the first time she had found out her name — Helen — scribbled in the front with a number and Hallow Croft's address. Samantha could only assume it had all had little value to the previous matron. She would mention it to Diane at some point; she could at least post the jewellery on when she went back into Nether Dale.

The potatoes plopped into the pan, a drop of water hissing as it hit the halogen ring.

'What's for tea?' Lily asked, her towel twisted in her hair and already in her pyjamas after a shower.

'A delicious meal of tinned potatoes, frozen sweetcorn and penne pasta.' Samantha picked up a half-empty packet. 'At least I think it's pasta, the packet's pretty faded.'

'*MasterChef*, here she comes.'

'Hey, you will be amazed at the magic I can perform with a little salt and butter.'

Lily picked up the TV remote and began clicking through the five terrestrial channels, settling on a reality TV show about a couple house hunting in the Dordogne.

'Mum, can we get Netflix?'

Samantha poured boiling water over the pasta, a splash hitting her arm.

'Shit.'

'Mum, I *said* can we get Netflix?'

'For God's sake, Lily, we've barely unpacked the boxes, give me a chance, will you?'

'Alright, I was only asking.'

Samantha ran her arm under the cold tap. 'I'm sorry, Lily, it's been a weird day, that's all.' She turned the tap off, brightening her voice. 'What have you been up to?'

'Not much. I took Finn for a walk,' Lily said, not looking away from the television.

'Oh yeah? That's nice. I bet Jonathan and Diane were pleased?'

'Magpie!' Lily shouted, putting her hand to her forehead to salute the solitary bird that had landed on the window-sill, peering into the room. She turned to Samantha. 'Mum, salute it, quick.'

Samantha smiled and flipped her middle finger at the bird, who flew off.

Lily shook her head in disgust, mumbling something about the swear jar that Samantha couldn't hear above the bubbling pans. She corralled a piece of pasta out of the burning water and popped it into her mouth, waving her hand frantically as it scalded her tongue.

The two ate the meal in front of the television. Samantha had always insisted on eating at the table previously, but here in the flat, space was scant. Lily plunged a fork into the eclectic mix of food and filled her mouth. Samantha caught her eye, waiting for a verdict, and Lily nodded.

'Not bad at all. Luckily I love salt.'

Samantha smiled. 'Cheeky so and so.'

The storage heaters had finally warmed the flat and Samantha had managed to put up a couple of their favourite prints. She allowed herself a small feeling of satisfaction; they had been here only a couple of days and already things were starting to come together. She smiled at Lily.

'What?' Lily said, her face scrunched.

'Nothing, this is just nice, isn't it?'

'Eating dinner?'

'Not just that, I mean the two of us starting a new adventure together.'

Lily shrugged, stuffed another forkful of pasta into her mouth and asked, 'Did you know about the curse?'

Samantha picked up a glass of wine from the floor and took a sip. 'What curse?'

'The curse of Hallow Croft?'

Samantha laughed. 'No. I don't know about a curse, enlighten me.'

'Well, when I was walking Finn, he ran off.'

'What? Did you get him back? If you lose that dog . . .'

'Yes, yes, that's not the point. Well, when I found him, he was sniffing round these standing stone things, the Nine Ladies.'

Lily looked at her mum as if she might know what she was talking about.

Samantha shook her head. 'The Nine Ladies?'

'Apparently, there were once nine women who danced on the Sabbath and were turned to stone for punishment.'

'Oh wait, I remember something from years ago. We just thought the people of Nether Dale were a bit weird.' Samantha smiled.

'Jonathan told me about the stones when I got back, and anyway, I googled them and saw this other thing about a curse.'

Samantha was momentarily distracted by someone on the television storming off.

'Mum.' Lily's voice broke through the house-hunting couple's argument.

'I'm listening — the curse, you said.' Samantha took another sip of wine.

'Yes, something to do with a murder, *here* at Hallow Croft. Annie was her mum, a local woman.'

'Whose mum?'

Lily became agitated. 'The murdered girl's mum.'

That got Samantha's attention. She put down her fork and contemplated her daughter a moment. 'Now you mention it, I do remember something about a young girl dying around here. But it was years ago, before I was even born.'

'Doesn't that freak you out? That someone was killed here?'

'Not really, people die all the time in terrible circumstances.'

Lily looked at her agog.

'I'm a nurse, Lily, if death and trauma shocked me, I couldn't do my job.'

'It's not just death, Mum, it's *murder*. Anyway, I'm going to find out more.'

'Leave it be, Lily. You'll only dig up silly rumours. Every village around here has them. Besides, this is Jonathan's family home, you don't want to upset him, do you?'

Lily turned away, sulking as she always had when her mum used logic.

'Listen. It's all nonsense made up by people who have nothing better to do. If someone died here then that's awful, but it's the past. Any talk of a curse is rubbish, that I can promise you. Just like saluting lonely birds.'

Lily pursed her lips, her face still turned away.

'I have ice cream.'

Her daughter turned to her, shaking her head at her mother's obvious attempt to bribe her back into her good books, but the smile on her lips betrayed her.

Samantha took their empty plates to the sink. She slid them into the washing-up bowl, turned on the hot tap and squeezed washing-up liquid into the flowing water, creating an expanding mass of bubbles. She wished Lily hadn't spoken to Jonathan and seen that article. Local gossip and superstition irritated her, busying bored minds. It was part of the reason she was glad to leave Nether Dale in the first place. She wasn't about to give air to it now, much less have her daughter becoming obsessed.

Samantha peeled the lid off the tub; icy particles covered the yellow ice cream she had found at the back of the freezer, just out of date but salvageable. She scraped the ice away and spooned coils of dessert into two bowls.

'Will you walk Finn again?'

Lily nodded, testing the ice cream using the tip of her spoon. 'I hope so.'

'Just do me a favour: lay off the rumours of curses and demons. It's superstitious clap-trap and there are much better things for you to fill your time with, like working on your art portfolio.'

Lily rolled her eyes as she licked remnants of ice cream from her spoon, long-since murdered girls forgotten. Her attention was now on the television. A wave of love came over Samantha as she watched her daughter smiling at something silly on the screen. The feeling turned to sadness. She knew that these moments were fleeting, and soon, like all children, she would be gone.

74

CHAPTER 12

The dining room at Hallow Croft residential home was quiet, other than the nerve-jangling screeches of metal scraping across porcelain. Samantha stood at the end of the room in front of a medicine trolley, popping pills into small plastic cups and mixing orange powders into beakers of tap water.

'Can you give this to Mr Alderton?' said Samantha, handing Debby a cup with thick orange liquid in it.

Debby passed the gloopy medicine over and Mr Alderton dutifully drank, wincing as it passed down his gullet. It was Lily's first day at the new school. Samantha felt nervous for her starting mid-term, but had marvelled at how confident she had been that morning, while Samantha had been riddled with angst for her daughter. If Lily wasn't happy there, then her plans of a new start would be seriously scuppered.

'Have you seen Renee this morning?' Samantha asked.

Valerie had sat down at the side of the breakfast room and was reading an old magazine.

'No, I haven't, shall I go and get her?'

'I'll go to her.'

The older woman nodded and went back to her magazine.

'Valerie?'

'Yes, Matron?'

Valerie looked irritated at having to look up from the magazine again.

'Perhaps Debby might need a hand?'

'What?' Valerie glanced over at Debby, who was balancing a large jug of orange juice and several glasses on a tray. 'Right, I see.'

Samantha wheeled the trolley a short way down the corridor.

The door to Renee's room was ajar. The scent of flowers wafted from a squat white candle on her dressing table. Samantha knocked gently.

'Renee?'

The door opened and Renee beamed back at her.

'Good morning, Matron.'

'Morning, Renee, how are you today?' Samantha held out a small pot of pills to her. 'I have your medication.'

'Come in, have a sit down.'

'I haven't really—'

'Nonsense, you've got five minutes, I'm sure.'

'Two minutes, and no whiskey.'

She locked up the trolley and pushed it into the doorway, but kept the door open. If anybody wanted her, they would be able to find her easily.

'Do they mind you having a candle lit, Renee?'

'Not as long as it's blown out at night and I'm in the room. Mr and Mrs Shuttleworth are very sensible like that. They don't mollycoddle us, not like most places.'

Samantha glanced at the framed photo of a young girl next to the candle.

'Your daughter?'

'Not mine, no, but I was close to her. Sit yourself down then.'

Samantha did as she was told, looking around the room at the pictures and photographs that covered the walls. Renee with a small boy in her arms. A café where the grocery-shop-cum-post-office now stood. Nether Dale from the 1970s and 80s.

'You grew up here?'

'Born and bred, for my sins. You, where are you from?'

'I've moved from Manchester but I grew up in Heather Brook, not too far away.'

'Ah, the posh part of the Gatherings,' Renee smiled.

'It didn't seem that way at the time, not on our little estate anyway.'

'How is your daughter settling in?'

'Very well, thank you. She's made firm friends with the Shuttleworths' dog—'

'Ah, Finn!'

'Yes, that's right.'

'I wish they'd let him come into Hallow Croft still.'

'Why don't they?'

'There was an incident.'

'What kind of incident?'

'The poor beast found his way up to Mrs Dawson's room, didn't he? One of the carers had left the door slightly open, got distracted by her mobile phone, no doubt. Anyway, she must have had food in there or something and he wandered in.'

'What happened? Did he bite her?'

'Not at all, quite the opposite really.'

'What do you mean?'

'Well, whatever she did he made such a racket they heard him all the way over at the cottage and came running. Valerie was shouting blue murder and the dog was cowering and shaking.'

'Did Valerie hurt him, or Mrs Dawson?'

Renee shook her head. 'They didn't find anything physically wrong with him, but he wasn't right for a week. Off his food, not wanting to go out. They thought he might have to be put to sleep he got that weak.'

'God, the poor thing.'

'Valerie, she's—'

The medicine trolley rattled forward and Valerie appeared at the door, her stature almost filling the frame.

'If the mountain won't come to Mohammed, then Mohammed must come to the mountain!' she chirped, carrying a plastic tray of food. 'Has Renee had her pills yet, Matron?'

Samantha smiled. 'No, she hasn't, and they're to be had with food so good timing, Valerie.'

Samantha stood up to leave, pushing the medicine trolley out.

'Nice to see you again, Renee, I'll see you later.'

Valerie closed the door behind her as Samantha stepped into the corridor. Mr Alderton called to her, waving an empty medicine pot.

'On my way,' she shouted out, before stopping and moving back to the door. She stood close, her ear to the wood. The door opened swiftly again and Samantha jumped back, feeling her face flush.

'You forgot these, Matron.'

Valerie held up the keys, jangling them from side to side. Her eyes fixed on Samantha's, a thin smile tight across her red lips, lipstick running into the threadlike wrinkles around her mouth.

'Oh, thank you, Valerie. That's not like me,' she said, taking the keys and putting them in her pocket.

Valerie's face relaxed, falling into a warm smile, eyes wide. 'You have to be careful here, Matron. These old folks will be having a rave if they get hold of what's in that cabinet!'

Samantha smiled. 'I'm sure they would.'

As she rushed the trolley down the corridor to meet Mr Alderton, she thought about Mrs Dawson upstairs and the poor dog. She felt her phone vibrate and took it out of her pocket, smiling at the thought of Lily texting her during the day. But she didn't recognise the number. She clicked on the icon and felt her heart pounding in her chest as a single-word message appeared.

Leave.

CHAPTER 13

Samantha tapped at the steering wheel, trying to get her thoughts in order.

Leave.

What sort of person would write something like that, without saying why or who they were. What did it even mean?

She heard the bus approaching before she caught sight of it coming over the hill. Its headlights shone through the dusk, causing her to squint.

'Jesus Christ.'

It looked like something from the 1970s, black smoke chugging from behind rising into the dusk of late afternoon. It was a yellow and sage-green monstrosity, seamed together with rust. Samantha watched as it came to a stuttering stop and three figures rose from their seats and made their way down the aisle.

Lily stepped down first, followed by a couple of other students who were sharing a joke, one grabbing the other's bag and threatening to run off with it. Lily walked alone ahead of them as they splintered off and disappeared down the hill. Samantha turned the radio off as Lily got into the car.

'How was your day?'

'Good.'

'Just good?'

'Yeah, it was good.'

Samantha started the engine.

'Going back tomorrow, then?'

'Yes.'

'Oh, how I enjoy these chats.'

Lily just groaned and began scrolling down her phone.

'Is there anything you want for your birthday?'

'We haven't had Christmas yet.'

'It's only a couple of days after. I was thinking maybe we could see if Sophie wants to come and stay as it's the holidays? I could take you both for a meal in town.'

Lily scrunched up her nose.

'It's your sixteenth, Lily, it's special.'

'I don't think it's a *thing* anymore, Mum. Besides, it will just get swallowed up by Christmas as usual.'

'I always try to make it special, don't I?'

Lily grunted, and Samantha, determined not to have an argument about it, focused on the road instead.

The drive up to Hallow Croft twisted and turned, framed by ornate shrubbery at one time meant to impress visitors, but in the faint light of the occasional lamp post it was a difficult road to navigate. Samantha peered up to the moon above the trees.

'Mum, stop!' Lily screamed.

Samantha slammed on the brakes and the two of them lurched forward, their seatbelts jamming them in place. Out of the window there was nothing but tarmac and trees.

'For Christ's sake, Lily! Don't do that again, you'll finish me off.'

'Something crossed the road up ahead, or someone, I'm positive.'

Samantha gestured towards the window. 'There's nobody there.'

'There was, I promise, Mum. I just saw a flash of something — they, *it*, ran over that way.'

Samantha turned the engine off, put on the hazard lights and opened the car door.

'Don't leave me alone, Mum.'

'It was probably a rabbit, or maybe Finn has got loose. Stay here.'

Samantha slammed the car door shut. Behind her, Lily clicked the locks. Samantha walked through a gap in the hedge, the brambles catching on her uniform. An owl called out into the clear night air, its hoot echoing across the grounds. On the other side of the shrubbery, the lawn fell away to the edge of woodland. She wrapped her cardigan tightly over her uniform, feeling suitably underdressed as usual, as she peered about her.

It must have been a wild animal, she decided. She turned to go back to the car, then stopped. In the half-light she could just make out something gouged into the ancient bark of a thick tree trunk. A pattern. She ran her finger over the mark, a circle within a triangle, a line scoured at the top, bottom and each side, as if the triangle had been placed over a cross. There was something familiar about it.

'Hello there,' a voice called behind her.

Samantha screamed louder than she had ever done in her life. She spun round, brandishing her keys as a weapon.

'Jesus, Valerie,' Samantha sputtered with relief at the sight of the older woman. 'You nearly gave me a heart attack.'

'Your car,' Valerie said. 'It's blocking the road.'

Samantha took her hand away from her chest and attempted to slow her breath. 'Of course, sorry about that. Lily thought she saw someone crossing the road.'

Lily appeared through the hedge. 'Are you OK, Mum?'

'Yes, Valerie just gave me a start, that's all.'

'She's a bundle of nerves your mum, Lily.'

Samantha ignored the comment. 'Are you sure all the residents are in the house?'

'All present and correct, I've just checked on them.'

Samantha thought back to her first night. 'And Mrs Dawson?'

'Sleeping like a baby, I've only just left her.'

'Right, then investigation over. Must have been a fox or something.'

'A big fox,' Lily grunted.

Samantha followed Lily back through the hedge, followed by Valerie. Silence reigned but for the sound of their footsteps. A swish of snow that lay across the branches brushed her arms, leaving flecks of frost on Samantha's clothes. A shudder ran up her spine, that spooked feeling a woman has when footsteps follow behind at night.

'You OK, lovely? You look a bit pale,' Valerie said.

'Yes, I'm fine. Just tired, I think.'

Samantha got back into her car, manoeuvring around Valerie's. She looked in the rear-view mirror, her eyes narrowing as Valerie didn't get back in her car, but instead disappeared through the hedge again.

'What's wrong, Mum?'

Samantha put her focus back on the road. 'Nothing, love.' She pasted a weak smile on her face. 'I'm just tired.'

'Maybe it *was* a fox,' Lily offered, 'or the Beast of Bodmin has moved up north!'

As they pulled up to Hallow Croft, Samantha glanced up to Mrs Dawson's window, a dull glow of orange light seeping through the curtains.

CHAPTER 14

By 9 p.m. the night staff had gotten most residents settled for bed and were sitting in the staff room waiting for the alert of buzzers. Samantha let herself in through the side door, careful not to make too much noise. She still couldn't find her bottle opener, and figured no one would mind if she borrowed one. She padded down the corridor towards the kitchen, but stopped to peek into the television room. An elderly women sat on one of the sofas, crocheted blankets pulled tightly over her knees. Samantha walked over, unable to remember the woman's name. Her head was bowed in sleep, hand still clutching the remote with bony fingers. Samantha gently prised it from her, switched off the television and continued on her way to the kitchen.

The place was spotless. The cook had cleaned and polished every surface and piece of metal until it shone. A stack of laminated health and safety checks, all ticked and signed, leaned against a giant refrigerator, which whirred softly in the corner. Everything was bathed in the violet light of a fly catcher high on the wall. Samantha flicked through a folder of weekly menus on the counter. Pasta, roasts, pizza and Chinese. She felt her stomach rumble.

Everything in the kitchen was industrial-sized, from the colanders that sat high on shelves, to the tins of custard and bags of flour. Metal utensils jangled in the first drawer opened as she sorted through potato peelers and slotted spoons. Surely there was a bottle opener here somewhere. Then her skin caught something sharp and she felt a rush of relief. She withdrew the spiral bottle opener and dropped it into her pyjama pocket.

Resisting the urge to pillage the multi-packs of crisps before she left, Samantha closed the utensil drawer and turned to leave.

As she swung round, the door to the kitchen opened. Aparna clutched a heavy book and shuffled towards her.

'Aparna? Are you lost again?'

The old woman muttered under her breath, sleepy dialogue barely audible. Samantha walked to her, placing an arm gently over her shoulders and trying to guide her out of the kitchen. Aparna resisted, her feet planted firmly to the laminate floor.

'Bad, bad night,' she whispered.

'You're having a bad night?' Samantha said, her voice quiet and reassuring. 'Would you like a hot drink to take to your room?'

'They're coming back,' Aparna said, the words coming out in a low growl as if another had spoken them.

Samantha wondered if she were sleepwalking, still in some nightmare that had taken her voice and replaced it with something more sinister.

'Have you had a bad dream, Aparna?'

Aparna mumbled, agitation clear in her voice as she hissed the word: 'Jinn.'

Samantha smiled. 'Yes, gin would be lovely, but not on a school night.'

Aparna tilted her head, her eyes fixing on Samantha's.

'Jinn evil.'

'They don't call it mother's ruin for nothing.' Samantha put a hand on Aparna's shoulder. 'Come on, I think you need to sleep. I'll bring you some Horlicks, that will help.'

Aparna looked out of the window, her brow creased with concern. She turned to Samantha, then took a black stone out of her pocket and placed it in Samantha's palm.

'Protect yourself,' she said, her voice twisted.

Samantha looked down to the shiny jet stone. 'I can't take this, Aparna. It looks precious.'

Samantha tried to give it back, but the woman wrapped her hands tightly around the book she carried.

'No. For protection,' the woman insisted.

'I will protect myself, Aparna, I promise. Not much gets past me.'

Samantha wondered how she could hurry this up. As much as she felt for the old woman, all she wanted right now was to be sprawled out on the sofa with a glass of wine.

'Come on, let's get you back to bed.'

Gina, one of the night staff, burst through the kitchen door and slapped her hand to her heart when she saw Aparna. 'There you are! Oh, hello Matron, everything OK?' The care assistant eyed her Snoopy pyjamas and grinned.

Samantha looked down to her nightwear, wishing she had more sophisticated attire.

'I just needed to borrow a fork.' She patted the pocket. Her lie was quick but necessary; she didn't want her staff thinking she had a drink problem.

Aparna clutched the heavy golden book in her arms like it was a precious child. Gina put a hand gently on Aparna's shoulder and led her from the kitchen. 'Come on, Aparna, let's get you to your room and I'll bring you a nice warm drink.'

'Aparna?' Samantha called. 'How did you know I was in here? I mean, to give this gift to.' She clutched the shining stone.

Aparna's eyes suddenly met Samantha's as if seeing her clearly; a crawling sensation ran up Samantha's spine. Aparna pulled away from the care assistant.

'We cannot undo what has been done, the bloodline is her only hope.'

Gina stood behind, smiling sympathetically, then took Aparna's arm and led her gently through the door.

'Come on, ducky, I think you've been watching too many late-night films.'

* * *

Samantha twisted the spiralled spike deep into the cork. Aparna's strange behaviour wasn't unusual in a dementia patient; God knows Samantha had heard all sorts in her time caring for the elderly. It was her eyes, one moment dazed and unfocused, the next boring into Samantha's as if she could read her every thought. She pushed down the lever and the cork popped out. As the wine flowed into the glass, she peered over, trying to catch sight of Lily's sketch book from college. She relaxed into the sofa and moved idly through the pages, a feeling of pride at the beautiful sketches her daughter had created. She stopped on the final page, eyes narrowing.

The graphite had been pushed into the page to form the circle and triangle, the spikes shooting up and out. It was the same symbol that had been etched into the tree. She pushed the sketch pad away, turning it over as if not seeing it would mean it didn't exist. She took a sip of wine and wished she'd replaced the battery of her vape.

From down the hallway she heard a door open.

'Lily?'

There was the sound of footsteps and her sleepy daughter peered in at her.

'What?'

'These drawings you've done. The symbols, what are they?'

'What drawings?'

Samantha opened the art pad and showed Lily her work, searching her daughter's eyes for signs of recognition.

Lily scrunched her face up. 'I don't know, they aren't anything, just doodles. Can I go to the toilet now?' she said sleepily.

'Of course. Night night, hope the bed bugs don't bite.'

Samantha listened as Lily washed her hands and returned to bed. She'd ask again tomorrow when Lily was more awake.

She glanced down at the sketch book, then something occurred to her. She got up from the sofa, went to her bedroom and reached across the bed for the ex-matron's diary. She flicked through the pages until she found what she was looking for. There, staring up at her, were the quick doodles that her predecessor had drawn. The same triangle and circle in front of a cross.

Samantha slammed the book shut and lay back on the bed, unease skittering through her body.

CHAPTER 15

1975

'Sylvia rang.' Kevin left the sentence hanging in the air, waiting for Annie to explain.

Annie's stomach flipped. 'Did she say what it was about?'

'I didn't ask.'

'Oh right, it will be about doing more hours, I expect.'

'Skivvying for her, I don't like the idea of that.'

'Someone has to earn money.'

Kevin turned his attention back to the egg and chips on his plate. Annie saw the hurt in his eyes and regretted her words. Still, he had no right to dictate to her who she cleaned for.

She watched as he pierced the egg with a chip, and a satisfying explosion of yolk ran down onto the plate. He took a slug of tea and swallowed the lot down in one go. She grimaced. He saw the look on her face and sighed. 'What? Aren't the common folk good enough for you anymore, with your posh friends?'

Annie looked away. She wasn't in the mood for an argument.

'I've heard she's into all that black magic stuff, devil worshipping.'

Annie rolled her eyes. 'Don't talk daft, Kevin. Besides, I'm just a cleaner there, I keep myself to myself.'

He stuffed another forkful of chips into his mouth, slapping his chops together.

'Old Joe at the Skull & Feathers reckons that Sylvia's a witch.'

'Don't be bloody daft. Old Joe thought aliens were going to come down and take over when the sixties ended. He's full of stories.'

'I've heard it from others too. They reckon there's a group of them—'

Annie felt the back of her neck prickle with heat; she needed him to stop before the questions got more difficult.

'That's enough, Kev, you'll scare me, and we need the money.'

He nodded. 'Just don't you go getting involved in anything. I don't want my wife to be the talk of the pub.'

Annie scoffed at that. They had both been the talk of the entire village since Emily's death; the pitying looks were crippling, the silences draining. Before it happened, they had led a quiet life, but they had had good friends. Party invites every other weekend, coach trips to the seaside. The invites had dried up quickly. At first it was too soon, but as time went on nobody knew what to say or how to act and so it became easier to not invite them. Annie didn't mind; her heart had blown into a million pieces and there was no way of fixing that to make others feel better.

'She asked if you could go to her house at 7 p.m.'

'It must be to babysit Poppet then.'

'That's a kid's job . . .'

He trailed off, the memory of Emily's babysitting duties for Sylvia filling the air between them.

Annie stood up from the table and scraped her plate, still half full of chips, into the bin. She slid it into the sink and ran water into the bowl, watching as the remnants of yolk and grease washed away.

'I'll do the washing-up when I'm back.'

CHAPTER 16

Samantha's hand froze holding the mother-of-pearl hairbrush in the air. She looked out of the window, watching as Diane chased Jonathan into the quadrant. She was shouting something. Even at this distance, Samantha could see the full face of make-up was distorted by anger.

'What have you seen?' asked Renee, already rising from the chair.

She pulled her cardigan tightly around herself and stood next to Samantha, both transfixed by the performance outside. Jonathan had stopped now and turned to his wife, waving his arms too, mirroring hers.

'He'll give in to her, he always does.'

'Do they argue a lot then?' Samantha asked.

She didn't like to gossip, especially with patients, but the question had left her mouth before she'd been able to stop it.

'Like cats and dogs,' Renee replied, her eyes still fixed on the pantomime below.

'Really?'

'Oh yes, it's some of the only entertainment we get here.'

'Apart from the magic show later. Are you going?'

'You try and stop me, It's the only time there's an open bar here.'

Renee opened her handbag to reveal a small silver hip flask. She tapped it with a pink-painted nail, winking at Samantha. 'Just in case you're stingy with the gin.'

Samantha smiled. 'A little bit of what you fancy does you good, I say.'

Their attention was drawn back outside as Jonathan stomped to his car, red-faced, his greying hair flapping in the blustery wind. Diane stuck two fingers in the air and spun on her heels, marching back towards their cottage. Renee returned to her chair and Samantha continued to brush her soft grey curls.

'He won't be getting tea on the table tonight,' Renee said, looking at Samantha through the large dressing-table mirror.

'Too right. He's a grown man, he can get his own food.'

'You're one of them, are you?'

'One of what?' smiled Samantha, knowing full well what was coming.

Renee regarded her, her eyes narrowing. 'Are you married?'

Samantha plumped Renee's hair with her hand and reached over for a can of hairspray.

'I was never asked.'

'Lucky escape, if you ask me. You've got a job where you can look after yourself anyhow, you don't need a man.'

'There, what do you think?'

The two women looked in the mirror, Renee turning her head from side to side.

'Hairdressing's loss is our gain,' she winked.

'What do they argue about?' Samantha asked, in spite of herself. She felt at ease with Renee, like having a trusted aunt.

Samantha picked up a necklace and placed it around Renee's neck.

'You name it, they argue about it. But it's never about what it's about, is it?'

'What do you mean?' Samantha connected the clasp and let the silver chain cascade over Renee's lavender cardigan.

'I mean, you can bicker all day long about whose turn it is to make cups of tea, where to go on holiday and so on, but it's what's unsaid that's the problem. The little things are just a symptom of something bigger. In their case, it's usually Harry, Jonathan's son, the heir to all this. I don't think she likes the competition. Well, that and she'd rather be in Spain than here.'

Renee ran her fingers down the silver chain, stopping at the black oval stone that hung from it. Samantha was reminded of the mobile in the shop, the same dark stones that glinted in the light. The gift from Aparna.

'What are these black stones? I keep seeing them.'

Renee smiled gently. 'Just good luck charms. Protection.'

'Protection from what?'

'Oh, nothing really, just local superstitions. Can't hurt, can it? Now then, if you've never been married, who's Lily's dad?' said Renee.

Samantha was momentarily taken aback, then she laughed. 'Someone who wasn't ready to get married.'

'Maybe he was worried you wouldn't want to make his dinner at night.'

Samantha put Renee's Zimmer frame in front of her and walked her out of the room. 'And he'd have been right about that.'

CHAPTER 17

1975

Annie tapped her fingers rapidly on the side of her mug. Sylvia reached out and patted her hand.

'How have you been, Annie? We've been thinking about you all week.' Sylvia lit a gold-tipped cigarette, her eyes fixed on Annie as if looking for the answer before she spoke. Annie looked from Sylvia to Ginny and then the others, no-one giving anything away.

'I've been OK.' Her hands trembled, and she held one tight within the other, conscious of the eyes of the other women on her.

'Thank you for bringing Poppet back the other day. She wasn't supposed to go into the village without me. You know what the local kids are like.'

'Little shits,' said Donna.

Annie nodded, disinterested in the well-meaning gratitude. As if sensing this, Sylvia sat up in her chair and addressed Annie more formally.

'The decision hasn't been easy. Had it been a direct curse on Henry Shuttleworth alone, I think it would have been much easier, but you are asking us to curse a future child. Have you thought this through, Annie? Can you live with this if we go ahead?'

Martha and Ginny looked to their mugs of tea, but Donna stared directly at her.

'You may still be alive when it happens, Annie — are you strong enough to see it through?' Corinne said.

'I want to be alive and here when it happens.'

Sylvia raised an eyebrow. 'You are really committed to doing this?'

Annie nodded. She lifted her head and looked at each member of the coven in turn.

'OK, then we'll put you out of your misery, darling,' said Sylvia, her manicured hand resting on Annie's. 'We've talked it through many times, there has been much debate and more than one meeting, but we have decided to help you.'

Annie heard a tiny gasp leave her mouth. Sylvia continued, 'As long as you're one hundred per cent certain it's something you want us to do.'

'Yes,' Annie said, squeezing Sylvia's hand, 'yes I do.'

Annie turned to the others again, tears pooling in her eyes and falling down her cheeks.

'Thank you, thank you all,' she said, wiping her face with the sleeve of her jumper.

Ginny smiled kindly, the others nodding but remaining serious.

'It's not something we take lightly. We are talking about another life, a future life being taken.'

Annie didn't register her words, just nodded furiously, still gripping Sylvia's fingers, her mind on Mr Shuttleworth and the pain the curse would bring.

'There are things we need in order to carry through the curse. Things you will need to do.'

Annie's cheeks were shiny with tears and red with relief. 'Anything.'

'Does Henry Shuttleworth know you? Have you ever seen him face to face?'

'No, they never covered it in the papers expect for a small mention. I never went up there again after that night. I couldn't face it, I—'

'You'll need to go to Hallow Croft.'

'What? Why?' Annie's skin pricked, ice-cold. 'Can't someone else go?'

Donna scoffed, shaking her head. Annie watched as Sylvia glared at Donna, who turned her attention to her nails, which were filed into points.

'We'll disguise you, just in case, but it has to be you, Annie. If the curse is to have the best chance of working, *you* have to get what's needed.'

'And what do we need?'

'Some of his hair and a possession of his, something small enough to fit in a poppet's body.'

'How will I get in?'

Martha leaned forward, clearing her throat before she spoke. 'My sister is friends with the housekeeper up there. She heard they needed extra help with the cleaning and—'

'You want me to clean? For *him*?' Annie felt herself well up, a ball of pain sticking in her throat.

'It's just for a morning. For this. Then you can walk away.'

Annie thought for a moment, her heart racing at the prospect of being in the same house as that man. Clearing away his dirt. Washing his pots.

'If you want us to do the curse, I'm afraid it has to be you. It's more powerful that way,' said Sylvia.

Donna sat back in her chair, exhaling plumes of cigarette smoke.

'OK,' Annie said. 'When?'

'You start tomorrow,' Martha said.

'Tomorrow?' Annie felt her stomach tighten.

'The sooner the better, Annie.' Sylvia said. 'It's a full moon on the twenty-seventh, that's this Saturday, and we can only do the ritual then — if not we have to wait another month.'

Annie nodded, sniffing away her tears.

'Say nothing to anybody, not even Kevin. If any word of this gets out then it will be the end of us,' Sylvia warned.

'I won't, I promise.'

Corinne walked over to a walnut cabinet and brought out a crystal carafe filled with green liquid. The mood lightened as she laid out six crystal tumblers. She placed a tiny slotted spoon over the first glass and rested a sugar cube on top. Next, she poured pale green liquid over the sugar, the drink tumbling into the glass. She patted her pockets, looking around, as Donna leaned over, handing her a lighter with which she lit the alcohol-soaked cube, the sugar slowly melting. She repeated with each drink then handed them to the women.

Each held the glass in front of them.

'To the coven, blessed be,' said Sylvia, raising her drink.

'Blessed be,' they repeated in unison.

Six glasses raised to the air, a toast to their strength, their resolve and their vengeance.

CHAPTER 18

A white van pulled up outside Hallow Croft. On the side was a large decal of a grinning, tuxedo-wearing man pulling a rabbit from a hat. Above it, *Merlin the Magician* in large blue writing. Samantha put down her mug of tea and left the office to meet it at the main entrance.

'Welcome to Hallow Croft,' she said.

Merlin exited the van, holding his lower back and groaning. He was much older than the decal suggested, but with his dyed black quiff and pale blue eyes, was still easily recognisable. A young woman got out of the passenger seat. She was petite, with golden blonde curls and a perfectly made-up face. She glanced up at Hallow Croft, unease turning her pale.

'The building is a little overwhelming, isn't it?' said Samantha.

The woman nodded. 'Always did give me the creeps.'

'Kelly!' Merlin scolded.

'So you've been here before?'

Before she could reply, Merlin had commandeered her. 'Take this.' He handed her a large black case which she strained to carry. 'I'll need my suit steaming too.'

Samantha flashed a look of sympathy to the young woman as she struggled past, clearly resigned to her role as his glamorous gopher.

'Is Kelly your dau—'

'Girlfriend,' he interjected.

'Oh . . .'

Merlin moved to the back of the van and hauled out a large black box. He wheeled it over the gravel, the wheels catching on the stones.

'Here, let me.'

Before he could protest, Samantha pulled the box from the other side and manoeuvred it up the ramp and into reception.

'Merlin!' Valerie exclaimed.

The magician stopped pushing, the box coming to a halt.

'Hello, Valerie.'

His eyes twitched as he spoke, his brash demeanour fading slightly.

'We're all looking forward to the show. Nothing like a magic trick to cheer up a gloomy December day.'

'Aye, well, I do my best,' he said, his eyes averted away from her. Merlin pushed at the trolley, forcing Samantha forward as they headed into the day room.

Samantha looked back to Valerie, the woman's expression darkly amused by the arrival of Merlin and Kelly. It seemed no face at Hallow Croft was free from her derision — no one except Lily, that is; she was at least thankful for that.

CHAPTER 19

Debby poured out the Horlicks into a waiting row of white mugs, before handing them out to the gathered residents in the communal lounge. Myrtle, a silver-haired woman of ninety-two, winced as her lips met with the hot liquid. Next to her, Colin, a retired airman, polished his medals with a cotton handkerchief.

'Horlicks, Colin?' Debby held out the mug.

He looked up, his brow creased. 'Major Hillard to you, young lady.'

Debby shook her head as she handed over the drink. Colin peered down to her feet. 'And those shoes could do with a good polish.'

Don entered the day room, a protesting woman shuffling before him.

'I was enjoying *Pointless* in my bedroom, why do I have to come here?'

'You'll love it, Joan. It's not often we get a real-life magician in our midst, is it?' Don caught Samantha's eye and shrugged.

'Come on, Joan,' Samantha rallied, 'it's going to be quite a night.'

Joan gave Samantha a look that revealed she didn't share the matron's enthusiasm.

'How about a glass of wine?' Samantha offered.

Joan's eyes brightened.

'Valerie, can you get Joan a glass of our finest, please?'

Valerie pushed a trolley towards them, her long fingers clutching the handle tightly.

'Sorry, Matron, our Joan can't have alcohol. She's on a strict diet.'

Joan's face dropped.

'Well, I'm sure one won't hurt, will it. Red or white, Joan?' Samantha was aware of all the residents' medical needs, including the advice that Joan could do with losing a pound or two. Something which Samantha felt wouldn't be scuppered by a small glass of wine as a treat.

Joan's eyes skittered from Samantha to Valerie, who raised her body, chest out. Her eyebrows twitched in fury.

'I had strict instructions from the old matron not to give Joan any sweet foods or alcohol.'

'Well,' Samantha replied, 'I'm the matron now and I say she can have a glass.'

The room fell silent as residents and staff alike witnessed the stand-off.

'Joan, red or white?' Samantha asked again, ignoring Valerie.

Joan spoke quietly, her eyes to the floor. 'White, please.'

Samantha straightened herself up and smiled sweetly at Valerie, speaking slowly and calmly.

'One glass of white wine, please, Valerie.'

'But—'

'Now, Valerie.'

Valerie unscrewed the bottle top and poured the wine into a glass. She handed it to Joan, pushing it so hard into her hand that the contents splashed over the top.

'Well don't blame me when she falls into a diabetic coma.'

Joan held the glass in both hands and sipped eagerly at the wine. Don led her to an empty chair as Valerie stormed off with the trolley, glass bottles clinking violently against each other.

There were mild protests from those on strong medication as the drinks trolley passed them by, but no amount of pleading would result in a stiff drink. Samantha made a mental note to purchase her own silver hip flask before old age kicked in.

In the corner of the communal lounge Merlin the Magician and his assistant were busy constructing a glittering silver backdrop. Not yet in costume, Merlin was still wearing a short-sleeved shirt printed with palm trees, and jeans held up with a heavily buckled belt. His hair was the colour of coal, the black dye evident by the colour that had seeped beyond his hairline. His assistant scurried here and there, placing a multi-coloured box at the front of the stage, a box of bunting beneath the magician's table. Samantha admired her ability to carry off skin-tight white jeans, not just for the fit but for managing to keep them pristine.

'Can I offer you guys a drink?' Samantha asked.

Merlin and his assistant turned to her as Samantha continued, 'Sorry, I didn't introduce myself properly earlier. I'm Samantha, the matron here.'

The assistant appeared to curtsy slightly. 'I'm Kelly.'

Merlin smiled, white teeth glistening, and took Samantha's hand, his dry lips puckering on her skin. 'Elvis Monday to Friday, Merlin at the weekend.' He raised his head again and curled his lip, 'Uh-huh.'

'Oh, right.' Samantha smiled politely and extracted her hand. 'Tea, coffee or something stronger?' She gestured to the trolley that Debby was wheeling around the room.

'I'd love a wine,' said Kelly.

Merlin fixed her with a look. 'Tea on a work night,' he said, then, darkly, 'Booze and sawing people in half don't mix.'

'Tea it is then,' said Samantha, eager to leave them to it.

She caught up with Debby, who had taken over the alcohol trolley and was free-pouring whiskey to excited residents.

'Could you give the magician and his assistant two teas when you've got a minute, Debby?'

Debby nodded, never once making eye contact. Her eyes always looked somewhere between Samantha's nose and lips, and Samantha instinctively reached to her mouth to make sure there wasn't anything there.

A collective groan rippled around the television room when Valerie took the remote control and turned the TV off.

'I was watching that,' Colin shouted.

Samantha winced, annoyed at Valerie's lack of communication with the residents. She was clearly still seething after the altercation, and Samantha needed her back on side.

'I asked Valerie to switch it off, Colin, the show will be starting soon. Maybe I was a bit too eager though, as it looks like it's going to be another half hour or so.'

She looked to the magician and his assistant, who were arguing over a velvet cloth, Merlin yanking it from the table and flapping it in the air. 'If they don't have a full-on domestic before curtain-up, that is.'

Valerie scowled and switched the TV back on, rumbles of gratitude spreading like a Mexican wave over high-backed chairs and clacking knitting needles.

'Thank you,' said Samantha.

It was dark outside, so she went to close the multiple heavy velvet curtains that framed the large room, looking up at the night sky. Fat clouds weighed heavily overhead, sending spikes of icy rain to the earth. Across the way, a small figure was momentarily lit up by a Victorian-style street lamp. Lily. Her daughter ran towards the back entrance, a folder held over her head for protection. Debby passed, carrying two mugs of tea to the makeshift stage. Samantha called out to her, 'I'm just going to see if Lily wants to watch the show. I'll be right back.'

Debby nodded and proceeded on to Merlin and Kelly, who appeared to have reached a truce and were now walking through their act.

The key turned in the lock and Samantha stepped into the living room, expecting to find Lily on the sofa, but it was empty. From Lily's bedroom, she heard the familiar sound of rustling, so she knocked twice and opened the door. Lily was elbow deep in a cardboard box.

'Are you coming to the magic show tonight?'

'Can you knock before you just come in?'

Samantha was blindsided by this unfamiliar welcome, a flush of rejection coursing through her.

'I did knock.'

'Yes, but you didn't wait for me to answer.'

Samantha hadn't waited, but this was a rule change made without her knowledge. It seemed communicating with a teen was a constant case of avoiding potential landmines.

'OK, next time I'll wait. Are you coming to the entertainment downstairs? Merlin the Magician, all the way from the sunny village.'

Lily pulled a face. 'No thanks, I'm going to watch telly.'

'I suspected as much.'

Lily threw down the paintbrushes she had just taken out of the box.

'Then why did you even bother asking?'

'Because I want you to be there? Come on, it'll be fun.'

'Sitting in a room full of old people isn't my idea of fun.'

'Don't be mean, Lily, it doesn't suit you.'

'It's not fair.'

'Life's not—'

Lily held a hand up. 'Don't say it.'

Samantha didn't retaliate. When she was Lily's age she was crashing on friends' sofas until the morning, not returning home until lunchtime. There she would find her mum, arms crossed, waiting for her at the front door ready to give her hell. Now she was a parent herself, she understood.

'Come on, for me?' Samantha pleaded, aware there wasn't time for an argument or sulking.

Lily's shoulders hunched, her face drawn.

'Oh, for God's sake. OK, if I *must*.'

Lily dragged herself to her feet and pushed the box back under her bed. She went to her drawers and pulled out a grey hoodie. She reached to take off her T-shirt, pausing when she saw her mum was still there.

'Well?'

'OK, OK,' Samantha said, backing out of the room.

Samantha waited in the lounge as Lily stomped around her room. Drawers slammed shut and shoes were kicked around the floor. The bedroom door opened and Lily marched to the front door of the flat.

'Well? Are we going or what?'

Samantha sighed and followed her daughter out, wondering if Merlin had a magic trick to make teenage attitude disappear.

By the time Samantha returned to the lounge with Lily, the lights had been dimmed and Valerie was sitting in a chair at the front, holding the remote control.

'Hello, lovey,' Valerie beamed at Lily, 'come sit next to me.' She took her cardigan off the empty chair next to her and patted the seat.

Samantha scanned the room for somewhere to sit.

'Over here, Matron,' Renee called out from the side of the room.

Samantha was about to make her way to the seat when Don tapped her on the shoulder.

'And here's our MC for the evening!'

Everyone turned to look at Samantha.

'Me?'

Don handed her a microphone. 'Knock 'em dead, Matron.'

She took the microphone and stared around the room. At least not all eyes were on her. Myrtle was pleading with Debby for a second glass of wine, Colin had walked over to the window and opened the curtain, staring into the darkness. Lily was picking at her nails, her mood still sullen. Valerie, however, was staring straight at her, thin mouth fixed in a smile.

'Right, OK.' She took a deep breath. 'Ladies and gentlemen, welcome to our very special show where we hope you will be dazzled by our entertainment tonight.'

A loud snore rumbled through the air, followed by Renee breaking into stifled giggles.

'Nether Dale's very own Merlin the Magician and his glamorous assistant Kelly!'

As she walked away from the stage, Don chirped, 'You're wasted in the care industry.'

'Yep, first Nether Dale, next Las Vegas,' Samantha retorted.

A single light shone on the stage and Merlin and Kelly walked out to the muted applause of the staff and a smattering of the residents. Ever the professionals, the two smiled widely before Merlin began addressing his audience.

'Ladies and gentlemen, welcome to the Magical Merlin show—'

'Louder!' a smartly dressed man called out.

'No heckling, Bert,' chastised Valerie, 'or we'll have security throw you out!'

Bert sat back in his chair, grumbling under his breath. Merlin coughed and continued through rattling trollies and buzzers for toilet visits.

Samantha leaned into Renee. 'Tough crowd.'

Renee sipped at her gin and tonic. 'Last month we had a Beatles tribute band, and poor old Edna croaked halfway through "Love Me Do".'

Samantha gave a cursory look around the room, checking that all residents were still alive and well.

Outside, sleet began battering at the large windows, making it even harder to hear. The whistle of hearing aids hissed throughout the room as residents tried to tune in to the act.

For the first trick Kelly rolled out a large coffin-like box to the front of the stage. She gestured at it like a game-show hostess, the sparkles of her diamanté leotard catching the lights.

'Ladies and gentlemen, what could be better than one beautiful assistant?' Merlin looked out to the puddle of blank faces, continuing regardless. 'Two of her, of course — more to go round!'

He lifted the lid of the box and held Kelly's hand as she clambered inside, giving a little wave to the crowd before ducking her head and reappearing through a hole at one end. Merlin closed the lid and reached down to the floor behind the box, reappearing with a handsaw, touching its serrated edge with his fingertips and giving a dramatic pained look. Kelly's head turned to the audience, her eyes wide and mouth open.

A buzzer sounded. Samantha checked the board to see who it was and went over to Bert.

'Are you OK, Bert?'

'I know how this is done.' He pointed at the box.

'Well, don't spoil it for the rest of us,' the resident seated next to him grumbled.

'She's right, Bert, let's leave it to everyone's imagination.'

Bert crossed his arms and slumped back in his chair.

Merlin proceeded to saw through the middle of the box, causing a resident at the back of the room to cry out.

'It's OK, Audrey,' Don shouted across the room, 'it's not real.'

Merlin grimaced at Don and began to saw with renewed vigour. When he had finished, he raised the saw in the air before putting it back down on the floor and taking a guillotine blade, inserting it into the gap between the boxes. He held his hands in the air with a flourish before dramatically pushing the boxes apart, revealing what appeared to be a severed Kelly. There were oohs and ahhs from the audience. Samantha watched as Aparna clutched her book to her chest. Merlin rejoined the boxes and removed the metal sheets, opening the box for a complete Kelly to appear, stretching her satin-gloved hands into the air, beaming to all. A crack of lightning bled through the curtains and she faltered slightly, Merlin reaching out to steady her. Samantha clapped, holding her hands up around the room to encourage others to join in as Kelly stepped down and prepared for the next trick.

Before the first act had finished there had been four toilet breaks, three heckles and an emergency alarm go off when a visiting relative had yanked the wrong cord in the toilet. During the intermission, Samantha made sure the act had refreshments. Merlin decided to break his no-alcohol rule and opted for a lager, with a large gin for Kelly.

By the time the second half started, many of the patients had gone to bed at their own behest. The audience were now down to a handful. Unsurprisingly, Samantha noted, mainly those who were able to take advantage of the complimentary alcohol.

As the music started, Merlin produced a red-eyed, white-furred rabbit, much to the delight of the audience.

Renee called out, 'How lovely!'

Lily clapped her hands together, beaming at the small animal. A fleeting thought of buying Lily a rabbit of her own crossed Samantha's mind. Maybe a hamster.

Kelly waved her arms around the stunned rabbit as Merlin lowered it into a box and put a lid on.

'It won't be able to breathe,' called out Bert, looking to Valerie for a response.

'He'll be fine, Bert, it's a magic rabbit,' Renee said, patting his arm.

'Magic my eye, this is animal cruelty, this is.'

Lily watched intently as Merlin waved a wand over the box and then lifted the lid to reveal it was empty. Renee stopped Bert from getting up. Oblivious to any audience distress, Merlin put the lid back on, drew his satin cape over the box again and called out:

'What do we say to bring the rabbit back?' He put his hand to his ear.

A lacklustre call of 'Abracadabra' petered out to silence as Kelly pressed a button with her foot, sending a small bang and cloud of smoke into the air.

With a flourish, Merlin pulled the lid off and the four sides fell down to reveal an empty box. He looked to Kelly, who shrugged, then to the floor around them. Bert hobbled to his feet. 'Right, that's it, I'm calling the RSPCA.' Suddenly, all the buzzers began to ring out at once, though nobody seemed to have pressed them.

'What the hell?' Samantha said, circling the room to check everyone was OK.

Aparna rose to her feet, her hands in the air. She spoke in tongues through the din and chaos. Before Samantha could reach her to sit her down again, the lights in the room extinguished and they were left in darkness.

'You've fused the lights, Bert,' Renee accused.

'Can someone put the lights on?' Merlin shouted from somewhere on the stage. 'I need to find my rabbit.'

Samantha tried the switches but nothing worked.

'Valerie,' Samantha called, fumbling for the torch app on her phone, 'do you know where the fuse box is?'

Before Valerie could answer, there was a crackling sound and one by one the lights came on again.

'Oh Lord,' cried Renee, her eyes fixed on the space behind Samantha.

Samantha turned to see a small woman, the silhouette of her frail body visible through the thin cotton nightie. Her hair was fine and tangled, gentle knots sticking out at angles.

She was cradling something in her arms.

'She's killed my rabbit!' cried Merlin.

CHAPTER 20

A herbal aroma hit Samantha as Valerie flew past her, heading towards the doorway.

'Now then, Mrs Dawson, what are you doing down here?'

Valerie tried to navigate her out, but Mrs Dawson squirmed away from her touch. In her arms lay the white rabbit, limp and lifeless.

Samantha had only seen Mrs Dawson that first night, during the tussle with Valerie in the quadrant. The distance and gloom had made recognising her now near impossible. The old woman looked malnourished, her eyes sunken and lips pale. Her wrinkles were deep and bones jutted out underneath transparent skin. A snake of unease slithered up Samantha's spine as she watched Mrs Dawson move away from Valerie and walk slowly into the room. The unease grew when Samantha realised she was aiming straight for Lily. Her daughter caught Samantha's eye, fear and apprehension washing over the young girl's face. The rabbit's ears flopped towards the floor, its eyes fixed open.

'Christ,' Samantha muttered.

She too headed towards her daughter, tripping over the wire and cursing Merlin for not securing it better. Before Samantha could reach Lily, Mrs Dawson was stood before her. She placed the rabbit gently in the girl's lap. Lily winced, eyes closed, and drew as far back in the chair as she could.

The room watched transfixed as the rabbit flinched on Lily's lap; a tiny spasm of life, or was it the last throes of death? It opened its red eyes and pulled itself upright, sitting on Lily's lap as its nose twitched, bright eyes surveying its surroundings. Lily's body relaxed; she sat forward, looking on in amazement at the animal.

The old woman reached out and touched Lily's hair, a crooked smile appearing on her face, pale blue eyes watery and bright.

'It's you,' she whispered, her fingers feeling at Lily's cheek as if she might not be real. Lily looked to her mum, seeking reassurance.

Samantha watched intently, wary not to frighten the elderly woman, but also aware that if her mood changed suddenly she needed to intervene to protect her daughter and the other residents.

The old woman cupped Lily's chin with her frail hand, 'Is it you?'

Merlin pushed forward. He snatched the rabbit from Lily's lap and cradled it like a newborn baby, checking it over with his hand. Samantha went to her daughter.

'Are you OK?'

Lily nodded, her eyes still on Mrs Dawson, who regarded her with fascination.

'Come along, Mrs Dawson, let's get you back to bed.' Valerie marched over, taking the woman by the shoulders and turning her towards the door. 'What a naughty thing you are, taking that poor rabbit.'

When she had left, Lily asked, 'How did she get the rabbit?'

Samantha shrugged. 'God knows, but what a finale to the show.'

Aparna was still reciting verses to herself. Samantha went to her, the touch of her hands causing Aparna to flinch.

'It's OK, Aparna, everything is OK.' Samantha put a comforting hand on her back, feeling the tremor in her spine.

She turned to Debby. 'Debby, could you take Aparna to her room and make sure she gets a warm drink?'

Debby nodded, leaving the drinks trolley and heading over. As she was about to leave, Samantha remembered the black stone, still in her pocket. She took it out and tapped Debby's shoulder, whispering, 'Can you put this back somewhere safe in Aparna's room?'

Debby looked down at the stone. A flicker of uncertainty crossed her face.

'She gave it to me, but I can't accept it,' Samantha said.

Debby hesitated, then took it, dropping it in her pocket, guiding Aparna out of the room.

Renee's fingers fidgeted with her onyx necklace, watching as Merlin and Kelly packed up their props; the rabbit was now eating a carrot in a mesh pet carrier. Renee let go of the chain and helped herself to a large sherry from the unattended trolley. She joined Bert and Lily at the front of the room.

'What a shame, I was enjoying the show,' said Myrtle, on her way to bed.

'I wasn't,' grumbled Bert, 'I've seen better at the arse end of Skegness.'

'Albert!' Renee tapped his hand sharply, winking at Lily.

'Well, that's not magic, not real magic. Just tricks and sleight of hand.' Bert curled his finger, signalling for Samantha to listen, and leaned towards her. 'If you want to know about *real* magic, you want to have a chat with that mad old bird.'

'Mrs Dawson?'

Bert raised his eyebrows. 'Oh aye. Haven't you heard yet about the—'

Renee dropped her glass of sherry, claret liquid splattering across the paisley carpet.

'Oh dear!' she cried. 'What a waste.'

'You clumsy thing,' Valerie said, marching back into the room.

On seeing Valerie, Bert quietened again.

All talk of magic disappeared with Merlin and Kelly as they made their exit, trailing cases and props behind them.

Samantha turned, surprised to see Valerie back so quickly. She had already taken a tissue from her pocket and was kneeling down on all fours, dabbing at the carpet.

'She said "*is it you?*" to me, what did she mean?' Lily asked

Valerie looked up. 'Oh, I'd ignore her, love, she doesn't know what day of the week it is half the time. I suspect she was just happy to see such a young and pretty face.'

Samantha noticed raised eyebrows passing between Renee and Bert.

'What a night!' Samantha exclaimed. 'A small glass of something? I'm officially off duty now.' She poured wine into three glasses and handed one each to Renee and Bert, holding the other out. 'Cheers.'

Renee beamed. 'Cheers, love.'

Samantha caught Valerie watching Lily, an intense look of concentration on her face. Lily idly sucked from a carton of orange juice, scrolling through her phone. Valerie caught Samantha's eye and offered a brief smile before leaving the room.

CHAPTER 21

Annie sat in the centre of the circle she had created with a thin line of table salt. North of the circle was a small Tupperware bowl filled with soil, to the east a joss stick burned. Behind her to the south, a candle flickered in the dim light of Emily's bedroom, and to her left, the west, a small bowl of water. The four elements of earth, air, fire and water, there to invoke the spirit of protection.

She took the small piece of paper and lifted the lighter to its edge, the flame catching hold and crawling upwards and across the words *Protect me*.

When the paper reached her fingertips she dropped it into the bowl of water, the flames hissing as they extinguished. She closed her eyes for a moment, repeating the words over and over in a whisper as the incense swirled around her body.

Protect me.

Annie felt the sensation of the spirit moving through her, giving her strength. When she opened her eyes again she drew her arms around her body, holding herself, waiting for the feelings to settle. She blew out the candle and swept up the salt in her hands, making a mental note to hoover up the stray granules later. Kevin hadn't been into Emily's bedroom since her death, and though she doubted he would ever again, still she needed to hide this part of herself.

Annie emptied out the soil and washed the bowls in the kitchen sink, drying them and placing them in a cupboard she had reserved for sacred implements and offerings. She folded the tea towel and hung it on the small radiator, then made her way out of the back door.

At the bottom of the narrow strip of grass that passed for their garden was a shed, its Perspex window cloudy with cobwebs and dust. Inside was the familiar smell of creosote and rotting cardboard, and propped to one side, Emily's bike. Pale pink with a white seat and small basket on the front, Kevin had built it for her and given it to her on her thirteenth birthday. Annie couldn't remember a time when either had looked happier.

She yanked at it, pulling it free from the detritus that held it like a bound animal. She was relieved to see the tyres were still fat with air and the chain still in place.

She stood with the bike in the alley that ran behind the houses and lifted her leg over the cross bar to sit on the padded seat, her toes just touching the slushy ground. The innocent snow had now been replaced with dragged footprints and sodden cigarette butts, dropped by the teens who gathered in the alleyways at night. She put her foot on one of the pedals, the bike tilting slightly, and pushed away. It had been years since she had ridden a bike and she fought with the handlebars to keep herself upright down the bumpy pathway. Passing the closed gates to her neighbours' houses, the sound of chatter and smell of fried breakfasts carried in the air from beyond them.

Though small in frame, Annie was strong; years of cleaning had seen to that. When she got her balance she rode at speed through Nether Dale, past the café as Mrs Harby washed the window with a yellow chamois leather. A young couple embraced on the wooden bench outside the Skull & Feathers, wrapped up in each other, oblivious to the cold. Annie pushed up the hill, her thighs burning from the effort, each laboured breath a visible puff in the air. She glanced at Sylvia's house as she passed, the heavy drapes still closed.

Her disguise had been light: a pair of clear-lensed glasses, a headscarf and an outfit only slightly dowdier than the one she usually wore. Her cheeks flushed as she pushed further up the hill, stopping when she reached the track to her right. She put a foot to the ground and caught her breath, the cold air sharp in her throat. The last time she had travelled down this lane it was by car, Kevin speeding across the uneven road as they rushed to find their daughter. Now she had time to see the iron filigree sign in the hedge.

Hallow Croft.

She fought to keep herself together. She had come this far, she just had to get in and out with the things Sylvia had requested. That was it. Annie pushed away again, making her way round the twists and turns, dwarfed by the giant hedges either side of the driveway. Crows cawed angrily above, swooping through the trees that surrounded the house.

Barely anybody in the village knew what the Shuttleworth family looked like; the children went away to school and the grocery shop delivered their food each week. She knew this because the shop owner took great pride in telling whoever would listen what they had ordered that week. Annie did know that Henry Shuttleworth's wife had long since left, now living with a titled man in Gloucestershire according to village gossip. Perhaps things would have been different if she had still been around, if . . . She stopped herself.

'Are you Joyce?' a woman shouted from the side of the house.

Annie paused for a moment. Martha must have given her a false name. She nodded, dismounted her bike and walked towards her. The woman was red-faced, a duster hanging from a floral tabard.

'Hi,' Annie said, holding out her hand.

The woman looked flustered, half raising her hand to meet Annie's. Her skin was red raw and damp with wash-ing-up liquid and hot water.

'I'm Dorothy, you'll be helping me today. I've been on my own for weeks now — you'd think people would be queuing up for good honest work, wouldn't you?'

Annie glanced up to the large windows, heavy curtains gathered at their centres with golden tie backs. A shadow moved across the room within and she jumped back.

'Bit nervous, are we?' said Dorothy, her forehead crinkling.

'No, not at all,' Annie said, trying to keep her nerves together.

Dorothy watched her a moment longer. 'Good, we're just here to clean, not get involved in their business.' She gestured for Annie to follow her, 'We're this way, the *servants'* entrance.' She rolled her eyes and led Annie past a stone statue of an angel looking to heaven, down thick stone steps, through a narrow wooden door and into a farmhouse-style kitchen, with black and white tiled floor and a large wooden island in the middle. A tatty armchair covered with a tartan blanket sat by an iron stove. A dog's bed, almost as big as a single mattress, lay by a wall. The kitchen smelled of stews and casseroles, homemade bread and the remnants of good wine spilled on the side. A giant dog padded into the room; Annie took a step back, her hands reaching out to the side, catching a pile of bone china plates that rattled under her touch.

'Don't be afraid of old Grantley. He spends most of his time down here. Mr Shuttleworth isn't a fan of the old mutt. Come on, I'll show you where you're to start.'

Annie edged past the dog bed, the animal barely lifting its nose to sniff her.

'Poor old bugger can barely see now.'

'If Mr . . .' the name stuck in her throat like a knife, 'Shuttleworth doesn't like dogs, then—'

'It was Mrs Shuttleworth who had a thing for them. When she left, the son needed something to keep him company, so he let him have one. This is the third Irish Wolfhound he's had; it's become a bit of a tradition, I suppose you could say. I reckon it's a way of keeping his mum close.'

They walked out into a large open hall. Light shone down from above through a giant window in the high ceiling. Annie's eyes were drawn up to the intricate cornicing lining the ceiling edges.

'These stairs are a bugger, I'm afraid, but with my back I'm not able.' Dorothy pulled the duster from her tabard and presented it like a magician producing a bunch of plastic flowers. 'You'll find polish in here,' she handed her a bucket of bottles and tins. 'Start from the top and work your way down. When you've finished, you'll find me in the drawing room over there.'

Dorothy nodded towards a large oak door. Annie clutched the bucket handle and turned to look up the vast wooden stairs that ran centrally from the hall up to the first-floor landing.

'If Mr Shuttleworth comes down, don't speak to him, he's not the sort to make light chat. Mind you, he spends most of his time in the attic working on his so-called *art*.' She rolled her eyes again, clearly at the end of her tether in her role as housekeeper. 'His bedroom is the first on the left. I'll let you clean that one, far too many knick-knacks for me to deal with today.'

Annie felt her heart thud at the thought of coming face to face with him, bile rising in her throat. She swallowed it down and nodded, before making her way to the top of the stairs as Dorothy left her for the drawing room.

When she reached the top stair, she put down the bucket and rummaged through the various tins. She selected a small tub of polish, prised the lid off and began to rub at the dark wood. The faint sound of classical music carried through the air. She looked back to where it came from. Was *he* there? She turned her attention to the job in hand, the whites of her knuckles visible through pale skin as she pushed the duster hard against the stair.

By the time she was a third of the way down her knees began to ache. Annie stood and stretched her body, reached her hands to the ceiling, her back arched. When a door opened behind her she stumbled and turned.

A young man bounded through the main door. He was tall, with a mop of chestnut-brown hair and wore smart jeans and a sports jacket. He threw a holdall to the ground, which landed with a thud, holding his arms out and beaming as Grantley ran towards him.

Grantley's claws tapped against the wooden floor, before he leaped into the air, his paws on the upright man's shoulders, tongue licking his cheeks. The young man greeted him with boyish enthusiasm, ruffling his fur and kneeling on the floor as the dog jumped down and rolled over.

'Well, look what the cat dragged in.'

Dorothy was stood by the drawing-room door, her arms folded across her chest. She was beaming.

The man got to his feet and went to her, Grantley following close by his side.

'Dorothy!'

She let her arms drop and embraced him, he returning the warmth.

'We've missed you here, Jonathan, glad you're back for the holidays.'

Grantley pushed at his leg, aching for attention.

Dorothy smiled. 'He's missed you most though, been moping about the kitchen for the last few weeks.'

As the young man turned to the dog, he caught sight of Annie and paused. Annie put her head down.

'That's Joyce, she's come to help me. These old bones won't be around forever.'

'Nonsense, Dorothy,' he said. He called to Annie, 'Hi, Joyce, nice to meet you.'

Annie nodded, twisting the duster in her fingers.

'And don't listen to Dorothy, she'll be here when my children are running around causing mayhem.'

Dorothy shook her head, laughing. A wash of guilt ran through Annie at the mention of his hypothetical children. There might be the sound of children running around these grand halls one day, but for at least one of them, if he should have a girl, it would be short-lived.

* * *

It was one o'clock before she had finished the final stair. Dorothy had invited her to the kitchen where they ate warm cheese and tomato sandwiches on thin white bread.

'Sugar?' Dorothy had her back to Annie, swirling sugar into her own mug.

'Not for me, thanks.'

Dorothy sat opposite her, pushing the mug across the table.

Annie smiled. 'Thank you. Have you worked here long?'

'Far too long, I used to manage fine on my own but my back's buggered now, I'm too old for this game. Needs young blood like you.'

Annie wondered if Dorothy knew anything about the night Emily was murdered. Had she noticed Mr Shuttleworth's behaviour? Heard anything? She shuddered.

'Are you shivering? Don't worry, you'll soon warm up once you get cleaning,' Dorothy said. 'As you can see, it's a big house.'

They ate their sandwiches in silence, Dorothy reading her horoscopes in a magazine while Annie concentrated on her task ahead. There had been no sign of Mr Shuttleworth all morning so she felt confident she would get what she needed before leaving and never coming back. Annie pushed her plate away, half of the sandwich uneaten. Her stomach was in knots.

'You not eating that?'

She shook her head and, without asking, Dorothy took it from her plate and bit into it, talking as she chewed. 'No wonder there's nothing of you.'

Annie pushed her chair back and grabbed the bucket of cleaning products.

'I'd better get on, I have to be home to make my husband's tea.'

'That's one thing I can be grateful for.'

Annie waited for Dorothy to continue.

'I've not had to worry about what to feed anyone else since my husband was killed in the war.'

'I'm sorry.'

'Don't be, he was a miserable bastard, not unlike him up there,' she looked to the ceiling. 'She got it right, buggering off to the south.'

'Why didn't she take her son?'

'Money gives you power, that and being a man. She tried but he . . . let's just say he's not got the best of temperaments. I wouldn't be surprised if she hadn't gone to Gloucestershire at all and was still here.'

Annie's brow furrowed. Dorothy smiled a wicked smile, but her words jolted Annie.

'Six foot under the floorboards.'

CHAPTER 22

Jonathan was washing his car, an old Jaguar, when Lily approached. Finn ran around the driveway with a bright yellow sponge in his mouth, throwing it up into the air and retrieving it again. He bounded up to her and dropped the sponge at her feet; as she went to pick it up, he snatched it from the ground and ran off again.

'Morning, Lily,' Jonathan said, dropping a wet chamois cloth into a bucket.

Lily waved and approached him.

'Can I take Finn for another walk?'

'Of course. Are you sure though? Wouldn't you rather be with your friends?'

She shook her head.

'It can be tough settling into a new place where everyone knows each other.'

Lily felt around in her coat pockets, her fingers playing idly with a key and a lone sweet wrapped in cellophane. She avoided his eyes and the pity they would exude.

'I hated the village when I was growing up.'

Lily stopped messing with her clothes and looked up at him.

'Did you?'

'God, yes. I didn't go to the same school as everyone else, I wasn't in the "in crowd". For that matter, I wasn't in any crowd.'

'But you lived *here*,' she gestured around, taking in the cottage, the grounds and Hallow Croft.

'I'd have much rather lived where everyone else lived. A place like this is OK when you're older, but for someone like you, I know it can be a bit . . . a bit isolating. I wished I'd moved for our son's sake, but Diane wouldn't have it. You get used to the space, you see.'

Lily hoped she'd get used to it, at least until she could get away to university.

'Early days,' Jonathan reassured. 'I'm sure you'll make plenty of friends in time. Until then we'll take full advantage of your services. His lead is in the kitchen, would you mind?' He gestured to his soapy hands and arms.

'Of course.'

As Lily entered the cottage, Finn paused behind her, then lay across the porch and pulled chunks off the sponge. She heard Jonathan calling for him to drop it as she disappeared into the hall.

It was dark in the cottage and the cold air from the open door swirled around the narrow space. Lily expected cottages like this to be cosy, with low beams and open fires, but Laburnum Cottage wasn't picture-postcard, it was an afterthought.

As she passed the living room, she heard a low voice. It was Diane speaking on the phone. Her voice was strange, distorted and unsettled.

'He's refusing to listen. Oh, I know, God only knows why I thought I'd be able to persuade him . . . Yes! A complete power cut and then she appears from nowhere with a rabbit! Oh, I don't know, it was the magician's or something. Looked all but dead and then came back to life by all accounts. No, I'm not drunk. If he won't leave here then I'll go myself, I'll stay in the villa for a few months. I'm not having it, Sheila, I've had enough now, what with all that matron stuff.'

The mention of the previous matron piqued Lily's curiosity. Her mum had so far been unable to find out why she had left so suddenly; perhaps she could find out now. Lily peeked through the crack in the door to see Diana taking a sip from her wine glass. Lily looked at her watch: 10.30 a.m.

'I'm just not sure how much more I can take here. I'm barely sleeping, even the pills don't work anymore . . . I'm beginning to question my own sanity these days.'

'Did you find it?' Jonathan called from the front door.

In the living room, Diane jumped up from her chair and hid the wine glass in a cupboard. Lily stood back, embarrassed she may have been caught snooping. Diane threw open the door, her face changing from anger to confusion when she saw Lily.

Jonathan was in the dark corridor now. 'The lead?'

'I forgot which door was the kitchen,' Lily said, feeling her cheeks redden at the lie.

'Straight ahead there,' he pointed beyond her. 'I'll get it, need a glass of water anyway.' He brushed past her in the narrow hall, leaving her with Diane.

Lily smiled innocently. 'I'm taking Finn out.'

Diane raised a perfectly pencilled eyebrow. 'Right, well, be sure to keep him with you.'

'I'll look after him, I promise.'

'He's the one that does the looking after,' Diane replied, glancing at Finn as he nosed at the gravel outside the door.

Lily nodded, feeling the extra weight of responsibility. She was relieved to see Jonathan come back through the kitchen door.

'You not dressed yet, Diane?' Jonathan said, his voice light.

'Are we going somewhere?'

'I thought we might take a drive out to Nether Dale.'

Diane let out a spiked laugh before going back into the lounge and slamming the door.

As Lily hooked the lead onto Finn's collar, Jonathan appeared on the porch, his car keys in hand.

'She's just a bit under the weather at the moment. It's not been easy here with not having a matron.'

Lily nodded. 'What happened to the last matron?'

Jonathan fumbled with the bunch of keys until he found the right one. He turned it in the lock. 'As I said, not everyone is suited to such a remote location.'

But he didn't catch her eye.

CHAPTER 23

Samantha flicked through the files in the cabinet drawer. There were only three Ds, two of which had *Deceased* written in red sharpie across the front, and the third a male and very much alive and kicking: Bert Denton. She went back to the As, slowly checking each one in case Mrs Dawson's file had been mistakenly put in the wrong place. By the time she reached Myrtle Worthington she knew it was a fruitless task. Samantha pushed the filing drawer hard and it slammed shut. As matron she should have access to *all* residents' information. Family history, medical history, next of kin, she should know about them. The office door opened and Samantha spun around, her back flush to the cabinet.

'Would you like a cup of tea, Matron?' Debby asked, poking her head into the office.

'Erm, right, yes please.'

'Are you OK, Matron?'

'You made me jump, that's all. I was just looking for something and I—' She stopped talking. She knew Debby wasn't interested in what she was doing, it was just something inside her that was unravelling. She felt foolish, like the child at school left out of the game. She needed to get a grip, stop letting this place get under her skin.

Debby held out the cup and Samantha took it from her.

'Thank you, Debby.'

Samantha walked around her desk and sat down as Debby went to leave.

'Oh, Debby.'

Debby turned, her eyes flickering around the room, unable to make eye contact.

'Can I borrow you a minute?'

'Valerie's told me I've to—'

'It won't take a minute. Close the door, will you.'

Debby did as she was told and reluctantly sat down.

'Can I ask you about Mrs Dawson?'

'What about her? I don't know much.' Debby's response was quick, stumbling over the words.

'You know more than me.' Samantha smiled. 'What exactly did she do to the previous matron to make her leave?'

Debby looked down to her hands, picking the tough skin around her nails. Silence hung in the air between them.

'Debby?'

She snapped her head up. 'I don't know, they don't tell me anything, I'm just a care assistant.'

'Did she hurt the matron in some way?'

Debby lifted her hand subconsciously to the small bald patch on her head.

'I don't know. I know that she's mad though, Mrs Dawson. Always trying to escape, to get to the woods. I've no idea why though, no one does. Valerie knows her best, so . . .' she trailed off.

Samantha took a deep breath.

'You know, I can see you work really hard here, Debby, and if you'd like to, I'm sure we could arrange for you to do your NVQ, you know, help you progress in your career.'

Debby's face brightened. Samantha doubted anybody had ever spoken to her about the possibility of career progression.

'Do you think? I'd love to be a nurse one day.'

'Well why don't we look into that for you?'

'Yes please, I'd—'

The door flung open and Valerie appeared, her face flushed, pupils sharp.

'There you are! I've been rushed off my feet!'

'Sorry, I was just—' Debby jumped to her feet like a startled cat and backed away from Samantha.

'Valerie,' Samantha said, 'please could you knock before coming in, we were having a private chat.'

Valerie's eyes narrowed, her jaw tensing as she clamped her teeth together. Debby looked to the floor. Samantha kept her gaze on Valerie, not letting her intimidate her the way she did others.

'Well I'm sorry,' she retorted, no contrition in her voice, 'but Mr Gladwin has had an accident. I can't lift him alone, it's health and safety, as you know.'

Samantha waited a moment before turning to Debby. 'You can go, Debby, we'll chat about things later.'

Debby nodded, her eyes still focused on the floor. Valerie looked at the girl curiously before turning on her heel and storming out.

She listened as Valerie began interrogating Debby as soon as they had left the office.

'What things is she going to talk to you about? She has no right to speak to me like that, Mr Shuttleworth would be furious.'

Samantha closed the door behind them and turned the key to make sure there were no more interruptions. She reached for the old matron's small diary in her pocket and opened it on the front page. She dialled Helen's mobile number and was met with a flat tone: it had been cut off. She flicked through to the back where there were further contacts, determined to get an answer from somewhere, and hopefully speak to her predecessor about Mrs Dawson.

She picked up the phone and dialled the number with the same surname; a faint voice spoke from the other end of the line.

'Hello?'

'Hello, this is the matron from Hallow Croft Nursing Home. I just—'

'*Why are you calling me? Don't you think we've been through enough?*'

Samantha sat up, thrown by the turn in the conversation.

'I'm sorry, I just wanted to ask Helen a few questions, that's all. I—'

'*Ask her a few questions? Are you winding me up? It was that place that drove her to it.*'

'I'm sorry, I don't understand, I—'

'*Her death.*'

CHAPTER 24

Finn pulled back. No matter how much she tugged on the lead, Lily was unable to budge the giant dog.

'Come *on*, Finn.'

But Finn sat firmly on his haunches.

Lily reached into her pocket for the small bag of treats Jonathan had given her. Finn tilted his head at the familiar crackle of the plastic bag.

She held one out, close enough that he could see it, but far enough away that he had to come to her to reach it. After a few steps she let him have it, then took out another. When they finally reached the trees, he stopped again and emitted a high-pitched whine.

'It's OK, boy.' She ruffled his head. 'Nothing to be scared of.'

Lily frowned at the dog. Finn had bounded quite happily into the woods before. Tempting him forward with treats, they got as far as the clearing where the ancient stones stood when Finn froze again and no amount of dried liver could drive him any further. Lily sighed. She wanted to investigate the stones properly. She was fishing out yet another treat when she saw what it was that had spooked Finn.

Lily crouched behind a mound of earth, urging Finn to stay beside her. Her hands shook as she clutched the fur on his trembling back.

She recognised the old woman from the magic night, the one who had handed her the rabbit. Now she wore a velour nightgown wrapped around her, the hem lightly kissing the ground as she danced in circles, weaving in and out of the standing stones. Her thin fingers pointed up at the gloomy sky above. Her fine white hair was still tangled from a night's sleep. On her feet her slippers were sodden.

A bunch of wilted flowers Lily recognised from the reception at Hallow Croft lay in the centre of the circle. The old woman's thin lips appeared to be repeating something over and over again, the words lost in the cold air.

She stopped dancing and took out a small doll from her pocket, gently wrapping thin ribbon around its entire body until it was bound. She then placed it in the ground by the flowers and spooned dirt over it using her hands. She laid the flowers on top and closed her eyes, lifting her arms to the sky once again as she continued to chant in a low growl, the words unintelligible as they scrambled in the wind.

Finn continued to whine, his eyes fixed on the woman. Lily felt the tension on the lead, aware he might bolt at any minute. The old woman drew her hands together as if praying and then turned and walked away, disappearing into the darkness of the woods.

When Lily was sure the old woman wasn't coming back, she pulled on Finn's lead, dragging him over to the circle. Her heart jolted. The grave Finn had dug up had once again been opened. The goat skull was now sitting by the flowers on top of the doll's shallow grave. She walked around it, touching the standing stones tentatively, before daring to venture toward the centre.

She moved the earth and pulled the doll out of the ground, shaking off the loose soil that clung to the silk ribbon. Its wool hair was yellow, now stained with soil which Lily tried to brush away. She looked towards the trees, reminded of the dolls that hung there like macabre decorations. Dolls that looked like this one. Its face was expressionless, two cross stitches for eyes and a line for a mouth. Lily stroked its hair, fascinated by its oddness. She looked to where the woman had disappeared and then scanned the trees to make sure she wasn't being watched before putting the doll in her pocket.

There was a rumble of thunder in the distance. Finn began to bark and Lily let him lead her away, the face of the golden-haired doll poking expressionless from her pocket.

As she led Finn back out into the open, with the quadrant in view, she saw Valerie walking with Bert in the grounds. Valerie towered over him, holding a large black umbrella over their heads as Bert held onto her other arm. Valerie caught sight of Lily and waved with the arm that Bert was holding, causing him to stumble. Lily glanced around to see if Mrs Dawson was anywhere to be seen, but she had gone.

'Hello, lovely,' Valerie said, looking beyond her to the woods, 'you've not been wandering around in there, have you?'

'I thought Finn would like the woods,' said Lily, 'then I saw that old woman and—'

'Old woman?' Valerie's eyes narrowed.

'The one with the rabbit.'

Lily noticed Bert lower his eyes to the floor as Valerie spoke. 'Oh dear, she's at it again. Must have slipped out without me noticing, the little monkey! Is she still there? I'd better go—' she went to let go of Bert, who took a stumbling step forward.

'No, she left before me. She seemed a bit confused. I was going to come and get someone but in the end she left.'

Valerie took hold of Bert again, the resident shooting her a disapproving look.

'What have you got there?' Valerie looked down to the doll sticking out of Lily's pocket.

Lily put her hand to her pocket, pushing the doll down. 'What?'

Valerie smiled knowingly. 'Is it a little dolly?'

Lily blushed, pulling the doll out of her pocket and showing Valerie. Bert flinched, his body pulling away.

'I found it in the woods. I liked it so I—'

'That's Mrs Dawson's doll. Don't ask me why an old woman keeps dolls, these old folk do all kinds of loopy things, half of them don't know what time of day it is.'

'Lunchtime,' Bert huffed.

'Present company excepted,' said Valerie.

She winked at Lily, who returned a smile.

'Now then, you give me that doll and I'll take it to Mrs Dawson. I'm sure she'll be missing it.'

Lily begrudgingly handed it over, fat raindrops hitting its face and soaking into the material.

A crack of lightning echoed from the grey skies.

'We'd better get you in, Bert, don't want you struck by lightning, do we?'

'Why not? Better than the slow decline I've got to look forward to.'

'A regular ray of sunshine, this one.' Valerie winked at a smiling Lily.

Valerie edged him round and headed back towards Hallow Croft.

'I'd like to meet her again,' said Lily.

'Mrs Dawson? Oh, I don't think that's a good idea, love.' Valerie smiled. 'Sometimes people aren't quite what they seem.'

CHAPTER 25

1975

Annie closed the bedroom door behind her and stifled a sneeze. The air was thick with the odour of old leather and dusty fabrics. If Dorothy had cleaned this room, it hadn't been for months. She ran her finger across the dark wood of the four-poster bed, a thick layer of dust gathering on her fingertip. Annie didn't need to clean in here, all she needed to find was a hairbrush and something personal to take to the coven, but the part of her that hated disorder had her dusting the bed's woodwork.

Annie walked over to the dressing table, on which were a few framed, faded photographs. Mr Shuttleworth proudly holding a limp pheasant in the air, a shotgun cocked over his shoulder. In another, his wedding photo, he was in an army uniform, his beautiful bride in silk and lace. She wondered why he had kept that photograph, a daily reminder of what he had lost. Did his wife leave because she knew the truth of what he was capable of? Had he done something like this before?

The en suite bathroom was clad floor to ceiling in off-white tiles, like something from a hospital. Vast, echoey and inhospitable. By the sink was a hairbrush, its thick bristles bound by greying hairs. She plucked at them and placed them in a brown paper bag she'd brought with her. There was nothing else but a worn toothbrush and a curled-up tube of toothpaste by the sink.

Annie went back into the bedroom and rummaged through the dressing-table drawers. If he had anything personal, surely this would be where it would be stored. A discarded wedding ring or family jewellery, anything to connect him to the curse, to bring sadness and pain to his family. A small wooden box revealed a jumble of cufflinks; she sorted through them, mostly plain silver. One pair caught her eye, gold ovals with the initials *H.S.* She dropped them into the paper bag and gently closed the drawer.

The bedroom doorknob creaked suddenly. Annie spun round, her heart racing, hand clutching the bag behind her.

Henry Shuttleworth glared in at Annie, his small dark eyes piercing through her. With his sunken cheeks and wild greying hair, he would have looked more at home in the nearest town's halfway house than creeping around Hallow Croft. He wore a white coat, splattered with dark hues of indigo, black and grey paint. When he spoke, his gravelly voice was like polished cut glass.

'Who are you?'

Annie was blinded by fear. She tried to remember the name she had given; eventually it came to her. 'Joyce. I'm the cleaner.'

'Where's Dorothy?' he grunted, waving a paintbrush in the air.

'In the drawing room, I think. I—'

'I don't like strangers poking through my things, get Dorothy now.'

Her eyes were drawn to his hands, the long fingers pointing at her, the fingers that had curled around her daughter's throat. Annie held onto the dressing table, trying to keep herself upright. She felt nauseous; the fusty air was oppressive, his presence suffocating.

Annie pushed the paper bag into her pocket and went to leave the room. As she passed Mr Shuttleworth, he grabbed the top of her arm, holding her tightly, his sharp eyes surveying her face.

'You look familiar,' he said, his tone curious and faintly amused.

Annie dropped her head to the floor, muttering, 'I don't think so, I'm new to the area.'

His fingers dug into her flesh; her skin burned as he kept her there, like a small animal trapped in a snare.

He released her arm. 'Fetch Dorothy.'

Annie scrambled away, stumbling as she tried to hold in the tearful rage and fear that burned inside her. She felt his eyes on her as she ran down the stairs and into the drawing room.

'Finished already?' Dorothy said, lightly dusting a marble whippet that sat among a pack of multiple stone breeds.

'It's Mr Shuttleworth, says he wants *you* to clean his room.'

Dorothy huffed, puffing her cheeks out and wiping her hands on her overall. 'That man will be the death of me.'

Dorothy grabbed her bucket and stropped out of the room, leaving Annie alone with the canine menagerie. She watched Henry's son in the garden outside, throwing a tennis ball to Grantley.

Henry Shuttleworth still had his child at home, he still sat down to dinner with him each evening to talk about his life. She felt her fists clench at all the things she would never have. Countless birthdays, a wedding, and then maybe there would have been grandchildren.

Then she thought about the curse and the small bag in her pocket. Henry Shuttleworth might have his child, but the coven would see to it that he would never have a female heir, at least not beyond her sixteenth birthday.

CHAPTER 26

'You shouldn't have been out so long in the rain,' Samantha said, placing the digital thermometer underneath Lily's tongue.

Lily had woken in the night, tossing and turning, disturbing dreams keeping her awake. She had managed to go back to a fitful sleep, only to wake at 6 a.m. with a coughing fit, bringing her mum to her room.

Samantha took the end of the stethoscope and held it against Lily's back, the cold metal causing her to flinch.

'You sound very chesty.'

Lily could hear the bubbling of her breath crackling beneath her ribcage. Her mum took the stethoscope away and left her bedroom, returning with pills and a glass of water. She sat on the edge of the bed and took the thermometer from Lily's mouth, peering at the tiny screen.

'Thirty-eight. It's high but not too bad, nothing a few days in bed won't sort.'

'Mum,' she protested.

'I know you always think you know best, but not this time Lily. I'm the nurse.' She jabbed at her Matron badge to seal the point. 'You can draw, read, sleep.'

Samantha handed the pills to Lily, who sat up, took the glass of water and swallowed them down.

'I'll have my phone with me, so if you need anything just text, OK?'

Lily nodded.

'I'll come back in a couple of hours to make you some lunch, but in the meantime, try and sleep.'

'Yes, Mum.' Lily put her hand to her forehead in salute.

As soon as the flat door was closed, Lily slid down in the bed, pulled the covers over herself and closed her eyes, hoping the painkillers would take away the throbbing pain in her head.

Hours later, she opened her eyes again, unsure if she was still dreaming. Was the person standing by the side of the bed really there? She blinked to try and focus. Her head was pounding again and her body weak as she tried to push herself up.

'Hello, lovey, how are you feeling? Goodness, you *do* look poorly.'

Lily squinted, a sharp pain rumbling behind her eyes. 'Valerie?'

'Yes, love. Your mum said you weren't feeling well, and it was my break, so I thought I'd bring you some orange squash from the kitchen.'

Lily took the glass from her and sipped, the ice-cold drink a brief relief from the heat that raged in her body.

'Thank you,' she croaked, surprising herself with her lack of voice.

Lily felt the bed sag as Valerie perched on the edge, a hand to Lily's forehead. 'Goodness, you could fry an egg on there.'

When Lily tried to speak, Valerie put a finger to her own lips. 'Now then, you just rest. I've something here to bring that temperature down. My own mum used to swear by it.'

Valerie took out a small bottle from her pocket, squeezed the rubber top and unscrewed the lid.

'Open wide and stick out your tongue.'

Lily did as she was told and Valerie pressed the rubber top, drops of bitter liquid hitting Lily's tongue. She screwed her face up and shook her head, clamping her mouth shut.

'You'll get used to the taste soon enough.'

Lily gulped and gestured for the glass of squash. Valerie handed her the glass. 'Have a little sip then, not too much.'

Lily took a small drink, but before she could take more Valerie swiped the glass away and put it just out of reach.

'Another five minutes or so and you'll feel the benefit of that. *Magic drops*, that's what my mum used to call them. Never failed to cure, no matter what the illness.'

Lily felt a tingle in her throat; she began to cough, and once she started felt it escalate until she coughed so hard, she heaved. When she caught her breath again, she looked up at Valerie, who was smiling gently.

'Better?'

Lily still felt weak, but her head was no longer pounding and her body felt slightly cooler.

'Yes, a little bit.'

Valerie winked. 'Told you so, there's a lot to be said for the old cures. None of these chemicals from goodness knows where. There's something else I have for you.'

Lily sat up in bed, dropping straight back down on the pillow as her head swirled. She blinked her eyes, trying to get them to focus as Valerie took something from her pocket. Her vision was blurred and there were three or more of Valerie spinning slowly in circle. Valerie put something in the palm of her hand, a silver chain that came in and out of focus.

'It's nothing fancy, just a piece of jewellery I found that I thought a young girl like you might like.'

'My head, I feel fuzzy.'

'Oh, that's just the magic doing its thing, it'll pass.'

Lily raised the pendant closer to her face, a silver disc with a tree engraved on the front. She turned it over to see the familiar symbol of the circle and triangle.

'What is this?' Lily slurred, pointing at the symbol. 'I keep seeing it.'

She looked up at Valerie, who was still in triplicate, three thin red mouths, six eyes staring back at her.

'It's supposed to be good luck, it's to keep you safe,' Valerie said. 'Wear it at all times and I'll never be far from you, I promise.'

Lily felt the cold skin of Valerie's fingers as she took the chain from her hand and secured it round her neck.

'That looks lovely!' Valerie exclaimed, her hands resting on her heart. 'Now then, you get some rest and I expect you'll feel completely better by the time you wake up.'

Lily watched Valerie's blurred figure moving away from her bed, but before she had reached the door everything turned to darkness and Lily's head fell back on the pillow.

CHAPTER 27

Samantha had hoped for more poise when she sat down opposite Diane, but the chintz sofa was plush and she sank right into it, her feet coming off the floor.

'Can I get you a drink?' Diane offered.

'No, thank you.' Then, after looking to the window, 'Is Jonathan around?'

Diane shrugged and poured herself one, looking up at the grandfather clock in the corner. 'He should be back by now, I don't know what's holding him up.'

Samantha was conscious of the time passing, the medication round due in thirty minutes. Diane would have to answer her questions.

'The previous matron, Helen, wasn't it . . . ?'

She noted Diane pause mid sip, her eyes widening.

'Why didn't you tell me that she had died?'

Diane lowered the glass, gulping down the sip of wine as if it contained splinters of glass.

'It would have been good to know, to not find out by speaking to her mother.'

'Her mother? How—'

Diane had paled; even her deep Majorcan tan couldn't hide her surprise at the question.

'I found Helen's, the matron's, diary in the flat. As nobody else would tell me, I wanted to speak to her, and when I couldn't reach her, I called her mum.'

'What did she say?'

'Nothing really, she hung up on me. But she blames this place. Did she slip? Hurt her head? Crash her car, what?'

'Suicide,' said Diane, her voice weak.

'While she was here?'

'She jumped from her flat window. I'm sorry, we should have told you, but . . . well, we didn't want to put you off.'

'The flat me and Lily are in?'

Diane nodded slowly, not able to look Samantha in the eye.

Samantha felt a chill ripple across her skin. She let the information process for a moment, aware that Diane was also upset.

'That must have been a terrible shock.'

'Yes, particularly as it was me who found her body.'

'Oh God, I'm sorry, Diane.'

Samantha had seen her fair share of 'jumpers' and the terrible aftermath. Wheeled into A & E, some already passed, but worse were those having to cling onto a life they no longer wanted.

'She might have survived . . .' Diane took another sip of wine, this time it went down smoothly, 'but she hit her head on the statue by the back door. Ironic, really, that it was an angel that saw her off.' Diane recoiled, the words seeming too light for the subject matter.

'How do you know it was suicide? I mean, she might have slipped while opening a window or—'

'We knew something wasn't right with her weeks before. She was late for shifts, her mood low. It all came out at the inquest.'

'I see. Did you have any idea what was wrong, what made her late for her shifts, depressed?'

Diane shrugged. 'She was a very positive woman at the start. I liked her, she brought a bit of life to this place. I even

141

invited her to the villa for her holidays, but she just changed. It's this place, Samantha, it . . . gets to you, its . . . history.'

'The murder?'

Diane snapped her head up, her eyes searching Samantha's. 'You know about that?'

'Not really, just the stories people told in the park when we were kids.'

Diane nodded slowly. 'It's been a terrible blight. Samantha, I . . . I think you should leave.'

'Leave?'

'Yes, leave Hallow Croft,' Diane urged. 'Something bad is going to happen, I can feel it. People say it's just idle talk, but I live here, *I know*. I'll make sure you have a good reference and pay — just get away, tonight if possible.'

'But you were desperate for a new matron to come, Jonathan said. You were both run ragged.'

'No, he was. I was secretly hoping Hallow Croft would close and we'd be free to leave for good. Get away from whatever it is that haunts this place.'

Jonathan called from the hallway and Diane shrank back, her hands cupping the glass of wine.

The living-room door opened and Jonathan appeared, brushing the rain from his head.

'Quite a storm out there again.' He looked at the two women. 'What is it?'

'Nothing, Jonathan, nothing at all. Lunch will be ready soon.'

'Would you like anything to eat, Samantha? I'm sure Diane has made enough sandwiches for an army.'

Samantha shook her head, 'No, thank you. I've taken up enough of your time and I need to get back to the residents and Lily — she wasn't well this morning.'

'What's wrong with her?' Diane asked, concern etched across her face.

'Nothing serious, just a bit of a cold, she was out in the rain and got a chill.'

'Send her our best,' Jonathan said.

'Yes,' Diane said, her mind somewhere else, 'I hope she's well again soon.'

As she approached Hallow Croft, Samantha thought back to the text message: *leave*. Exactly what Diane had just said. She passed the angel statue by the stairs, with its chipped wing and mournful gaze, and a shudder crawled up her spine.

CHAPTER 28

1975

Annie ran from Hallow Croft, her hand tight to her trouser pocket and the paper bag containing his hair and cufflinks. She glanced back to see Dorothy glaring down from Henry Shuttleworth's bedroom, duster clenched in her fists. Annie grabbed Emily's bike and pushed herself away. As she turned a corner, she heard the sound of an engine, the roar getting louder as it approached. She felt herself wobble as the car passed, and turned the handlebars towards the hedge. She hit a rock as she slammed on the brakes and felt herself tip, falling to the ground and pinned beneath the bike.

The car screeched to a halt and Mr Shuttleworth's son ran back up the hill to help her. She turned her head, straightening her glasses and pulling her headscarf down. Blood was seeping from a gash on her knee onto the dusty road.

'Here, let me help you.'

She kept her hands pressed against her knee. As soon as he lifted the bike from her, Annie scrambled off the floor and stood up.

'I'm fine,' she said, her head down, refusing to look him in the eye.

'Your bike, it needs looking at. I can fix it.'

Annie glanced at the bent wheel and chain that had slipped.

'It's fine.' She could kick the damn thing, but instead limped off down the lane, pushing the bike along.

'Hey, you need someone to look at that knee!' Jonathan shouted.

Annie began to jog. Anything to get away from that kind voice, so unlike his father's.

She hobbled all the way back to Sylvia's house. Poppet came to the door. Her bright smile faltered when she saw the dark stains seeping into the denim of Annie's knees.

'Sylvia!' she called.

Annie had never heard Poppet call Sylvia 'Mum'; it was just one of the many disconcerting things that made the child different from her peers.

'I've told you not to shout from room to room.' Sylvia marched down the hallway, stopping still when she saw Annie. 'Goodness, Annie, what happened up there?'

Sylvia brought Annie into the kitchen and took out a box from a cupboard above the kettle. She opened it up to expose rows of small glass bottles, which she sorted through, a pleasant clinking of thin glass jingling around the room. She found what she was looking for and then picked out a handful of cotton wool balls from another glass jar.

Annie was perched on a stool by a thin wooden breakfast bar. She flinched as the ointment was wiped across the skin, bloodied cotton wool thrown straight into a bin. Over her shoulder Poppet watched in fascination.

'Where's your bike now?'

Annie nodded towards the window, 'I've left it over there by the shed.'

Sylvia looked up from the knee, her eyes boring into Annie's.

'You should have asked for a lift. Henry Shuttleworth might have recognised the bike from when Emily went up there.'

'He didn't see me arrive or leave.'

Sylvia pondered for a moment. 'Did you get what you went for?'

Annie took the paper bag from her pocket and put it on the breakfast bar. Sylvia washed her hands at the sink before opening the bag and taking out the contents. She placed them on the side, gently separating the small mat of hair from the gold cufflink. Poppet raised her hand to touch them.

'No,' said Sylvia, tapping her hand away.

Poppet scowled and crossed her arms tightly over her chest.

'Perfect,' said Sylvia, 'these are exactly what we need. The full moon is on Saturday; we'll meet here and walk to the standing stones together.'

'But you said I didn't need to go back there—'

'I meant into the house. We need to perform the ritual at the place she died, that's where it will be most powerful.'

Annie felt a wave of sickness in her belly, but she had come too far to stop now. This time at least the others would be with her, and at night she was unlikely to see anybody from Hallow Croft.

'Saturday is fine, I'll tell Kevin it's a Tupperware party or something.'

'Will he even notice you're gone, Annie?'

'Only if I haven't put his tea out,' she joked.

Sylvia shook her head, 'The age of romance and all that.' She turned to Poppet. 'Could you fetch me one of your dolls?'

Poppet smiled, looking pleased to be a part of the plan at last. She ran out of the kitchen, sharp taps sounding as she bounded up the stairs.

'Perhaps one day she'll be the head of a coven,' Annie said.

'God help us all if she is. I don't think there would be much group decision-making in her case — when Poppet wants to do something, nothing stops her, just like her father.'

Sylvia had never spoken about Poppet's dad; it was Ginny who had told Annie about him. A Wiccan priest gone

146

bad, she had said. The rest of the coven knew better than to ask Sylvia about it, and until now she had never mentioned him. If Annie was going to delve further, she was stopped by Sylvia switching the kettle on and talking about last night's telly. Poppet returned breathless, holding out a small male doll and handing it to her mother.

'Perfect, Poppet.'

The small girl beamed as Sylvia held up the raven-haired doll and uttered her thanks to the powers that be for such a perfect poppet.

CHAPTER 29

Samantha was on her way to the flat when Don caught up with her.

'Matron, I think you should come and see Renee.'

Don looked panic-stricken, breathless from running to get her.

'What's wrong?'

'I don't know, she's suddenly taken a turn for the worse. It doesn't look good.'

Samantha glanced up to the flat windows, Lily's curtains still drawn.

'I should really check on Lily, she had a temperature and—'

Don's face darkened. 'I don't think she's got much time left.'

Samantha took her phone out of her pocket and began typing.

Hi Lily, hope you're feeling better. Got to go see a sick resident, be home very soon. Love you xxx

Samantha hadn't been prepared for what she found when she entered Renee's room.

She placed a hand on Renee's forehead; she was cold and clammy and her skin ashen. Her mind went to Lily's illness

— was there a virus going around? Samantha took her phone from her pocket and scrolled through the contacts.

'Hi there, it's Matron from Hallow Croft, we have a doctor visit booked for Renee Pickford. Yes, please could I request it as urgent. Thank you.'

She ended the call and looked back on the notes. Renee had been given all the meds she could have for the moment. Samantha drew a small case from her pocket and took out a digital thermometer, easing it into Renee's mouth.

104 degrees.

She went to the small sink and wet a flannel, folded it, and placed it on Renee's forehead. Renee murmured and opened her eyes to thin slits. She held out her hand and Samantha took it.

'You just have a bit of a temperature, Renee, the doctor is coming to see you soon.'

Renee went to open her mouth, her lips dry and cracked. Samantha took the flannel and dabbed them before replacing it back on her forehead.

'Just rest, sweetheart,' said Don, holding her hand in his.

A strange noise left Renee's mouth, a long 'Aaaaaa.' She blinked, her eyes watery, a weak tear escaping and falling down the side of her face to the pillow.

Samantha pulled a cord by the bed and outside the room a bell rang intermittently. It was only a matter of seconds before Debby popped her head around the door.

'Could you get me a jug of iced water, please?'

Debby peered over at Renee, her eyes widening. 'I'll go get it now.'

'Aaaaaann,' Renee croaked, the noise turning into a hoarse, dry cough.

'Try not to speak, Renee. Debby is going to get you a drink, it won't be long. We'll have you up and about by lunchtime.'

They were platitudes she was used to giving. Countless offerings of 'don't worry' and 'you're going to be fine' to fill the gaps between cries of agony or desperate final breaths.

Debby ambled through the door clutching a Perspex jug of water and plastic tumbler full of water and ice.

'Don, can you help me lift Renee a little,' Samantha asked.

Don hooked his arm under Renee's armpit, Samantha taking the other.

'On three. One, two, three.'

They pulled Renee gently to half sitting, and she began to mumble again.

'She has a fever,' Samantha explained. 'Here's a drink, Renee, take a sip.'

Samantha held the cup to her lips, which were moving rapidly, as if she were trying to form a sentence. The water pooled in her mouth, dripping down the sides, a small gag as a drop hit the back of her throat.

'Let's lay her back down, hopefully she'll settle.'

Renee became agitated, flinging her body from side to side, a limp hand catching Don's glasses and sending them flying to the floor.

As he crouched to find them, Renee called out again, this time her voice cracked and deep, a growl from the pit of her stomach.

'Aaaannniee.'

Samantha gulped back emotion, trying to lay Renee down on the bed.

'Renee, please, you need to relax.'

Beads of sweat began to form on Renee's forehead, her eyes rolling back in their sockets.

The window to the room flew open and a blast of cold air surrounded them.

'Jesus!' Samantha looked behind her to see Valerie standing in the doorway, her brow furrowed.

'What's happening here?' she said. She crept nearer to them, her arms behind her back, watching Renee. Samantha caught Don's eye and they exchanged a stony glance. Valerie marched to the other side of the bed and edged Don aside, taking hold of Renee's hand.

'Now then, Renee, what's all this fuss?'

'We're fine, Valerie, best not to overwhelm her with too many people now. Can you go and wait for the doctor, they'll be here any minute.'

Samantha caught Don's eye, gesturing for him to take back Renee's hand. Valerie was now looming over Renee like a bird of prey, holding onto the woman's hand with a vice-like grip.

Renee began to call out again, her words jumbled and unintelligible, as if she were speaking in tongues, just as Aparna had done the night of the magician. Samantha took out her phone again and rapidly jabbed the screen. When she got an answer, her voice was desperate.

'It's Matron again from Hallow Croft, can you tell me when the doctor will get here?'

As the receptionist on the other end of the line tapped slowly away, Samantha watched Valerie stroke the side of Renee's face. Valerie smiled a crooked smile down at Renee, who seemed to focus again, her eyes wide, pupils enlarged. For a moment Samantha thought Valerie had calmed her down. Then Renee stopped and took in the face above her.

Fear contorted Renee's features and, with what seemed like every last speck of energy the woman had, she began to howl, her body convulsing. Samantha dropped her phone and ran over, pushing Valerie out of the way and trying to hold Renee to the bed. Renee fell limp.

'Renee?' Samantha felt for a pulse.

Nothing.

She leaned her cheek against Renee's mouth but felt no breath.

'Lower the bed down now, Don. Valerie, call an ambulance.' Valerie looked shocked. 'Now, Valerie!' Samantha pressed the emergency alarm on the wall and the bell rang out in a constant beep.

Valerie turned on her black plimsoles and left immediately. Samantha began CPR on Renee, blowing into her mouth and then placing her hands on her chest to perform compressions, fifteen to each of her three breaths. Renee's body flayed with each of the pushes down on her chest.

'Come on, Renee, come back to us.'

Samantha's voice was edged with desperation. Don watched helplessly, his face unsure, looking to Samantha for direction.

'I'll keep going until the ambulance gets here.'

Beyond the door they could hear the gathering of voices, curious residents and staff waiting. When the sound of sirens echoed outside, Samantha felt a rush of relief, the adrenaline pulsing through her body coming under control as she heard the heavy footsteps of paramedics approaching down the corridor.

She stepped out of the way, calling out a brief explanation of Renee's history and how she had been this morning. The paramedics listened as they continued the CPR, Samantha stepping back and leaning against Renee's dressing table.

Don looked across, shaking his head slowly. Samantha watched the ambulance crew share a familiar glance and then step away from Renee's lifeless body. The woman turned to Samantha. 'I don't think it would be fair to continue.'

Samantha forced a small smile. 'OK.'

The paramedics began to pack up their equipment as Samantha approached Renee, taking her arms and placing them by her side, gently closing her eyes and pulling a white sheet up to her neck, tucking it neatly under the mattress. Samantha's hands shook slightly as she tried to lift the mattress, the shock of losing a resident so full of life, and so quickly, never getting easier.

'Don, would you mind getting some flowers from reception?'

Without a word, Don left the room. Samantha heard the anxious whispers behind the door, all eager to know what was happening. She was pleased to hear Don ask them to get on with what they were doing. Death was inevitable in her work, even more so in a nursing home, but still each one came as a jolt. Renee even more so, as she was the resident Samantha had taken to first. She felt a buzz in her pocket and reached for her phone, tapping on the message.

Get away from here.

She hit delete, furious that at this time, in this moment, a stranger had decided to interrupt her with more threatening doom.

The paramedics left and Samantha was alone with Renee. The previously chaotic scene was now a tranquil one.

She shuddered as an icy draught rippled through the room. The curtains billowed and there came the tinkle of breaking porcelain. She shut the window and bent to pick up the broken figurine, slotting its head against its shoulders. She placed the pieces on the dressing table, suddenly aware of the mementos of Renee's life before her. The mother-of-pearl brush set, a black-and-white wedding photo framed in silver filigree.

The photo of Renee with her friend. Both smiling widely, young women with their futures ahead. Samantha squinted and brought the photo closer to her face. The blonde woman was familiar, thin-framed and delicate with bright blue eyes.

She was relieved when Don entered carrying a vase of white lilies, glad not to be alone. He placed the flowers on the side table by Renee's bed. Their overpowering scent soon faded in this room of sudden loss.

CHAPTER 30

'What did she give you?' Samantha demanded, trying to keep her voice steady.

Lily didn't take her eyes away from the sketchpad as she began shading the teeth of an animal's skull. 'I don't know, some herbal stuff.'

When she had returned to the flat, Samantha had been full of concern. It was irrational, but what had happened to Renee and the parallels to leaving her feverish daughter had shaken her. She was surprised to find Lily out of bed, drinking squash on the sofa, and catching up on her artwork as if she had never been ill.

'You shouldn't just take something if you don't know what it is, Lily!'

Lily put the pencil down and turned to her. 'It worked better than the tablets you gave me, so does it matter?'

Samantha gritted her teeth. 'And you shouldn't let anyone in when I'm not here, OK?'

'I didn't, I just woke up and she was in my room.'

Samantha put down the mug of tea she was cradling and sat by Lily.

'I locked the door, I'm sure I did.'

'I thought you must have given her a key or left the latch on.' Lily went back to her drawing, pushing the soft lead hard to create the blackness of the empty eye sockets.

'Why would I give her my keys?'

Lily shrugged.

'What's that?' Samantha pointed at the drawing.

'Just a skull I found . . . well, Finn found.'

Though bones and anatomical pictures were nothing new to Samantha, she had never known Lily to take an interest before. Since her daughter had begun painting, the walls had been covered in pictures of flowers and portraits of faces that had caught her eye. Her daughter's talent was a mystery to her; her own artistic endeavours were limited to stick figures and childlike houses.

'It's a bit . . . macabre, isn't it? Is that what your art teacher wants?'

Lily scowled and turned so that the drawing was out of sight of Samantha. 'They want us to draw things that inspire us,' she said dryly.

Not wanting to cause an argument, Samantha didn't pursue it further. She got up from the sofa and went to make Lily a cheese sandwich. She then cut up an apple, piling the pieces on the small plate.

'I need to get back to work, call if you need me, OK?'

Lily nodded, taking the plate from her.

'And call if anyone else decides to make an impromptu visit.'

Lily rolled her eyes, enough to let Samantha know she had been heard. Samantha grabbed an apple from the side and headed out the door, unable to shake off the irritation of Valerie having been there.

* * *

When Samantha reached the day room, she noticed a small group gathered at the French windows. Valerie, Debby and two of the residents, Edna and Sue. Aparna wandered past

155

them, towards Samantha. She smiled, but the smile belied a look of worry etched across her small forehead. Poor Aparna, Samantha thought, the elderly woman perpetually stuck in a world of anxiety.

'Are you OK, Aparna?'

Aparna looked up at her, regarding Samantha's face with solemn eyes. 'Bad things coming.'

'What bad things, Aparna?'

Before Aparna could reply, Valerie let out a hoot of laughter, which instantly bristled Samantha, like fingernails down a chalkboard. Aparna wandered off, leaving Samantha alone again. Despite herself, she approached the window, curious to see what the women were watching.

'He's for it now,' Valerie gloated.

'Who is?' Samantha said.

The group turned and quietened, like naughty school children caught passing notes in class.

Debby looked to the floor and the two residents remained quiet. Valerie crossed her arms under her bust and tilted her head, enjoying her moment.

'The prodigal son is back, isn't he?'

'Whose son?'

Valerie paused, then raising an eyebrow exclaimed, 'Jonathan's son!'

'Oh,' Samantha wasn't sure why this was news, 'I didn't know Jonathan and Diane had a son.'

'They don't,' said Valerie. 'That's the problem.'

Samantha narrowed her eyes, waiting for more information. Valerie fixed her eyes on Samantha, clearly enjoying her confusion.

'He's not Diane's,' said Debby.

'*Debby*,' Valerie admonished, 'that's not your story to tell.'

'Well, it's not yours either,' she mumbled, her cheeks red.

Valerie took a deep breath, her chest filling out like a balloon, her eyes piercing into Debby's downturned head.

Samantha turned to Debby. 'Debby, could you do the lunches, please? Start with Dot and then Agatha?'

Debby nodded and turned, heading towards the kitchen, her cheeks still ruddy from the conflict. Valerie went to follow, but Samantha put her hand on her shoulder and she swung round, her stony gaze fixed on the matron.

'Valerie, could I have a quick word before we get them through to lunch?'

Valerie didn't answer, but stayed where she was.

'I understand you went to see Lily earlier.'

Valerie pushed her tongue to the side of her cheek, her mouth clamped shut.

'And you gave her some tincture? Some herbal remedy?'

She remained silent, forcing Samantha to continue.

'Well, in future, please could you speak to me before you consider treating my daughter with anything, even herbs? I like to know what is happening.'

'How is she now?'

'She's much better, but that's not the point, it's—'

'Surely her wellness is more important than her mother's dented ego?'

'I'm sorry?' Samantha could feel herself rising to the bait; she caught a glimpse of a resident shuffling across the dining room, using the backs of the chairs to balance as she walked.

'Look, just . . . can you ask next time?'

Valerie's defiance dissolved into contrition. 'Of course, Matron, it won't happen again.'

Samantha felt the relief wash through her. Valerie went to help the resident to her chair.

'Oh, and one more thing — how did you get into the flat?'

Valerie shook her head and waggled a finger playfully. 'You only went and left the door open, didn't you. Good job it was just me that ventured up there. Could have been any old stranger.'

Samantha thought about the morning. She was always so careful to lock doors, a childhood full of return trips home with her mum 'just to check'. Had she forgotten? Her memory had gotten worse lately. That said, it was highly unlikely a boogey man was going to find his way up the maze of corridors and happen across her unlocked flat. Then again, Valerie had.

Samantha looked out of the window. A dark blue Porsche was parked in the car park, its private plate conspicuous among the dilapidated staff run-arounds.

She walked into the dining room, residents arriving one by one and taking their usual seats. Debby was sitting next to Dot, carefully spooning something beige into the elderly woman's mouth, trying to coax her along.

'Are you OK, Debby?' Samantha asked, smiling at Dot, who looked blankly back at her.

Debby shuffled in her chair, her eyes flickering around the room.

'Yes, Matron.'

'You know, it's OK to speak up for yourself, that's very brave.'

Debby wiped Dot's mouth clean.

'How long have you known Valerie?' Samantha sat down next to Debby, confident that no one else could hear their conversation.

Debby kept her eyes on Dot. 'Everyone knows Valerie, she's lived in Nether Dale forever.'

'Are you from Nether Dale?'

'Yes, my family have lived here for years.'

'Valerie does seem to have an influence on everyone,' Samantha said, a half-smile lacing the words.

'People are scared of her, that's why.'

'Oh, why?'

'I don't know. She's all right really, she looks after me.'

Dot swatted Debby's hand away, splattering a spoonful of the beige mush across the carpet. Debby reached down to wipe up the spill, her hand resting on the spoon for a moment.

Debby handed Dot a sippy cup of water. The veins in Dot's hands bulged as she gripped the plastic container and suckled the spout.

'Did you know about the last matron?' Samantha waited to observe Debby's reaction.

She looked anxiously around the room.

'I already know about the suicide,' Samantha assured her.

Dot turned her eyes to Samantha, watching her curiously as she sipped at the drink.

Debby stuttered, 'I wasn't here, I mean, when it happened.'

'Was she depressed?'

'I don't know. I know there'd been some barney, though. She'd tried to get involved with Mrs Dawson, there was a row and then she changed.'

'Changed?'

'She had seemed happy before, everybody liked her. She was nice. But after that, she was moody and bad-tempered, as if she didn't want to be here. It was horrible to be around her, like someone had body-snatched the old matron away and replaced her with this miserable one. That's why we look after Mrs Dawson now, she knows us.'

'I'm sure it wasn't directly to do with Mrs Dawson. Depression can be like that, a dark cloud taking over, no tangible reason. It's a terrible—'

'It wasn't that, it was something here that did it. Something in that room, *her* room.'

'Mrs Dawson's?'

Debby nodded. Jonathan entered the dining room, beaming at his residents. Debby took this as an opportunity to pick up the near-empty bowl and sippy cup and scuttle off towards the kitchen.

'Ah, there you are, Matron.' Jonathan turned to Dot. 'And how are we today, Mrs Jones?'

The elderly woman nodded blankly, a confused look on her face.

'Hi, Jonathan,' said Samantha.

'How is Lily doing? Nothing serious, I hope?'

'Just a slight fever, she seems much better now.'

'Excellent. I was sorry to hear about Renee, a terrible shock. A lovely woman.'

'From the short time I knew her, I'd have to agree.' After a pause, she reached out and touched his arm. 'I meant to ask, are there other keys to my flat? On a general bunch somewhere? It's not that I mind, but—'

'No, there are only two keys, and I gave them both to you.'

'Are you sure?'

Jonathan smiled widely. 'Yes, of course, your flat is private, I wouldn't dream of letting anyone else have a key. Why do you ask?'

'Oh, nothing. I, er, ignore me, I'll check Lily has the spare.'

Jonathan nodded and went back to his business.

Samantha peered over at Valerie, who was sat chatting to another resident. As if feeling Samantha's gaze, she looked up, a small, tight smile pulling across her lips. A moment later, Valerie reached into her pocket and took something out. She clutched it in her fist, spinning it, her fingers twisting and curling over a small object. Samantha watched, transfixed, as Valerie's fingers began to open, revealing a bright silver key in her palm.

CHAPTER 31

A silence blanketed Hallow Croft for the next two days, all going about his or her duties without fuss or comment — residents dressed and fed, beds made and pillows fluffed. Samantha prepared Renee's room for her next of kin's visit. Her son, who had long since moved to Kent, was travelling up to make arrangements for her funeral and to collect her belongings. Samantha straightened the crocheted blanket across the bed and wiped the fallen lily pollen from the side table. She unwrapped some purple carnations from their cellophane and placed them in a vase of fresh water. It was usually a clinical task, to make relatives feel better about the passing of a loved one, but she wanted to do more for Renee, to make it more fitting for her somehow.

She had looked in on Lily on her break. Her daughter was now recovered, but still weak from the fever. Samantha had been pleased to find a note saying that she had 'gone out for fresh air'. Though Valerie's visit had angered her, Samantha had to admit, if not out loud, that the herbal remedy seemed to have cured her.

'Cuppa?' Don called around the door.

'Yes please,' she said, stretching out her back. She gave the room a last once-over before following Don to the staff room.

Don stood just outside the staff-room door, blowing cigarette smoke into the cold air. Samantha stood the other side, looking out towards the woods.

'Want one?'

He held the cigarette packet out to Samantha.

'Nope, I'm going to be good, well, kind of.' She took the vape from her pocket and drew on it. Vanilla vapour surrounded them.

'Renee was one of the good ones,' said Don.

'I didn't know her that well, but still.' She turned to Don. 'She seemed so full of life, no illness, not even a slight cold, and then suddenly . . .'

Don inhaled on the cigarette and spoke in puffs of smoke. 'And then there's the like of Mrs Potter that refuse to go, living on purely to bring misery to our days.'

Samantha laughed, then stopped herself. 'You shouldn't talk about the residents like that. Honestly . . .'

'Maybe it was Mrs Dawson's appearance? It's enough to send the healthiest over the edge,' said Don, flicking ash into a plant pot. 'From what I gather, they used to be good friends back in the day.'

'Mrs Dawson and Renee?'

'So Valerie says. That's why they kept them apart mainly. Mrs Dawson would get too upset when she saw Renee, probably something in the back of her mind reminding her of how she used to be.'

'Do you know who put Renee to bed the night before she died?' said Samantha.

Don thought for a moment. 'I did Albert and the top floor, Debby was helping me, so it must have been Valerie, I suppose.'

Samantha stared out beyond the low wall that encircled them, over to the moors and the woodlands.

'Shall I ask for you?'

Samantha turned back again. 'No, no. It's OK, I'll go over everything later when I finish the report.'

A phone rang in the staff room and Samantha leaned in and picked up the receiver.

'Yes. Oh, OK, tell him I'll be there in a minute.'

She dropped the vape in her pocket. 'Renee's son has just arrived.'

Samantha made her way back to her office, taking a deep breath before opening the door. She was surprised to see Jonathan sat on the other side of the desk.

'Ah, Matron, this is Sergeant Pickford.'

Sergeant Pickford rose to shake her hand.

'Call me Dave, please.'

Samantha took his hand and shook it gently, a balance between formality and sympathy.

'I'm sorry for the loss of your mum. I hadn't known her long, but I was very fond of her.'

He smiled as she took a seat by the side of the desk.

'I was just telling Dave that you did everything you could to try and save Renee,' said Jonathan. 'He wanted to thank you himself.'

'I'm very grateful, Matron.'

Samantha smiled, shrugging. 'She was a lovely woman, she'll be very much missed.'

Sergeant Pickford nodded, tears welling in his eyes.

'Right then,' Jonathan said, standing up, 'shall I take you to her room now?'

Jonathan and Samantha watched silently as Dave wandered around Renee's bedroom. He lifted up the framed photo of two young women from the dressing table.

'Does Mrs Dawson know?' Dave asked.

Samantha saw Jonathan's eyes twitch, flickering first to her and then back to Dave.

'I'm afraid Mrs Dawson doesn't really know where she is anymore, so it's very difficult . . .' he trailed off.

'Of course,' said Dave, placing the photograph on top of a cardboard box, which he carried out of the room.

Samantha and Jonathan followed.

'Right then,' said Jonathan, 'I'll be in touch soon.'

Dave released an arm from the box to shake Jonathan's hand.

'If there's anything more we can do, please do call.'

Jonathan left Dave and Samantha in the hallway.

Something shiny caught Samantha's eye and she bent to pick it up, showing it to Dave.

'It's her medal for good service in the police force.'

'Renee was a police officer?'

'For many years, reached a high rank too. She was an inspiration to me.'

'I had no idea.'

'Well, she wasn't one for boasting, especially round here. She solved many cases, but there was one she never could, and she'll take that disappointment to the grave.'

'The murder at Hallow Croft?'

He nodded, clutching the medal. 'But she more than made up for it in other cases. Anyway, thank you again — I'll send my son to collect the rest of her things in the next day or so. He's a painter and decorator and has a van for the bigger bits.'

'Didn't follow into the family business then?'

Sergeant Pickford smiled. 'He's got more sense.'

Samantha gestured to the photograph he carried. 'It's a lovely photo of her, she looks so young and carefree. Can I ask, who's her friend?'

Sergeant Pickford looked down at it. 'That was her good friend, the mother of the young girl that was murdered here. It's Annie, Annie Dawson.'

CHAPTER 32

Samantha waved Dave off from the main door, a rising wind pushing against him as he made his way to his car. A bin had fallen over at the side of the house, empty pasta and biscuit packets swirling across the gravel. She ran out to retrieve them, chasing them in circles until she managed to catch them with the tips of her fingers. As she made her way back, she caught sight of Lily walking up the drive, Valerie by her side. They were laughing, each clutching their coats tight to them and Lily brushing her hair from her face. That familiar feeling of unease rose up in Samantha. She shouted to Lily but her voice was swallowed up in the wind and carried away to nothing. The pair disappeared round the back of the house. Samantha considered following them for a moment, then thought better of it and returned to her office.

She was surprised to find Jonathan sitting back at her desk. He was deep in thought, not noticing her presence until the office door closed behind her.

'Sorry, Matron, I'll be out of your way shortly.'

'Do you need me to do anything?' Samantha offered.

Jonathan looked up. 'Renee was always very good to me when I was growing up, you know. She looked out for me after my mother left.'

Samantha sat down in the chair opposite. 'That must have been tough.'

Jonathan's brow furrowed, his thoughts in another, darker place.

Samantha took a breath. 'Why didn't Renee spend more time with Annie here?'

Jonathan's head snapped up. 'You heard me explain to Dave, it upset Mrs Dawson.'

She was taken aback with the sharpness of his tone. 'I just think it's a shame. Renee's son said they were good friends, and she obviously thought well enough of Mrs Dawson to keep that photograph of her up all this time.'

'It's years since they were friends, I don't know why she bothered.'

'You know, Jonathan, as Renee was dying, she was trying to tell me something. I think she was trying to call for Mrs Dawson.'

Jonathan stood up, gathering himself as if returning to the present.

'I should get back to Diane, gifts to wrap and all that. Which reminds me, what are your plans for Christmas?'

'Oh, I hadn't really thought about it. I'm working, of course, so will make something for Lily after and watch a bit of television, I suppose.'

'Absolutely not. I insist that you and Lily join us for Christmas dinner. You finish just after lunch?'

Samantha nodded.

'Well, Lily can come over earlier, can't have her alone at Christmas, and you can join us when you've finished your shift.'

'It's very kind of you, but—'

'No buts, I'll ask Diane to set the table for five. My son will be there and he'll have had enough of us by then. You would be doing me a favour.'

There was no way for Samantha to refuse. She would rather just get into her PJs and watch crap TV with Lily, but he was right. It wasn't fair on Lily to be alone all day and, if

166

she were honest, the idea of someone else making the dinner was very appealing.

'As long as you let me do the washing-up.'

'Deal.'

As Jonathan left the room a buzzer began to sound. Samantha looked up to the board in the office: Mrs Dawson. She reached up and switched it off with her key, hoping that Valerie hadn't already seen it. She rushed out of the office and ran up the stairs, determined to meet Annie properly at last.

CHAPTER 33

1975

Under the light of the full moon, the coven walked single file along the track, the sound of footsteps on gravel echoing in the silence. Each wore a heavy black cloak, hoods pulled over their heads, faces hidden. The bells of Nether Dale church rang in the distance, striking eleven o'clock: one hour until midnight, when the curse would be sealed.

Sylvia led the women, turning off the track and heading across a field up to the woods. Annie glanced to her left, where the faint lights at Hallow Croft could be seen. She felt an urge to turn and run, a deep sickness of fear and uncertainty that made her knees buckle. As if sensing her fear, Ginny put a hand on her shoulder and whispered, 'Keep going, Annie.'

Annie looked away and followed Sylvia into the woods. Twigs and dead leaves crunched beneath their feet as they weaved through the jagged trees. The full moon threw shadows through the branches, each woman illuminated and sent into darkness with each alternating stride. Not even the sudden swoosh of wings from an owl swooping down distracted them from what was ahead.

The moment Annie caught sight of the standing stones, her steps faltered, her ankle twisting beneath her as she fell to the ground. Ginny pulled her up.

'You OK?' she asked.

Annie flinched as a stab of pain shot through her ankle. 'I'm fine.'

Sylvia stood in the middle of the stones. She held out a silver knife and turned slowly, creating a sacred space for the women to stand in. The women formed a circle, and when Sylvia went to untie her cape, they each followed suit, the cloaks sliding down their skin, the bluish white light of the moon illuminating their naked bodies. Sylvia wore a translucent robe beneath, secured in the middle by a gold belt. On her head, a crown with horns twisting towards the night sky.

Their toes sunk into the icy dirt, bare feet gripping the lichen-covered stone as they twirled over them, dancing in circles, arms writhing snake-like in the sharp wind that prickled bare skin. They commanded energy to their bodies, golden light swirling through their fingertips and into veins, fizzing down to empty stomachs. They danced around a wild fire, flames dancing with them and orange light reflecting on their skin.

Together they howled and cried like wild foxes, their bodies swaying from side to side. Gigantic shadows followed them on the moonlit ground.

Martha began to beat a drum, slow, steady beats as the women's cries continued. Annie was brought out of her trance by the crackle and spit of dry twigs in the woods.

As the drum beat three times in quick succession, the women knelt within the circle. Sylvia held up the doll that Poppet had given her and, taking her small knife, dug into the material, cutting a hole in its belly. She stuffed the hair and cufflinks into the doll's body and then, taking a needle and thread, darned the hole with two large stitches. As the other witches watched, still swaying from side to side, Donna poured a flask of water into a bowl and presented it to Sylvia, who submerged the doll, sealing the curse. She then placed the poppet on a silver tray and held it up to the sky, chanting to the spirits. The women watched as Sylvia crouched and placed the doll into a deep hole in the ground that Corinne had dug with the silver blade. Each woman dropped soil over the doll until it was completely covered. They took each other's hands and formed a tight circle around the freshly formed mound. They spoke together.

We bring this curse to being for the life of Emily.
May her life be celebrated, and her death avenged.
The guilty family will suffer, no longer escaping consequence.
We take the life of the first female-born child.
To die at sixteen on the last full moon.'

A crow called out from the trees, answered by another. The women's hands dropped free from each other, breathless; they closed their eyes, each offering a silent prayer to their god. When their bodies had calmed and their minds were clear once more, they dressed, before silently walking away into the night.

CHAPTER 34

Lily sat on her satchel, knees bent and back against the standing stone, drawing pad resting on her thighs. She took a graphite pencil from a case and began to sketch a circle of twigs and stones she had arranged on the ground. She pulled a tissue from her pocket and blew her nose; if her mum were to catch her sitting on the damp ground, she would have a fit. She carried on with her drawing.

'Hello there!'

Her heart raced as her head snapped round to see a man stood watching her. She guessed he was in his late thirties as he approached her, waving his hand in a friendly manner. On the other side of him, Finn trotted on the end of a lead, his tail swishing wildly when he saw Lily. She pushed away the twigs and stones, sending them scattering across the ground, not wanting this stranger to see.

She didn't reply, just managing a small, confused smile. Finn pulled on the end of the lead, his body lunging towards her.

'Looks like Finn knows you,' he beamed. 'I'm Harry.'

She suspected from the way he announced himself that she was supposed to know who he was; her silence prompted him further.

'Jonathan's son.'

Harry unclipped the lead from the collar and Finn bounded over to Lily, his giant body clumsy and enthusiastic. He knocked the art pad from her knees, sending it flying onto the damp ground.

'Get down, Finn!' Harry shouted, the dog obediently keeping all four feet on the floor, its body sweeping across Lily's waist. 'Sorry, he can be a pain.'

'I'm Lily,' she said, as Finn lapped at her face with his tongue.

'The new matron's daughter? Ah, I've heard a lot about you — all good, don't worry.'

She smiled, ruffling Finn's shaggy mane.

'You clearly have a fan here.'

'I walk him sometimes. I always wanted a dog of my own but with Mum's job . . .' She shrugged.

'Yes, they do take a lot of commitment, too much for me alas, that's why I enjoy having Finn when I'm here.'

Harry looked familiar, a younger, fresher and less tanned version of Jonathan.

'I hear you're joining us for Christmas dinner,' said Harry. 'Am I?'

He nodded. 'What's that you have there, Finn?'

Finn was now pushing the twigs and stones around with his snout.

'Oh, it's nothing, just a nature thing.' Lily pushed her art pad back into her satchel.

'Do my dad and stepmum know you come up here?'

Lily shrugged. 'Jonathan does.'

'Well, don't let Diane know, she'll have you drowned in the nearest pond.'

'Sorry?'

'I'm just joking. Let's just say Diane is slightly obsessed with old wives' tales and rumours. Finn! Come here, boy.'

She watched Finn gallop back to Harry.

'See you on Christmas Day then,' he said, reclipping Finn's lead and dragging the giant dog back towards the woods.

Lily nodded, waving at Finn, who whined as he was led away. She rearranged the twigs and stones until they were back in their original position, and took her pad out again. She sat back and began to draw again, her thoughts not on her work but on what Harry had said. If she got a chance, maybe Diane might tell her what happened at Hallow Croft all those years ago.

CHAPTER 35

Samantha looked up and down the corridor, checking that nobody else was coming to answer the bell. She pushed open Mrs Dawson's door to find the room in darkness.

'Annie?'

She heard a small voice calling out as she edged into the room.

The bed was empty, sheets and blankets pulled back. Samantha looked around the room, the chill in the air causing her to shudder. She felt the radiator, snatching her hand away from the ice-cold metal. Samantha crouched down to check the controls: it was on full heat. She tapped at the metal as if this would miraculously bring it to life, but there was just a hollow echo.

She had expected the decoration to be like all the other bedrooms, framed prints of fruit and flowers, porcelain animals and crocheted blankets. However the walls in Annie's room were soft pink and adorned with posters of The Rolling Stones and David Bowie. She turned to the far wall: a beautiful oil portrait of a young girl dressed in blue satin, a girl not much older than Lily. On a dressing table was a photograph of six women in flowing dresses, flower garlands placed on their heads.

'She's really gone, hasn't she?' she said, her voice cracking.

Samantha walked slowly towards the high-backed chair facing the window, fine strands of white hair just visible. Outside in the garden Don sat with a resident who was bundled up in blankets, both looking to the sky of greyish clouds heavy with snow. Annie stared beyond them, out to the woods.

Samantha placed a hand on the arm of the chair and crouched down beside Annie.

'Who has gone, Annie? You mean Renee?'

'How did it happen?' Her words curled and faded as she spoke.

Samantha shrugged. 'I . . . I'm not sure. She had a fever and then—'

In one arm Annie clutched a worn teddy bear, her other hand clenched into a bony fist, the whites of her small knuckles exposed. Samantha edged back, uncertain if she was about to be landed with a punch.

'Her heart just stopped?'

'Yes, that's right. When I saw her the night before she died she was as bright as a button, but by the morning—'

'Like Matron?'

Samantha froze. 'Matron? But she committed suicide, didn't she?'

Annie turned her head slowly to look up at Samantha, her expression dark and tortured. The woman seemed to have aged further since the night of the magic show, dark circles beneath tissue-paper-thin skin.

'Leave this place,' her eyes narrowed, 'and take her with you.' Annie, still looking straight at Samantha, pointed a crooked finger towards the quadrant outside.

Samantha looked out to see Lily walking across the grounds, her satchel slung over her shoulder.

'We're not going anywhere, Annie. I'm staying here with you. This is my job, I'm happy here, I—'

Annie got hold of Samantha's hand and squeezed it so tightly that Samantha thought her fingers might break.

'I'm warning you to leave before it's too late,' Annie hissed. 'It'll be the full moon soon and then she'll die.'

'Don't say such awful things, Annie. You've had an upset — Renee was your friend, I know that, but—'

Samantha tried to prise Annie's fingers from hers but each time she lifted one it snapped back down, harder than before. Annie pulled at her arm until Samantha's face was inches from hers and whispered, *'She'll die . . . she'll die!'*

CHAPTER 36

Samantha stormed into the kitchen carrying a tray of mugs. She slammed them down on the metal work surface, making Cathy jump.

'These mugs are dirty.'

Samantha handed one to Cathy to inspect.

'Dishwasher must be playing up or something.'

'Make sure in future they're all clean before putting them on the trolley. Residents pay a lot of money to be here, the least they can expect is clean cups.'

Valerie appeared beside her, raising her thin eyebrows at Cathy, who returned a bemused look.

She left the two women to whisper as she left. Annie had got under her skin in a way no one else had managed to. There was something wrong at Hallow Croft, she knew that, but as far as she could see, it was just bullish personalities and ego, rather than anything sinister. Annie had scared her, because that wasn't just silly stories about curses and past crimes. It was specifically about Lily. But Samantha could put it down to dementia or some kind of psychosis brought on by the loss of her own daughter.

They had clearly let it all build and created some kind of hysteria in the home between the residents and staff. If she did nothing else during her time here it would be to put an end to it, once and for all. She would make sure to keep Lily out of it, though; she didn't want her scared and asking to leave. Whatever warnings came, Samantha was determined to see this job through.

Samantha found herself in the lounge and went over to sit next to Bert as he drank his medicine from a small plastic cup. The day room was filling up post lunch as the television blared Christmas hymns from the corner. Aparna shuffled in and sat herself the other side of Samantha. Samantha smiled over at her as the old woman arranged her clothing in the seat.

'She was a good woman, Renee,' Bert said, handing back the plastic cup.

'Yes, I was very fond of her,' said Samantha, turning the cup in her fingers. 'Did you know her before she came here?'

'Oh yes, everyone local knew Renee. Once caught a robber red-handed and chased him over the green, tackled him to the floor as well. Don't be fooled by her size — she was a warrior when it came to doing the right thing.'

'I believe she was very close to Annie Dawson?'

Bert's fingers tapped at his lap, his eyes forward. 'For a long time.'

'Did they ever spend time together here?'

'They keep a tight rein on Annie here,' Bert looked around the room as if checking the coast was clear, then turned to Samantha, his voice low and deep. 'She isn't like most people, she's been through . . . a lot, what with her daughter and all.'

'The murder?'

Bert nodded. Samantha thought about the painting on the wall. She didn't think she could survive if anything happened to Lily. What that poor woman had been through was unimaginable to anybody else here, and now they punished her for her distress.

'Did they ever catch who did it?' Samantha asked, leaning in, though she already knew they hadn't.

'That's just it, nobody was ever charged, though she was convinced she knew.'

Samantha waited.

Bert put his hand to his mouth and spoke in a hushed tone. 'Annie swore blind it was old Mr Shuttleworth senior, Henry. He'd been painting her girl's portrait that night, he painted lots of local beauties. But he always said someone had broken in and attacked them. Swore up and down he got hit over the head and she'd tried to escape but ended up killed instead. There wasn't any of that DNA malarky back then, you see, and no witnesses apart from Mr Shuttleworth, so people chose to believe him. He had half the village living out of his back pocket, so it wasn't hard to keep them on side or at least quiet.'

'Poor Annie.'

'Poor Annie nothing, she took her own revenge.'

'What do you mean?' Samantha asked, trying to ignore Aparna, who was now tugging at her arm.

'I shouldn't say anything, they don't like idle gossip around here.'

Samantha waited, and sure enough he continued, 'The Nether Dale witches, you see, Annie was a part of all that.'

'Witches?'

'Oh, I don't mean flying around on broomsticks and wearing pointy hats and all that rubbish, I mean *real* witch-craft. My Jean used to run the café in the village and she was terrified of them, swore blind they put a curse on her Victoria sponge cakes — she never had one rise again after a to-do with Sylvia one day. Not that you'd know there was anything odd to look at them. They were just normal women. After the murder they say Annie persuaded them to put a curse on the Shuttleworth family.'

'What kind of curse?' Samantha asked, then, turning to Aparna, who was jabbing her with a finger, 'I'll be with you in a moment, Aparna.' She turned her attention back to Bert.

'There were all kinds of rumours — Nether Dale's like that, as you know. Some said the village would burn down at the millennium, others that a plague would come and wipe out all the residents.'

'Well, you're still here,' Samantha smiled, relieved that the curse rumours were so outlandish. 'It was back in the seventies, wasn't it? I think it's done now.'

'Full moon coming,' Aparna interrupted.

'Yes, so I've been told, will we all start spouting hairs on our chests and howling?' Samantha joked, patting Aparna's hand.

Aparna snatched her hand away, a look of irritation on her face.

'*That's* the other rumour,' Bert said glumly.

'What other rumour?'

'That the first-born girl of the Shuttleworth family will die.'

'Do they have any girls in the family?'

'Not as far as I know,' he replied. 'Looks like Jonathan's son better keep his trousers on though, he's the last Shuttleworth.'

'Right, well, let's hope that rumour disappears along with the plague and the village going up in flames.'

'Five days,' Aparna interrupted again.

'What's in five days?'

'The next full moon.'

Samantha shook her head and stood up, worried that if she listened to any more then she'd end up loop the loop in a high-backed chair alongside Aparna.

'There is a full moon every month, Aparna, I shouldn't worry about this one.'

Samantha had a sudden urge to get back to the flat and have a glass of wine. Take a break from the madness.

'Come on, grumpy, fancy a smoke?' Don said, meeting her in the corridor. They went out through the side door in the staff room, he with a cigarette, Samantha with a mug of tea. 'That's the problem with a place like this, no one's got anything better to do than make up stories.'

'But there *was* a murder though, wasn't there? Mrs Dawson's daughter was killed. Does Jonathan ever mention it?'

'And scare off potential residents? No way. Besides, as you probably know, the rumours were all about his father.'

Poor lad came back from boarding school to all that. I mean, by all accounts his dad was a right bastard, but he *was* his dad and we always want to believe the best, don't we? He'd already lost his mother.'

The wind curled around the walls, catching Samantha's neck. She pulled her collar up.

'What about Matron's suicide?'

Don looked sheepish. 'Well, I didn't want to tell you about that, it's not nice, is it? Especially with you being so new and all.'

'Why do you think she did it?'

He shrugged, blowing smoke into the air. 'Who knows why people do these things? I know she was happy here at first, got on well with everyone except for Valerie.'

'Valerie?'

'Valerie didn't take to her and made it very clear — the daily evil eye from her is enough to send anyone off the edge. She's all right, Valerie, but she doesn't take well to new blood, might knock her crown a bit, if you know what I mean.'

'But suicide?'

'Listen,' Don extinguished his cigarette and put it in the small metal bin attached to the wall, 'you just keep doing what you're doing and you'll be fine. The residents love you and the Shuttleworths seem happy.' He looked out to the grounds, 'Speak of the devil.'

Samantha looked across the way; Valerie was walking with Lily again. Jesus, what did they have to talk about so often? Samantha frowned at the way Lily smiled up at the woman, taking in her every word. Valerie placed a parental hand on Lily's back, the other hand waving in the air to illustrate some point Samantha couldn't hear.

'Come on, best get back to it,' said Don. He walked in through the staff-room door. Samantha looked out to the grounds, but Valerie and Lily had disappeared from sight.

CHAPTER 37

1975

Poppet was waiting for Annie at the end of the alleyway, her eyes dark and eager. The older woman handed the young girl the envelope.

'Take it to Hallow Croft in the morning.'

Poppet nodded.

'Tell no one, not even your mum, OK?'

Poppet shook her head. 'For Emily.'

'Yes, Poppet, for Emily.'

Poppet turned and skipped away, the envelope poking out from the top of her coat pocket. Though young, Annie knew Poppet was capable of almost anything. She was sure it was the child who had persuaded her mum to do the curse and turned the unsure witches to her favour. One day she would be a priestess in her own right, Annie was sure of it. Poppet had loved Emily like a sister; Emily had cared for her and understood the strange child in a way no one else did.

There was a fear in the coven of what Poppet would become, what powers she might have and how she would use them. Emily had once told her mum that Poppet had fallen out with a child at school, and that same child had had an accident on the way home and broken his leg; he didn't go back to school for a month. Coincidence maybe, but Annie knew about Poppet's father, the man cut out from every photograph in the house. The man who had been thrown out of his own coven for an evil that no one wanted to be associated with. He had long since died but had left a powerful legacy behind in the form of Poppet, and nobody really knew which way she would fall.

Annie watched her disappear around the corner, out to the road. The thought of Henry Shuttleworth opening her letter over his poached eggs on toast thrilled her. Her only wish was that she could be there to see his face when he read it.

CHAPTER 38

There was a knock on Lily's bedroom door.

'Are you ready, Lily?'

Lily clenched her throat. 'I'm feeling a bit coldy.'

Samantha opened the door and Lily pushed her phone under the covers.

'Not too ill for YouTube, I see.'

Why did her mum care so much about her phone use? It wasn't as if she had a bunch of friends she was neglecting because of it. If anything, it was the only way she had been able to keep in touch with her old friend Sophie. She should be pleased.

'Aren't you coming then?'

Lily thought for a moment.

'Come on, it's Christmas Eve, *my day off*! Don't you want to come to town?'

Lily rubbed her forehead. 'I need to sleep, Mum.'

Her mum eyed her with concern. 'Do you want some painkillers?'

Lily shook her head. 'No, I think sleep will help.'

'OK, well, I won't be long then. Phone me if you need anything.'

Her mum looked sad, a fleeting pang of guilt washing over Lily. 'Have fun.'

Her mum came into her bedroom and kissed her forehead as Lily lay back down, pulling the duvet high to her neck. She felt the gentle stroke of her mum's hand across her cheek, almost sending her back to sleep.

'Right, wish me luck with the crowds!'

And she was gone. As soon as Lily heard the latch click into place, she sat up in bed, pulling out her phone and unlocking the screen. She tapped into the search engine.

Witchcraft Nether Dale Hallow Croft.

Lily scrolled through the results. Mostly pictures of Hallow Croft, a couple of the village green, and then one of a platinum-blonde woman wearing a flowing kaftan and sat in front of a table of candles and silver ornaments. She tapped the link.

Nether Dale Guardian 1975.

VANDALS APPREHENDED BY KEEN-EYED POLICEWOMAN

Three teens have been caught vandalising a property in the sleepy village of Nether Dale. The teens were apprehended when PC Renee Pickford noticed paint on their clothing that matched an earlier report of vandalism made by Sylvia Crowther of Sage End. It's not the first time Crowther has been a victim of such a crime. In November of 1968 Robert Lee of 12 Alvin Close was cautioned for graffiti daubed on the walls of Sage End.

A controversial figure in the village, self-styled 'High Priestess' Ms Crowther had this to say following the incident.

'I am shocked and saddened that once again, my property has been defaced as a result of malicious rumour and misinformation. There is a huge misconception around myself and the work I do, which unfortunately results in such crimes. I am thankful to PC Pickford for her sharp

eye and support to myself, yet disappointed to hear that once again, no action will be taken by those higher up.'

The graffiti has since been removed, but is said to refer to accusations of witchcraft and devil worship, the latter of which Ms Crowther strongly denies.

CHAPTER 39

1975

Donna and Ginny were on their hands and knees, scrubbing the bricks with soapy cloths. When Annie approached Sylvia's house, they looked to her and then away, their faces solemn.

'Who did this?' Annie asked, reading the newly daubed graffiti.

Death to the Witches.

It took a moment for Donna to answer, and when she did it was tense with anger. 'Someone told Henry Shuttleworth about the curse, didn't they?'

Annie tried to feign surprise. Had Poppet lost her nerve and told Sylvia? She felt sick instantly; these women were her only friends, her only support, and she needed them for the curse to remain. If they doubted her, they might reverse it to save the coven from the retaliation of the Shuttleworth family.

'Who would do that?'

'Oh, I don't know,' Donna said, 'someone impatient for him to know he was going to be punished?'

Annie reddened, turning to Sylvia's front window to see her stood there, her finger curling as she gestured for Annie to come to her.

'I'd get your excuses in order if I were you,' Donna said, wringing out another paint-soaked cloth.

Annie took a deep breath and made her way to Sylvia's front door, her head down to avoid the woman's looming wrath. The door was ajar, and Annie entered, the hall in half-light from the open door to the kitchen where she knew Sylvia was waiting. Footsteps scuttled across the floor above and she heard small breaths somewhere on the landing.

The kitchen was alight with candles, hundreds of flames dancing across the walls and artwork. Sylvia kept her back to Annie, watching the fading light outside.

'Is everything OK, Sylvia?'

There was an excruciatingly long pause. Annie wished Sylvia would speak, say something, anything. Just get it over with.

'Why did you do it, Annie?' Sylvia said, finally.

Annie paused, the sickness rising as she imagined more of her life falling apart if she lost her place in the coven.

'Do what?'

Sylvia snapped around, 'Don't! Just don't.'

Annie flinched. Even Sylvia's perfectly coiffed hair and emerald satin kaftan did nothing to detract from the anger that was etched across her face.

'He wouldn't have done that.' Annie pointed towards the wall, noticing Ginny and Donna making their way back with the buckets.

'Of course he wouldn't, he got the local teens to do his work on his behalf. What exactly did you say to him?'

Annie pulled a chair from the table, the wooden leg scraping against the tiled floor. She sat down and rested her elbows on the table, her head in her hands.

'I'm sorry, I just wanted him to know. How would he know it was us? Me?'

'Who else would write that but the mother of the child he killed? He might be old, but he's not an idiot. You should have spoken to the coven first. It wasn't your place to put us all at risk.'

Annie lifted her head, tears streaming down her face. Sylvia continued, 'You could bring us all down with this, Annie. For years we have been the subject of gossip and rumour, nothing more. Now you have given tangible evidence that something has been done to curse his family.'

'But he's old! If he went to the grave never knowing, what's the point? Where is the punishment?'

Sylvia slammed her hand on the table, causing Annie to jump.

'We already went over this, Annie! It is not your place to decide how and when he knows. We are a coven, six women who decide everything *together*. Nobody takes it into their own hands to act and put the rest of us at risk.'

Annie sensed the presence of Ginny and Donna in the hallway, the shuffle of clothing and feet trying to be discreet.

Annie's voice shook as she asked, 'How are we at risk? What will happen?'

Sylvia sat on the chair next to her. 'I don't know, I just don't know. But this? The insults, that might just be the start. Why, Annie? Why?'

'Half the village knows what an evil man he is, they wouldn't care.'

'Don't be so bloody naïve. Who do you think pays for all the carnivals, the local school? Who puts the new roof on the church when it fails? He's a powerful man, Annie, and could call on any number of people to do his work for him, regardless of their morals. We find ways to let people know things, Annie, through village talk. Keep it as unprovable rumours, laugh it off, take the odd bit of abuse. But now they know . . .' they both looked out of the window as two teens in dark clothing passed by the drive, glaring into the window. 'Now they know.'

CHAPTER 40

Lily jumped out of bed and got dressed. She dragged a brush through her tangled hair and pulled on her beanie.

Valerie was waiting for her in the car park, her small car's engine chugging grey smoke into the cold, clear air.

'Don't you look a picture on this grey day!' Valerie beamed, opening the passenger door and dusting down the seat before letting Lily in.

Lily clicked in the seat belt and glanced around the car. A cardboard tree hung from the rear-view mirror, its red colour now fading to pink. She turned to the backseat, Valerie's handbag, with its contents falling across the seat. A tube of lipstick, a purse and a vial of liquid that looked like the medicine she had given Lily when she was sick.

'How are we feeling today, Lily?'

'Good, thanks,' she smiled.

Valerie reversed the car and turned down the drive, passing glum-looking visitors clutching bags of presents as they trudged towards the doors of Hallow Croft. They drove down the hill towards Nether Dale, turning into the gravelled drive of a large Victorian house. It was the kind of house Lily dreamed about living in. She had only ever known small rentals with just enough room for her and her mum; she longed for a place that had a room she could draw and display her art in. Mum had never let her use Blu-Tac and drawing pins on walls that didn't belong to them.

Valerie put the handbrake on and opened her door. 'Here we are.'

She reached over, scooped the contents back into her handbag and lifted it from the backseat, almost catching Lily's head as she swung it around, stepping out of the car.

'*Mi casa es su casa*,' she proclaimed, gesturing for Lily to get out of the car.

Valerie took a large bunch of keys from her bag and opened the purple door. Inside, Lily marvelled at the intricately tiled flooring and the walls covered in photographs from another time. She was about to ask who the people were, but Valerie had already disappeared into another room; there was the sound of a kettle heating up and mugs being clattered.

Lily followed her into a large kitchen diner with a huge round table surrounded by wooden chairs. She had pictured Valerie living in a bungalow somewhere, alongside retired couples who tended to their roses each summer and organised neighbourhood watch meetings as the nights drew in. Two cats sat on a sofa by the bay window, both turning to her and watching her with their green, almond-shaped eyes.

'Don't you have a Christmas tree?'

'Not my kind of thing. Besides, there's only me and the cats so it'd be a lot of work only to be taken down a few days later.' She pointed at the cats, 'That's if these little monkeys didn't claw it down first! Tea?' Valerie held out a mug.

Lily peered into the greenish-yellow liquid. 'Do you have any milk?'

Valerie laughed. 'You don't sully good tea like that with milk, Lily. That's herbal tea.'

Lily sipped out of politeness rather than want, relieved to find it tasted sweet, like a hot mint squash. She held out her fingers to the cats, making a kissing noise to try and tempt them closer. Instead, they put their heads back down and went to sleep.

'Don't mind them, not very sociable. Now Baal is much more interactive, he'll be hiding out somewhere until he's sure you're safe company.'

Lily looked around to see if she could spot the third cat.

'Why don't we go into the lounge, it's comfier there and I've got that book you wanted to see.'

Lily followed Valerie out of the kitchen and into the front room. The smell of burned wood in the fireplace filled the air. A worn sofa was strewn with patchwork blankets and velvet cushions, beside it a long burned-out joss stick stuck in a wooden holder surrounded by soft flakes of ash. Lily sat down as Valerie swept out the ashes and remade the fire, lighting it with long matches taken from a silver tin.

'There now, I'll make us some food and we can chat some more. You OK?'

Lily nodded, the warmth from the fire making her feel sleepy as she sank further into the sofa.

* * *

'Hey there, sleepy head.'

Lily blinked, Valerie's face inches from hers. The pencil-thin eyebrows were raised with apparent concern.

'Sorry, I must have nodded off.' Lily pushed herself up, her throat dry and head woozy. Plates of food lay on the coffee table before her.

'I left you for a while, looks like you needed a sleep. I suspect that flat isn't all that warm, is it?'

Lily thought about the layers of hoodies she wore every night, the piles of blankets as she and her mum watched TV. She reached for her phone to check if her mum had messaged, anxious she might have slept too long. It was still early afternoon and there were no messages on the screen.

'Now then, why don't you have something to eat, I'll have to get you back soon.'

'Could I use your toilet?'

Valerie paused for a moment, then smiled. 'Of course, lovey. Just up the stairs, turn left and it's at the end of the landing.'

Lily got up, supporting herself with the sofa arm. Daytime naps always left her feeling jet-lagged and disorientated.

'Steady she goes,' Valerie giggled.

Lily fumbled along the wall for a light switch at the bottom of the stairs, but couldn't find it. The wooden stairs creaked with each step, and the space got darker as she got to the top. When she reached the landing, she looked around in the gloom, turning right at the banister. A black door to her left had a key in the lock, further along there was another door which she assumed was Valerie's bedroom, and then the bathroom.

When she had finished on the toilet, she flushed the chain and washed her hands. She looked in the mirror. A thin tuft of hair stuck up on the top of her head, much shorter than the rest. The ends were jagged, as if a razor had sliced through the lock. She touched the hair, trying to flatten it down, cursing herself for constantly pulling her hair back into ponytails, making it weak.

She walked back onto the landing. From downstairs came the sound of Valerie eating her lunch, spoon hitting bowl, and pouring more tea. Lily crept along the landing, unable to resist peeking into the next room. A double bed-room, walls painted in muted orange, a sense of neglect not overcome by the bright floral duvet tucked neatly into the bed. More framed photographs across the walls, a glamorous blonde woman in a picture by the bed. Lily closed the door softly and went to the next, the locked black door. Her hand reached for the key, faltering as Valerie called up the stairs, 'Have you fallen down the toilet?'

Lily hurried along the landing. A cat jumped down from the banister and hissed at her, its back arched and teeth bared. She edged around it, her hands clutching the banister, and jogged down the stairs, her footsteps echoing along the cavernous hallway.

Valerie held out a plate already loaded with food; it looked like a salad she would see on Instagram. A remote Nordic restaurant serving berries and leaves. She thought about her mum in town, eating fried rice at her favourite chain, and a spike of longing hit her.

'Thank you,' Lily said, taking the plate.

'Good for a growing girl that, all natural. Was that Baal I heard making a fuss up there?'

'Yes, I think I scared him.'

'Oh, nothing scares Baal, he's just protecting his territory. Not like the other two, they barely register a stranger in the house.'

Lily picked up a thin, dry stem, dark berries hanging like decorations on the Christmas tree. She picked one off and put it on her tongue.

'Sweetest fruit you'll ever taste.'

She bit the berry with her teeth, juice bursting out and dribbling down her chin; she wiped it away with her sleeve, red juice streaking across the pale hoodie. It tasted like an unripe strawberry. Valerie watched her, a smile pasted across her face. 'Well?'

Lily nodded, smiling weakly at the pile of food she had to get through.

'It's magic food, that's what it is. Like that medicine I gave you. All these factories making food in test tubes when Mother Nature has already provided it.'

Lily chewed on a leaf she thought she recognised from the side of paths, and looked around the room. Her eyes landed on a painting in the corner, a symbol she recognised — more than recognised. The familiar circle and triangle, painted in black against a red background. She put her hand to the pendant around her neck, Valerie watching her.

'That's right, Lily, you can never have enough good luck symbols around you.' She glanced at Lily's plate. 'Bless you. Give it here. You did well to eat all that you did, you're not used to good food yet, that's all. Too much sugar has spoiled your tastebuds. My mum started growing the herbs herself in the garden, I've done my best to keep them all going.'

Valerie wandered over to an oak cupboard, groaning a little as she bent down. 'Speaking of which, on our little walk the other day you said you wanted to see her special book, didn't you? It's in here somewhere.'

After some shuffling through papers and glass jars, Valerie lifted out a large leather-bound book and shut the cupboard doors with a swing of her foot. She put the book in front of Lily, its cover worn but the letters still visible.

Grimoire.

'She was into her magic and all that. Hers was a bit airy-fairy for my liking, but you're welcome to have a look as you're interested.'

Lily tentatively lifted the cover, revealing pages of hand-scribbled notes. Icy shards of sleet began to tap at the bay window, the light so low that a lamp outside had begun to glow. She read the instructions on how to grow herbs, nothing more than she would have found in one of her mum's unread 'Grow Your Own' books at home. When she turned the page there were cuttings from other books among the handwritten words. Spells for cleansing homes, getting a lover, and yet more for ridding yourself of negative people. It all felt a bit childish.

'See, it's not that sinister, is it?'

Lily smiled. 'No, not at all.'

'These folk who go on about witchcraft don't know what they're talking about half the time. It's mostly crystals and good thoughts, you see. Anything you can use for your art project there?'

Lily kept turning the pages, trying to find the darkness she now wanted to portray in her art.

'Not yet.'

She ran her fingers over a greying lock of hair that had been taped to the page. Valerie watched her with narrowed eyes.

'Now that's for curses.'

Lily snatched her fingers away, causing Valerie to let out a loud laugh. 'You won't get cursed just by touching it. You have to do all sorts of other things for it to work . . .' She paused. 'Or so Mum used to say.'

Lily turned the page. 'Does it tell you somewhere how to do a curse?'

'Oh, that takes years of practice, Lily, you can't just read something from a book and then expect to be an expert. Besides, imagine all the bad things that would be happening if everyone could just do that?' Valerie winked at her.

Lily nodded, wondering who she would curse if she could. The older girl who'd bullied her at primary school? The dinner lady who'd made her eat cold mashed potato? Her vengeful thoughts were interrupted by Valerie.

'I'd best get you back. Your mum will be wondering where you've got to.'

Lily looked at her watch; her mum would be home any minute. Time had gone ridiculously quick; it felt like she'd only been in the house an hour or so.

'Would you like to borrow it?'

Lily looked up, questioning.

'Mother's grimoire. I know you'll take good care of it. Mind your mum doesn't clap eyes on it, though, not everyone's understanding about these things. We don't want to worry her, do we?'

Lily clutched it to her chest. 'I'd love to, thank you.'

'There's something else I'd like to give you, it's come all the way from South America.'

Valerie walked over to a shelf and stretched her arms up to retrieve a parcel wrapped in brown paper. She handed it to Lily.

'Just a few bits and bobs if anything in Mother's book takes your fancy. Only the good spells, mind.'

Baal padded into the room and Valerie scooped him up into her arms. She ran a hand from his head to his tail, the cat letting out a deep purr. 'See, he's just a teddy bear at heart.'

Valerie nuzzled her face into his fur; all the time the cat kept his eyes on Lily.

They walked out into the hall, Lily stopping by the photograph of the blonde woman holding a baby; the centre of the picture had been torn at some point and now clear tape held it together. On the other side of the tear stood a dark-haired man; he wore all black, a long chain around his neck with some kind of pendant hanging from it. Two antlers curled back from a crown on his head. His cold eyes made Lily shudder.

'Who's that?' she asked.

Valerie turned and gazed at the picture, smiling, 'Oh, that's my dear father.'

'What's that on his head?'

'A crown. He was a high priest, you see, a most powerful man. Too powerful for the likes of Nether Dale.'

Lily thought about her own dad; she often spent fleeting moments wondering what he looked like, where he was, and if she had any siblings she'd ever meet — a recurring dream of appearing on *Long Lost Family*, open arms and tears of regret for the years he'd lost with her.

'You'll meet him one day,' Valerie said.

'Pardon?'

'Your dad. That's what you were thinking of, wasn't it?'

'How did you know?'

'Call it female intuition, if you will.'

'Is that you?' Lily pointed at the baby in the blonde woman's arms.

Valerie laughed. 'Yes, that me. Little baby Poppet.'

CHAPTER 41

Samantha rolled out the wrapping paper and placed the set of watercolours on top. She took a pair of scissors from the coffee table and sliced through the reindeer-dotted paper in a satisfying swoosh, folding the paper over the present and holding it in place with the scissors while she felt about for the roll of tape. She got up and looked in the kitchen drawers, but found only odd utensils, unidentifiable cables and old bank statements she had to find a place for.

She went down the hall and gently opened the door to Lily's bedroom; her daughter was fast asleep under the covers. Samantha hoped the full day's rest would mean Lily would be back to normal for tomorrow; she was now looking forward to a Christmas dinner she hadn't slaved over herself. She tip-toed over to the chest of drawers by Lily's bed, sorting softly through the books and pencils and retrieving a roll of tape. She glanced at her sleeping daughter, noticing a silver chain around her neck. Lily stirred as Samantha lifted the pendant. She didn't recognise the piece of jewellery with its engraved tree. She turned it around to see a familiar triangle and circle symbol. Confusion raged through her.

'What the hell is this, Lily?'

Samantha held the necklace up to her daughter's face. Lily peered from the duvet; her eyes went wide when she saw the pendant in her mother's fingers. She snatched it back.

'It's mine.'

'Where did you get it?'

Samantha waited for Lily to answer.

'Valerie gave it to me,' said Lily finally, sitting up in bed. 'Why are you being so dramatic about it, it's just a necklace?'

Samantha raised an eyebrow. She might not be a believer in the occult, but she knew that this symbol was not a lucky four-leaf clover or St Christopher.

'This is the symbol carved into the tree — is it some kind of witchcraft thing?'

'I thought you didn't believe in all that stuff?'

'Never mind what I believe in, why did Valerie give it to you?'

'Can I wake up properly before my interrogation, please?'

'Well it's not staying, harmless or not. It's weird, and Valerie had no place giving it to you.' She pulled the necklace and it snapped away from Lily's neck. 'And all these skull drawings you've been doing, you can stop that too.'

'Mum, what the heck's wrong with you?'

Samantha stormed out of Lily's bedroom. She heard her daughter scrambling from the bed and footsteps running up behind her.

'Give it back!' Lily screamed.

Samantha blazed, registering in the drama that Lily was in her clothes, not the pyjamas she had left her in. 'It's all going in the bin.'

She stamped on the pedal to open the lid. Lily snatched at the necklace in Samantha's fist, but Samantha yanked it away, dropped it and let the bin slam shut.

'I hate you!' Lily screamed, her face level with Samantha's. 'Why did you bring me here if you don't even want me to make friends?'

'With Valerie?' Samantha scoffed. 'For Christ's sake, Lily, she's in her fifties, surely. Can't you make friends your own age?'

'I did, and you took me away from them!' Lily spat, her cheeks red and tears pooling in her eyes.

'You'll make friends at college.'

'I'm making friends here. I like Valerie, she's kind to me, she doesn't try to tell me what to do or what I can or can't have.'

'That's because she's not your parent — it's my job to be your mother.'

'Be my mother? All you've done is uproot me and drag me to the middle of nowhere because you couldn't keep your legs closed!'

Samantha's hand drew back and slapped Lily across the cheek before she could stop herself. She gasped, horrified. 'I'm so sorry, Lily, I didn't mean to—' Samantha tried to embrace her but Lily stepped back sharply.

'I loved Manchester, I had friends there, and you had to ruin it all by sleeping with that stupid married doctor!'

The truth burned, not least because Samantha wasn't aware that Lily knew why they had had to leave. How much had she seen or heard on those nights he had popped round while feigning late nights to his wife? Did she know about the fallout at the hospital? How she'd had to give up her job so that a more senior man could stay and keep his? Her stomach churned.

'It will be fine here, Lily, I promise. I'm sorry. I shouldn't have taken the necklace, it was stupid.'

Samantha opened the bin and found the pendant in an empty tin of baked beans. She ran it under the tap, thin orange liquid swilling down the plughole. Lily snatched it from her and stormed back to her room, slamming the bedroom door so hard that the thin partition walls shook.

Samantha's phone buzzed on the side and she looked to see a message alert from the mystery doom-monger. She didn't open it, instead swiping to delete. She leaned against the sink, trying to make sense of everything, then peered over to the presents, still unwrapped on the floor, and sighed.

'Merry bloody Christmas.'

CHAPTER 42

1975

There had been no word from the coven for a week. Annie picked at her food, a racing heartbeat and churning stomach stealing her appetite.

'What's up with you?' Kevin said through a mouthful of egg and toast.

Annie pushed the plate away and got up from the table, stumbling slightly as the blood rushed to her feet.

'You'll just be skin and bone soon if you're not careful.'

She felt his eyes scanning her body through the cotton nightie she had lived in for seven days. The toast cascaded into the swing bin, a crust breaking free and falling to the floor; she left it there. Dropping her plate in the sink she left the kitchen and Kevin, who shook his head in apparent bemusement. A slurp of tea signalled the end of his concern.

Annie lay on Emily's bed, clutching her favourite teddy bear, staring up at the oil painting. She had slept in her daughter's bed for the past week, the scent of her now barely there. It had been stupid of her to tell Henry Shuttleworth about the curse, she knew that, but surely not bad enough that she was cast out from the only friends she had. Even

Ginny, the most understanding of them all, hadn't picked up her calls or answered the door when she'd knocked.

It was the grief and bereavement all over again, as if she had lost Emily only yesterday. She closed her eyes, praying exhaustion would take over and she might finally sleep again. As she reached that state between wake and sleep, the telephone rang out downstairs, jolting her awake. Annie strained to hear as Kevin picked up the phone.

'Annie. It's for you.'

She dragged herself up from the bed and pushed a strand of greasy hair behind her ear. As she reached the top of the stairs, Kevin put the receiver down on the table. 'It's that Ginny woman.'

Annie felt a surge of hope stream through her veins as she ran down the stairs, her hand gripping the banister. She grabbed the receiver.

'Ginny?'

There was a pause; for a moment she thought they had been cut off and panic started to rise again until Ginny spoke: *'Annie, I thought you should know before anyone else told you . . .'*

Annie felt herself stumble to the side, steadying herself with a hand on the table.

'It's Sylvia, she's dead.'

Annie let the phone drop from her fingers as a wave of nausea swept over her. As she crumpled to the floor, she was aware of a figure watching her from a doorway, a young girl still and solemn. A hand reaching out . . . then, darkness.

When Annie awoke she was in her own bed. She blinked her eyes, trying to get her bearings when the news hit her again.

Sylvia was dead.

She began to cry, streams of tears that soaked her pillow as she pushed her face into it. Did this mean the end of the coven, her only chance at having any kind of life at all? Annie hadn't heard the front door open, and when the door to the bedroom creaked she expected to see Kevin demanding breakfast.

'Annie?'

Annie recognised Ginny's voice as she lay staring out of the window. She felt the mattress rise as the woman sat next to her and stroked her lank hair.

'Come on, Annie, you have to get up.'

'How did she die?' she said, her voice barely audible.

'A car accident. She was driving up from Nether Dale in the storm, heading home when another car drove her off the road.'

'The Shuttleworths?'

Ginny shrugged. 'More likely his young cronies, I don't know, they haven't found the other driver yet. It was a farmer who saw it, he wasn't quick enough to see who was driving. Just heard an engine revving and looked to see a car force her from the road. She skidded through the hedge and her car overturned in a ditch.'

Annie began to sob again, then turned to face Ginny. 'Why her though, why not me? I asked for the curse.'

'They've been after her for years, Annie. Sylvia was going to move away some time ago, the threats were becoming unbearable. She had too much influence over the village, capable of things that money alone couldn't buy. We persuaded her to stay, not to let a group of rich men drive her out. They believe that without her, the rest of us are powerless.'

'But I made it worse.'

'Maybe, but they would have carried on hounding her anyway. We should have let her go years ago. We all feel to blame.'

'The others must hate me, and Poppet? She'll never forgive me. Who's looking after her?'

'She's with her aunt and uncle — she barely knows them but they're who she's been entrusted with for now. But listen, you must stop feeling sorry for yourself, Annie, we need you now more than ever. The coven must continue — it's what Sylvia would want. As for Poppet, she needs you too. She's sick with revenge, and if someone she truly knows and trusts doesn't speak to her soon then I fear what she will do.'

Ginny helped Annie up from the bed. 'When did you last have a shower, Annie?' Ginny pegged her nose with her fingers, causing the first smile to form on Annie's lips in days.

She caught sight of herself in the long mirror on the wardrobe. Ginny stood next to her. Kevin was right, she looked close to death. Her hair hung in greasy tendrils, framing a pale, gaunt face that she barely recognised as her own.

'Come on, let's get you back to the land of the living,' Ginny said, picking out some fresh clothes and taking her to the bathroom.

Ginny went downstairs to make a cup of tea as Annie took a shower. She instantly felt better as the hot water hit her skin, washing away the sweat and tears. She rubbed a rough, soapy flannel across her body, bringing her senses back to life. When she had finished, she wrapped a towel around herself and cleared the condensation from the mirror above the sink, seeing a flush of colour return to her skin.

She combed her hair and pulled on the jeans and an embroidered top that Ginny had chosen for her and made her way downstairs to where Ginny was busying herself in the kitchen.

'You don't need to do that,' Annie said, as Ginny began washing pots in the sink.

'Rubbish, it's no bother. You sit down and get that toast down you.'

Annie did as she was told, though she struggled to eat more than half a slice, her stomach so unused to food these days.

'Once I've cleaned up in here, we're going to take a walk to the village and get some fresh air.' Ginny must have noticed the reluctance on Annie's face as she added, 'It's an order, not a request.'

Annie nodded. There wasn't much in life she was thankful for, but right now her gratitude for the coven was stronger than ever.

CHAPTER 43

Lily refused to come out of her room; not even the obliga-tory watching of *It's a Wonderful Life* could tempt her to join her mum on Christmas Eve. Samantha felt wretched; she had never so much as tapped her daughter's hand before. The worst thing was, it was her own shock and frustration that had seen her hand strike Lily — her daughter had only spoken the truth.

The married doctor had been a mistake, and not for the obvious reason. When it came to the reckoning of who would suffer the fallout of their brief affair, he had scuttled away like a mouse through a skirting board. The man who healed the sick and was treated like a god was no more than a frightened boy when the shit hit the fan, leaving her to take the flack along with her P45.

Samantha switched aimlessly through the channels as snow began to fall outside the window. She wanted to leap up and get Lily, to show her, but knew she would be rebuffed and feel even worse than she did now. Tomorrow all would be well, presents would fix it.

Samantha poured another glass of red wine and opened her laptop.

It didn't take long for her to find forums discussing the curse of Hallow Croft. Conspiracy theorists, ghost hunters and the occasional occultist, all with differing views. She clicked on a photo embedded within an article, the same photograph that was hung in the Shuttleworths' toilet. Samantha zoomed in on who she presumed was Jonathan, a striking young boy with dark curls and a friendly face. Still so familiar somehow.

She scrolled to the figure behind, his father. Thin-mouthed, with cold, dark eyes that seemed to look beyond the camera lens. This was the man Annie thought had killed her daughter. Samantha knew better than to judge anyone by looks alone, but those eyes made her shudder. Next to him was Jonathan's mother, a porcelain-skinned beauty who wore her hair in a high chignon, an empire-line Lurex dress to her ankles.

There was one thing Samantha didn't understand about it all. If Annie thought Jonathan's father was responsible, why on earth would she decide to spend her final days in his former home? The very place her daughter had been killed?

She rubbed her temple and put the wine down on a coffee table, closing the laptop and switching off the TV.

The presents were laid out beneath the small plastic supermarket tree she had bought last minute. Next year they would have a real tree; next year they would watch their film together.

Samantha reached out for the curtains, looking out of the window at the falling snow. The moon was fat, but not quite full, shining silver light onto the pale blanket that settled on the ground below. Beyond the quadrant and into the woods she noticed smoke curling above the trees, a smudge of orange glow rising to the sky.

She reached for her mobile and brought up Jonathan's number, then swiped it away. He would be relaxing with his family and she didn't want to cause a drama unnecessarily. If it was kids messing about in the woods, the falling snow would extinguish any fire before he could. It was far enough away to not be a danger. So she drew the curtains.

As she passed Lily's bedroom, she leaned her ear against the door, her knuckles raised to knock, but thought better of it. Instead, she whispered goodnight and made her way to bed.

CHAPTER 44

The other side of the door, Lily was tossing around in bed, pulling the duvet with her. Though in sleep, she was conscious of something, somewhere, pulling her. Heat rose from her toes up through her body as she squirmed across the mattress, a mumble of words leaving her lips.

Dull orange light hit the window, a gloomy illumination on her skin, beads of sweat forming on her forehead. Roused but still groggy, she reached out in a sudden thirst for water, and took a sip from the glass by her bedside, heavy gulps cooling her throat.

She kicked the duvet from her body, soothed by a cold breeze curling through the gaps in the windowpanes. She clutched the pillow with both arms, its cotton cover now damp with sweat. From the corner of her eye she saw the blur of a spider scuttle across the ceiling, then another and another, until it seemed the whole ceiling was swarming with insects. Her breathing quickened as she peered at a stitch-eyed doll that crawled across the room. She jolted up in bed, still holding the pillow in her arms, and looked to the window.

The orange light faded and the room returned to darkness. Lily reached over and switched on her lamp, breathless and dazed. She looked to the ceiling, now clear of spiders. She took a long breath and drank more water, then opened her bedside drawer and took out the small bottle Valerie had given her. She squeezed the pipette and let five drops of the herbal remedy dissolve on her tongue.

Within minutes her body relaxed, and she was pulled into sleep.

CHAPTER 45

Valerie looked into the fire, a rictus grin spreading across her face as the flames licked and crackled before her. She stroked the goat's skull with her hand, a chant of thanks for its protection and power. In three days, the full moon would be here in all its powerful glory, and the curse of Hallow Croft would finally be fulfilled.

She took out the snippet of golden hair secured at the end with a length of knotted string; there were fifteen knots, one for each year of the child's life. She held it before the flames, her palm flat, fingers stretched. With her other hand she released pale powder onto the hair and string.

'Curse the child that walks the ground of Hallow Croft.

Complete the circle of vengeance for those that passed before.

Bring her to me so that I may be, the last one that her eyes will see.

My father's strength is at my core, may his darkness help me for ever more.

When the full moon comes I start the end, I bring her here, my deathly friend.

Hail, Baal, I give to thee, in honour of my mother and dear Emily.

A life for a life was the promise we made.

Two children will be lowered into the grave.'

She placed the hair over the skull and dripped blessed water over the offering, a dark prayer for the moon's power and Baal's blessing.

The trees around her swished in the howling wind, a badger screeched from somewhere beyond, the elements drawn into her chaos. She held her arms to the sky, crying out, quietening the call of the wild animal.

Valerie walked trance-like through the woods, a fizz of adrenaline running through her veins. She reached the tree of bodies and smiled at the figures dangling above her. Little doppelgangers of Kevin, Renee, Matron, a bullish school-teacher, an unfaithful lover. She reached up and touched the bare, crooked branch, her fingers running along the damp wood, curling them and feeling the life within the veins of the tree. Her body lit with the anticipation that soon the blonde-haired doll would hang along with them.

CHAPTER 46

In the early days Samantha would have done anything to put a stop to the 5 a.m. Christmas morning wake-up alarm from Lily. Now, as she sat alone in her Rudolph pyjamas cradling a cup of tea at 8 a.m., she would go back in time in an instant.

She shouted from the lounge, 'Lily, are you up yet? I have to be in work in an hour.'

There was the faint sound of shuffling bedcovers before Samantha heard a bedroom door open and Lily appeared in the lounge. Samantha put her tea down and went to her, embracing her in a hug. She felt Lily's tense body relax a little, then relief as she felt her daughter's arms wrap around her waist.

'Happy Christmas,' Samantha said, her face buried in Lily's hair. 'How did you sleep?' She stood back, pushing a strand of Lily's hair behind her ear.

'OK, I think.'

'Ready for presents?'

Lily fell back on the sofa, her eyes still not fully open.

'Or tea first?'

Her daughter nodded lazily, curling up in the foetal position as Christmas hymns sang out from the TV.

Samantha boiled the kettle again and stuck two slices of bread in the toaster. The snow outside had stopped, but enough had fallen that there was a white glow lighting the room.

'Maybe we could make a snowman later? It's rare to have a white Christmas.'

Lily grunted.

After the fuel of tea and toast, Lily began to come to life and Samantha felt relieved that it was tiredness and not their previous fight that had made her unresponsive. She watched as Lily opened her presents, the joy of giving her daughter gifts never getting old. When she opened a soft package revealing a caramel-coloured teddy bear, the fifteen-year-old squeezed it tightly, her eyes closed. Next, a new palette of watercolours and an art book featuring the botanical paintings of the Belvedere Museum in Vienna.

'I thought you might take some inspiration from the pictures,' said Samantha hopefully.

Lily raised a knowing eyebrow at her mum.

'Just, when you're bored of painting skulls and stuff.' Samantha smiled.

Lily ran her fingers over the glossy hardback cover. 'Thanks, Mum, it's beautiful.'

After the last present, an assortment of make-up and toiletries, had been opened, Samantha got up from the floor. 'Right, I'd better get ready for work.'

'Wait,' Lily said.

She reached under the tree and pulled out a small present. Samantha took the gift, feeling around the paper and shaking it by her ear. There was a jingle of soft metal; she widened her eyes and Lily smiled.

Samantha undid the paper and opened the lid of a small box to reveal a heart locket on a silver chain.

'Oh, Lily, it's gorgeous, thank you.'

'Open it,' Lily urged.

Inside, a tiny picture of Lily faced an old photograph of Samantha.

'Where did you find that?' Samantha said, pointing to the photo she had long forgotten existed.

'When I was sorting out boxes, it was there with my beginner's violin certificate and a crayon drawing of a cat that looked more like a rabbit.'

Samantha laughed. 'Ah, the catrabbit, I remember it well.'

She leaned forward and held Lily tightly. 'Thank you, Lily, it's lovely.'

'Valerie helped me put it together.'

Samantha paused, a drip of bitterness souring the moment.

'That was kind of her,' Samantha managed to get the words out, despite them threatening to stick in her throat.

'I'm sorry for saying what I did yesterday about you and that doctor, I just—'

Samantha stopped her. 'It's fine, you have nothing to be sorry about. The remorse is all mine. Let's not mention it again. Deal?'

'Deal.'

Samantha put the chain around her neck, fumbling with the clasp. Lily took it from her and secured it, Samantha holding the locket in her fingers.

'I feel bad leaving you here alone. When are you going over to Jonathan and Diane's?'

'Dunno, I expect I'll go over about twelve and maybe walk Finn. I'll work on my art until then,' she said, holding up the paints she had just opened.

'Great, well, I'll see you there about two, OK?'

Lily nodded, already breaking into the paint box. Samantha went to get changed, hoping that today would be a fresh start.

CHAPTER 47

1975

Poppet opened the box, a smile creeping across her face when she saw the small brooch.

'It was—'

'Emily's,' said Poppet, taking it out of the box and holding it up to the candlelight.

'Happy Christmas,' Annie said, pleased to see the child smiling.

Metal trays clanked in the kitchen, the smell of turkey carrying through the house. Poppet glared at the door.

'It's nice your aunty and uncle have come to look after you,' Annie said, knowing full well how much Poppet hated strangers. 'It must be very tough for you today, so soon after your mum . . .' Annie's voice faltered; she clenched her fists, trying hard not to cry in front of the child.

'They hate me,' Poppet said, turning her glare to Annie.

'They don't, Poppet,' said Annie, 'it's just a difficult time. I'm sure they're doing their best.'

'They bought me this.' Poppet held up a dress, far too young and flowery for her. 'They don't know me at all and I don't know them. I want Sylvia.'

Annie embraced the child, Poppet's body remaining unresponsive to the affection. 'I miss her too.'

'Are you staying for lunch?' a head popped round the door, Poppet's uncle.

Annie let go of her. 'No, that's very kind, but I have to get back to make dinner for my husband.'

'Very well.' He glanced nervously at his niece before disappearing again.

'Be nice, Poppet. I know it's tough, but they're trying.'

She grunted, scowling as Annie rose to leave.

'There's something else I need to tell you, Poppet.'

The girl looked up at her.

'The curse — I've decided to ask the coven to reverse it.' Poppet opened her mouth in protest, but Annie continued, 'It's gone far enough now. We need to bring peace back to the village.'

Poppet spoke in a low growl, 'But *Emily* and *my mother*.'

'I know, but enough is enough. I can't keep feeling this pain anymore. I've decided and that's that. If they agree, we'll reverse it.'

The girl's voice rose with each word: 'No, no, no, no!'

'I don't want to talk about it anymore. It's for the best for all of us, you included.'

Poppet stood up and screamed at the top of her voice, 'Noooooo!'

Annie put her hands to her ears as the room shook, paintings jangling on the walls and glasses tinkling together on the shelves. In the kitchen a woman cried out as a tin tray crashed to the floor, the sound of a roasted turkey bouncing across the tiles.

CHAPTER 48

There was a steady stream of visitors throughout the morning at Hallow Croft. Some chatted animatedly with their loved ones, exchanging gifts; others sat beside elderly parents who no longer recognised them, recounting stories of Christmases past in the hope of a flicker of recognition.

Christmas carols played from a large speaker that Jonathan had placed in the lounge. An elderly woman sat alone, mouthing the words to 'Silent Night', knitting needles click-clacking between nimble, crooked fingers.

The staff were in good spirits and, despite her agitation, Samantha even found herself wishing Valerie a cheery 'Merry Christmas' when she had appeared wearing a tinsel belt and bauble earrings. Gifts were handed out to those that had no one to be with them.

'What did Santa bring then?' Don asked, an elf hat on his head.

Samantha took the locket in her fingers and held it out. 'From Lily.'

'Oh, how lovely,' he said, the small bell on his hat tinkling as he leaned forward to take a better look.

'Let's see,' Valerie said, forcing him out of the way. 'Oh, it suits you, I knew it would.'

Samantha gritted her teeth, 'Thank you, Valerie, and what did Santa bring for you?'

'Oh, I don't celebrate Christmas really, I put this facade on for the old folk,' she jangled her Christmas earrings with her finger.

'Well, I've got you a present, Valerie, I shall take it back if you didn't get me one,' Don jibed.

Valerie ignored him, turning her attention back to Samantha. 'I saw Lily making her way to the Shuttleworths'. She looked a picture.'

Samantha smiled. 'I'm sure she did, she has style — gets it from her mother.'

Why did this woman bring out this snarky, unpleasant side of her? Samantha was annoyed with herself.

'Blimey,' Don poked Samantha's arm. 'I love me, who do you love?' he joked. 'What are you doing tonight, fancy a drink with me and my fella at the Skull and Feathers?'

'Jonathan and Diane have invited me and Lily round to theirs.'

'Ooh, get you, teacher's pet,' he teased.

'You'll meet the prodigal son today, I suppose,' Valerie said.

'He's a looker,' Don marvelled, his eyebrows raised. 'You'd better hope they've got some mistletoe up somewhere — if not, I'd take your own.'

Samantha smiled. 'No thanks, it's just me and Lily for the time being, and I'm more than happy with that.'

'Yes, well, you haven't clapped eyes on him yet.'

A dinner bell rang out and the care assistants began to gather residents for Christmas lunch. Relatives that had their own festivities to go to said their goodbyes, hugging loved ones with promises of the next visit in the New Year. A couple of residents had been taken earlier in the day to enjoy Christmas elsewhere, and the few relatives who had wanted to stay led their elderly family members to the dining room.

Staff buzzed about the kitchen as a red-cheeked Cathy held plates announcing the various dietary requirements and regimes. Giant trays of roast potatoes and stuffing lined the counters, gravy bubbling in a large metal container.

Cathy held a tray up, its dish covered with a silver cloche. 'Mrs Dawson's tray. Where's Valerie to take it?'

'Put it under the warmer for now,' Samantha said. 'I'll go and get her.'

Harassed by requests for plates minus Brussels sprouts and 'plenty of gravy', Cathy did as she was asked, and Samantha left the kitchen, passing Valerie, who was caught up in a dispute about table seating between two male residents.

By the time Samantha had persuaded Annie to come out of her room, the Christmas cheer at Hallow Croft was in full swing. Residents and staff were chatting, the hymns now changed in favour of Cliff Richard and Wizzard. The smell made Samantha's stomach rumble, her own dinner still hours away. Annie dug her nails into Samantha's arm, the skin almost pierced before Samantha managed to unclamp her hand and take hold of her wrist to guide her along.

'You shouldn't be up there all on your own today, it will do you good to mix with some of the others.'

Annie stared forward, shuffling down the corridor as if being led to her grave. They passed Mrs Potter, who paled when she caught sight of Annie, giving her a wide berth as she crossed her chest. Samantha bristled at the treatment the old woman received; she was no different to any of the other residents. Certainly some could inflict a slap or tongue-lashing on an unsuspecting victim, but it was the staff's job to manage it, not shut residents away like caged animals.

The festive chatter rippled to a silence as Samantha and Annie came into view. A cracker snapped and echoed, the winner of the small plastic frog letting their prize fall to the floor as they looked up with fear etched across their brows.

'What's going on out—' Valerie burst through the kitchen door, her bauble earrings swinging, face searching.

When she saw Annie, her mood changed in an instant, her mouth pulled tight. She turned the stereo off, Elton John silenced.

'What is she doing down here?' she demanded.

'Annie is going to enjoy Christmas dinner along with everyone else,' Samantha said, ignoring the burning looks from the room.

'She should be back in her room, I'll bring her her lunch,' said Valerie, marching over and trying to take Annie's arm. 'She shouldn't be here.'

Annie pinched Valerie's skin, causing her to pull away.

'See? She's not supposed to be with others, you don't know what she's capable of.'

Samantha led Annie to a table for one in the corner, helping her sit down and placing a napkin across her knees.

'Now then, Valerie, I'll sit with Annie while you bring her lunch. Enough of the silliness. Annie is going to start coming downstairs to eat.'

Samantha listened to Annie's heavy breath, her heart pounding behind protruding ribs. She placed a hand over the older woman's, still wary about her ability to lash out.

'You're to have Christmas dinner with everybody else, Annie. I'll take you to your room straight afterwards, I promise. OK?'

Samantha scanned Annie's face, but there was no hint of emotion at this promise. All eyes turned to Valerie as she marched, chest out, chin up towards the kitchen. A heated exchange between herself and Cathy followed that was clear enough for all to hear. She returned with a tray, dropping it onto the table with a clatter.

'Mr Shuttleworth will hear about this,' she hissed at Samantha.

Samantha smiled graciously. 'I'll tell him myself over dinner.'

Valerie snorted like a horse expelling air, muttering to herself as she stormed out of the dining room.

'Can you turn the music back on, Debby?' Samantha asked.

In time the dining-room chatter returned, wary eyes occasionally darting to the corner where Annie picked at her food.

'Eat some vegetables, Annie, there's mince pie for dessert.'

Annie whispered something.

Samantha leaned in. 'What was that, Annie?'

'Where is she?'

'Who? Valerie?'

Annie dug her clawed hand into Samantha's. 'The *girl.*'

Samantha felt a shudder scuttle up her spine at the mention of her daughter.

'With the Shuttleworths. I'm going to see her in a bit for—'

'If you won't leave, keep her close to you.'

'She's a young woman, Annie, I can't keep tabs on her 24/7.' Her words faded as she remembered what had happened to Annie's daughter.

For a moment Samantha was at a loss as to what to say, but then she noticed Aparna rise from her seat and begin to make her way over. She focused in on Aparna's long grey plait that curled over her shoulder and braced herself. Annie slowly craned her head to watch the woman's progress. Samantha observed Annie closely. Sweet Aparna was no match for the viciousness Samantha knew Annie was capable of.

Annie's crinkled skin softened as she met the gaze of Aparna. Aparna reached out a hand, her fingers searching for Annie's. Then Annie raised her hand to meet Aparna's, their fingertips gently touching before lacing together. Around them the other residents exchanged worried looks.

Aparna tilted her head, her failing eyes pooling with tears. She moved closer until she could reach around Annie's head and pull it towards her stomach. Annie let her body be cradled by Aparna, her face uncertain at the offer of affection.

Aparna stroked the thin wisps of hair on Annie's head.

'I'm here, Annie my love, I'm here.'

CHAPTER 49

'She's over there, Mr Shuttleworth.' Valerie's voice seemed to whip across the room as she stormed through the door, followed by Jonathan.

Aparna pulled away and Annie sank back into her seat like a startled bird. The other residents looked back to their empty plates, except for Bert, who seemed to be enjoying the event.

Jonathan was still wearing an apron, a splatter of gravy evidence of deserted Christmas-dinner preparations. Valerie led him to the corner, stopping by Samantha with her arms crossed tightly under her bosom.

'Merry Christmas, Mrs Dawson, how are you today?' said Jonathan.

Annie looked up at him, her mouth opening and closing, but no words arriving.

'She's done really well, Mr Shuttleworth,' Samantha smiled, 'I think it's done her good to be with the others.'

Samantha avoided any eye contact with Valerie. She patted Annie's hand and tucked a stray piece of hair behind her ear.

'Well, she does seem OK,' Jonathan offered to Valerie. 'Perhaps she could stay for dessert and then you can take her back to her room?'

Valerie opened her mouth to speak, but Samantha interrupted. 'I think it's time we brought her down for all her meals, not just today. She's enjoyed being down here, haven't you, Annie?'

Annie looked up at Samantha, nodding gently. Valerie looked to Jonathan, shaking her head and sucking in her cheeks. Jonathan looked from Valerie to Samantha, and then to Annie.

'Let's see how she is in the morning, Matron. No need to make any decisions now. We can speak later.'

Samantha felt even a little hope was a victory for Annie, and for her battle against Valerie's dominance in the home. If she was going to change the difficult atmosphere that had been allowed to fester here, she knew it started with Valerie.

'Why don't you get Annie her mince pie, Valerie?' Samantha asked.

Valerie's eyes blazed, only softening a little when she glanced at Jonathan, who offered her an understanding smile.

'Very well.' She unfolded her arms and marched off to the kitchen, residents and their families watching her intently.

'Right, well, now that's sorted I'll get back to the cottage. Diane is cooking up a feast and she'll be missing her sous chef.'

Samantha smiled and nodded, eager to get through the dessert with Annie and begin Christmas herself. Jonathan left the table and did a cursory tour of the other residents, waving his hand and wishing all a merry Christmas.

CHAPTER 50

Samantha walked out of the quadrant and onto the shale pathway that led to Jonathan and Diane's cottage. She carried chocolates and a bottle of wine she had bought in Nether Dale. She had managed to find a sheet of tissue paper to wrap it in, an attempt to heighten its value a little.

There were three cars parked outside the cottage: Diane's Range Rover, Jonathan's Jaguar, and the navy-blue Porsche, which had been spotted by eagle-eyed residents and staff alike on its arrival. After work she had thrown on a clean pair of jeans and a suitably sequinned jumper; she looked down at her slightly battered boots, wishing she'd made more of an effort. She knocked on the cottage door, expecting to hear Finn bounding down the hall, but there were only footsteps.

Jonathan ushered Samantha into the hallway. The smell of roast dinner permeated the air, making Samantha's stomach rumble.

'Happy Christmas, Samantha.'

Jonathan was wearing beige cords and a bright golfing jumper; he had clearly been given aftershave for Christmas as the scent of woody musk fought with the food cooking in the kitchen. Samantha returned the greeting, looking down the hallway.

'Where's Lily?' Samantha asked.

'Where do you think?' Jonathan smiled.

'Finn?'

'She should be back anytime now, she left about twenty minutes ago.'

'I guess she knows her way around,' said Samantha.

'Here, let me take your coat.' Jonathan took her jacket and threw it over his arm, leading her to the lounge.

Diane smiled thinly when she saw Samantha at the door.

'Here, it's nice and chilled.' Jonathan put a glass in Samantha's hand as she sat down on the sofa; this time she rested on the edge so as not to disappear into the soft furnishings.

'Dinner smells lovely, Diane,' said Samantha.

'Diane makes a mean roast dinner, Samantha, we're all in for a treat.'

His wife sneered. 'He appreciates my cooking, if not my opinions.' Words had clearly been had in the cottage, and now Samantha was sat in the fog of animosity.

'Diane is canvassing for a New Year's getaway to the villa.'

He smiled nervously. Samantha felt sorry for them both. When she had arrived she'd felt Diane to be cold and entitled, now she knew she was just scared of Hallow Croft and the supposed 'ghosts' of its past. Jonathan, like Samantha, was just trying to be rational.

'I don't blame you, Diane, a lovely bit of winter sun.'

'Two against one!' said Jonathan, ignoring the daggers from Diane.

They were saved by the sound of the front door opening. Samantha caught Lily's voice, and then another, a man's.

The door to the living room opened and a bedraggled Finn trotted in, ignoring the new visitor in favour of the dog bed by the fire. Lily walked in followed by Jonathan's son.

'Harry, meet Samantha, our new matron.'

Samantha looked up at him, that dark wavy hair, those brown eyes and playful smile. Her mind raced back to the photograph in the toilet and online: that's why the young Jonathan had looked so familiar. She choked on a mouthful of wine. Diane shot up and began slapping her back. Samantha tried to gesture to her that she was fine, while trying not to spill any more from the glass that danced with each gasp for breath.

When she managed to catch her breath, she took another sip to coat her throat. She focused on the glass, not wanting to show her face. If the floor could have swallowed her up, she'd have jumped in head first. For a split second she considered running out of the room, dragging Lily with her. Memories flooded her mind: their first kiss, the smell of Calvin Klein aftershave when she lay her head on his shoulder, the terrible jokes that made her laugh until her stomach hurt.

'Samantha?' Harry said. 'Samantha from Heather Brook?'

'That's right,' said Jonathan brightly. 'Do you two know each other?'

Samantha peered up, meeting Harry's gaze. He looked at her in the same way he had done when they were teenagers. Back then he wore second-hand Levis and T-shirts emblazoned with the bands of the time. Now he stood before her in a more conservative outfit of beige cords and a navy jumper, clearly the Shuttleworth male uniform. He still looked good.

Lily looked from her mum to Harry and back again. 'Mum?'

Samantha drained her glass.

'Hello, Harry,' she stuttered.

Jonathan was at the ready with a top-up. 'Small world!'

'We knew each other once upon a time,' Samantha said.

Harry laughed, 'From way back when. Misspent youth sitting in the snug at the Skull and Feathers.'

Diane was now paying attention, eyes narrowed as she looked from one to the other, waiting for an explanation.

'The pub you showed me on the first night?' Lily asked. Like Diane, she had also perked up considerably and was looking quizzically at her mum.

'It was a long time ago, Lily. We were young and there were a lot of kids in the different villages. I don't remember every face I met.'

She caught Harry's look, somewhere between amusement and confusion.

'Well, I had no idea you knew each other,' Jonathan said. 'Then again, Harry was always sneaking out when he was supposed to be doing homework.'

'Dad, it was much-needed down time.' He smiled.

As she looked at him, Samantha was transported back to those walks through Nether Dale at night, his hand holding hers. The unrealistic promises of forever love.

'Well, you look like you've done well for yourself,' Samantha smiled.

'I've done OK, yes — travelled the world, ticked off a few things from the bucket list, you know.'

Samantha didn't know. All she had done since they had last seen each other was study, work and look after Lily. Swimming with sharks and scaling the Golden Gate Bridge had never been options.

Jonathan clasped his hands together. 'Well, now we're all here, shall we go through for dinner? I for one am starving.'

Samantha's appetite had dwindled to nothing; she wasn't sure she would make it to the dining room without passing out. She watched as Lily followed Harry out of the room. Diane switched into hostess mode as she mumbled about gravy and the pressures of timings. Jonathan held a hand out to Samantha; any other time she would have balked at the old-fashioned gesture, but now she was thankful and held onto it, pulling herself up.

The table looked beautiful. Gold placemats and sparkling silver cutlery; shiny red berry wreaths twisted around cream candles, the flames flickering in the dimmed light. Samantha had hoped to sit as far away from Harry as she could, so her heart dropped when she saw the handwritten place cards.

'You're over here, Samantha, next to me,' Harry beamed.

Jonathan took his place at the head of the table and Lily and Diane sat opposite Harry and Samantha.

'Tell me, Lily, what are your favourite subjects at school?' Harry asked.

'Art's what I love best.'

'Lily is going to go to art school,' Jonathan interjected, 'she's very talented.'

Harry looked surprised to hear his dad was so knowledgeable about Lily.

'Very good. I'm afraid I don't have an artistic bone in my body,' Harry said to Lily. 'That family talent seemed to stop at Grandfather.'

Jonathan looked to the floor at the mention of his father, Harry appearing to regret his words also.

'Did you go to the comp?' Lily asked.

'I'm afraid not, my wicked father sent me away to boarding school,' Harry grinned.

'Anyone for more gravy?' Diane asked.

Finn raised his head and barked, his teeth bared at the small leaded window. Harry got to his feet to check, peering from side to side. Samantha sat upright.

'Nobody there, Finn.'

Diane shuddered. 'Can you go and check, Harry? Finn doesn't normally bark unless someone is around. It'll be those damn women.'

'What women?' Samantha asked.

'Not on Christmas Day, Diane. Besides, that daft dog would bark at his own shadow,' said Jonathan.

'Christmas means nothing to them,' Diane said coldly.

'I'll go and have a look,' said Harry, wiping his mouth with a napkin and dropping it on the table.

'I'll join you,' said Samantha, putting her knife and fork down. She wanted to see whoever *these women* were for herself.

Jonathan tried to quieten Finn. Lily left the table to help him, distracting Finn with a shred of turkey from her plate.

Outside the air was crisp and the layer of snow now crunched underfoot. Harry shone the torch on his phone into the gloom around them, walking twenty feet from the front door and peering into the distance.

'Nothing, must have been a badger set him off or something.'

He walked back towards where Samantha stood at the front door, part of her disappointed not to see who these mysterious visitors might be.

Harry leaned against the wall, putting his phone back in his pocket.

'So how come you're here, I thought you couldn't wait to get away?' he asked.

'I did get away, for a time. I just, well, life happens, doesn't it?'

She felt his eyes scanning her face; she didn't want to look at him, afraid of what she might do or say.

'How has working-class life treated you?' she said, her eyes fixed on a family of wicker deer in the garden, covered in fairy lights.

He took out a packet of cigarettes and lit one; she glanced down to the proffered packet touching her arm. The urge had never been stronger, but she shook her head.

'I had to fit in with you all,' he said.

'You should have just been yourself.'

'Do you think the likes of Mobsy and Darren would have let me hang out if they knew I was a boarding-school boy from the big house?'

A giggle escaped Samantha's mouth at the mention of their former acquaintances. 'No, you're probably right. But you didn't have to lie to me, I wouldn't have cared.'

'Really? I heard the way you all joked about the *big* houses and the snobs that lived in them.'

Samantha felt herself redden, remembering they had all spoken freely of their disdain for those that lived in the nicer houses.

'So you made up an imaginary aunt you were visiting and a comp you never attended?'

'I'm in politics now,' he smiled.

'I was told you'd moved away years ago. If I'd known I might bump into you, I'd never have come back.'

'Charming.'

A cry rang out in the distance, a screeching sound like tom cats fighting.

'What the f—' Samantha stopped herself cursing for once.

'It'll be kids messing around,' said Harry.

'Shall we go and check?'

'No,' he said, 'I only came out to keep Diane happy.'

'You get on OK with her?'

Harry paused, his face thoughtful, as if trying to formulate the words.

'Let's just say I understand her. There's a lot of history to Hallow Croft that she has to live with. I don't blame her for wanting to leave.'

'You don't believe all that curse crap, do you?' Her laugh dissolved when she saw he was serious.

'Not everyone is as cynical as you, Samantha.'

'Let it go, Harry, I was sixteen.'

'You broke my heart.'

'I'm sure it took you all of a week to get over it. Besides, I didn't have a choice — my parents split up and I was sent to live with Dad in Manchester.'

Another cry in the distance, screeching like nails across metal.

'Shouldn't we?'

'Come on, let's go back in.'

'What did Diane mean by *those women*?'

'The local Wiccan women, been in Nether Dale for years. They gather sometimes by the standing stones. Harmless really, just Mother Earth type stuff.'

His tone was light, but his brow furrowed.

'What?' she said.

'Why didn't you keep in touch?'

She wasn't prepared for this, her face flushed.

'I needed to start my life, away from here. I was busy, that's all — nursing college.'

'Huh?' he mused. 'It wasn't me that drove you away?'

'Don't flatter yourself,' she chided. 'I told you, I had to go with my dad to Manchester.'

They followed the echo of chatter through the hall and into a small dining room with low beams and a redundant iron fireplace. The three were watching, waiting for their return, worry etched on Diane's face.

'It was nothing, just kids in the woods,' Harry smiled.

The two took their seats, and Samantha realised to her dread that she was going to have to spend the next hour or so reinventing the past in order to keep the future she wanted.

Jonathan's praise of Diane's cooking skills had been justified. The roast potatoes were perfect and the homemade stuffing the best Samantha had ever tasted. She watched as Lily dug into the home-cooked food, a break from the pre-prepared offerings she was providing at the moment. Diane pushed her plate aside and sipped on the garnet-coloured wine from the heavy crystal glasses.

'The food is delicious,' Samantha said, noting Harry's smirk and raised eyebrows.

Diane smiled, her lipstick slightly smudged.

Jonathan piped up, 'Harry, why don't you take Samantha and Lily for a drink at the Skull and Feathers one night? Soft drink for Lily, of course. I'm sure she'd enjoy seeing something other than old people like us for a change.'

'Charming,' said Diane.

'Or take them for a spin in the Porsche.'

'No,' Diane said sharply. Samantha turned to her, grateful for the intervention but surprised at her tone.

'I'd like that,' Lily said, her eyes fixed on Harry.

Samantha turned to her daughter, who was purposely avoiding eye contact with her. Harry smiled at Lily, then looked over to Samantha, his smile fading when he saw her expression.

'I wouldn't want to take any of your time away from visiting your family,' said Samantha.

Harry held his hands up, stuck between Lily and Samantha. 'Listen, I'm here for a few more days, let me know. If you're busy, Samantha, I could show Lil—'

'She's busy too.'

Jonathan looked curiously at Samantha, and Lily's head shot round, glaring at her. Samantha remained steadfast. 'It's really kind of you, Harry, but we're both still settling in and Lily has an art project to complete.'

Lily opened her mouth, 'But—'

'Lily,' Samantha warned. 'No.'

Samantha couldn't help but notice that Diane seemed pleased with her refusal; it was almost enough for her to change her mind. But Harry would only be here for a few more days. The more she could keep her and Lily away from Harry, the better.

CHAPTER 51

After dinner at Laburnum Cottage had wrapped up, mother and daughter made their way back to the flat, Lily heading straight up, Samantha taking the scenic route via the residents. In the lounge, carols played on the television and those that were still awake sang along, faint voices echoing many Christmases past.

'Have you had a nice day, Aparna?' Samantha asked.

The woman smiled, a cup of tea in her hand.

'I bet it was nice to have your grandson here today, he's a handsome boy.'

Aparna nodded. 'And Annie.'

'It's funny, I thought you were afraid of her?'

'Afraid *for* her,' whispered Aparna.

'Well, you seem to be in the minority there,' Samantha joked. 'If it was up to everyone else, she'd be locked in her room indefinitely.'

Aparna put a hand on Samantha's and Samantha held the woman's fingers in her own. 'I knew Annie years ago. We met when we both got jobs at the new supermarket in town, we got the bus together. She . . . she took me under her wing.'

'So you were friends?'

'Yes, there was a group of us, she introduced me. It was another world — it *is* another world.'

'That's nice.'

Aparna began to shake. 'She's losing her powers, Matron. Soon it will be too late.'

Samantha sighed. Poor Aparna. It was lovely to spend time with her when she was lucid, however brief.

'I should get back to the flat now, spend some time with my daughter — if she'll tolerate me, that is. You know what teenagers are like.'

'It's her birthday soon, isn't it?'

'Yes it is, how did you—'

'There is only so much we can do to protect her, you must get her away. Beware the full moon — when it comes, it is time.'

Samantha heaved herself up from her chair, stretching as she yawned. 'Shall I get someone to help you to bed?' she asked Aparna.

Aparna lowered her cup to her lap, her head down as if defeated. Samantha called Caroline from the night staff over to help her, and said goodnight to the other residents. She had no time for more stories of curses and doom; a much more immediate issue had arrived at Hallow Croft and she had no idea how she was going to deal with it.

CHAPTER 52

The following morning, Lily made her way down the narrow stairs that led to the back door carrying a rolled-up page from her drawing pad. Instead of taking the door outside, she entered the one that led to a corridor within the nursing home. Her mum's voice carried from the office to her side as she crept past, making her way towards the stairs. She listened at the doors until she heard Valerie's voice. She knocked lightly and Valerie appeared. When she saw Lily, her eyes widened and she blocked the gap in the door with her body.

'Yes, love?'

'Sorry, am I disturbing you?'

'Not at all, Mrs Dawson's just having another one of her tizzies. A bit too much excitement yesterday, I expect. Taking her out of her room has set her back.'

Lily grimaced in understanding and held out the rolled-up paper. 'I wanted to give you this, for Christmas, and as thanks for the necklace and for being so kind.'

Valerie clutched her chest and smacked her lips together. 'Oh, that's so sweet, Lily, thank you.'

'I've been working on it all week.'

A growling voice came from somewhere in the room, 'Is that the girl?'

'Nothing for you to worry about, Mrs Dawson,' Valerie called back, before returning her attention to the picture and unrolling it to see the pencil drawing of the skull and twigs.

'It's a bit dark, but it's all I've managed so far.'

'Nothing of the sort,' Valerie studied it further, 'I love it!'

'Happy Christmas.'

'Happy Christmas, lovey.'

The voice called again, 'Is it her?'

Valerie rolled her eyes and whispered, 'I'd better go back.' She furled the picture back up with a smile. 'Oh, I almost forgot — that thing we talked about on our walk, the beginner's spell?'

Lily nodded, glancing nervously around. Valerie rummaged in her pocket, taking out a small folded piece of paper.

'You should have everything you need in that parcel I gave you.' She held the paper out to Lily, an eyebrow raised conspiratorially.

Lily put it in her pocket and turned to go, as Valerie retreated back into Annie's room. She glanced into the open doorways of residents' rooms as she passed them, Bert giving her a wave and calling out to wish her a belated merry Christmas. At the end of the corridor she was met with Aparna. Lily wasn't sure if the old woman had seen her as her eyes remained forward, as if in a trance. As she passed, the old woman reached out and clutched Lily's arm, digging her fingers into her skin.

'Stay with me,' Aparna hissed.

Lily looked around for a care assistant, the woman's grip getting tighter.

'Do you need help?' she asked, speaking slowly and carefully, as if to a child. 'I'll get someone for you.'

'Jinn,' Aparna urged. 'Jinn.'

'I'll take you downstairs, someone there will be able to help.'

As Lily tried to guide Aparna away from the landing, her mum appeared at the top of the stairs.

'There you are,' Samantha said. She looked at Aparna's hand clutching Lily's arm. 'All OK?'

Lily shrugged. Samantha took Aparna's hand in hers.

'Come on, Aparna, let's get you back to your bedroom.' She began to lead the woman away, turning to Lily, 'I'm done after I sort Aparna — fancy watching some TV together and finishing those mince pies?'

'I'm going to go into town,' Lily replied.

'Really? On Boxing Day?' Lily saw the brief disappointment in her mum's face, quickly replaced by a broad smile. 'Well, I could come too. I suppose there'll be some good sales on and—'

'No. I'm only going for a couple of things, I'll get the bus.'

She watched her mum's face drop again. A car crunched by on the gravel outside; they both looked to the window to see Harry's Porsche disappear down the road.

'Why don't you go out with him? Just for a drink,' Lily asked, eager to get her mum off her back.

'I want to spend time with you.'

'What is it you keep saying to me? Get some friends your own age?'

It was cruel and Lily knew it, but she couldn't help herself. She left her mum on the landing and made her way down the stairs.

CHAPTER 53

1975

Sylvia's funeral took place just after Christmas. Annie had spent Christmas Day in a daze, which had gone unnoticed by Kevin. He had started drinking at 11 a.m. and managed to stay awake just long enough to eat the dried-out turkey and burned roast potatoes she had served up. There were no crackers or board games, and as Kevin slept off his dinner, Annie had spent the afternoon in the company of the coven making wreaths for the funeral.

Nobody had realised just how well-known Sylvia was until the day of her funeral. Black cars drove in procession through Nether Dale, and curious villagers who had previously snubbed her now stood out on the streets transfixed. Flowers and paisley maxi dresses blended with diamonds and furs in the small church graveyard. Annie, Poppet, Ginny, Donna, Corinne and Martha walked behind the coffin towards the grave. Poppet held her head high, her pale face solemn. When they reached the graveside, Poppet turned, her eyes dry and cold as she looked down into the dug-out ground.

Annie didn't hear what the vicar said as the coffin was lowered into the earth, her thoughts focused on Poppet and what would happen to her now she had no mother or father. An auburn-haired woman who wore emerald earrings and a fur coat wept into a handkerchief, her husband's arm resting on her shoulder. The vicar's wispy grey hair blew in the breeze, standing on end as if he had been shocked. Two little girls giggled and pointed, until their mother tapped them both sharply on the shoulder.

When the interment had finished, a queue of mourners took handfuls of soil and scattered them into the grave as Poppet watched. Mourners began to move away, leaving the child alone at the graveside. Once suitably distant the gathered mourners began to chatter and point in the direction of Sylvia's house, where sandwiches and tea were waiting.

Ginny put a hand on Annie's shoulder, 'You coming?'

'Yes, just waiting for Poppet.' She turned to Ginny. 'I heard they know who did it. One of the gardeners from Hallow Croft.'

'Yes. Hasn't been seen since. He's probably been paid off by the family and living it up in Spain as we stand here.'

'I doubt he'll ever pay for this.' Annie said.

'Go fetch Poppet, let's get back to the house.'

Annie joined Poppet at the side of the grave, both looking down on the wicker coffin. She reached for Poppet's hand but the child snatched it away.

She looked up at Annie.

'He'll pay.'

Annie regarded the child. She had no doubt that Poppet was capable of dark magic, and unlike her mother there would be no meetings or joint decisions.

'Let's not think about that now, let's go and honour her life with the others.'

Poppet followed Annie and Ginny out of the churchyard, all accepting a lift from Martha who was waiting, engine running, by the gate.

When they arrived at Sage End the house was alive with chatter about Sylvia, the good times and the bad. Sylvia had had so many different lives, travelling the world, learning from occultists and witches everywhere. Annie had always been in awe of her experience and power, and now she was gone.

Poppet sat alone by the window, playing with one of her dolls, squeezing its body and talking to it, the words unheard through the other guests' tears and condolences.

'What do you think will happen to her?' Corinne asked.

Annie looked across to Poppet.

'I don't know,' Annie said. 'I don't know if there are any other relatives. Her aunt and uncle have refused to look after her beyond the funeral. I don't expect there'll be a queue.'

When Annie had walked through the door she had been shaking with anxiety at the thought of seeing those mourning the loss, but she needn't have worried. The coven gathered her up and held her, each blessing her with kind words and spoken spells of protection and everything felt safe again.

Poppet came to Annie's side and Annie put a protective arm around her, the girl's body ice-cold despite still wearing a heavy woollen coat. A woman with a dried flower wreath atop long auburn hair eyed Poppet and then backed away, turning to make conversation with a man who wore a long velvet coat and a top hat with feathers sprouting from the brim.

'Something to eat?' Annie said to Poppet, offering her a thin sandwich of fish paste.

Poppet clamped her mouth shut and shook her head.

'Why don't you go and have a nap then, perhaps you'll be hungry after.'

The mourners watched in silent sympathy as Poppet padded through the room, the lounge door slamming behind her, causing a woman to cry out in shock, her hand to her chest.

As the last of the buffet was picked at, the sound of a ball began to echo from above. A slow *duff duff*, familiar to the women when Poppet was angry.

'Do you think we should try and find her dad, maybe he would look after her?'

'No chance. Sylvia would never forgive us. Besides, he left for America years ago, I doubt anybody knows where he is now. She'll probably go into foster—'

'She can't!' Annie said, so loudly that the mourners turned to look. She lowered her voice. 'No, she can come and stay with me awhile. I'll look after her.'

And even though Poppet couldn't possibly have heard, the ball above silenced.

CHAPTER 54

Samantha swished the damp sponge over the coffee table, then covered it with a patchwork cloth she had bought on a holiday in Spain. Memories of teaching Lily to swim in the hotel pool calmed her.

She emptied the last of a box of Quality Street into a blue bowl and filled the kettle. As she went to answer the door, she sprayed perfume into the air, an expensive alternative to the air freshener she had forgotten to buy in the village.

'Come in,' she said, keeping a fixed smile on her face as Valerie entered the hallway.

'Oh, you have made this a little home,' said Valerie as she walked ahead, inspecting every nook and cranny as she went.

'It's getting there,' said Samantha. 'I'm going to paint through in the spring, really make it home.'

'You think you'll still be here come spring?' Valerie winked.

Samantha was momentarily taken aback. 'Yes, of course. Why wouldn't I?'

'Oh, no reason. Like I said before, this place isn't for everyone.'

'Well, I come from here.'

'And Lily?'

Samantha gestured for Valerie to take a seat on the sofa. 'Yes, she seems to be settling well.'

'She certainly is a joy to have around,' said Valerie, helping herself to a chocolate. 'Obviously I love the old folk, but it's nice to have a young'un around. Is she not here?'

'She's gone into town.'

'Oh, I thought you'd be together on Boxing Day. She's an independent soul, isn't she?'

Samantha wasn't sure if that was a dig or not; she chose to think not.

'Have you got children?' asked Samantha.

Valerie laughed. 'When I say it's nice to have them around, it's also nice to give them back.' She rescued a crumb from her chin, scooping it back into her mouth. 'No, I never had any interest in adding to the population myself, I prefer cats.'

Samantha raised her eyebrows. 'Well, I guess they're a little cheaper to maintain.'

Valerie gave her a thin smile.

'I'm glad you could come and have a cuppa, we don't seem to have much time to chat while we're on the job,' Samantha said.

It was the last thing she felt like doing on any afternoon, but she had decided that part of her role was to start bringing people together, and if she expected that from everyone else, she was going to have to make the effort herself. Besides, she lived by the adage: *keep your friends close and your enemies closer.*

'I wanted to apologise for yesterday.'

'Oh?'

'I should have warned you I was bringing Annie down to the dining room. I appreciate that after all your hard work with her it must have been a shock to see her there.'

Her apology appeared to surprise Valerie.

'I appreciate that, Matron. You see, we don't keep her away for her own good. We do it for all the others.' She sat back on the sofa with a mug of tea, wincing as the hot liquid touched her lip.

'Well, as you can see now, we can manage her well enough—'

'Matron, forgive me, I don't mean to be rude, but you have barely been here five minutes.'

Samantha clenched her jaw, trying her hardest not to show the flash of irritation Valerie was already provoking. She let her continue.

'I have known Annie for a long time, long before she came to Hallow Croft as a resident. Her struggles are not new.'

'She lost her daughter.'

'More than lost, Matron — her daughter was murdered. That has had a crippling effect on the woman, as you can imagine. She was only in her thirties when it happened. Something like that can send a person to a very dark place.'

'That's as maybe, but as health carers it's our job to see what we can do to improve things, not just shut her away.'

The wind rattled at the windows as rain began to fall, washing the last flakes of snow away from the windows.

'Tell me, Matron, why did you leave the area all those years ago?'

Samantha shrugged. 'My parents separated and I went with my dad. My mum moved away—'

'But she didn't, did she?'

'Sorry?'

'I think I'm correct in saying she still lives in Heather Brook?'

Samantha felt a brick of anxiety drop into her stomach. How could Valerie know this? She had changed her name, the village was far enough away, and God knows her mum never spoke of her after she left, of that much she was sure.

'Have you told Lily this?' Samantha asked, trying to keep her tone calm.

'Of course not, dear, your business is your own. The secrets you keep are yours and yours alone.'

'It's not a secret, Valerie. I'd just prefer it if she didn't know. We didn't have the best relationship back then. As far as Lily knows, she moved down south years ago. I stayed with my dad, so she has a grandad at least and—'

Valerie put her cup down and picked up a chocolate as she stood, taking a small bite before speaking. 'I understand, Matron. I'd just ask that you have the same respect for *my* need to keep Annie safe in her room. There are things you don't know about her that are best kept that way. I can help her, I aways have been able to. She trusts me.'

Samantha nodded, despite herself. 'Of course.'

'It's OK, dear,' Valerie soothed, 'you're still learning our *strange* ways here, but we know best.'

Samantha didn't know exactly who she was referring to in that *we*, but she was prepared to back down on the Annie issue if it meant keeping her own mother out of her life.

CHAPTER 55

1976

Kevin opened his mouth to protest as Annie changed the television channel. He glared over at Poppet, whose narrow eyes stared back at him. There was a crackle of aluminium as his fist clenched a half-empty beer can.

A lion bounded across the screen, in fast pursuit of a gazelle.

'Poppet likes nature programmes, don't you?'

Annie glanced at the girl, who returned a satisfied smile then sat back on the sofa, clutching a glass of fruit squash.

'I like snooker,' Kevin mumbled under his breath.

It was the end of January now and the child had been with them a month. Kevin had tried to put his foot down but to no avail. Annie earned the money, prepared the meals and cleaned the house; the power was hers.

He slurped down the rest of his beer, followed by a drawn-out belch. Annie scowled at him.

'What?' he protested.

'Do you have to do that?' she said, her voice tight with disgust.

He shrugged and lit a cigarette. Poppet coughed.

Annie stood up and walked across the room, pushing the net curtains aside and opening a window. 'You shouldn't smoke around Poppet, she's sensitive to it.'

A blast of air whistled into the living room, the stacked newspapers on the table fluttering.

'Then she should be outside playing.' He drew on the cigarette.

Annie caught Poppet sneering at him and shot her a quelling look. Though she had little time for her husband or his bad habits, it was still his home and she was wary of Poppet trying to exude power over either of them.

Poppet drew her mother's old book onto her lap, flicking through the pages and scanning the words and images.

'She prefers adult company, she always has.'

Kevin grunted. 'Don't you think it's about time she went back to her own family?'

'*Kevin*!' Annie remonstrated, looking to Poppet, who was once again staring at him.

He shot the young girl a look, but seemed unnerved by her, and lay back in his chair. He laced his hands across his belly and closed his eyes. Annie sat back down to watch the television, as the lion ripped at the gazelle's body, tearing off chunks of flesh.

Poppet began whispering something, a mumble of words in the strange language Annie knew only too well.

Kevin cried out, clutching his chest and crumpling forward, a guttural cry bubbling up in his throat. Annie jumped up and slammed Poppet's book shut. 'Enough!'

Her husband woke from his sleep, beads of sweat trickling down his cheeks. He appeared dazed and disorientated, his hand still at his chest.

'Bad dream?' Annie said.

He steadied his breath, jerking his head as if bringing himself round from a deep sleep. Annie glared at Poppet, who shrugged, a thin smile on her lips.

'Fetch me a glass of water,' he said, his breathing settling.

On her way to the kitchen, Annie caught the eye of the girl and put a warning finger in the air.

No more.

CHAPTER 56

Lily got off the bus and made her way down the road. As the skies above opened, she considered calling her mum for a lift, but decided against it. She needed quiet and space to think, not an interrogation about who she had seen and what she had done. She looked across the fields at the sheep taking shelter by the drystone walls. Rain needled down onto their backs, resting on the thick wool. She wrapped her coat around her satchel to protect the contents within.

A car whizzed past, its brake lights shining red through the mist. Lily slowed her walking, looking back up the road, a sense of unease creeping through her. As she approached the car, she gave it a wide berth, trying not to look. The window lowered and Harry stuck his head out.

'Do you need a lift?'

Lily relaxed, a small laugh leaving her lips. 'I'm going to the village.'

'No problem, hop in.'

She crouched down to get into the Porsche, the smell of new car distinctly different to her usual experience. There were no receipts or empty packets of mints on the dashboard, just a suitcase lying on the backseat.

'Nice car,' she said.

Harry smiled, 'Thanks, not quite made for these hills but good for London.'

'When do you go back?'

'A few days. We close down for Christmas and the New Year.'

'Nice work if you can get it,' Lily joked.

Harry smiled. 'I hear it's your birthday tomorrow? Any plans?'

'Not really, maybe just a meal with Mum.'

She thought about her friends back in Manchester, the parties they would have. She suddenly felt very sorry for herself, part of her wishing she'd taken up her mum's offer of having Sophie visit.

'How old will you be?'

'Sixteen.'

He tapped at the steering wheel, his forehead creased in thought.

'Do you get to see your dad much?'

'I don't know him,' Lily said, fastening and unfastening her satchel.

She had stopped asking Samantha a long time ago; she and her mum had always been fine, so in the end it hadn't mattered to her.

'Have you ever wanted to know? Does it bother you?' he asked, indicating to pull up by the village green.

'Not really, my mum covers all parenting bases.'

Lily hoped he might offer to take her out again. She liked the car and he was fun. He didn't speak until the car pulled up in the village. Lily got out of the car, thanking him for the lift.

'Could you tell your mum to call me? I'd like to see her before I go if possible.'

'Sure,' Lily said.

'And happy birthday for tomorrow!'

Lily smiled, watching as Harry's car moved off back up the hill.

CHAPTER 57

1976

'I'm afraid, Mrs Dawson, one can't live as he has done and avoid the consequences. He has the lungs of an eighty-year-old and a liver so pickled it should be in a jar.'

Annie pulled the bedroom door to as Dr Mardle spoke, the two of them standing on the landing.

'Can't he have treatment?'

'I'll prescribe antibiotics for the bronchitis, which should help ease things. His liver test results, however, are not as promising. He'll be referred to a specialist, but in the meantime I'd suggest he limit alcohol, and as for the cigarettes? I'm sure you don't need me to tell you.'

As if on cue, Kevin began to cough and splutter on the other side of the door, the doctor flinching as it reached a crescendo and ended with a heave of the lungs.

'I have some herbal remedies I can—'

'Mrs Dawson,' he sighed, 'there comes a time when man needs more than nettles and hocus pocus to get well, and I'm afraid Mr Dawson is well beyond that point now. Stick to proven science, dear, it's your best bet.'

Annie watched as the doctor climbed into his car and drove away. Upstairs, the sound of blackened lungs gurgling continued unabated. She went to the kitchen to make Kevin a cup of tea, finding Poppet already by the hob, the kettle beginning to whistle.

'I was going to make Kevin a drink,' Annie said.

'No need, all in hand.' Poppet smiled, pointing to a mug with a picture of two kittens on it.

'Thanks, Poppet. I'm going to have a lie-down in the lounge for a bit, I haven't slept with the noise all night.'

'You relax, I'll make sure he has what he needs.'

Annie lay on the couch, listening as Poppet knocked on the door upstairs, the low rumble of voices before the girl left and went to her own room. Annie felt guilty that she wasn't more concerned about her husband, that it was only a sense of wifely duty that kept her carrying and fetching for him. He had left her in all but body three years ago, not giving a second thought to her need for support or care; a part of her resented the fact she would be forced to look after him now.

Annie awoke to the sound of voices passing by her window. She looked at her watch. She had been asleep for hours. The light outside was fading and the room was in darkness.

She got herself a glass of water from the kitchen and made her way upstairs to the bathroom. She turned on the taps and poured in lily of the valley bubble bath. She relaxed back into the hot water, soft bubbles rising and spilling over the side of the tub. She lifted her head from the water, pushing back her soaked hair. From the bedroom she heard Kevin begin to cough again. The grating noise pushed her head under again until the hacking became a dull, imperceptible blur. When the coughing didn't stop, she stood up in the bath, stepped onto the tufted bathmat and wrapped a thin towel around her body.

He was gasping, the coughs so severe he couldn't catch his breath. Annie ran to him and placed a damp arm across his back as his face reddened.

'Try and breathe,' she urged, as his body jolted, the bubbling lungs expelling air in blasts. 'Poppet!'

The girl ran to the bedroom door, rubbing her eyes.

'Call 999.'

Poppet went downstairs to the telephone as Annie tried to calm Kevin, whose body was now in spasms, specks of blood splattering the handkerchief he clutched in his fist.

'Are they coming?' Annie shouted, panic rising in her body.

Poppet was back at the door. 'Yes, they said they'll be here as quickly as they can.'

There was a pounding on the wall, the next-door neighbours finally at the end of their tether. The paper-thin walls did nothing to hold the horrendous coughing within the room. Kevin made a strange gagging noise, as if something were stuck fast in his throat. Annie smacked his back, but it was no good. His face began to turn blue as he held his own throat, his wide eyes staring at Poppet as he fell back on the bed.

'Kevin?' Annie cried, trying to rouse him as blood trickled from the corner of his mouth to the bedsheets.

By the time the sirens turned the corner on their street, Kevin had gone.

'Is he . . . ?' Poppet asked.

Annie stared at the girl, scanning her face for signs of shock or upset — there was nothing. Poppet turned and went back to her room, the crackle of a radio filtering down the hallway as she searched for her favourite station.

After they had taken him away, Annie cleared up the kitchen. Guilt pierced her insides for her earlier thoughts. Had she brought this on somehow? Were her thoughts so powerful that her wishes, however fleeting, had been granted?

Then she spotted the kitten mug. She slowly moved towards it, lifting its handle and peering inside. She recalled how Poppet had made a drink for Kevin. It occurred to her that it was the first time since she had come to live with them that Poppet had done anything for him at all. And now he was gone.

Annie sniffed the dregs at the bottom. A tiny dark speck was stuck to the side. She slid it out with a finger and lifted it to the light, knowing what it was even as she did so. A tiny speck of skin from a belladonna berry.

CHAPTER 58

Lily began the walk back up the hill. She hadn't wanted to ask Harry to drop her at Valerie's house. She knew her mum resented their friendship and Harry might have told her.

As always, Valerie was overjoyed to see her.

'I've something for you,' the older woman beamed, leading her back out to the drive and telling her to cover her eyes.

When Lily took her hands away from her eyes, she gasped, 'Is that for me?'

Valerie rang the silver bicycle bell with her thumb.

'A young girl needs to have a bit of freedom, so I thought you'd like it. An early birthday present before the big day tomorrow.'

Lily walked across Valerie's drive and reached out for the pale pink bike, running her hands across the handlebars.

'You shouldn't have, I mean—'

'It's second-hand, I've just cleaned it up a bit for you. It was rotting away in the shed, so I thought I'd give it a new lease of life. It's a bit old-fashioned, I know, but better than nothing.'

'I love it! Thank you.'

Lily got on the bike and rode in circles around the gravel driveway, Valerie beaming like a proud parent each time she passed. Lily rang the bell and Valerie clapped her hands.

'Now then, you seem proficient to me, so why don't you cycle back to Hallow Croft? I'll follow behind, make sure you're safe.'

Lily put the brakes on and a foot to the ground. 'I don't have a helmet.'

'Oh, don't worry about that, I'll keep an eye on you. Health and safety madness these days.'

Lily thought for a moment, wanting to heed all the warnings her mum had given her over the years about road safety, but also not wanting to disagree with Valerie.

'You'll be fine, I promise. Come on, I'll be right behind you.'

Lily hesitated, before putting her foot on the pedal again and pushing off towards the road. She waited until Valerie was behind her in the car and set off up the hill to Hallow Croft. Her thighs ached as she ascended the hill, pushing as hard as she could so that she didn't roll back into Valerie's car, which was edging slowly up the hill behind her. The skies were grey and the moors around her coated in bleakness, ragged sheep fleeing as she cycled past. She turned the corner onto the drive towards Hallow Croft and her legs relaxed, the relief of flat ground causing her to speed up, feeling the cold air blast through her hair.

Lily heard Valerie's car parking up behind her as she carried on round to the quadrant. Blank faces appeared at the windows as she sped past. When she reached the grass squares she noticed the blur of a figure standing there watching her through an open window on the top floor. Lily took a hand off the handlebar and waved to Annie, the bike wobbling as she sped across the pathways.

Lily squeezed the brakes, bringing the bike to a grinding halt as she reached the gravel driveway. A fat drop of rain hit her rosy cheek, followed by a gust of wind. When she looked again, Annie had disappeared from sight, the window closed. Birds swooped in the sky, heading for the shelter of the woods.

Lily dismounted and pushed the bike towards the back entrance of Hallow Croft. She managed to get it down the narrow stairs and into the hallway, leaning it against the wall. She swished her hands through her damp hair and bounded up towards the flat.

'Where have you been?' Samantha shouted from the lounge.

Lily called back, 'Nowhere,' and went to her bedroom. She closed her door, took off her wet clothes, and got straight into the Snoopy pyjamas Diane and Jonathan had given her for Christmas.

She took her sketch pad out of her satchel and flipped through the pages, the multiple symbols she had scratched in pen and pencil having an hypnotic effect on her. Lily held onto the pendant round her neck until the feeling took hold. Then, taking a red felt-tip she began manically sketching the lines and circles again and again until her fingers ached. By the time night came she had filled the entire drawing pad with the strange symbol that she didn't yet understand.

CHAPTER 59

The next morning Samantha was sat on the lounge floor blowing up balloons. She tied off the end of the final one, throwing it up in the air and batting it towards the others, where Lily's presents had lain waiting for the past two hours.

She tore idly at her toast, as *The Wizard of Oz* played to itself on the television. Lily hadn't come out of her room the previous night. All dreams that this move would provide them with quality 'mum and daughter' time were dissolving by the day. Samantha was trying to be patient, to give her the space that all the child manuals implored parents to do. Lily was too old to be forced to spend time with her mum, and if she were honest, it was depressing watching Lily pretend to enjoy these times when Samantha knew she'd rather be in her room staring at the ceiling or messaging on her phone.

Samantha threw the remainder of the toast in the bin and drained her mug of tea. She knocked on her daughter's door again, standing back and waiting. Lily groaned a response.

'Happy birthday, Lily! Are you coming out to open your presents?'

'I need to sleep,' Lily croaked back.

Samantha thought about waiting, but better to go out now and return when she was sure Lily would be up and in the mood for her birthday.

'OK, I'm just nipping into the village. I'll only be an hour, don't open anything until I'm back, OK?'

Lily groaned a sleepy response and Samantha leaned against the door. 'I love you.'

* * *

Samantha drove down the familiar roads that linked the Gatherings villages. Each had their own identity. She drove through Bradlock, its cement works providing work to most of the community. Three miles away, Scartle was little more than a cluster of limestone houses and a telephone box that was now filled with books to read and swap.

A pair of hikers trudged along the pavement, map in hand as they pointed into the gloomy distance. Samantha had never appreciated the scenery that surrounded these places, the high peaks and heather-clad moors that seemed to go on for miles. As a child it was a mystery why tourists would travel from the lights of the city and its bars to spend the night in a cramped B&B, or worse still sleep under canvas on the local farms. Nightlife back then had been sitting on the wall by the bus stop, or those occasional nights cadging lifts to the Skull & Feathers.

She shuddered, a memory of the first time she'd set eyes on Harry piercing into her head. All of the girls had liked the new boy. He was an occasional visitor from Sheffield, invited by another boy who lived in Nether Dale. The two of them must have been in collusion, concocting a lie about his identity so he would fit in with the *commoners*.

It made Samantha angry to think that she had fallen for it, a whole story of a 'bad lad' who regularly got suspended from the city comp. The two of them sniggering to each other. At the time she had thought the laughter came from their schoolboy antics; now she knew it was from the deceit.

She should have known from the first kiss. He smelled of expensive aftershave, not the cheap knock-offs the others bought from the village shop. Less Hai Karate, more Calvin

Klein. His hair should have given him away, a Hugh Grant foppishness — but the accent? She smiled to herself when she thought about it, a strong Sheffield burr: 'It's reyt good.' 'You're nesh, you are!' — straight from the pages of *The Secret Garden*, no doubt. With hindsight, Harry had never been the cheeky working-class Dickon; more the spoiled Master Colin in disguise.

It had crossed her mind to tell him about Lily over the years, of course it had, but there was never a right time. Lily had asked when she was younger, usually when school made Father's Day cards, which Samantha found screwed up in the bottom of her bag year after year.

The truth was, the longer it went on, the harder it was to go back there. Besides, with the portrayal of the petty-thieving, school-dodging teen he had given her, she hadn't exactly had high hopes for the influence he might have had on her daughter. He would be gone any day now, then at least for the time being she would be able to continue the charade. Lily barely liked her as it was right now; an emotional bomb like this might shatter them for good.

All thoughts of that current crisis paled as Samantha drove into Heather Brook, transported back sixteen years in an instant. The ruddy-cheeked village butcher putting out his sign for cut-price meats, the village shop with the same nativity figures displayed year after year, the post woman riding her bike down the windy lanes.

Samantha drove up the street and parked outside a row of houses with low walls and identical doors. An inflatable Santa in one of the gardens swayed in the wind, snowflakes sprayed on each window of the house. She edged down in the car seat as she looked up to her old bedroom window, the same curtains hanging. She wondered what they had used the room for when she had left — was it a memorial to her? More likely, she mused, it had become a craft studio for her mum, or a display room for the endless ornaments she always bought.

A woman in a carer's uniform got out of a car and flung a large bag over her shoulder. Samantha watched as she walked up the street towards her and into her mum's front garden. The carer let herself in and closed the door.

Samantha waited for a moment, then opened her car door and crossed the road, disappearing down a small ginnel between the houses. When she reached the back garden, she climbed over the wall and hid behind a small garden shed. She edged her way to the back door and slowly moved along the wall, to peer in the window past the archway that opened the kitchen up to the lounge.

She took a sharp intake of breath. Her mum was sat in a high-backed chair, the carer with her back to Samantha, sorting through a pill case, picking out the ones she needed to take. Her mum was just sixty-seven years old, but her frail arms shook as she raised the glass to her mouth, swallowing the medication. She smiled sweetly at the young helper, who sat in a chair opposite as they spoke.

Samantha turned away, her back to the wall. A rush of emotion filled her. She had expected the same old hard-faced parent, the rule-giver and fun-thief. When she returned, she had expected to feel the same hatred for the woman who had forced her to go away to have her baby. All she felt now was regret and pity.

The last sixteen years felt like they had flown by, that no time at all had passed, but the mum she had left behind all those years ago had changed almost beyond recognition. She wondered if her mum would even recognise her now, or whether the shock of seeing her would be enough to kill her off.

She looked back through the window. The carer was gathering her things, ready to leave. For a moment Samantha wanted to run and meet her at the front door, ask about her mum, but she was frozen to the spot.

Her mum raised a hand to wave goodbye. Then she turned back to the television, a plaid blanket draped across thin knees. Samantha pulled herself away, thoughts scrambling in her head. She climbed back over the wall and turned back up the ginnel.

'Who's that?' a voice called out.

Samantha turned to see her old neighbour, Clive. He was holding a bag of bird seed and a wire tube of fat balls. Although greyer and markedly thinner in face, he was as recognisable now as he had been back then.

'It's me, Samantha.' She smiled, walking back towards him.

He appeared confused for a moment, his eyes narrowing, scanning her up and down.

'By God, it is you, young Sammy. Well I never. How are you doing?'

'I'm good thanks, you?'

'Can't complain — our Denise is away at the moment, went to see Kelly for Boxing Day while I stayed home with the dog. It's a shame, she'd have loved to have seen you. Have you been in?' he said, gesturing to her mum's house with the bag of seed.

'No, she had company, so . . .' she drifted off, knowing the excuse was weak at best.

'I bet she'd be over the moon, love, why don't you knock and see.'

'Another time.'

'It's never too late, you know. These daft family arguments, they can be fixed.'

Samantha bristled. A reminder that in a small village, their business was everybody's business. It was naïve of her to think they wouldn't all have asked where she and her dad had disappeared to. They had probably sat and listened to her mum give them all the details over cups of tea and chocolate biscuits.

Samantha smiled. 'Give my best to Denise and Kelly, will you?'

'Course I will,' he walked over to the bird table, 'and hope to see you again soon, eh?'

Samantha checked her phone when she got back into her car, a message from a number she didn't recognise.

Hi Samantha, can we meet? Just need to chat about something before I leave for London. H.

Her heart raced. Jonathan must have given him her number. What did he need to talk about? Suddenly the idea of running back to the house and making up with her mum seemed like an attractive proposition. Perhaps she could hide out in her old bedroom until Harry left again. She stared down at the screen, her thumb hovering.

Sure, how about this afternoon?

The reply came straight back.

Skull & Feathers? I'll pick you up outside Hallow Croft at 4.

CHAPTER 60

Lily watched as Valerie shuffled the cards between her hands. Cathy, Hallow Croft's cook, sat opposite her as she presented the deck. They were in a small room filled with books for residents to borrow; in the centre was a table and four wooden chairs. The curtains were closed with a single light above switched on.

'Split the deck three times, Cathy, and while you're doing it, think of what you want the cards to answer. Are you thinking about something?'

Cathy nodded her head and carefully split the deck face down into three piles. Valerie turned the top card of each over and Lily strained to see the pictures. She didn't recognise the usual pentacles and swords of the decks she had seen in magazines. These cards were of fine pen-and-ink drawings of animals and fantastical beasts, the thin edges rimmed with metallic red foil.

Valerie grinned. 'Oh I say, this is a good hand, Cathy. Have you had a falling-out with anyone recently?'

Cathy nodded vigorously. 'I most certainly have, I—'

Valerie held her hand up. 'Don't say any more, let the cards do the talking.' She tapped the card entitled *Botis* with her fingernail. 'Botis is the demon of reconciliation, he can bring together the deepest of enemies. Is it a family member?'

Again, Cathy nodded, this time saying nothing more.

'Is it about an inheritance?'

Cathy looked to Lily, her eyebrows raised. 'Yes, it's our—'

Valerie held up her hand again. 'Valac. This card tells me that you're going to be receiving what's rightly yours soon.' She turned over the third card and sat back, shaking her head in relieved understanding. 'Ah, Baphomet. The card of financial prosperity. It all makes sense together, see? What belongs to you will be in your hands soon.'

'How soon?' Cathy asked.

'The demons are good, Cathy, but they don't guarantee a date.' She winked at Lily. 'Now then, your turn, birthday girl.'

'Me?' Lily asked.

'Of course, why not? It's only a bit of fun.'

Lily shrugged. 'OK, but—'

'Don't tell Mum.' Valerie smiled. 'I know, she worries too much about you. The tarot is no more than a harmless card game.'

Lily took Cathy's place as the cook began messaging on her phone.

'Just telling Simon we might be going on holiday after all,' she beamed.

Valerie gathered up the three piles and began to shuffle the deck in swift motions, the cards weaving in and out of each other. Valerie closed her eyes, taking deep breaths as Lily tried to think of a question to ask. When she had done preparing, Valerie opened her eyes and fixed them on Lily.

'Have you thought of something?'

Lily nodded.

'Same as before: cut twice, making three piles. No rush, see where your hand is drawn to.'

Lily hesitated. Each time she reached a place in the deck she was tempted to move her hand again.

'Just go with your instinct, Lily, there's no right or wrong.'

Lily made the first cut just as the door to the room opened and Aparna appeared. When she saw what they were doing she reached out her hand, her face crumpled in fear. 'Stop!'

Lily looked from Aparna to Valerie.

'It's OK, Aparna, we're just playing cards, that's all,' said Cathy, looking up from her phone.

Aparna stood still, watching the light above them swinging gently. The bulb flickered.

'Close the door, Aparna, you're letting a draught in,' Valerie said, her face taut.

Aparna started to talk to herself, rambling as her eyes rolled back in her head.

'Is she OK?' Lily asked, getting up from her chair. Valerie stood up and stopped Lily, walking over to the door herself.

'I'll be out in a minute, lovely, you just wait in the day room,' she told Aparna.

Aparna turned, spectre-like, and left the room. Valerie went to shut the door, but another draught swept across the room and it slammed shut. The light flickered on and off again.

'Should we check she's OK?' asked Lily.

'She'll be fine,' said Valerie. 'Now, where were we?'

Lily glanced back at the door, not sure whether to check herself, but not feeling able to leave the chair she was sat in.

'Split the deck, Lily.'

Lily placed two piles of cards on the table and gave Valerie the third. Lily watched as Valerie turned over the top three cards: *Lucifer, Moloch* and *Ipos*.

Lily knew nothing of demons, but she knew Lucifer. The card depicted a plump cherub sat atop a mound of skulls. She felt a shiver crawl up her spine, a sudden urge to leave the room and forget about the cards. Valerie must have sensed her hesitation, as she rested her hand on Lily's.

'These are good cards, Lily. Sometimes a warning can help you avoid bad things.' She looked down at the cards, gently skimming the first with her index finger. 'Lucifer, he may be the card of death, but that can mean the death *of* something, not you. The cards are rarely literal. Lucifer gives

263

you insight, Lily, you must look within you to see what it is you need to free yourself from. See Moloch here?'

Lily nodded.

'Moloch is the devil card.'

'The devil?'

'It's not about you, Lily,' Valerie repeated. 'He represents those who wish to make you worse off — it's just a warning. Is there a friend you don't trust? A family member making things difficult?'

Lily opened her mouth to speak but Valerie stopped her. 'Don't answer that, it's between you and the cards. Just be aware that not everyone has your best interests at heart, Lily.' Valerie rested her hand on the final card and smiled. 'Ipos. He speaks of the past and the future and he shows you that you can use that information to make better decisions going forward. So when you take the warnings, also take comfort that the power is within you to live your own life.'

Lily tried to take it all in, wishing she'd had a more straightforward reading like Cathy, who was already scanning holiday sites on her phone.

'So . . . I just need to be careful who I trust?'

'Exactly, Lily. Know those that have your best interests at heart and stick with them.' She winked. 'Like me.'

Valerie gathered the cards together and placed them in a red velvet pouch, quietly thanking them for their knowledge.

As they walked back into the home, a bell rang. Valerie looked at her watch. 'Break time's over, no rest for the wicked! Why don't you go and get some fresh air, Lily? Does a girl good to get outside and see a bit of nature.'

Valerie headed off towards the day room and Cathy back to the kitchen.

Lily looked over to the day room, unnerved to see Aparna staring straight at her. Valerie's dark warnings flitted around in her head.

When she got back to her room, she tried to draw a landscape from a photograph she had borrowed from the school library, but no matter how much she tried to create a likeness, everything she drew turned into a grey mess. She ripped the paper out and scrunched it up, throwing it across the room. As the afternoon wore on, the discarded paper piled up as her frustration grew from nowhere.

Sometimes Lily missed who she used to be; she missed the way her mum used to look at her like she was the best thing in her world. Now her mum was always annoyed with her, their bond stretching and twisting out of shape. Lily didn't know how to get back to before, and the sadness and anger she felt was all-consuming.

Lily opened her satchel and took out a bundle of velvet. She stood up and let the dark cloak she had bought hang to the floor. It was the most beautiful thing Lily had ever seen. Velvet with silk ribbons and a large hood. She swung it around her shoulders and tied the ribbon, lifting the hood over her head. In the mirror she saw her reflection, a girl morphing into a woman.

She opened her bedside-table drawer and pulled open the brown paper parcel Valerie had given her. Small vials of liquids and herbs, instructions on how to use them and maybe create her own one day, so that she could add to the grimoire. Valerie saw something in her, she understood her.

Lily began to fix her drawings to her bedroom wall, filling all the available space with her new artistic creations. She stood back and admired them, silently thanking Valerie for inspiring her to think for herself and stop listening to those that didn't have her interests at heart.

She ran her fingers down the cloak. It was just as Valerie had asked her to get. In fact, she now had everything that Valerie had requested. Her ceremony was going to be very special, she knew that. Finally, she would feel part of something and belong.

CHAPTER 61

1976

Donna sat back in her chair, waving her hands around at the décor in Sylvia's kitchen.

'Don't you want to make your own mark in here, Martha? Isn't your style more conservative?'

Martha looked up from her notes to the golden buddhas and pot plants that trailed to the floor.

'It was part of the agreement to rent the house: keep it exactly as it is, nothing removed. That way it's ready for Poppet when she inherits it at eighteen.'

'Imagine owning your own house at eighteen years old,' Annie said.

'I'm sure she'd prefer having a mother,' Martha said coldly.

Annie hung her head. 'Of course, I just meant . . .'

There was silence around the table, the empty chair beside them a ghost of their leader.

'Corinne, is your friend coming tonight?'

Corinne looked up, her face drawn and pale. She glanced at her wristwatch. 'Yes, she should be here any moment.'

Ginny made the women an absinthe each and they raised their glasses. 'To Sylvia, blessed be.'

Annie put the glass to her lips, bumping her teeth when the knocker banged against the brass plate on the door. Corinne pushed her chair back and left the room as the others waited for their guest. Voices carried down the hall, footsteps clipping across the tiled floor. As the door opened, the coven turned to see their potential new recruit.

Corinne put an arm around the woman's shoulders. 'Ladies, this is Aparna.'

CHAPTER 62

Samantha wished she hadn't agreed to Harry's request to see her. She could easily have avoided him until he left, and from what she had gathered, his visits were few and far between. She went into Lily's room and took a hoodie from her wardrobe, pulling it over her head, on the front a decal of a Care Bear sat on a cloud. She shook her head as she looked in the dressing-table mirror, but her attention was caught by the reflection of Lily's wall behind her.

She turned slowly, attempting to take in the mass of sketches before her.

What the hell?

Samantha moved closer, her eyes scanning each one. Drawing after drawing of creepy dolls in trees, and that symbol. It looked like the daubings of a lunatic. Her first instinct was to tear them all down, but she stopped herself. It was Lily's room, her space, and somehow she had to try and respect that.

It's just a stage, she told herself, *it will pass.*

In the kitchen she made herself a cup of tea, biding time until her daughter returned. Her mind raced, and for a fleeting moment a desire rose up to get their things together and leave as she had been warned to.

She looked towards the hall as a key turned in the door. 'Lily?'

Lily appeared in the doorway; she looked sheepish and unnerved.

'What's wrong?'

'Nothing,' her daughter replied, shrugging. She looked at Samantha's top, her face dropping. 'That's my hoodie.'

'You don't mind, do you? I've borrowed your clothes before.'

'You went into my room.'

'I always go in your room — who else do you think picks up your mess and washes your clothes?'

'In future I'll tidy my things and do my own washing.'

Lily turned to go to her room.

'What's wrong, Lily?'

She stopped and looked back at her mum. 'Nothing is wrong, I'd just prefer it if you didn't snoop around my things and didn't take my clothes.'

With that, Lily stormed to her room and slammed her bedroom door. Samantha stood for a moment, then she thought again of her own teenage years and, suddenly, she couldn't blame her daughter.

She looked up at the clock: it was just gone 4 o'clock.

Shit.

Samantha grabbed her bag and keys and ran out of the door and down the back stairs out to the car park.

Harry was waiting for Samantha, the engine running. She was glad for the warmth of the car and the heated seat she relaxed into. Though she didn't want to be here, with him, it was at least time away from Hallow Croft, the flat and her moody daughter. She just wished there wasn't so much of her past that she had to protect; that she could just go out and have a drink and relax. The car was taking her away from the frying pan and precariously close to the flames.

'Sorry I'm late. Lily . . . never mind.'

Samantha went to put her keys in her handbag, noticing something different. She held them in her palm, waiting for the answer to appear. Her key ring wasn't attached.

'You OK?' Harry asked.

'Yes, I just— it's nothing.' She dumped the keys in her bag, hoping that a resident wouldn't stumble across the key ring.

'Nice top,' said Harry.

'It's Lily's.'

'You don't say.'

Samantha looked at him, suddenly wondering if she'd rather be feeling the wrath of Lily again.

'This is a friendly drink, right? I'm not in trouble?'

'Shit!' Harry swerved the car to avoid a sheep lying in the road.

He pulled over to the kerb and stopped the car, putting the hazard lights on and getting out. Samantha unclipped her seat belt and followed him, joining him beside the animal.

'Is it . . .'

'Dead? Yes, must have been hit.'

'And they just left it?'

Harry nodded. 'Seems that way. Can you help me move it?'

The two of them wrestled the stiff body out of the road and lay it by a five-bar gate leading to the field.

'Look,' said Samantha, 'the others . . . Are they . . .'

Harry jumped over the gate and walked into the field as Samantha slowly edged towards him.

'What the hell happened here?' he said.

'We should call someone. Do you know the farmer?'

Harry shook his head. 'Dad might, I'll give him a ring.'

'Must be a disease or something.' Samantha looked down at her hands, rubbing them against her sides. 'Damn it!'

'Better not let Diane know.'

'Why?'

'According to her, right before the curse hits the village a plague will befall the livestock and harvest.' He held his hands in the air like claws, 'Mwuhahaha.'

Samantha shook her head, a slight smile on her lips. 'You're still an idiot.'

Harry lowered his arms and looked at the dirt and blood streaked across her pale pink hoodie. He called Jonathan, who promised to find out who the farmer was and get them to visit the field.

'Still up for that drink?' he said.

Samantha nodded, then looked down at her clothes.

'I have a spare jumper in the car, you can borrow that.'

They made their way back to the car in silence, Samantha trying to avoid looking down at the sheep corpses dotted about them.

Beams of lights burned through mist as a tractor made its way past them on the road to Nether Dale. Samantha looked up at the driver, a solemn-faced farmer making his way to the field, the bucket extended at the front, ready to scoop up the bodies.

Harry pulled into the pub car park; neither spoke until they were in the Skull & Feathers.

The pub was just as she remembered it. A small bar with a line of pumps, wooden bar stools lined up for the regulars, who sat in the same spot every night. Beyond the snug where they stood was a door to a back room, where the pool table had once been. That's where she'd first met Harry.

Samantha was relieved to find the corner of the snug unoccupied and went to claim it.

'What can I get you?' the barmaid said, her eyes lighting up as Harry approached the bar. 'It's Master Shuttleworth, isn't it?'

'Harry,' he smiled. 'A pint of Theakston and . . .' he turned to Samantha, who was sitting down.

'Malbec please, large.'

Harry brought the drinks to the table, Samantha noticing the barmaid's eyes following him.

'You have a fan.'

'I'm sure I wouldn't be so alluring if I wasn't heir to the manor.' He smiled.

'Oh, I don't know, when you were plain old Harry from the high-rise block you were fairly attractive.'

'Fairly?'

'Slim pickings in Nether Dale.'

Harry regarded her, his eyes narrowing. Samantha felt panic rise in her stomach — he had something to say. This wasn't a social get-together, that much she knew. She took a sip of the wine; it didn't taste like Malbec, it barely tasted of wine. She winced.

'It's Lily's birthday today, isn't it?' Harry asked.

'Yes,' said Samantha, her fingers tracing the rim of her wine glass.

'Have you anything planned?'

Samantha felt a wave of defensiveness rise within her, Lily's rejection of her offer of a cinema trip or tea out still hurting.

'We're doing something next week instead, there's a film on she wants to see in town.'

Harry nodded slowly. 'Hmmm. How old is she today?'

Samantha considered lying. By the time he found out from Diane and Jonathan she could escape. To where? The cleaning supplies cupboard at Hallow Croft? Build a shelter in the woods?

'Sixteen. Do you want some crisps or nuts?' Samantha looked in her bag for her purse.

'So, you became pregnant with her in the spring of 2007.'

Samantha paused, as if trying to work out the dates herself. Harry watched her every expression and move. 'Yes, I suppose so.'

Harry said nothing more, leaving it up to her to create another diversion, to weave herself further into her own web of lies.

Part of her still felt anger at him for lying. As far as she had known, he lived in a city miles away. Had she for a minute suspected he came from Nether Dale, that he was connected to Hallow Croft, she never would have returned. The gig was up though, she couldn't run from this any longer, and so she put her bag down and looked him straight in the eye.

'What do you want me to say, Harry?'

CHAPTER 63

Lily sat on her bedroom floor and unfolded the piece of paper Valerie had given her. Lily needed her mum to stop interfering in her life, to let her be her own person. This spell, Valerie had said, would do exactly that. Using a teaspoon, she measured the herbs and powder, dropping them into a glass jar. She took a small bottle of oil and added ten drops. She took out the key ring she had taken from her mum's chain, shuddering at the moniker *Sexy Samantha* as it whirled around in her fingers. Holding the container up to her eyes, she watched as the slick liquid dripped down the side of the glass and soaked into the mixture, covering the key ring.

As she lit a small red candle, Lily spoke the words written in the book, gently repeating the incantation over and over. When she was done, she tipped the candle over the top of the jar, turning it so the wax sealed the lid to the glass. She blew out the candle and placed the jar by her bedside.

Lily heard a *clink* at the window. She turned to see a cat looking into her room.

'Baal?'

Lily ran over to the window; she urged the cat to move slightly so she could open it. When she did, the cat slinked past her, jumping down to the floor.

'How did you get here?'

His fur was soft, with no evidence of having travelled the three miles or so from Valerie's house.

Lily looked out to the grounds and down the wall of the building. She turned back to her room to see Baal stretched out on her bed.

The cat purred with each touch, its amber eyes looking into hers. Lily knew Valerie had already gone home for the day, so she reached for her phone and scoured the contacts.

'Hi Valerie, it's Lily. Thank you, yes, I'm having a nice day. It's just that Baal has turned up here and . . . yes, of course . . . I'll bring him back now. No, I don't mind at all.'

Lily scooped him up and took him down the stairs to where her bike was. Baal stepped from her arms into the basket as if he had always travelled like this, settling down until only his head was visible above the wicker.

Lily opened the door and pushed the bike outside. The air was cold against her cheeks as she pedalled across the grounds and out of Hallow Croft. She spun down the hill, almost driven from the road by a tractor that passed by; she saw the pile of dead sheep stacked up in its front bucket, and her foot slipped from the pedal, causing her to wobble. When she reached Valerie's house, Baal jumped from the basket and disappeared through a side gate into the back garden. Lily got off her bike and walked to the gate, peering through the wooden slats.

Coloured bunting hung from the trees, their branches still bare. A wooden table on the grass was laden with bowls of food and glasses filled with pale cordial. Balloons tied with string bobbed in the air. A crow flew down to the table, pecking at a triangle sandwich. Baal jumped up, and the bird flew off to the safety of a nearby branch. Lily heard the faint sound of singing. '*Happy birthday to you, happy birthday to you, happy birthday dear . . .*'

Valerie appeared around the wall, carrying a cake alight with candles.

'. . . *Lily, happy birthday to you!*'

'Thank you,' Lily said quietly, overwhelmed by the sudden attention.

Valerie opened the wooden gate and ushered Lily in.

'It's the talk of Hallow Croft! A sixteenth birthday is special.'

'How did you know I'd be here now? I only came because of—'

'Baal?'

Lily scoffed. 'He didn't bring me here, *I* brought *him*.'

'And here you are!' Valerie exclaimed. 'Come and sit down, I've made sandwiches and cakes, all for you.'

Lily sat at the table, her chair sinking into the wet grass.

'I can't be too long, my mum doesn't know I'm out.'

Figures moved around in the kitchen, scuttling back and forth.

'Who's that?' Lily said, pointing towards the house.

Valerie smiled. 'Just some friends from the village who wanted to help you celebrate. Now then, blow out the candles and make a wish.'

Lily closed her eyes and blew, a vague wish fleeting through her mind. When she opened her eyes, she gasped. A group had gathered round the table, men and women, staring down at her. Their faces were solemn until one smiled and it caught like a wave, flowing along the faces until they were almost on the verge of hysteria. Ripples of 'Happy birthday, Lily!' repeated from their mouths.

Lily, overwhelmed, tried to focus on the crowd around her. The man with shaggy dark hair, the school bus driver. Another woman she was sure had been to Hallow Croft to visit a relative. The couple from the diner that first night, no longer silent but giggling and muttering birthday wishes.

'I think I'd better get home now. Thank you for all this though, it's amazing.'

'Not yet, Lily, you've only just arrived. We have party games.'

The gathering nodded enthusiastically.

'Please stay,' one pleaded.

Another grabbed her hand and pulled her to her feet, dancing in circles and taking Lily with him. Soon the others joined the circle and began to sing. She noticed Baal watching from the gateway, his eyes narrowed. As she was spun around, the cat disappeared out of view and the people surrounding her began to blur.

'I need the bathroom,' Lily shouted above the singing.

The dancing stopped, the party looking to Valerie. Her face broke into a warm smile. 'Of course, you know where it is.'

Lily stumbled, still dizzy from the spinning, and made her way to the back door as Valerie called after her, 'Don't be long, we've got cake to eat.'

Everywhere Lily looked there were lit candles; tea lights had even been placed on each step as she climbed to the landing. She noticed the black door that had been locked previously was now open, orange and white light flickering against purple walls. Curiosity pulled her towards the room; she would just peek, nothing more. She pushed the creaky door further to see hundreds more flames dancing in the draughts of the old house. In the centre of the room, drawn in white chalk, was the symbol she had sketched over and over, so familiar to her it appeared in her dreams. A dress had been hung up on a wardrobe door, a pale blue satin slip. Lily walked over and touched the soft material, turning to try and make sense of it all. Was this part of her birthday celebrations, was the dress a present?

'Oh, Lily, you've spoiled the surprise!' Valerie stood at the door, her hands on her hips.

Lily tried to edge past her. 'I was just comin—'

The other guests were stood behind Valerie, watching her with fixed grins on their faces.

'Do you like your special present?' she asked. Lily nodded mutely as Valerie walked past her and took the dress down. 'Now you go into the bathroom and pop it on. It wouldn't be a proper party without a party dress, would it?'

'No,' said Lily, 'I suppose not.'

The group parted to let her through, and she took the dress into the bathroom, locking the door behind her. She looked behind the toilet to see if there was a window she could get out of, panic rising. She reached into her pocket but her phone wasn't there; it must have fallen out in the garden.

She put her ear to the door: the voices outside were now muted. Carefully, she slid the bolt and pushed the door open slightly. Through the crack she saw that they must all be in the purple room. Only the back of one woman was visible in the doorway. Lily took a deep breath and ran down the stairs, kicking tea lights, which tumbled and extinguished as they fell. She heard the footsteps above scrambling across the room. She pulled at the front door but it was locked. She glanced left and right but there was no key. Footsteps were pattering down the stairs. Lily ran to the kitchen, feeling the air from the open back door.

In the garden she sprinted towards the wooden gate. She flung the gate open just as Baal jumped down from the wall, his claws out, scratching her face. She touched her cheek with her hand. Blood smeared across her palm. The cat hissed as she scrambled onto her bike and took off towards the road. Footsteps followed her across the gravel until there was silence. Then Valerie's commanding voice: 'Let her leave.'

Tears streamed down Lily's cheeks as she pushed the pedals harder and harder up the hill, pain searing her thighs. She longed to be with her mum, to have her nagging her about the mess in her room, or the amount of time she spent on her phone. Then she remembered the spell she had cast and the stupid glass jar that Valerie had given her, and sickness rose inside her. If she could get back in time, she could do something to stop it — she needed to stop it.

The giant wheels rumbled up the hill behind her, but Lily didn't look back. She just kept on pedalling as hard as she could. The vehicle began to slow, and she felt a fleeting wash of relief. It was just the school bus trying to pass her. She glanced up at the window, only to see the bus driver's stoney eyes and grin facing her.

It was no use; no matter how hard she tried she couldn't outpace him and there was nowhere to go but forward. The bus clipped the side of the bike and she felt herself falling to the ground, the bike clattering across the road.

For a moment, everything went silent. The grass and sky became one and she twisted on the ground, trying to crawl across the road. She heard a car pull up and footsteps coming slowly towards her, sounds muffled as though someone had stuffed cotton wool in her ears. She felt a pair of hands grasp her as she was pulled off the ground.

CHAPTER 64

Harry stared down at his pint, eyes blazing as his fingers tapped manically against the glass.

Samantha felt her heart pounding, a sickness swirling in her stomach. Her eyes darted around the Skull & Feathers. A fire burned in the grate, a shaggy whippet stretched out in front of it on a threadbare rug. Two old men played dominoes nearby, cheeks ruddy from the warmth of the fire.

She returned her gaze to Harry, urging him to look at her. 'Say something then.'

His chest expanded and deflated, his mouth opening and closing as if the words couldn't form themselves.

'All this time, Samantha, everything I've missed.'

'We were so young, Harry. You might think it would have been all birthday parties and trips to the zoo, but it's a lot more than that.'

'I'm not an idiot, Samantha, I understand that.'

Samantha felt her cheeks burn; she knew she was trying to justify a decision she had made that was indefensible. He should have been told. It hurt her to see Harry's crumpled face; he looked like he had aged five years in the last thirty minutes. He had regained his voice now, and Samantha let the inevitable tirade fly at her.

'You thought you could just airbrush me out of your lives, her life, *my* daughter's life. Who the hell do you think you are, Samantha?'

The barmaid looked over, idly drying a pint glass as she watched the two of them. When Harry caught sight of her, he lowered his voice, clutching his ale.

'Did you never think for a moment that I might have wanted to know I had a child? That I might have wanted to be involved for all these years?'

'I wasn't ready for a relationship, and neither were you,' she said, trying to keep her voice steady.

'Maybe not us, but I might have wanted to see Lily. You had no right to make that decision for me. She is half of me too, and I bet she's asked about me more than once.'

Samantha looked down at the table, her mind trying to gloss over those conversations with her daughter.

'What did you tell her? That I was a feckless man? An abuser? What?'

Samantha thought she might throw up right there and then. Lies swirled around her head, but realising the truth would out one way or another, she confessed.

'I-I told her it was a one-night stand and that when I told you about the pregnancy, you went off with someone else.'

Harry shook his head in disbelief.

'Why didn't you stick around here? Surely you'd have been better with your mum's support too?'

Samantha shook her head. 'She wasn't best pleased to find her straight-A student daughter had become pregnant by a teenage tearaway who'd left school at fifteen.'

Harry flushed, the blame bouncing back and forth between them like a ping-pong ball.

'They were already rowing all the time and my news just made everything worse. I couldn't take it, I had to get away. When Dad decided to leave, I chose to go with him.'

'Does your mum see Lily?'

Samantha took a sip of her drink. 'Soon after we left, they divorced. Mum blamed me and I just felt so guilty I decided to get on with my life. I sent the occasional Christmas card and photo, but I just felt it was better to stay away.'

'And not face up to anything?'

Samantha went to argue but it was futile; she knew he was right. She avoided difficult conversations and conflict as much as possible in her private life, and now she had been caught out.

Harry slumped back in his chair, running his hands through his hair. 'Jesus, Samantha. I suppose at least you didn't tell her I'd died — that would make telling her now a little bit more awkward.'

'*You* can't—'

'What? I can't tell her? Are you serious?'

'I didn't mean that, I meant that it should come from me. It'll be easier for her then.'

'Well, I want to be there. I need to tell my side of the story too. The *full* story.'

Samantha nodded; the narrative was no longer in her control, the least she could do was to let him tell Lily his side.

He was about to continue when the door to the pub flew open, the whippet shooting to its feet and cowering beneath the legs of the domino player.

Don tried to catch his breath, bent over with his hands on his knees as he spoke through pants, 'Samantha, it's Lily!'

Samantha stood up at once. 'What is it? Is she OK?'

'She had an accident on her bike. I was driving past and saw the car hit her—'

'A car? Is she OK? She's not . . .'

'She was conscious, broken bones at worst. The ambulances round here take forever so I took her to Longston Peak Hospital.'

'Why didn't you call me?' Samantha said, trying to process the information, then looked down at her phone, remembering she had turned it off to have the difficult chat with Harry.

'I can give you a lift,' said Don.

Harry got his coat and pushed his arms into the sleeves. 'It's OK, Don, I'll drive you, Samantha.'

'Thanks for taking her, Don,' Samantha said, squeezing Don's arm, then rushed off after Harry as the mutt whined from somewhere beneath the table.

Samantha held onto her seat as the Porsche careered down the country lanes, heading out of Nether Dale and towards Longston Peak. From memory she knew there was a hospital there, but doubted it had the facilities to take care of anything more than a sprained wrist or broken toe.

'She doesn't even have a bike,' said Samantha.

Harry shrugged. 'Maybe she's borrowed one from a friend.'

'She doesn't have any, she barely knows anyone apart from the residents and staff.'

She caught Harry looking at her quizzically. 'She prefers the company of older people.'

Harry hit the indicator and they turned into Longston Peak, the largest of the Gatherings villages. Like Nether Dale there was a village green, though this one had a large Christmas tree in the centre with coloured lights, its base protected by low wooden fencing.

'I think it's up there on the left,' said Samantha, pointing ahead.

They pulled into the small car park, the hospital itself more like a large bungalow than a medical facility. Samantha had undone her seat belt and was opening the door before Harry had turned the engine off, running towards the hospital entrance. She flew into reception and up to the desk.

'I'm Lily's mum.'

The woman with a pinched mouth and thin blonde hair peered up at her from behind thin spectacles.

'Lily?'

'Rawley, Lily Rawley. She came in after falling off her bike.'

The woman tapped at her computer screen using two fingers, waiting for the information to load. Harry joined Samantha at the desk, his breath heavy.

'Is she OK?' he asked.

Samantha didn't answer, her mind focused on the computer that slowly flickered to life.

'Ah yes, Lily Rawley. Came in about an hour or so ago?'

'Yes, that's her. Is she OK, which ward is she on?' Samantha looked around for a board with the wards listed, but there was none.

'Discharged herself,' the woman said, giving Samantha a satisfied smile.

'What? How could she, she's only fifteen! Well, sixteen today — it's her birthday.'

'She will have had an adult with her to do that, unless she lied about her age on admission.'

The woman scanned the screen with her finger, mumbling the notes in front of her.

'Valerie Delway, her guardian.'

'She's not her guardian! Christ, do you even check these things?'

'Valerie?' said Harry.

The woman shrugged. 'We can only go on what we're told and—'

Samantha didn't wait for her to finish; she grabbed Harry's coat sleeve and dragged him back out to the car park. She tried Valerie's number as they swerved through the winding village roads, but the signal wouldn't let the call connect.

Harry spun right into the drive of a Victorian villa-style house.

'I'm sure this is her house. I had to drop her off once, when she was sick.'

Samantha ran out of the car and banged on the door. When there was no answer she tried the handle, but the door was locked. She moved to the large bay window and peered into the darkness, her hands against the glass.

'Any signs of life?' Harry asked.

Samantha shook her head and ran round to the side of the house looking for a way in. A wooden gate stood open. Harry followed her through to the garden. Balloons dragged across the wet ground and a black cat pawed at the lefto-ver food, jumping away when it caught sight of Samantha. Samantha picked up a glass and sniffed the contents, wincing at the strong herbal smell. There was a cake on the edge of the table, its iced lettering distorted by the rain, only just legible.

Happy Birthday Lily x

The gate creaked as it swung back and forth. Samantha noticed something on the ground and bent to pick it up.

'It's Lily's phone.'

Harry ran to her, looking down at the home screen, a photo of Lily and Sophie.

Samantha snatched it from him, looking at the phone. 'She was here.'

'Before the accident?' said Harry.

Samantha picked up a bedraggled paper streamer. 'She had some kind of party — I knew nothing about this.'

She went to the back door and pushed it open. The house was in darkness, the smell of burned-out candles overwhelming. She ran up the stairs, cursing as she kicked a tea light that rat-tled down the stairs to the hallway. Samantha passed the toilet, burst into the next room and turned the light on, a single bulb swinging from the ceiling shining scant light on the room.

'Jesus, Harry.'

Harry joined her, his face dropping. The two of them walked into the room, trying to dodge the hundreds of extin-guished candles scattered about the floor and surfaces. There was a single table at the end, covered with a purple velvet cloth. Samantha picked up a silver goblet, her face distorted in the reflection. A small bone-handled knife lay next to it, alongside vials of herbs and some kind of animal skull. Then she noticed the photographs. Samantha recognised the girl in the first: it was the same young, carefree smile she had seen immortalised in paint in Annie's room. Emily Dawson, the murdered girl. Another photo stood next to it, another blonde-haired girl of a similar age whose image caused an overwhelming sense of sickness in Samantha's stomach — it was Lily.

'What's this?' Harry said, pointing at a large symbol on the floor.

Samantha clutched Lily's photograph, turning to follow his gaze: it was the familiar circle and lines of the triangle.

'Where is she?' Samantha sobbed.

Then she remembered Bert's words: the first Shuttleworth girl born was cursed. She still didn't believe in witchcraft, but she knew enough to believe in real evil.

'Harry, we have to find her!' Samantha cried.

'Let's go back to Hallow Croft, Valerie might have taken her back to your flat.'

'Lily has had a road accident, she might have broken bones, and Valerie has discharged her and taken her. Why would she do that? And why have a party for her without telling me?'

Harry shrugged. 'We'll ask her when we find her, come on.'

Samantha let herself be pulled out of the house and into Harry's car. As he zipped through the narrow lanes, she found herself gazing up at the perfectly round moon. What had Aparna said?

Beware the full moon.

Harry's Porsche pulled up outside the main entrance and Samantha shot out, pushing through the main doors and into the reception. Mrs Potter was calling out from the day room. Bert was waiting by her office door, demanding to see the management, and several of the residents were wandering back and forth as if not knowing where they were going.

'Have you seen Valerie?' asked Samantha, shaking Caroline's shoulders.

'I don't know, she might have been here earlier,' the care assistant stuttered, her eyes blinking as if caught in a blinding light.

'What about Lily?'

'No, I only came on an hour ago and it's been madness here ever since. I know they say the full moon sends everyone doolally, but this evening is something else.'

Samantha looked up at the board, lights flashing in all the rooms. She took her phone out again and jabbed at the screen.

'You've reached Valerie Delway, I'm not able to take your call at the moment. Please leave a message after the beep.'

'Valerie, it's Samantha, have you got Lily with you? Could you call me as soon as you get this?'

Samantha unlocked the flat door and ran in, followed by Harry. She pushed open Lily's bedroom door, noticing a mess of clothes and small bottles everywhere, then dashed into the living room. Her birthday presents remained unopened, the balloons now gently bobbing across the carpet.

'She's not here,' she called to Harry.

Harry was in Lily's room, staring at the pictures of pop-pet dolls and strange symbols.

'Yeah, I know,' Samantha said, seeing the shock on his face.

'Come on, let's try Dad, he might know.'

Samantha nodded, trying to suppress the rising fear that shook her body. Lily would be fine, Valerie would probably just be giving her some herbs to try and heal her and prove a point. Samantha knew Valerie didn't like her, that her authority irked the woman, but Lily? From the moment they had arrived she had gone out of her way to take her under her wing and spend time with her. There was no reason to believe she would hurt her.

'Come on, we'll find her,' said Harry.

Samantha couldn't help but notice his pained expression didn't match the calm words coming out of his mouth.

* * *

Harry burst into the cottage, followed by Samantha. Jonathan and Diane were in the living room reading.

'Whatever is it?' said Diane, letting her magazine drop to her lap.

Harry spoke first. 'Have you seen Lily and Valerie?'

Diane shook her head and looked to Jonathan, who thought for a moment before responding. 'Not since this morning. Valerie was taking Bert out for a walk round the gardens. Why, what's the matter?'

'Lily was hit by a car.'

Diane shot up from her chair, the magazine swishing to the floor as she clutched at the diamond cross on her necklace.

'Is she OK?'

'We don't know, we can't find her. She was at the hospital and Valerie discharged her.'

'Valerie? Why would she do that?' Jonathan said.

Samantha noticed Diane looked pale.

'Diane?'

'Now don't start, Diane,' Jonathan warned.

'Start what?' demanded Samantha.

The room fell silent, a war of wills erupting as Jonathan dared Diane to speak. Diane looked from her husband to Samantha.

'She deserves to know—'

'It's rubbish, Diane!' Jonathan shouted, his anger startling Samantha, 'And these ridiculous rumours could destroy us — you have to stop.'

'Tell us, Diane,' pleaded Samantha. 'Whatever it is, it might help make sense of it all.'

Diane took a deep breath. 'From the minute I first moved here I had a bad feeling. Everyone just said it was moving from a city to village life, but I know there's something bad coming and it's something to do with that Annie Dawson woman.'

'What do you mean?' said Samantha, impatient for her to get to the point.

'Jonathan's always had a soft spot for Annie, feels sorry for her despite what he's been told.'

Jonathan interjected, 'And you've always had a *weak* spot for idle gossip.'

'What has this got to do with Valerie and Lily? Will somebody please tell us what's going on so we can find my daughter?' She felt Harry's eyes burn into her at the use of *my*. She looked back at him — now wasn't the time.

'There's a curse on this place,' Diane continued, looking at Harry. 'Your dad won't admit it and he's hidden it from you, but Annie has something to do with it.'

'There's nothing to admit to, it's poppycock,' said Jonathan. 'The poor woman had a terrible loss and the village saw fit to demonise her for it. I may have been away at school for most of the time, but I know a fairy tale when I hear it. The poor woman can barely remember her own name these days.'

'What kind of curse?' Harry said.

'I don't know the full details, nobody really does except those involved at the time. If I were you,' urged Diane, 'I'd speak to Annie. She's probably got them both holed up in her room.'

Jonathan rolled his eyes to the heavens, 'Oh, for pity's sake, Diane.'

Samantha felt a shiver through her bones. Her mind went back to the night of the magic show, Annie's apparent fixation with Lily. What if she had seen Lily fall and some-how persuaded Valerie to bring her to her room and . . . Her head hurt with the insanity of it all. She just wanted her daughter in her arms again.

'None of it should affect you anyway,' he said. 'If I remember rightly, the so-called curse wasn't put on just any-one, it was the first-born girl of the Shuttleworths, and as Harry doesn't have any children yet—'

Samantha snapped her head to face Harry; he met her eyes.

'What is it?' said Diane. 'You both look like you've seen a ghost.'

CHAPTER 65

Harry paused by Annie's door as Samantha entered. When she saw Annie was in bed, she gestured for Harry to follow her.

The room was lit by a small lamp, its bunny-rabbit base in-keeping with the rest of the childlike furniture. Annie was lying on her bed staring at the ceiling, mumbling frantically to herself as a cold wind blew in through the open window. It was useless. Jonathan was right, Annie was barely conscious of the world around her most of the time, how was she going to help now? Samantha exhaled and turned to leave with Harry.

A guttural sound carried across the room and Samantha and Harry spun round to see Annie was now sitting up, her back against the wall. Her pale eyes stared at Samantha.

'I told you to leave,' she said, her voice cracked and dry.

Samantha's eyes darted around the room, unable to move. She felt stuck to the spot, unnerved by the woman in front of her.

Annie's eyes slowly moved to Harry. 'The father?'

'How—'

'Lily's in danger, Samantha, she has been since the day she was born.'

'What do you mean, Annie? How is she in danger? Valerie's with her and she likes Lily.'

'She doesn't *like* Lily, she needs Lily.'

'*Needs* her?'

'I tried to stop it, many times. To take back the curse, but Valerie is stronger, her magic . . . darker.'

'I went to her house. I saw the altar and the symbol. I don't believe—'

'Then you had better start believing, Samantha, because only then can you save her.'

'From what? Where is she?'

'You know about the murder?' Annie rasped.

Samantha looked up to the oil painting. 'Yes, and I'm sorry for your loss, but I don't understand what it has to do with me and Lily.'

Annie blinked her eyes slowly, taking a laboured breath, her ribcage dramatically rising and falling.

'The curse . . .' her voice faded with her breath.

That word was beginning to chip at Samantha. 'Annie, what is the curse?'

Annie looked at the two of them, trying to hold her body up, taking a breath that seemed to give her renewed energy.

'After Emily was murdered by *his* grandfather,' she jabbed a crooked finger at Harry, 'I wanted justice. But it seemed that justice wasn't for the likes of me and Emily.' She took a painful breath.

'So what happened?' Samantha asked impatiently. 'What did you do?'

Annie turned her head to the window, staring out towards the grounds.

'I stopped the curse,' she said, looking back to Samantha. 'Eventually. I knew how to reverse it.'

Samantha felt relief coursing through her. She turned to Harry, reaching out to hold his hand, expecting to see him mirroring her own feelings. But his expression wasn't one of happiness.

'Then the so-called curse isn't in place now?' he asked warily.

Annie's head trembled as she turned to look at him, her eyes narrowing.

'I wasn't the only one deeply affected by Emily's death. Valerie loved Emily almost as much as I did, and when she found out that I had reversed the curse she took things into her own hands. Valerie put it in place again, but stronger.'

Annie looked her straight in the eyes, her own glazed with tears. 'The first-born daughter of Henry Shuttleworth's line will die before midnight on the nearest full moon to her sixteenth birthday.'

Samantha felt Harry's hand clench her shoulder. 'Tonight.'

Samantha stiffened, drawing her body upright.

Outside, the sky had darkened and moving clouds brought the round moon out of hiding.

'Yes,' Annie said simply. She turned to the window. 'It might be too late. She'll have taken her to the same place the curse was set — to the standing stones.'

Samantha thought back to the orange glow she had seen that night, the rising smoke. A fire.

As Samantha and Harry left, Annie called out, 'She isn't just avenging Emily's death now, but her mother's too.'

CHAPTER 66

1976

Poppet clutched Annie's coat as she walked down the stairs. 'Go back to your room, Poppet,' Annie said, not making eye contact with the girl.

'Don't do it,' Poppet spat.

'Do as you're told or I'll send you to live with your aunt and uncle.'

Poppet let go and stepped back. 'You wouldn't.'

Annie sighed. 'No, I wouldn't . . . Look, I know you don't want this, but trust me, it's for the best for everyone. It's time to make peace and move on — the village has been under one curse or another for too long.'

Poppet didn't answer, just backed away into Emily's room. Moments later, the sound of a ball bouncing against the wall.

Annie grabbed her keys and left.

* * *

Ginny took the thin, wet doll from the ground, its body caked in dirt. She handed it to Annie. 'Take care of it, Annie.

You must keep her safe until the end of your life to keep the curse reversed.'

Annie held the doll like a frail bird, the yellow hair now blackened and unravelled. Martha, Corinne, Donna and Aparna gathered around her, their arms holding each other as the clouds above swam across the moon, revealing a sliver of light that glittered in the night.

CHAPTER 67

1980

Valerie set down a handpicked bunch of flowers on Kevin's grave that lay in the shadow of Nether Dale church.

Annie smiled. 'They're beautiful, Pop— sorry, Valerie. It's still hard to get used to after all these years.'

Valerie ran a finger across the groove of the letters, *Beloved Husband*, a smear of greenish slime coming away from the stone. She stood, her dark hair pulled back in a ponytail, thin lips painted red.

'I can't believe you're eighteen, Valerie, it's a special day.'

Sergeant Pickford walked by the graveyard in uniform; Annie turned at the sound of footsteps.

'Hi, Annie,' she called.

'Hi, Renee. It's Valerie's birthday today, eighteen! Would you believe it?'

Renee gave a thin smile. 'Happy birthday, Valerie.'

Valerie lifted her head from the grave. 'Have you caught him yet?'

'*Valerie*,' Annie pleaded. 'Not now.'

Renee gave an apologetic look. 'Nothing new, I'm afraid. Enjoy your birthday, Valerie.'

Valerie sneered as the policewoman walked away. 'Bloody useless.'

'What did you expect? It's been eight years since Emily and five since your mum. If they haven't done it by now . . .' She shrugged. 'Come on, let's not spoil your birthday talking about him. Let's get you back, I've got a surprise for you.' She put her arm through Valerie's and led her from the graveyard.

* * *

'Happy birthday!' Annie turned from the kitchen counter, holding an iced cake with eighteen lit candles, shielding them from a draught that came in under the kitchen door.

Annie placed the cake in front of Valerie. 'Go on then, blow them out and make a wish.'

Valerie took a deep breath and blew the candles out, then closed her eyes tightly. When she opened them again a slow smile curled on her lips. Annie watched her closely, a feeling of unease at the cold look in Valerie's eyes.

* * *

Valerie took a framed picture down from a shelf and held it above the cardboard box that was stuffed with clothes and books. News that she could now move back to her mum's house was bittersweet. She would miss Annie, the way she cared for her like she was her own daughter and tried to teach her the ways of the coven. Valerie ran a finger over the photograph she held, her mother's beauty as she cradled her as a baby. Her father, now crudely reattached with sticky tape, stood by her side. She wondered if her mother had ever truly gotten over him. She could have burned his image, thrown him in the bin. Instead she had kept it with her grimoire and everything else she held precious. The coven thought that if they kept him out of her life then he couldn't influence her, but his blood swirled through her like snakes in a pit. Valerie only had to close her eyes and she could feel his magic in her, not that of the coven, and it felt far more powerful.

She put the photograph in the box and covered it with a swath of hessian. Something clicked in her mind and she rose, sneaking across the landing to Annie's room. Valerie knelt on the snagged carpet and reached under the bed, pulling out a large wooden box. When she opened it the scent of rosemary filled the air, causing her to recoil: a protective herb. She dug her hand in, through the velvet-encased goblet and bell, and pulled out the thin poppet doll she had made for her mother. Annie had washed its hair carefully and now the yellow wool was only slightly dull. She felt its belly, the hard edges of Henry Shuttleworth's cufflinks still safely encased.

Valerie put it in her pocket and returned the box underneath the bed. In her room she packed the last of her things before taking it all downstairs where Annie was waiting, a tear in her eye.

'I'm going to miss having you around. Are you sure you're old enough to live alone? You'll miss my shepherd's pie, you know.'

'I'll come back, Annie. You'll be sick of me before you know it.'

Annie sighed, wiping her cheek with her sleeve. 'Anytime, Valerie, if you need anything at all.'

Annie hugged the awkward girl, her body stiff and unyielding. She had never come to like or reciprocate displays of affection. Valerie tried to look regretful and sad, but inside a flame was growing, burning within. Now she would be free to work her own rituals and spells away from Annie's watchful eyes.

Now she could put the curse back on the Shuttleworth family.

CHAPTER 68

Lily blinked through the flames of the fire that raged before her eyes, her cheeks burning from the heat. She looked down to the pale blue satin dress, her feet bare in front of her. She had been bound to one of the standing stones in a seated position, the icy cold rock digging into her back. The light from the moon shone down over the trees, throwing slivers of light on the circle of twigs that had been woven around the fire.

She tried to pull away from the stone, but the ropes were fastened tightly and dug into her skin.

She called out, her throat dry and scratchy, 'Who's there?'

Lily caught sight of the cat skull within the circle, the night shadows drawing down the dark hollows of the eye sockets. The symbol she had drawn so many times was painted on its forehead in black charcoal. Footsteps were close by, twigs and leaves cracking beneath feet. Lily swung her head around to see who was coming. She began to tremble despite the heat of the fire as six dark figures appeared from the woodlands, each wearing a heavy black cloak with a hood that fell forward, hiding their faces in shadows.

Lily trembled as the figures took their place around the outside of the stones. One by one they let their cloaks fall to the ground to reveal their naked bodies. One of the women reached down and picked up a thorned crown adorned with antlers. She lifted it to the air as the final figure let her hood fall back, keeping her gown in place.

'*Valerie?*' Lily muttered, unable to raise her voice beyond the crackle of the fire.

Valerie's face glowed orange against the flames, her lips a thin line and arched eyebrows exaggerated by charcoal. She did not look at Lily, but down at the flames as the other women began to dance around the circle, each lost in their own meditative state as Valerie began to chant in a voice Lily didn't recognise.

'I bind this spell, be mine, be mine.
I bind this spell be mine, be mine.
Light and dark are turning,
Death be in the burning.'

Valerie held the blonde stitch-eyed doll up to the sky, her painted nails clutching it tightly. She took out a tuft of hair from her pocket and bound it around the doll's neck. Lily suddenly remembered the torn hair on her head that day at Valerie's house. She wanted to scream, was desperate to scream, but fear numbed her body. The dancing women began to chant as they continued to curl around the stones, lost in another place.

'When the moon winds blow,
Round and round and round we go.
When the moon winds blow,
Round and round and round we go.'

Valerie brought the doll to her lips and called out again above the women's chants.

'By my witch's breath and by the fire of witches' lore,
Send through the flaming door.
By my witch's breath and by sands of time,
This spell is mine and mine all mine.'

'Please stop!' Lily managed to call out, her pleas ignored by the women, whose eyes became white as they rolled back in their heads.

Valerie looked her straight in the eyes across the flames that licked the cold air. A small cry left Lily's lips as she recognised Debby, who handed Valerie two small silver goblets, the flickering orange flames reflecting the metal. Valerie held the drinks in the air, chanting,

'Halt now, coven, and let the spell be cast
Have us receive our vengeance at last.'

Lily noticed a figure behind Valerie, standing in the woods. Partially hidden by the trees, it was only when the light of the fire illuminated her face that she could see it was Aparna. Lily watched as the woman held her hands to her chest, her eyes closed and mouth speaking rapidly, words unheard.

The other women stopped dancing and faced the fire as Valerie moved forward, the doll held out in front of her just above the flames.

'We repeat nine times to cast the spell,
And swear to Baphomet we will never tell.'

The women began to chant together once, twice, three times.

'I weave, I bind this spell be mine.
I weave I bind this spell be mine.
I weave I bind this spell be mine.'

As the witches continued the chant, Valerie took a sip from one of the goblets, wincing as the liquid slid down her gullet. She walked forward to Lily and held the other goblet to her lips.

'Drink.'

Lily spat the drink out on the ground. Valerie held her mouth open, pouring it in as the girl coughed and spluttered.

As the coven reached the sixth chant she heard footsteps running through the woods. Was this the devil coming to take her?

Her thoughts were interrupted by the wind viciously blowing through the fire, the flames almost horizontal. The women stopped, then they heard voices calling out from the woods.

'Lily! Where are you?'

Lily gasped, her eyes searching the trees, trying to find her mum in the darkness. She took a deep breath and called out as loudly as she could, tears running down her face.

'Mum, I'm here! Please help me!'

The witches looked at each other, wide-eyed, then crouched to the ground, gathering up their magical tools. Debby watched them, going to get her own things, then standing back again, seemingly pulled between leaving with the other women and staying with Valerie.

'Keep going!' Valerie roared.

The witches didn't acknowledge Valerie's pleas; instead they ran from the stones and disappeared into the darkness of the woods, their cloaks trailing behind them. Debby took one last look at Valerie before following the coven into the night.

CHAPTER 69

Valerie opened her mouth to shout again, but froze, her hand reaching to her throat. Her eyes began to bulge as she choked up pale bile. Samantha ran into the clearing.

'Lily!' Samantha screamed, running towards her daughter.

Lily shook as her mum untied the knots that bound her, the girl collapsing into her arms. Samantha held her tightly, until Lily was able to pull away from the stone. Lily tried to look over to where Valerie lay, but Samantha turned her away.

Harry rushed over to Samantha and Lily, taking his coat off and placing it around the girl's trembling shoulders. Seeing Lily was safe with Harry, Samantha walked slowly over to Valerie, all the time checking to make sure she didn't make any sudden moves. When she spotted the trickle of blood running from her mouth to the ground, she knew she wouldn't be getting up again.

Samantha called the police and gave them all the details she could, which were scant to say the least.

'Do we need to stay . . . with the body, I mean?' said Harry.

Samantha shook her head. 'I'm not staying here a moment longer.'

Harry nodded. 'Come on then, let's get you both home.'

CHAPTER 70

Diane had run a bath for Lily, and Samantha now sat at the side of her daughter, the bubbles of lavender foam overflowing down the sides of the tub. They'd gone to the cottage so that they were not alone; Harry had nipped to their flat to grab Lily's nightclothes and toiletries. Samantha had checked Lily over as she got undressed, but other than a badly sprained ankle it was mostly grazes and bruises. She was happy that with rest Lily would recover physically. Mentally, however, she had no idea.

Now Samantha sponged soap across her back, the red indents from the stone criss-crossed over her skin like ancient hieroglyphs, her hair hanging in wet tendrils. She hadn't spoken since they had returned to Jonathan and Diane's cottage and Samantha was in no mood to rush her. To have her back was enough.

When Lily had dried herself and put her pyjamas on, Samantha tucked her into bed and sat on the edge, stroking her cheek. Lily looked up at her mum, her eyelids slowly closing.

Samantha crept out of the room, leaving the door open in case Lily called out. She side-stepped the camp bed Diane had set up for her. She could have laid down on it right then and slept for the rest of the night, but she needed to make sense of what had happened and, perhaps more importantly, what would happen next. She could hear Harry telling them about the night as she approached the door.

All eyes were on her as she entered the lounge.

'How is she doing?' Harry asked, a coffee clutched in his hand.

'She's asleep.'

Diane held out a glass of wine, but Samantha shook her head. 'No thanks, I need to be able to drive in case Lily takes a turn for the worse or something.'

'Turn for the worse? I thought she was OK?' said Jonathan.

'She's just been tied to a rock in the dead of winter by a mad woman, who she then watched being poisoned by her own hand. Poison that was likely meant for Lily.'

Jonathan blushed. 'Quite. I knew Valerie was a bit eccentric, but not this, not her.'

'Well, she's not the only one. There were a group of them. They scuttled like rats deserting a sinking ship when I arrived.'

'I told you, Nether Dale is like something from medieval times. We should have stayed in Sheffield, not come here,' Diane said.

'I thought you wanted to live in Hallow Croft? In the house, I mean,' Samantha said.

'Did I heck as like,' Diane scoffed. 'As soon as I moved here I was told about the murder; gossiping locals couldn't wait to let me know. And the rumours about Jonathan's dad.'

Jonathan stared into his whiskey glass as Diane continued. 'No. If we had to be here to make a business, I didn't want to be completely onsite. It was my choice to move into this cottage, not Jonathan's.'

Harry raised his eyebrows at this revelation.

'Did nobody suspect Valerie was convinced she was a witch? Weren't there signs of delusion somewhere along the way?' asked Samantha. 'Did nothing come up in background checks?'

'*Delusions* of witchcraft?' said Diane, her eyes narrowing. 'Did you not see it with your own eyes?'

'Everything I saw could be explained away by a good psychologist. It's not as if there were flying broomsticks and magic wands on show. Just mad women dancing naked around a fire wanting to please an evil woman who, for some reason, wanted to kill our daughter.'

Jonathan's head snapped up. '*Our* daughter?' He looked to Harry for an explanation.

Harry shifted in his seat. 'Samantha and I . . . Well, back when I was at school we went out for a bit and, well, Lily was the result.'

Diane looked at Jonathan, both open-mouthed.

'The curse, you see, the one you told us about — it was meant for Lily,' Harry explained.

'I've got a granddaughter,' Jonathan stated. 'I can't believe it.'

'How long have you kept this from us?' Diane asked.

Samantha looked to the floor. 'I only told Harry today. Obviously I had no idea he was your son until Christmas lunch. I would never have come here if I'd known.'

'It's a long story,' Harry said. 'Maybe one for another night.'

Samantha looked at him gratefully.

She was about to relax into the chair when something occurred to her.

Aparna.

She had been in the woods too, a confused old woman out in the cold.

'I need to go and check something in the home,' she said.

Harry went to stand up, but Samantha waved him back into his seat.

'No. You stay here in case Lily wakes up. You can always call me if it's a real emergency. My phone's turned on.'

Harry sat back down and, with that, Samantha ran back out into the stormy night.

CHAPTER 71

The room was empty, Aparna's bed still made. Samantha called one of the night staff over. 'Have you seen Aparna?'

'She was taken for a bath about half an hour ago. She'd been wandering, see, and—'

Samantha relaxed, relieved to hear she was at least back inside Hallow Croft.

'Where is she now?'

'Is she not in her room?'

Samantha shook her head. 'No, I've just checked.'

'Well, she's not in the day room, I've just come from there. Shall I help you look?'

'If you don't mind. You check the rooms on this floor, I'll look upstairs.'

The woman did as she was told and began knocking on doors, quietly calling through. Samantha went up the stairs, taking them two at a time. Most residents were asleep. As she passed Bert's open door, he called out, 'Are you doing night shifts now, Matron?'

'Just looking for Aparna, have you seen her?'

'Try Annie's room, I saw her heading that way a bit ago.'

Oh, God. Samantha glanced down the corridor to Annie's room. She suddenly regretted reintroducing the two of them if it now meant Aparna was in danger. She ran to the door and knocked. No answer. She pushed the door open to find Annie lying in her bed, Aparna sitting next to her, stroking Annie's forehead.

'She's fine, Annie, she's fine,' Aparna kept repeating.

'Aparna, are you OK?' Samantha said, rushing to her side.

The old woman turned at the sound of her voice but didn't quite make eye contact. 'The girl? Is she well?'

'Yes, Aparna. I'm sure it'll take a while for her to get over the shock, but at least she's safe now,' Samantha said. 'But I was worried about you, what were you doing in the woods?'

Aparna looked to Annie, who squeezed Aparna's hand gently.

'I went to help Annie.'

'What do you mean? Annie has been here all the time.'

'Exactly, Annie is weak. So I went in her place, to try to stop it.'

Samantha felt like she was in some weird abstract play where all the parts were mixed up and nothing made sense.

'You still don't believe, do you?' Aparna said.

'Believe in what? Curses? No, Aparna, I don't believe.'

'Even after what you saw with your own eyes?'

Samantha put a hand on Aparna's arm. 'Aparna, I saw a mad woman doing a terrible thing to a child.'

Annie sighed, her chest rising and falling rapidly. Aparna turned to her, her hands holding Annie's. 'Annie, what's wrong?'

'Something . . . someone, it's not done yet . . . I-I can see something.'

Samantha lifted her fingers to Annie's neck, feeling her pulse as it weakened beneath her thin skin. 'I'm going to call for the doctor.'

'What is it, Annie?' Aparna begged.

'There's another in her place.'

'What does she mean, "there's another"?'

Aparna shook her head. 'I don't know, I—'

'Get . . . me,' Annie took a thin breath, 'the scrying mirror.'

Aparna went to Annie's dressing table and felt her way across the ornaments and teddies, until her hand closed around a black disc that sat on a small stand. She brought it to Annie.

Samantha watched as the two women joined hands and rubbed the shiny black surface, both repeating words over and over again.

'Show me the face.

Show me the face.'

Samantha watched as the reflection of Debby's face appeared in the black mirror. She spun around. Debby was standing in the door.

'All OK in here, Matron?'

'Debby? What are you doing here, you're not working, are you?'

'No, Matron. I just came to collect something I left in my locker.'

'The girl's not safe,' Annie cried. *'The girl is not safe.'*

CHAPTER 72

Samantha left instructions with the night sister to call her with any updates on Annie. Any other time she would have stayed, even when not officially working, but her priority was Lily right now.

Jonathan, Diane and Harry were all still in the lounge. They had been joined by a policeman, who stood by the fireplace sipping tea from a floral mug.

'Do we know who the other women were?' Samantha asked, searching his face for signs of success.

The policeman shook his head. 'No. We searched the area, but there was no one. The body,' he cleared his throat, 'Valerie Delway, has been taken to the morgue. Hopefully we'll understand a bit more once the autopsy has been carried out.'

'I'd feel a lot better if you found out who they were. Have you been to Valerie's house?' asked Samantha.

'My next port of call,' said the officer, putting the mug down on the table. 'Thanks for that, Diane.'

'You need to find them,' Samantha insisted. 'There's only two hours until midnight.'

The room looked at her quizzically and Samantha flushed. 'I know it sounds silly, but there's some kind of madness, a superstition here. Whatever it is, for some reason Lily is at the centre of it. I just want to make sure it stops tonight.'

The sergeant nodded. 'Of course, we'll do our best to round the women up.' The policeman picked up his pen and pad from the table. 'I'll let you know if I find anything, Matron. In the meantime, keep an eye on your daughter, sounds like she's had a hell of a night.'

'Yes, just a bit,' said Samantha, trying to prevent her eyes from rolling at the understatement.

The cottage door opened. A wind chime tinkled in the wind before it closed again.

Samantha turned to the others. 'This place is fucking nuts.'

'Calm down, Samantha,' said Harry.

'I'm sorry, Harry, but you saw your daughter tied to a rock in the middle of the woods, surrounded by lunatics, and you want me to be *calm*? And what about all that *so-called* medicine Valerie was giving her? She could have been poisoned to death.'

'Maybe Lily was enticed by all the witchcraft stuff here. I saw the drawings she's been doing; maybe she got involved in something and it all went too far?'

Samantha narrowed her eyes at him, trying to resist an urge to tip the half-empty bottle of Portuguese wine over his head.

'Diane? You don't think something bad happened?'

Diane avoided her glance. 'I think we've all had a long night and it's probably best we go to bed.'

Samantha gasped. 'Right, well, OK then, let's just forget tonight ever happened, shall we? We can all wake up tomorrow and carry on.'

'It's not that, it's . . .' Harry took a moment before continuing, 'If there's any kind of scandal here, then . . . then we might have to close the home. If Valerie has accidentally poisoned herself then it's one thing, but to suggest any kind of cult, mass hysteria . . .'

Jonathan nodded. 'We can't have any more scandal at Hallow Croft. The residents would be taken out and we'd have to sell up. It will be all our jobs, the villa and inheritance gone. Which now includes Lily.'

Samantha chewed on her lip, her hands firmly on her hips as she leaned towards Harry.

'Isn't this kind of cover-up what started it all in the first place? Nobody doing anything? Are you going to let that happen again?'

'Samantha, for Christ's sake, you don't even believe in all the supernatural stuff, so don't let it ruin us all. At least it will have scared Lily off it now.'

Samantha looked to the door. 'Did anyone check on her while I was gone?'

'I checked on her half an hour ago, fast asleep still.'

Samantha ran up the steep staircase, bobbing her head to miss the beam that ran across the ceiling at the top. It took a moment for her to remember which room Lily was in and she ran to the door.

'Lily, are you OK?'

The bed was empty, the covers thrown back and the sweaty imprint of her daughter's body still visible on the top sheet. She screamed at the top of her voice, 'Harry!'

Harry was by her side within seconds, looking at the empty bed. 'What the—'

A toilet flushed at the end of the landing, and they looked at each other with knowing relief.

'Thank God,' said Samantha.

The bathroom door opened and Lily appeared, her eyes half-closed, sleepily walking towards the bedroom. Samantha went to straighten the bed, Harry waiting at the door for Lily and guiding her back into the room.

'See, nothing to worry about, she'll be fine,' he said.

Samantha helped her into the bed, tucking her in again. She looked up at Harry. 'Diane's changed her tune. The fear of losing the villa must be strong.'

Harry sighed. 'As much as she hates living here, she'd hate a cramped house in some city more.'

Samantha was too tired to argue.

'I'm going to sleep now, wake me if you hear anything from the police, won't you.'

'Will do,' said Harry. 'Night, Samantha.'

Samantha took her shoes, jumper and jeans off and crawled into the sleeping bag on the blow-up mattress by Lily's bed.

She made sure the volume was turned up on her phone, her eyes lingering on her screensaver: a picture of her holding a baby Lily in her arms, kissing her head. Putting the phone down, she squirmed about in her sleeping bag trying to get comfortable, hoping that with daylight some sense would come of the last few hours.

When Samantha woke up it was still dark. The sound of tapping had brought her out of a fitful sleep. She grabbed her phone. *11.15 p.m.* She twisted around in her bed, looking at the window. Tiny pebbles hit the glass again and she went across to look out.

'What the hell?'

Aparna and Annie were standing side by side in their nightdresses waving up to her. Rain was beating down, the wind blowing their hair behind them. Samantha blinked, feeling sure they would disappear when she looked again, but no.

Aparna gestured for her to come down, a finger to her lips.

Samantha scrambled on the floor for her jeans and pulled them on, ready to take the two women back to their rooms, when she noticed Lily's empty bed and the open bedroom door.

Samantha banged her fists on Harry's door and Finn began to bark downstairs. She didn't wait for him to reply, instead she ran down the stairs and outside.

'What's going on, Aparna? Annie? Do you know where Lily is?'

Aparna nodded and pointed to the sky and the moon. 'They have her.'

'Who, Aparna? Those women from the stones?'

Aparna nodded.

'Where have they gone? Back to the stones?'

'Valerie's house,' Annie said. 'The stones have lost their power now.'

There was a bark. The three turned to see Finn bounding towards them from the cottage.

'Jesus, not now,' Samantha said.

'We need to go to Valerie's house,' Aparna urged.

Samantha fished in her pocket for her car keys. Finn pushed at her legs with his long snout.

'Not now, Finn.' She pushed him away. 'Go home.'

Samantha opened the back door of her car and Finn leaped in, his body filling half of the seat. Aparna put her frail hand on the dog's back and got in next to him. Annie somehow found the strength to open the passenger door and let herself in.

As they drove down the road towards the village, Samantha looked in the rear-view mirror, at the strange image of Finn peering out of the window and Aparna next to him, muttering to herself. For a moment Samantha wondered if this day was payback for every bad decision she had ever made.

'Here,' Annie called out, pointing left as the satnav announced that they had reached their destination.

Samantha pulled up on the curb outside, not wanting the headlights to alert anyone to their arrival. The three women got out of the car, followed by Finn, who jumped out before Samantha had a chance to lock him in. The dog went ahead, sniffing the ground and cocking his leg on the low wall outside.

If Samantha thought that she would be the one responsible for the two older women, she was proved wrong as both walked ahead of her towards the front of the house. Candlelight flickered from every window, shadows dancing against the walls inside. She followed as Annie and Aparna walked up the steps, hand in hand. Annie paused for a moment, eyes closed, and placed her palm against the door. Aparna dropped her head as if in prayer.

'We must be quick,' Samantha urged.

'Shh,' Aparna whispered. 'We need to do this right.'

Samantha looked at her phone: *11.30 p.m.* Then up to the bright full moon.

Beneath Annie's hand, the door opened. They walked into the hallway, shrouded in darkness but for the flickers of orange light that came from the rooms to the right. A staircase lay straight ahead, at the top of which came muffled chants and distorted voices. Aparna turned to Samantha and whispered, 'Do nothing, leave it to Annie.'

Samantha followed as Aparna's feet disappeared up the stairs and out of view. A cat exited the kitchen, its amber eyes watching the three women walk slowly upstairs. The chanting grew louder with each step. Samantha's heart ached to find her daughter, but for once she wasn't going to be a bull in a china shop. She needed to trust that Annie knew what she was doing. That she was leading them to her daughter.

Samantha caught up with them at the top of the stairs. To their right, the door to the room where she had found the altar was now closed.

Annie turned to Aparna and whispered something in her ear. Samantha watched as Aparna took out a familiar black stone from her pocket and held it tightly in her palm, hissing a prayer-like verse. The two old women held hands tightly. Another cat appeared, hissing and arching its back, warning them to keep away.

With her free hand Annie pushed out her palm to the cat and spoke in a language Samantha didn't recognise. The cat retreated to where it had come from, padding backwards along the landing, all the time watching as if waiting for their next move. The chanting behind the black door quietened. Samantha felt her heart race, but the two women before her remained calm, even as the black door opened.

Samantha tried to look in, but Aparna blocked her view.

'Is Lily in there?' Samantha asked, her voice now weak.

Neither Annie nor Aparna answered. They only walked through the doorway, their small bodies disappearing into the darkness. Samantha stepped forward to push her way in, but no sooner had she reached the door than it closed. Though not before she caught a glimpse of her daughter lying in the middle of the room surrounded by hooded figures.

CHAPTER 73

Samantha hit the black door with her fist. 'Let me in! I want my daughter!'

As she lifted her fist to knock again, the door opened and she ran in, the sight before her stopping her in her tracks.

Annie and Aparna had joined the circle of women, chanting together. In the centre, in the middle of a large circle, lay Lily, her eyes closed.

'Is she—?' Samantha cried, trying to run to her daughter, but stopped by the press of chanting women.

'Aparna?' she pleaded.

Aparna ignored her, instead chanting with the circle of women.

'What are you doing? I thought . . .'

She looked around the circle: a familiar face from the garage that first night, the woman who had read her palm, one of the cleaners from the nursing home, and another, the barmaid from the Skull & Feathers.

Lily began to moan lightly, as if in a half-dream.

'Are you OK, Lily?' Samantha shouted above the noise, but her daughter didn't respond.

'Welcome, Matron,' a voice called from within a dark hood.

Samantha watched as the person's hands reached up and pulled the hood down. The other witches gazed on in dazed appreciation.

'Debby?' Samantha cried. 'What are you doing? What . . .'

Debby stepped forward into the light of the candles. 'Thank you for coming, we didn't want to do this without you.'

'Do what? Debby, what are you doing here?'

'Why wouldn't I be here? Not . . . intelligent enough?' She put on a childish voice. 'Just a lowly care assistant?'

'Of course not, but why? Is it Valerie? Did she make you?'

Debby smiled, her eyes narrowing. 'Nobody makes me do anything, Matron. Valerie is . . . was . . . like a mother to me, and I'm finishing this for her.'

Samantha turned to Annie and Aparna. 'You don't want this, you can stop this—'

'Give me the doll, Aparna,' Debby commanded.

Aparna took out the doll she had taken from the standing stones and handed it to Debby.

'No, Aparna!' Samantha cried weakly.

Debby took the doll with a lock of hair attached to its neck and held it up in the air, its cloth body now streaked in dirt.

Samantha launched herself at Debby, but two of the coven held her back. Debby began to chant as the other witches watched with frenzied glee. She placed the hair in a thin, stitch-eyed doll above a small cauldron of fire.

'Stop!' cried Samantha.

Outside the room, she heard a scuffle break out. Finn growled, a cat screeched, there was an ear-piercing yelp. Debby turned mid-incantation as Diane burst in, followed by Finn and Harry. Debby grinned manically and lowered the doll into the fire, Samantha watching in horror as her daughter squirmed on the floor.

Diane grabbed Samantha's hand, both of them powerless to stop what was happening in front of their eyes. Finn snarled at the witches, standing back as if held by an invisible wall. Samantha's attention was drawn to Annie and Aparna. She let go of Diane's hand, tilting her head and watching as the two women began to chant loudly, louder than the others and at odds with what they were saying.

Samantha looked from Lily, who had stopped squirming on the floor, up to Debby, who now looked frightened.

Suddenly Debby clutched her neck as if something were stuck in her throat, her face reddening and eyes wide.

Samantha gaped at her, and then at Lily, who had opened her eyes and was sitting up. Annie and Aparna held hands, repeating the chant over and over. The other women shook their heads, the spell broken, seemingly unable to carry on. One ran to Debby's side, holding her as she fell toward the floor.

Annie held her arms out in front of her, gesturing to Samantha to move forward. Samantha stepped into the circle and the gathered women drew back as she did so. As soon as she was close enough, she pulled Lily into her arms. They sat on the floor, Samantha stroking Lily's hair, holding her to her body, rocking her like the baby she had once been.

'What did you do, Annie?' Debby gasped.

'It was the hair I tore from your head.'

Debby touched the spot that had once bled and swore.

Aparna nodded. 'You can't hurt the girl anymore.'

Outside the window, a siren wailed in the distance, while nearby the church bells rang midnight. Samantha began to cry, her tears falling onto Lily's golden hair.

CHAPTER 74

Samantha sat next to Annie on the bed, the older woman's hand resting in hers.

Annie's voice was worn, her body once again frail and delicate. 'I'm sorry, Matron, for everything I started. I—'

'No, Annie, I understand why you were so angry back then. I don't know what I'd do if the same thing happened to Lily.'

'But I—'

'You didn't, though, in the end you saved her. Who's to know that Valerie wouldn't have done something herself anyway? She had many reasons to be angry with the Shuttleworths — not just losing her friend, but her mother too.'

Annie nodded. 'She grew up to become a force of nature even I underestimated.'

'But why come here, to be so close to a place she loathed?'

Annie smiled. 'Valerie didn't have the same emotions we have, she never did. If she wanted revenge, she would seek it no matter what it took. It also meant she could keep an eye on me. To try and stop me reversing the curse. She would never kill me, she couldn't, she loved me in her own way.'

'Why did Jonathan let her work here? He must have known about her, about the curse and his dad?'

'Jonathan doesn't believe in witchcraft. I think it soothed the family guilt about her mother, to give her work here. When Emily died, she was just a young girl, he can't have known how important she was to Valerie.'

The sound of buzzers ringing in the corridors alerted Samantha to the other residents needing her attention.

'One more thing, who came to the cottage and took Lily to Valerie's house?'

'The scrying mirror was right,' said Aparna. 'It showed her face.'

'Debby?'

Aparna nodded.

'She has keys to everywhere, waited until you were all asleep. Even the dog didn't stir. She is powerful, perhaps more so than Valerie ever was.'

'Annie, do you have any family you want me to call?'

'My family are waiting for me somewhere else.' She turned to look at the portrait of Emily and smiled gently. 'I'll see them soon enough.'

Samantha got up from the bed and straightened her uniform. As she reached the door she turned back. 'Annie, what happened to Valerie?'

The old woman opened her eyes and turned her head towards the door. 'Simple. Aparna switched the poison in the goblets — not supernatural, just sleight of hand.'

CHAPTER 75

As Samantha handed out tablets in the day room, she looked out at the quadrant where Lily sat with Aparna. The two of them had been as thick as thieves since that night, a week ago.

'I hear Valerie's left,' Bert said, accepting a pot of pills from Samantha.

'Yes, it seems a better opportunity came up somewhere else.'

'Well, I for one won't miss her,' he said, taking a sip of water. 'Something about her I could never put my finger on.'

Samantha took the empty pot from him and wheeled away the medicine trolley. In the corridor she saw Harry coming towards her, a large holdall over his shoulder.

'Where are you going?' Samantha asked.

'Back to London,' he said. 'I've got work and—'

'What about Lily?' Samantha said, looking around to make sure nobody could hear.

'You were right: you're better off without me. I should have come with you to Valerie's.'

'I couldn't wait for you, anyway, you came in the end.'

Harry chewed on his bottom lip, a slight frown on his forehead. Samantha continued, 'Lily will find out soon enough and she will wonder why you've left. Don't forget I was the one that cut you out in the first place, I can't imagine I'm up for parent of the year either.'

'You want to tell her?'

'Of course, she needs to know the truth. She deserves it. It's no longer about me and you, it's about Lily.'

CHAPTER 76

The three of them sat at a table by the fire in the Skull &
Feathers, Harry's eyes on Lily, concern plastered across his
face.

'So, does this mean you'll move back to Nether Dale?'
Lily asked.

Harry looked at Samantha and then back to Lily. 'No.
I'll be in London for a while yet. You can visit me there
though, and I'll come back here as often as I can.'

Samantha patted Lily's hand. 'That would be cool,
wouldn't it? A break from bleak old Nether Dale?'

The landlord coughed; Harry and Lily laughed as
Samantha reddened.

'I like it here,' Lily said, 'but London would be nice too.'

Harry relaxed his shoulders, a wide smile across his face.
'That's great, I'd love that.'

'Hey, does this mean that I'm the heir to Hallow Croft?'
Lily asked.

'Lily.' Samantha shook her head.

'I guess it does,' said Harry. 'Why? You don't have any
plans to see me off with any spells, do you?'

'As long as you keep your end of the bargain and visit,'
Lily smiled.

The door to the pub opened and Diane and Jonathan walked in, Finn padding behind. His tail wagged as soon as he caught sight of Lily. Diane went straight to the fire and warmed her hands.

'What can I get everyone?' Jonathan asked.

Samantha noticed the landlord straightening himself up and beaming in Jonathan's presence as he went to the bar.

'When do you leave, Diane?'

'Two days' time. I can't wait to feel that Majorcan sun on my back again.'

'Can I ask you something?'

Diane's excitement for her holiday dissolved.

'I had some texts warning me to leave Hallow Croft.'

Diane looked to the bar, where Jonathan was paying for the drinks, the landlord engaging him in animated chat. She looked back to Samantha.

'I had my suspicions about you and Harry.'

'What?'

'Who do you think used to drop him in the village without his dad knowing all those years ago?'

Harry smiled coyly, his cheeks flushed. Diane turned to Harry.

'You used to tell me about her, well, about this girl you were sweet on called Samantha.' Then to Samantha, 'As soon as Jonathan told me your name and that you used to live here, I put two and two together. When I found out about Lily I was frightened for you. I knew about the curse, of course, and rubbish or not I just . . . I just didn't think you should stick around. Whatever Valerie was, or wasn't, I knew she was bad news. I tried to get Jonathan to fire her many times, but he wouldn't listen.'

Jonathan approached the table, refreshing the empty glasses. 'Looks like a serious chat. What are you three conspiring about?'

'None of your business,' Diane said. 'Now then, Samantha, are you going to be alright here by yourself?'

'Hallow Croft is in safe hands,' Harry said, nodding at Samantha.

Finn whined and turned, walking towards the door.

'Mum, do you mind if I walk Finn for a bit?' said Lily.

'Of course, don't be too long though.'

Lily promised and jumped up from her seat, running to Finn and taking his trailing lead in her hand.

CHAPTER 77

Lily and Finn crossed the road, afternoon mist thick in the air. She opened the small iron gate to the graveyard and walked along the pathway until she came to the grave by the brick wall. She knelt down and reached out to touch the head stone, running her fingers across the carved name.

Emily Dawson ~ Our Beautiful Daughter, Forever in Our Hearts.

Lily reached in her pocket and took out a shiny black stone of protection, polishing it on her coat before pushing it into the cold earth.

'Rest in peace, Emily,' she said, holding her palm on top of the ground.

Finn huffed gently, his tail sweeping back and forth across the path.

The gate to the churchyard clicked open and Lily looked back to see her mum approaching.

'Come on, you, let's go back and get some dinner.'

Lily took her mum's arm. 'What treats lie ahead? A pie in a tin and packet mash?'

'How dare you? Beans on toast, I'll have you know.'

A single magpie landed on the wall by the gate and Lily smiled as she watched her mum raise her hand to her head and salute.

* * *

Back at the flat Lily carefully piled up the drawings she had taken down from her wall. To her credit, her mum hadn't mentioned them, or anything to do with witchcraft since that night. She placed the drawings in an art folder and pushed it under her bed, then felt around for the book Valerie had lent her.

She pulled the grimoire out, leafing through the pages until she found the spell she had performed so many weeks before. The jar was still on the shelf, sealed, the spell still bound and active, her mum's key ring still visible in the oily contents. It was not the ritual Valerie had hoped she would perform, of that she was sure. But it was the one she felt she needed most. Sylvia's recipe and instructions written in beautiful italic script, *Strengthen the mother & daughter bond.*

Lily had been spending time with Aparna, who had told her about the original coven and its friendships. How Ginny had made the best absinthe drinks and how Donna had taken great pleasure in shocking them with her stories.

Lily gathered some of the herbs together along with a bag containing a small metal bowl and matches, ribbon and scissors, and headed out to the woods. She called at Diane and Jonathan's on the way to pick up Finn.

The dog walked untethered by her side, sniffing at the ground as Lily reached up and cut the ties that each of the small poppet dolls hung from on the ancient tree. All previous targets of Valerie's curses. She placed each one carefully in her coat pockets and walked to the standing stones, Finn following behind.

In the centre of the clearing, she cast a circle with salt and gave blessings to the four elements of fire, earth, air and water. She lit a small fire in the metal bowl and placed offerings of twigs, leaves and winter berries around it. Finn lay by her side as she sat on the cold ground and began to bind each doll with lengths of satin ribbon, carefully wrapping them until they were completely bound.

She dug a shallow hole in the earth and lay each doll within it, side by side, reciting a spell from the grimoire. After gently covering them in soil, she gathered her things and left, calling Finn to her as they walked side by side, back towards Hallow Croft.

EPILOGUE

Samantha spooned mashed potatoes onto the plates as the kettle bubbled to a stop. She looked around at the kitchen she had left all those years ago. It was unchanged. The same willow-patterned plates were laid out before her. She stirred the granules into the boiling water and poured the thick gravy over the pie and mash.

As she carried the tray of plates through to the lounge, she smiled as she watched Lily trying to explain to her mum the rules of Pontoon. It was a game Samantha and her mother had played many times when she was a child, and now she watched as Lily tried to explain to her grandmother the value of the court cards.

'Dinner is served,' Samantha said, putting two of the plates down on the coffee table and the third on a tray attached to her mum's chair.

'So you *can* cook,' Lily teased, digging her fork into the pie.

'Less of the cheek, madam.'

Samantha left her plate on the table and tied a napkin around her mum's neck. 'I hope you're hungry, Mum.'

Her mum smiled up at her daughter, her frail hand reaching for Samantha's face, stroking her cheek. Samantha held it there, inhaling the scent of her violet perfume and kissing the soft skin.

'This is so good,' Lily said, swallowing another mouthful of food.

Samantha moved her mum's hand down to her side and began to feed her, one teaspoon at a time, dabbing her mouth with a paper napkin. Her mum smiled at her, as if there was a spark of recognition. Samantha wished she could say sorry for the past sixteen years, tell her that she wished she hadn't been so stubborn and had come back sooner.

'Who is she?' her mum said quietly, pointing at Lily.

'That's your granddaughter, Mum, that's Lily.'

'Oh, that's nice,' she said, opening her mouth for more food.

When they had cleared up the dinner plates and played another round of cards, Samantha and Lily put their coats on to leave.

'I'll be back tomorrow, Mum, OK?' Samantha kissed her forehead. 'I love you.'

'That's nice,' her mum said, her eyes focused on the afternoon TV, as Samantha and Lily stepped out into the cool spring air.

THE END

ACKNOWLEDGEMENTS

First and foremost, I'd like to thank Mhara Starling. A practitioner of traditional Welsh witchcraft. Our talk was *so* important for creating the central truth of the story. Your insight was fascinating, and I will be forever grateful to you.

My own coven:
To Gabriel. You are my son, my love, and now you're older, often annoyingly wiser than me. Mel Collins, you make me laugh, you give me ideas for killer lines, and your support throughout writing (and life in general) has been invaluable. You're a star. Angie Lopez, you never fail to make me smile and for some reason put up with my bossiness with the patience only a saint could muster. Katrina Atkinson, my sister. One of the kindest and most talented women I know (but who would *never* accept this compliment). Thank you for always supporting me and being there when I need you. Avril Farmer (AKA Mum). Thank you for all the love and care you have shown me throughout my life, you have given me the grounding to do all the things I've done (including the crazy things). I love you. Zoe Clarke, dog mama extraordinaire, thank you for the friendship, the ghost hunt and *all* the birthday props. Nicola Clark, my oldest friend

(forty-eight years and counting) and still able to make me laugh like a drain. Sash, we don't see each other often and I am the worst at replying to messages, but thank you for your friendship and support, I really appreciate it all. Michelle St John, my neighbour and most excellent friend. Thank you for the support and enthusiasm for all things writing and life in general. Sara Nadine Cox, thank you for that early pro-posal edit and your support, a magician with words. Stacey Harper, thank you for your enthusiasm, you have a heart of gold and your friendship is much appreciated. To Fi, for your support, humour, and encouragement. To my lovely agent Katie Fulford at Bell Lomax Moreton, and to those brilliant women at Joffe Books who need to do serious magic to correct my grammar. My editors, Emma Grundy Haigh and Hayley Shepherd.

I worked in care homes for several years and loved the time I spent with some incredible women. They taught me that life is precious and something to be grabbed with both hands. I will forever be grateful for that experience and those conversations. Annie, Kitty, Jessie, Vera, Gertie and Renee, I was truly blessed to have known you.

Also to all those who have supported me in other ways via letting me gabble on their podcasts, Frankie and Sarah at Read & Buried, Mike at Geek4 and Stu at British Murders. And those incredible bloggers who have supported my work throughout the year, I am forever thankful to you all. And finally to Joe, thank you for appearing, like magic.

THE JOFFE BOOKS STORY

We began in 2014 when Jasper agreed to publish his mum's much-rejected romance novel and it became a bestseller.

Since then we've grown into the largest independent publisher in the UK. We're extremely proud to publish some of the very best writers in the world, including Joy Ellis, Faith Martin, Caro Ramsay, Helen Forrester, Simon Brett and Robert Goddard. Everyone at Joffe Books loves reading and we never forget that it all begins with the magic of an author telling a story.

We are proud to publish talented first-time authors, as well as established writers whose books we love introducing to a new generation of readers.

We have been shortlisted for Independent Publisher of the Year at the British Book Awards three times, in 2020, 2021 and 2022, and for the Diversity and Inclusivity Award at the Independent Publishing Awards in 2022.

We built this company with your help, and we love to hear from you, so please email us about absolutely anything bookish at feedback@joffebooks.com

If you want to receive free books every Friday and hear about all our new releases, join our mailing list: www.joffebooks.com/contact

And when you tell your friends about us, just remember: it's pronounced Joffe as in coffee or toffee!

ALSO BY SALLY-ANNE MARTYN

STANDALONE PSYCHOLOGICAL THRILLERS
THE CLINIC